THE LAST GUY ON EARTH

THE LAST GUY ON EARTH

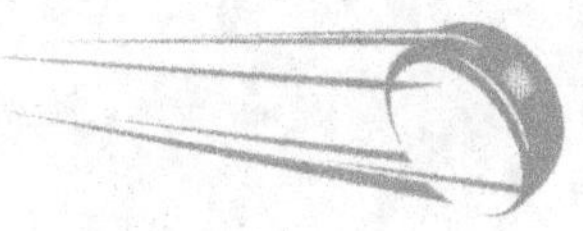

SARINA BOWEN

Tuxbury Publishing LLC

For permissions, contact the author at www.sarinabowen.com/contact

Cover illustration and design by Elle Maxwell.

Editing by Edie's Edits. Proofreading by Claudia F. Stahl.

The Last Guy on Earth is a work of fiction. Names, places, and incidents are either products of the author's imagination, or used fictitiously. Any resemblance to actual persons, living or dead, businesses, organizations, educational institutions, sports teams, events or locales is entirely coincidental.

ONE

Jethro

DECEMBER

LATER, when I'm cruising at thirty-thousand feet over the Great Plains, I'll replay the morning in my mind, trying to remember how I felt before my life was upended.

I'll recall trudging from my car to the practice facility under a pale winter sky—the same walk I've taken for nine years.

I've got no idea what lies in store for the day. All I'm thinking about is Christmas, and whether it's a good idea to pay a premium for that sold-out gaming console.

On the one hand, it will make Toby happy. On the other hand, I've officially become *that* parent—the kind who spoils their kid because gaming consoles are dope, and I don't know how else to show love.

Old Bob, the security guy, holds the facility's door open. I give him a nod of thanks the same way I always do. In the corridor, I'm a little surprised to see my agent waiting for me. Bess used to live in Detroit, though, so running into her isn't *that* weird.

Then I get a look at her face. Time slows as I take in the grim line of her mouth and the worry in her eyes.

"God, what?" I swallow and it's more difficult than it should be. "Christ. It's not my dad?" He's not in the best of health.

1

She gives her head a quick shake. "No, no, it's nothing like that. Management wants a meeting." She puts a firm hand on my arm and steers me toward the executive suite.

"Oh." I consider this for a moment as we enter the suite's double doors. "And they asked *you* to be here? Am I being reprimanded for..." I break off because I can't honestly think of a thing. I've had a slow start this year, but that's not a punishable offense. Either I'm being disciplined for something I said, or...

Another idea slices through me, but it's almost too outrageous to say out loud. "They didn't *trade* me."

Bess actually flinches.

"Jesus Christ," I sputter. "They wouldn't do that." But even as the words leave my mouth, I realize they could absolutely do that. We gave up my no-trade clause on the last contract negotiation in order to get other concessions.

Still, it doesn't make any sense. You don't get traded after fifteen years and a couple championships just because of a slow start to your season.

Or that's what I believed until right this second.

"Let's just go see what they say," she says quietly.

"But you think they're trading me." I can tell because Bess looks upset, and that never happens. She's steely in the face of adversity. Quicker to anger than worry.

"I got a bad feeling," she whispers.

"Jethro? Bess?" We both look up to see Carla, the General Manager's assistant, poking her head out of the GM's office. "If you could come right this way," she says, avoiding my eyes.

My heart drops even further. I gave *everything* I had to this team. Years of service, and it ends like this.

———

The next ten minutes are some of the most confusing and humiliating of my entire life. The jowly GM mutters platitudes about how difficult this decision was. And the head coach is all full of shit when he tells us how this new situation gives everyone involved an opportunity for the best possible season.

"They need your experience," he says. But all I can hear is the drumbeat of rejection inside my skull. *Traded. Traded. Traded.* They might as well throw me in the Detroit River. I'm not even listening when they explain who they traded me for. Some forward from Florida.

Florida. I picture the arena down there and try to imagine myself on the home team's bench. Impossible. In my panic, I lose the thread of the conversation again. They drone on and on. Turns out I'm a pawn in some kind of complicated, three-way trade.

I hear Bess say, "That must have taken weeks to put together."

Weeks? They've been setting up the gallows for weeks, and I had no idea.

How am I going to explain this to Toby? And *when?* A new wave of panic washes through me, because midseason trades happen fast. There's probably a plane ticket in my email inbox right now.

I glance at the clock on the wall and do the math. It's ten a.m. and Toby is at school. He doesn't get out until three o'clock. *Shit.* "Excuse me," I say, interrupting the conversation. "What's the time-line here?"

The coach and the GM stare at me for a beat. "Well, as you're aware, these things happen fast..."

"I know that," I say through gritted teeth, "so let me repeat the question, because I got a kid's heart to break after you're done breaking mine. Tell me the fucking timeline."

A shadow of something that looks like shame passes through my coach's eyes. "You're on a three o'clock flight to Denver."

"Denver?" I hear this word like a record scratch. "Why *Denver?*"

There's a deep silence in the room while three people stare at me. "As Coach was just saying," Bess says carefully, "Colorado needs seniority between the pipes..."

Holy hell. I missed a crucial detail about the three-way trade. They're not sending me to Florida at all.

"Are you kidding me?" I yelp, speaking before I've even processed this latest disaster. "I cannot play for Colorado."

More silence. Bess recovers first. "Let's head out now, Jethro. You'll process this news, and we'll discuss your options."

But even as she says it, the awful truth is sinking in. I don't have any options. I'm playing in Colorado, or I'm not playing at all.

That's when Bess stands up to shake hands.

Somehow, I force myself to my feet, allow my hand to be shaken, and my shoulders to be slapped. I hear a few more platitudes thrown my way, but fuck that. I don't have to pretend this isn't devastating. I don't owe them a fucking smile.

I let Bess herd me outside the facility, where she opens the passenger door to a rental car in a visitor's parking space and sort of shoves me inside. "I'll look up this flight they have you on. We'll make a plan. Do you want me to fly to Denver with you? Or should I stay back and help your dad?"

This question does the trick of snapping me out of my stupor. I turn to Bess and really look at her for a second. She's sitting in the driver's seat, body twisted toward me, concern in her blue eyes. I'm pretty sure I could assign her any task at all right now, and she'd do it. No questions.

I'm fucking grateful, but it still doesn't help the situation. "You don't have to fly out there with me," I say, my voice gravel. I clear my throat. "That's not the hard part."

"What *is* the hard part?" she asks carefully. "Why did you say you can't play for Colorado?"

I look away, out the window. Bess and I are pretty close, and I don't hold stuff back from her. Until now, that is. There's no way I can explain this. It's not even my goddamn right to talk about it, even if I wanted to.

Which I don't.

"You know Clay Powers, right?" she asks. "Weren't you in the minors together?"

Fuck. Her memory for details is often handy. But not today.

"Hmm," she says when I don't answer. "So you're not a fan?"

I shake my head, because I don't trust myself to speak.

"He must not feel the same, though," she says carefully. "Or he wouldn't have approved the trade."

"Right," I agree, just to move the conversation along. "Maybe he's forgotten all about me."

TWO

Clay

"WILL YOU LOWER YOUR VOICE?" Frank, my GM, scowls at me from behind his giant desk at our Boulder headquarters.

"No!" My pulse is pounding in my ears, and I can hardly think straight. "There's no pretending that this is a friendly chat, Frank. You've pulled some crap before, but this is straight-up bullshit. I didn't *want* this player. He's a dinosaur."

"He isn't," Frank hisses.

"No? Then how come you went *behind my back?*"

"I didn't have to!" he shouts. "Because. It's. My. Call." He thumps the desk with his meaty fist on each word.

"A call that's going to look pretty fucking bad in a few months when this player proves uncoachable!" I shout. "There goes our chances at the playoffs."

"Based on what?" he hollers back at me. "We needed some experience in front of the net. I got that for us. Our own goalie coach is practically jizzing himself with excitement to work with Jethro Hale, and you're throwing a goddamn tantrum!"

"I told you—"

"You told me nothing. Just that you don't want this guy."

"The word *no* is a complete sentence," I snarl.

"Come on, kid," he says with a patronizing smile that makes my blood pressure double again.

"Fuck you," I say icily, and his eyes widen. "I'm not your *kid*. If you want someone to kiss your ass, get a dog. And if Hale was the last goalie on Earth, I'd still think this was a bad move."

Frank's eyes are now so wide they're bugging out, but that's all I have to say on the matter. I'm practically shaking with anger, and possibly in jeopardy of getting fired if I stay in this office any longer. So I turn around, throw open Frank's office door, and storm out.

Three paces later I register all the people in the outer office. None of them were here when I'd stalked through to see Frank. My assistant, Liana, for one, looks mortified. Then there's Murph, my assistant coach. He's also red-faced for some reason.

Then I spot the man standing so still against the windows I'd almost missed him. But now that I'm conscious of his presence, my senses laser in on him, and only him. Same tall stature as when we were kids. Same broad shoulders. Sandy hair so familiar that I feel it like a burn inside my chest.

And anger burning in those deep green eyes.

Fuck me sideways. He probably heard everything I shouted at Frank.

Propelled by fury and physical momentum, I'm out of the room in three more paces. And having no better plan, I keep walking. Leaving the management suite, I hightail it across the catwalk spanning the open-plan gym below. A player salutes me from the weight bench. In response, I manage a stiff wave. But my mind is still too busy exploding to engage.

Jethro Hale, a man I've successfully avoided for a decade and a half is here in the building. The newest Cougar.

Here. In Colorado.

I can barely breathe, I'm so upset.

It's a quick jog down the stairs at the back of the building and out through the exit. My truck is waiting in my reserved spot, so I climb into it and turn on the heat against the December chill. Then I grab my phone and hit the number of the only person in the world who would understand what just happened to me.

"Clay?" my sister answers. "You okay? I got two minutes before my next patient."

I'm used to catching her in two-minute increments between appointments, so I talk fast. "Frank traded a goalie for Jethro Hale. After I told him not to."

"*What?*" The shock in her voice is gratifying. "Hale is there? In *Colorado?*"

"Yeah." I let out a heavy breath.

"*Why?*"

"Because Frank doesn't listen when I talk. But also, there was really no way for me to explain..."

"Yeah, okay," she says quickly, and we lapse into a shared silence.

Kaitlyn knows everything that went down between me and Jethro. But Frank doesn't. When Hale's name first came up, I mentioned playing with him when we were young and said we didn't get along. But there was no ethical way for me to hint at our very personal connection. I'd never out anyone.

"Clay, I'm so sorry," she says. "And—hell—the timing."

"The timing," I echo, and my stomach lurches. "Shit, you're right." It's the worst possible moment for Hale to show up here and remind me of the life I never had. Not with everything that's about to go down in Colorado.

She blows out a breath. "What are you going to do?"

"I have no idea," I admit. My job is all-consuming. I need focus. No distractions. And the thought of looking Hale in the face every day for the next six months makes me want to vomit.

"Clay, I'm sorry to do this but..."

"Go," I say, suddenly exhausted. "Heal the people of Seattle."

"I love you," she says.

"You too, babe. Thanks for picking up."

"Anytime!"

She rings off, and the phone makes that beep that tells you you're all alone.

I lean my head against the headrest and close my eyes. The first image I see in my mind's eye is Jethro Hale's brilliant green eyes.

THREE

Fifteen Years Ago

NOVEMBER

FROM THE THREADBARE SOFA, Jethro Hale watches the new guy pace between their kitchen stove and their small living room. Not that it's a long walk—just a few steps, really.

Clay Powers is a handsome dude, all flashing blue eyes and good muscle definition. He's older than Jethro by two years, but they're both newcomers to professional hockey, because Clay finished his degree at a fancy private university before suiting up to play for the Busker Brutes, their new minor league team.

Hale didn't get to finish his degree, and he's still bitter.

Jethro would have thought that being a rich college graduate would relax a guy, but Clay ("it's short for Clayton") Powers hasn't sat down for longer than thirty seconds since he moved in three days ago. He's wound up so tightly that Jethro feels tired just watching him.

"You want some pasta, right?" Clay says, grabbing a frying pan out of the cabinet and inspecting it. He makes a face like he finds it lacking. "I'm cooking."

"Uh, sure. Thanks," Jethro says uneasily. Truthfully, he would rather live alone. Except he's broke, so now he's sharing a small one-bedroom with a stranger. And it's tricky to find housing in the small city of Busker, New York, just outside of Utica.

The team's owner—a slumlord who also owns car dealerships—solves this problem by renting divey apartments to his players for cheap. The complex is called Double Oaks, and it's pretty run down.

Jethro and Clay are sharing a bedroom so small that their two double beds take up almost the entire floor space. Their bathroom is similarly claustrophobic. Jethro has bruises on both elbows from bumping his long arms into the walls of the narrow shower stall.

In the kitchen—which is really just the other end of the living room—Clay puts the skillet on the stove and turns on the heat. Then he grabs a funny-looking bottle of oil out of the cabinet, pours some into the pan, and adds a pound of ground beef a moment later.

With stabbing motions, he breaks the beef up with an ancient wooden spoon, while also talking a mile a minute. "There's something just *off* about this team, don't you think? You've been here longer than I have."

"Only by a single week," Jethro points out. He watches Clay attack the meat with speed and finesse, and wonders where he comes from. Like, what planet.

People often mystify Jethro, but Clay is truly baffling. For starters, he drives a BMW. Not a new one, but still. His clothes all look like they were designed and manufactured according to his exact musculature. And there are products in the bathroom that Jethro has never heard of. Styling foam, for example. And Clay's razor looks like it came from the James Bond lab—all matte metal and angles.

Clay opens another cabinet and frowns. "Is there a cutting board?"

"I...maybe?" Jethro has never used a cutting board in his twenty-two years on Earth.

Clay grabs a plate instead. Then he produces an onion from

somewhere and dices it quickly in several directions. As Jethro watches, several cloves of garlic meet their fate in much the same way. "Okay, but the team… There's all this *tension*."

"Because we suck?" Jethro offers. They've had three back-to-back losses since Clay arrived. As the goalie, Jethro has been too busy trying to stop shots to notice anything subtler than pucks flying at his face.

"No, it's bigger than that. The coach always looks like he wants to strangle Laytner." That's their team captain. "Which is weird because Laytner is the only decent player who's not in this room right now."

Jethro smiles at the compliment, knowing that it's true. He's busy keeping their losses to a minimum, while Clay Powers has done his level best to double their shots on goal.

But they can't do it alone, which is probably why Clay is so stressed out over there, cutting up a red pepper as if it's personally offended him. "How did Laytner get to be captain, if Coach hates him?" he wonders aloud. "And why is everyone so quiet in the locker room? It's just weird. But I have an idea. I think I know what we need to do."

Get some better players and a better coach?

"We have to throw a party."

"Wait, what?" Jethro has neither money nor friends, and you kind of need both to throw a party.

"Don't worry. I got this. Doesn't have to be anything special." He throws the diced vegetables into the pan with the sizzling meat, and Jethro's stomach growls.

In his experience, eating pasta means pouring some sauce from a jar over whichever spaghetti was on super sale. It never smells like what Clay's cooking.

Clay has a jar of pasta sauce on the counter, which he eventually adds to the beef. But he also adds some expensive looking olives, and… heavy cream? His new roommate is some kind of cooking-show guru. It would be more amusing if Jethro wasn't stressed about how to pay this guy back for sharing his food.

A colander that Jethro didn't know they had has appeared in Clay's hands. "Okay, I'll drain this, and we'll eat." He turns off the heat under the pot.

Jethro gets up and joins him in the kitchen space, which is awkward because there's barely enough room to turn around. Clay serves up two giant plates of pasta and then spoons generous portions of meaty sauce all over them.

"Hold up," Clay says when Jethro tries to take his. "Don't forget the cheese." He grabs a small container and sprinkles its contents heavily all over the plate. "Okay, you're good to go."

Their dining set is a shaky card table and folding chairs. They sit down together, and when Jethro takes a tentative bite, he has to hold back a moan. It's just so *good*. Meaty and flavorful and hot. Even the penne is better than he's used to. The flavor is almost nutty.

"Uh, thank you for this," he says. "Kinda great."

"De nada." Clay attacks his own plate, but the wrinkle of worry in his tanned forehead hasn't eased.

And who's tan in *November*?

"The team might turn around," Jethro offers, feeling he owes his roommate a little conversation while he chows down on this amazing food.

"It has to," Clay says. "Otherwise, we'll be stuck in this back-water forever, on this weird-ass team."

Whatever. Jethro's life is already complicated, and he's getting paid actual money to play hockey, even if it's barely a living wage. Besides—it's only been two weeks. Things could look up.

In the meantime, he clears his plate.

Clay does the same. Then he puts his elbows on the table and rubs his temples. "I got a headache coming on. This fucking team."

Jethro gets up to put away Clay's leftovers and scrub both pans. It's the least he can do. But when he's done, Clay is still sitting there, looking miserable. For a charming, rich guy, he's seriously anxious. "You get a lot of headaches?" Jethro hears himself ask.

"Sometimes," Clay mutters.

"Drop your head," he says, tapping Clay between the shoulder blades.

Clay obeys without asking why, a sign of trust that strikes Jethro as both unusual and possibly stupid. They don't even know each other.

Jethro puts a hand at the base of Clay's skull and digs his thumb into the muscle there.

"Damn," Clay whispers. "Harder."

A shiver runs down Jethro's spine, but he couldn't have said why. He massages Clay's muscular neck, using his other hand to grip the crown of his head where Clay's hair is softer than he'd imagined. "My, uh, mom used to get a lot of headaches. She hated the meds, so we tried massage. Just to release the neck and shoulder muscles. Like this." He moves his hands down to the juncture of Clay's neck and shoulders and applies an even pressure.

Clay groans.

"Drop your shoulders," Jethro orders, working his hands into the tight muscle. This dude seriously needs to relax.

"Trying to," Clay mumbles.

Jethro leans in, willing Clay's muscles to release. He's solid under his palms. Sturdy.

Then Clay lets out a sudden moan, and Jethro feels lighter inside. Like he's been useful. "Usually works," he says unnecessarily. But it's true—a man's body is far more predictable than his temper.

Clay sighs. "Your mom's headaches got better? Without meds?"

"Yeah," he lies. Because they could have. If she hadn't driven drunk into a telephone pole and died.

Clay sags happily onto the table. "Thanks, man."

"De nada," says Jethro carefully. And Clay laughs.

FOUR

Clay

IT'S GAME DAY, and I have a routine that I never break: greet the players, check in with the training staff, review any injuries. Later, there'll be a pregame video session followed by a coach's meeting to finalize the starting lineup.

That's how it's supposed to go. But today's routine has gone to hell. I can't function. I drive home in a daze, ignoring all my messages. I stare into my refrigerator, having no memory of what I bought for lunch.

I used to cook for him. He liked that a lot.

God, what is wrong with me? I grab the deli package of smoked ham and slap together a sandwich. I need to pull myself together. There's two games left before our brief Christmas break. And right after that...

I take a deep breath and try not to panic.

After a hasty meal, I drive into Denver and lock myself away in the small office I use at the arena. I sit down at the desk and pull a 4x6 card and a pen from the drawer. I write down the date and *Starting Lineup.*

But then I stall out, unable to finish a single lucid thought, because Jethro Hale and I are in the same zip code. And I'm suddenly twenty-four years old again, and heartbroken.

Fifteen years ago, I fell hard for him, and I thought he felt the same. But then he ripped my heart out and threw it away. A lot of time has passed, but this ache in my chest says I never really got over it.

Now I'm supposed to be his *coach*? If it weren't so awful it would almost be funny. Whatever I did to piss off the universe, it must have been big.

There's a quiet tap on the door.

"Yeah?" I say, knowing it's my assistant Liana on the other side. I lift my chin as the door opens, trying to look calm.

Liana appears, looking impeccable as always. Her hair is wound into a soft knot. Her suit is Cougar blue, her shoes shiny. And she's giving me one of her serious frowns. My assistant has the remarkable ability to say a lot with just one facial expression. Some of her serious frowns are thoughtful, some of them judgmental.

This one says, *What the hell, Clay?*

"Coach," she says slowly. "Is something wrong?"

You have no idea. "No, why?"

Her frown shifts to reflect incredulity. "Murph has been trying to reach you for hours."

"I had some things to take care of," I lie, hoping she doesn't ask what. "Anything I need to know?"

Her expression hardens, like she can't believe I'd stoop so low as to blow off all my responsibilities and then pretend like it's no big deal. And she's right—this isn't me. I always do what's necessary for the team, no matter what.

"Jethro Hale has arrived at the arena. You need to introduce him."

My stomach drops.

"And while we're on the topic of Hale, we're putting him up at the Four Seasons for a few days. But today I found him a rental in Rocky Bluffs that he can move into within the week."

"Rocky Bluffs?" That's the condo complex where I live. "Why there?"

Her frown returns in force. "Immediate availability of a three-bedroom, which he needs. And since I've been there to drop things off for you, I knew it had a playground. He has a kid."

A kid? A *family*. Holy crap. He must be married, and somehow, I never heard about it. It's not like I google him. But hockey is a small world.

Could this get any weirder? I'll probably meet his wife at the next charity event. I'll be standing there in my tux, a smile painted on my face, trying to forget how much her husband liked it when I used to get down on my knees...

"Coach?"

"Yeah?" I say, jerking back into the present.

"You look a little pale," she says, concern in her voice. "Are you coming down with something?"

"Maybe," I say, grasping at this excuse. "Haven't felt quite right all day."

"Oh hell," she whispers, giving her pretty head a shake. "We don't have time for you to get sick. I'll grab you one of the trainer's vitamin drinks."

"Great idea," I agree, as if my problems could be fixed by a little extra Vitamin C and zinc. "Thank you."

"Now shake a leg," she says. "Go greet the new guy. Half the front office heard your little shouting match this morning. It makes you look like a dick. And Coach?" She lifts her gaze to mine. "You're not a dick. So fix it."

"I will," I say, because I know she's right. "Then I'll find Murph and apologize."

She gives me a nod of approval, so I must be making more sense now. Then she disappears, closing my office door behind her.

I drop my head for a couple of seconds, allowing myself this one last moment to wallow. And then I push my chair back, lift my chin, and leave the room. I pace from the office into the rabbit warren of hallways winding through the arena's underbelly.

It's the usual game-night chaos—players and support staff everywhere. God only knows what I'm going to say to Hale when I find him. Probably a bunch of platitudes. *Welcome to Colorado. Nice to see you again. Hope you're settling in.*

I give myself a little pep talk as I peer into the various rooms we use for game prep. *Nobody ever died of awkwardness. It's been fifteen years. You're different people now.*

My inner twenty-four-year-old is unconvinced.

I turn another corner and suddenly he's in front of me—standing ramrod straight in a dark blue suit. He's so tall that he looms over Murph, who's talking fast and gesticulating wildly.

They both sense me at the same time. Murph shuts up and looks at me quizzically. But Hale's expression guts me. His familiar green eyes go slitty with anger. His jaw tightens, and his mouth forms a grim line.

I've seen Hale angry before, but never at me. And it's not fucking fair. But I'm the goddamn coach of this team, and I don't have the luxury of being pissy about it. I clear my throat and greet him as neutrally as I can. "Evening, gentlemen." I offer a hand to Hale. "Welcome to Colorado."

He says nothing. But he grips my hand in a brief, bone-crushing press and then drops it again, like I might have a communicable disease.

So this is going well.

"Where've you been?" Murph asks unhelpfully.

"Tied up," I say lamely. "Sorry about that. Mr. Hale, would you come with me a moment? We should talk."

"I have to suit up," he says gruffly. "So maybe some other time."

Seriously? Murph's jaw drops, right along with mine. "Now is a perfect time," I say icily. "It will only take a moment. Follow me."

I turn without looking to see if he'll follow. I'm banking on the fact that he knows a player can't just dismiss the head coach. Not ever.

Everything is weird and wrong. I want to go back home and start this whole day over—this time without Hale's disastrous trade.

I hear footsteps behind me as I move down the corridor. My office suddenly feels too far away for this charade, so I step into an alcove that contains the rolling carts we use for toting gear, and I turn around to face him.

Looking at Jethro hasn't gotten any easier in the last minute. It still makes me ache to catalog all the ways he looks the same. Those sandy eyelashes. That scruffy jaw. I used to run my knuckles across it.

Yet so much has changed. I'm looking at a champion now, not a broke minor-leaguer. He's a damn legend, and under different circumstances, I'd be thrilled to work with him.

Neither of us is thrilled, though. He stands a few feet away from me, shoulders squared like a fighter in the ring. And the anger in his blazing, green eyes makes me wonder if he's about to take a swing at me.

"Look," I say, jumping in with my apology. "I'm sorry for whatever part of my bad reaction you heard this morning."

"Which part?" he snaps. "The part where you called me a dinosaur? Or the part where you said that if your shaky team doesn't do well in the playoffs, it's probably my fault?"

"Hey—I didn't mean that. I was just reacting badly to..." I take a breath and look directly into his eyes. "The shock. That's all. I sincerely apologize."

"*The shock,*" he repeats acidly. "Really? Was your life upended this morning? Did your team yank the rug out from under you?"

I blink. Because the answer to both those questions is *yes*. But it's abundantly clear that Jethro can't see it that way. He thinks he's the only one with a reason to be upset.

And I don't know whether to laugh or cry, because it's the same problem all over again: he matters more to me than I ever mattered to him.

I'm the only fool who ever thought differently.

FIVE

Jethro

CLAY'S EXPRESSION tightens into something I can't read just before he averts his blue-eyed gaze. My life is moving at too fast a speed for me to process all the waves of aggravation rolling off him.

I'm so angry I can hardly breathe. Clay and I used to be *tight*. I trusted him in all the ways there are to trust a person. And the first thing I heard—along with everyone else in a five-mile radius—was that he wouldn't want me if I was *the last guy on Earth*.

Who says that about a three-time champion?

Now we're staring at each other, both of us angry. It wasn't his ass who got FedExed across the country this morning at the whim of my team's manager.

My former team. I wonder what they're all doing right now. It's probably business as usual in the dressing room. Smack talk and strategy. I was supposed to play St. Louis tonight. Now I have to suit up for a game against... I can't even remember who. I'm so disoriented.

"Listen," he says without meeting my eyes. "I'm sorry you're pissed off about the trade. A trade I had nothing to do with."

"You made that *abundantly* clear," I hiss.

He sighs and lifts his eyes skyward. And the gesture is so

familiar that it actually pierces the bubble of anger inside my chest. For a split second I can see the twenty-four-year-old Clay Powers, pacing in our little kitchen, angsting about something or other.

It's wild, really. That time in my life has been buried for so long, and now here it is, standing right in front of me in a sharp suit and a scowl.

It's almost too much to take in.

"The point is," he says, trapping me with a pair of knowing blue eyes that seem more familiar with every passing second. "I hope you can settle in and be happy here. I hope we can get past this awkward moment and play some great hockey. That was always your goal, wasn't it?"

"Yeah," I admit hoarsely.

He looks away again, and pinches the bridge of his nose, the way he used to do when he felt a headache coming on. "Good," he says firmly. "Please let Murph or Liana know if there's anything we can do to make your family more comfortable. Liana is a miracle worker, and the goalie coach is excited to work with you. Now if you'll excuse me, I have to tell my team about the trade."

Then? He steps around me, as if this little chat wasn't his idea in the first place. And he stalks away from me.

As he goes, I catch myself watching his confident stride. If you'd told me fifteen years ago that Clay Powers would become the youngest coach in the league, I would not have laughed. He was always the kind of guy who wanted things done right. He knew how to handle himself, and he knew how to handle others. It doesn't take a mental leap to see his star is still rising.

Meanwhile, my star has just been kicked to the curb. It's deeply embarrassing to start over at thirty-seven. Yesterday, I thought of myself as a valuable member of my hometown team. Today, I'm just the trash they're hauling out the back door.

It doesn't help that I'm the third-oldest player in the league. That's why it stung so bad to hear Clay call me a dinosaur. The whole office heard it. They know what their coach thinks of his newest player, and I don't know how to come back from that.

"Hale?" I look up to see Matt Murphy, the assistant coach, beckoning to me. He's a big guy with curly hair and an easy smile. "Coach Powers is just taking a moment to tell the guys that Cockrell was traded. But then we've got to get you suited up. Our equipment guy will make you a jersey."

"Okay," I manage. I follow him down the corridor while he asks me benign questions about my equipment so he can pass that data to the manager. He pauses outside the dressing room, where I can hear Clay's voice again as he addresses his players.

The room is dead silent. They clearly show him all the respect that a head coach deserves. And from this day forward I'm supposed to do the same.

I've spent the day suffering from a million emotions—my humiliation in Detroit, my anger, and my worries for my family— but now I can't stop thinking about just one. Clay Powers and I have a past together. A distant past, but it's still messy.

Now that he's my new boss, there's only one way to get through this. I have to put every memory of those old days in a fireproof safe and lock that shit up. Nothing good will come from thinking about what we used to be to each other...

"Hale?" Coach Murphy says.

I snap out of my reverie, follow him into the dressing room, and immediately feel like a monkey at the zoo. Heads swivel in my direction. The players all look a little shellshocked. They can't believe their backup goalie got zapped into thin air a few days before Christmas. They'll probably miss the guy.

Plus, it's a brutal reminder that it can happen to almost anyone. It's like seeing a news story on TV about a car accident and recognizing the intersection in the clip. You think: *that could have been me.*

Except this time, it *was* me, and their stares are making me twitch.

"Well?" I bark. "Where do you want me?"

Clay glances around the room until his gaze lands on a half-empty stall. "Banks!" he shouts.

An equipment guy comes scurrying in from another room. "Coach?"

"Set up Mr. Hale in Cockrell's old spot, please."

"Will do, sir." The young man hurries over to tidy up a stall next to Andrey Volkov, their primary goalie.

I head over to that spot and set down my bag. There's probably something I should be saying right now that would lighten the moment, but I don't know what that is.

Clay would know, my brain offers up unhelpfully. He was the talker. The charmer. I've always been terrible at conversation.

Luckily, the team captain—veteran player Ted Kapski—crosses the room to shake my hand. "Hi. Welcome to the team. I'm sure you're as surprised to be here as we are to see you. But it's an honor, man."

I shake his hand, but I don't feel all that honored. "Thanks," I say gruffly. "Merry Christmas to me."

"This really fucks up the Secret Santa chain," another player mutters. It's Davey Stoneman, one of their star forwards.

Kapski gives him an elbow to the ribs. "Dude, seriously?"

"I love my rituals," Stoneman says sourly. "But I'll prolly love not having to shoot past Hale next time we play Detroit. So welcome, man."

"Thanks," I say stiffly.

"Where are you staying?" Kapski asks. "The holidays are a rough time for a trade."

"You're telling me." I rub my temples. "My family is taking it hard. I'm in a hotel in Denver for a few nights. The team found us a condo. It's empty, though. I gotta get some beds and stuff before my dad brings my kid out here."

A defenseman rises to cross the room. "Hey, I got a furniture guy for you. He did my whole place in a few weeks. Looks great, too. You want the name?"

"Absofuckinglutely. Give me all the names. Or—better yet—wake me up from this nightmare."

There's an uneasy chuckle. But I don't know how to fake how I feel, and I don't see why I should try.

"You know you've got to suit up, right?" Kapski says. "They didn't call up a third stringer to back up Volkov tonight."

"Yeah. Sure. I'll get on that. Right after my breakdown."

Another awkward chuckle.

"Let's find you a jersey," Kapski says. "And I'll give you the nickel tour."

"And after the game, we'll take you out and get you drunk," Stoneman offers. "Something to look forward to."

"Sounds good," I lie, because I don't even drink. "Let's do it."

SIX

Fifteen Years Ago

DECEMBER

"ANY PROGRESS?" Clay's sister asks on their weekly phone call.

"A little," he grumbles, wiping down the kitchen counter with the hand that's not holding the phone. "We won a couple games this week, but the team is still a train wreck. No morale. Weird tension between the coach and the captain."

"Maybe the coach is just bad at his job?"

"Maybe? But he won the Frozen Four at his college gig. I dunno. It's just strange." He opens the fridge and squints at the contents.

"How's the apartment? How's the roommate?" Kaitlyn asks.

There's nothing good to say about the Double Oaks, so he tackles the second question. "He's..." Clay glances toward the door, double checking that Jethro isn't on his way in. He's always last to leave the rink, because he sharpens his own skates. "Jethro is the best thing about this place," he admits.

"Yeah? Would I like him? Is he hot?"

Clay snorts, as he's expected to do. Jethro *is* hot, and Clay thinks about it a whole lot more than he should.

"What's his nickname? And what do you like about him?" Kaitlyn presses, having no idea how confusing her second question is. And how often Clay reflects on it.

"Uh…They call him Jetty, I guess because he moves fast. So, yeah, mostly I like the way he saves goals."

"Obviously. But what's he like as a roommate?"

Another guilty glance toward the door. "He's nice and calm. No drama." Although that doesn't really do Jethro justice. He's quiet in an unflappable way that goes a long way toward soothing Clay's anxiety. "He likes my cooking, and he always cleans up the kitchen."

Again, it's all true, but it doesn't capture the dynamic that's blossomed inside these four walls. Evenings in Jethro's soothing company are the only thing keeping Clay sane. Most nights he putters in the kitchen, rehashing the day, while Jethro offers a quiet observation or two. Then they eat, with Jethro always so grateful to be fed.

Afterwards, Jethro cleans up the kitchen while Clay picks out something to watch on TV. There might be a hockey game that they need to watch. Or maybe there's a new disc from Clay's Netflix subscription waiting in their mailbox.

Either way, the angry world seems to reset itself in the peace and quiet of their shitty, little apartment. Sometimes Clay even gets a neck rub out of it, but he tries not to ask too often. He doesn't want to make it weird.

"Everyone loves your cooking," his sister points out. "He'd have to be dead not to. But I'm glad you made a friend."

It sounds so patronizing that Clay laughs. "Yeah, I'm playing nice with the other kids in the sandbox. You don't have to worry."

"I *do* worry about you," his sister admits. "How's the anxiety?"

"It's…eh. The usual."

She makes a noise of dismay. "Have you been sleeping?"

"Mostly. Falling asleep is hard, but after that, I do okay."

"Hmm."

"I'm *fine*, KayKay. How are you doing?"

"Great actually. Have you talked to Dad?"

"No. Is there some reason I need to?" Clay doesn't call home very often if he can help it. "My anxiety is bad enough without listening to Dad question all my choices."

"Fair," she says. "I called them last night to tell them I chose my specialty. Dad is underwhelmed."

"Wait, why?" he asks. His sister is in medical school, which is exactly what the Powers kids were groomed to do with their lives. "What did you choose?"

"Psychiatry."

Clay lets out a cackle of surprise. "God, really? Are you going to start charging me for these phone calls?"

"No!" she yelps.

"Seriously, why would that piss Dad off?"

"Because he's Dad? Because nothing is ever enough?"

That shuts him up for a second, because until now, it hadn't really occurred to him that his siblings could be any kind of disappointment. That's always been Clay's realm. *Business management?* His father had roared when Clay announced his college major at Boston College. *That's a fucking waste of money.*

Clay had pointed out that his hockey scholarship covered more than half of it, but the blow hadn't landed. And it never would, because as far as Dr. Powers was concerned, hockey was a waste of time, and a degree in business would never be worth the paper it was printed on.

"I'm sorry," Clay says to his sister. "Whatever he said, it shouldn't matter."

"I told him that his attitude was just proof that the world needs more psychiatrists."

Clay howls with laughter. "His head probably blew off."

"A little bit."

"So...a shrink in the family. Interesting. When do I have to start watching what I say?"

"You've got it backwards," Kaitlyn insists. "Patient confidentiality is the law. I'll take your secrets to my grave."

"Cool," he says, but he feels a prickle of guilt. Kaitlyn is the only sibling he's really close to, but she doesn't actually know his biggest secrets—the ones that are eating him alive lately. Not that she'd judge him. Not even if he told her all the gory details of a certain night he'd had last year. Spring break. A stranger in a Bahamas bar. Flirting with another guy for the first time in his life.

Then following that guy back to his hotel room...

He hears the sound of a key in the front door. "Hey, Kaitlyn? I should probably go soon. But congrats on picking your specialty."

"I'm excited. I *loved* my clinical rotation on the locked psych ward. I know that's a weird thing to say, but it's true. My mentor is doing such great work with those teens..."

Jethro's big frame fills the doorway. Clay looks up at him and smiles automatically.

His roommate's smile is slower to form, but no less genuine.

"Awesome, KayKay. I'm going to run now. Talk soon?" He hangs up with Kaitlyn as Jethro stacks a couple boxes from the liquor store inside the door. "Hey! What's that?"

"Got some booze for your party."

"You didn't have to do that," Clay says. Jethro is always short on cash.

"Payday." Jethro shrugs. He pulls an envelope out of his pocket, crosses the room, and tosses it to Clay. "Grocery money." After hanging up his coat, he drops his lanky body onto the small sofa beside him. "What smells so good?"

You. Clay gets a little rush every time Jethro is close to him. Which is often, seeing as this couch is undersized, and their beds are about three feet apart in the other room.

These days when he has trouble falling asleep, it's not always because of stress. Sometimes it's sexual frustration. Jethro's mostly naked body is a source of torture.

Clay turns his head to answer Jethro's question, and when their gazes meet, he feels an electric jolt inside his chest. "I made braised-chicken tacos for dinner. Should be ready in about an hour."

Jethro tilts his head back and inhales deeply. "I have to smell that for another *hour*?"

"You'll survive." He uses his knee to nudge Jethro's. Any excuse to touch him.

"Good scrimmage today," his roommate says, having no idea of the riot happening inside Clay's body. "Seems like your line is getting its shit together."

"Thanks. I'm cautiously optimistic."

Jethro turns and swings his feet up and over Clay's lap to rest them on the opposite arm of the sofa. He's so tall that he barely fits on the couch. "Who was on the phone? Got a date?"

"Nah. That was my sister. Kaitlyn."

"She hot?"

"Hey!"

Jethro laughs. "She into hockey players?"

"No, thank God." *That's only me.* "She's a med student at Stanford."

"*A med student.*" Jethro pronounces this like it's in a foreign language. "Christ, your family. Bunch of overachievers."

"You're telling me."

Jethro rests his lazy gaze on Clay again, and Clay takes the opportunity to study his eyes. They're a green-gray color at the center, with the most amazing dark green ring around the iris. They're framed by long, sandy lashes with pale tips. Clay studies them way too often.

"You know what *my* sister is up to?" Jethro asks, and Clay shakes his head. "Getting slapped around by some dickwad who deals pot to high school students."

"Fuck," Clay whispers.

"Used to be able to keep an eye on her, but now I'm trapped out here in Shitsville. Last night a friend texted me a picture of Shelby's boyfriend screaming at her in a parking lot."

"You're worried about her."

"Constantly. She's nineteen and clueless, but thinks she knows everything." He closes his eyes. "She ran off the rails after our mother died. I've been trying to convince her to figure out her life. I sent her some money so she could go back to school, but she spent it on *him*."

And here Clay thought he was stressed out. "That blows. I'm sorry."

"Couldn't sleep last night." He reaches back and grips the base of his skull. "Feel like you. All tight and angsty."

"Hey, lift up a sec." Clay nudges Jethro's legs out of the way. Then he stands and moves to the back of the couch. After setting his hands onto Jethro's shoulders, he digs his thumbs into the muscles there.

Jethro sighs, relaxing into his touch. And Clay goes to town, giving him a major-league massage and ignoring the way his own body hums at their proximity.

Until Jethro suddenly clasps Clay's wrist, stopping him.

Clay's heart stutters when Jethro turns to meet his gaze. "Thanks," he says gruffly.

"You're welcome," he whispers, unable to tug his eyes away.

Jethro doesn't look away, either. "Hey. Don't think I haven't noticed."

"W-what?" Clay's breath leaves his body.

"The grocery bill," Jethro says. "You've been lowballing it for me."

"Oh." He lets out a slow breath. "I buy organic, and it's spendy. Not your problem."

"Appreciate it," he says gruffly, releasing Clay's wrist.

With his heart galloping, Clay crosses to the kitchen to check the chicken.

SEVEN

Jethro

"BUT I DON'T *WANT* to move," Toby insists, his young voice radiating panic from my rental car's speakers. "I like my room the way it is."

My blood pressure climbs another notch. "I hear you, bud. But your room at Grandpa's house isn't going anywhere. You can visit in the summer. In the meantime, you'll also have a nice room here. It's a great townhouse. There's even a fireplace, so Santa can find you."

That last tip is courtesy of the real estate agent. *That's what my kids would worry about*, she'd said.

But not Toby, apparently. "Jeez, I'm not a *baby*," he scoffs.

I hold back a sigh. "Just keep an open mind," I beg. "There's a killer playground at the complex. That's why they showed this place to me. Lots of kids live around there. You can see it tomorrow."

"They can have it. I'm not coming!" he insists. "There's no reason I should have to!"

I hear a loud thump—the sound of a phone smacked down on the nearest piece of furniture—and then nothing more.

My father's voice comes through the speaker a moment later. "Hey. You still there?"

"Yeah. Unfortunately." I stop at a traffic light and look around.

Boulder is beautiful, but it's ruining my life. What's left of it anyway. And this intersection doesn't look very familiar. Did I miss my turn?

"He's pretty upset," my father says unnecessarily.

Like I didn't notice? "This will blow over, right? He'll get used to Colorado once he's here."

He'd better, because we don't have any other choice.

"Jethro." My father drops his voice. "You could just leave us here in Michigan. It's an option."

"No. I can't do that." The light turns green, and I follow the traffic ahead of me.

"You could," he says simply.

The awful truth is that I've already considered this. Yesterday morning, right after the gut-wrenching meeting with management, I'd left Bess and driven straight to Toby's school, where I asked to pull him out of class. I'd taken him to McDonald's, bought him a breakfast sandwich, and told him we were moving to Colorado.

The first thing he'd said was, "No way." The second thing was, "Go to hell." And the third thing was, "I hate you."

Right about then, I'd considered asking my dad to stay back in Detroit with him until the end of the season. Our lives have been so full of turmoil already. I was awarded custody of Toby only eighteen months ago. But my hellacious schedule means I can't be his only caretaker. So I'd given up my condo and moved into my father's brick two-story.

During that time, my once-absent father has held our odd little family together. That's why his suggestion is not that outrageous. But I'm the one with custody, so I'd have to go back to court to give my father the legal right to care for him.

Also, my father is a sixty-five-year-old man in an eighty-year-old body. He's suffering from a steadily weakening heart, probably exacerbated by previous decades of alcohol abuse. I can't leave them alone for six months. I just can't.

"Dad," I say carefully. "I'm sorry to disrupt your life. But I can't leave Toby in Detroit. I'm sure *both* of you hate me a little right now. But it's not forever. My contract is only another year and a half."

He sighs. "Yeah, okay. It's what Shelby would want, anyway."

There's also that, I guess. Fucking Shelby, who caused almost as much drama in my life as my terrible mother and my unreliable father. Shelby's opinion counts last.

I stop at another light and look around. That's when I realize I have absolutely no idea where I am. "Hey, Dad? I have to go. I'm going to be late for practice." On my first day.

"How do you want me to pack up your room?" he asks.

"I don't. Pack the Christmas presents we got for Toby and some clothes for the both of you. Then hire whichever overpriced mover Bess found for us, let them handle everything, and then get on a plane tomorrow morning. Now I really gotta go."

"All right. See you tomorrow, son."

I ring off with him. "Hey Siri!"

"Yes, champion?"

That's funnier when I'm not late. "Where is the Cougar Ice Barn?"

"The Cougar Ice Barn is located in Boulder, Colorado. It's the headquarters of the Colorado Cougars, a professional ice hockey team..."

"*Where*, Siri? Navigate to the Cougar Ice Barn."

"One moment, champion."

Sigh.

"Use the right lane to turn north onto Broadway..."

I flip on my blinker and start to change lanes when someone lays on the horn behind me. There's a flash of yellow, and a Jeep leaps out of my blindspot and passes me at warp speed.

Christ. I almost got into an accident. I hate Colorado.

Stressed out and tired from staying out until one a.m. with my new teammates, I finally arrive fifteen minutes later. After I jog into the building, I find the dressing room empty. I change as fast as I can, but I can't skate without stretching. So there goes another ten minutes. When I arrive on the ice, the team is already involved in drills.

"Good of you to join us," says Murph, the assistant coach.

Shit. It gets even worse when I glance at Clay, who's silently judging me. Arms crossed. Face grim. And then he actually averts his fucking gaze, as if I don't exist.

"I got fucking lost," I mutter. "Apologies, Coach."

Murph nods grumpily. And Clay says nothing. Like I'm as important as a wad of gum on the bottom of his shoe.

I skate out for my first practice.

EIGHT

Clay

"THIS LOOKS BAD," Murph mutters during the team scrimmage. "The new goalie's getting shelled. Are we in trouble, or what?"

He isn't hallucinating. I'm watching some of the most awkward goaltending I've seen in my adult life. "Don't rush to judgment. He doesn't usually practice at altitude. And bear in mind that he hasn't broken in a new team in almost a decade." The younger Jethro Hale bounced around to a couple great teams before landing in Detroit for the past nine seasons.

"Wait, I thought you hated this guy," Murph says.

I wince. It would be so much easier if that were true. "Hate is a strong word," I say carefully. "We don't get along. But he's one of the most decorated goaltenders in the league."

"He *was*," Murph says quietly. "But Detroit didn't want to carry him through the playoffs. So now we gotta, instead?"

"Seems so." And Murph's blunt little analysis of the situation echoes my own thoughts. Then again, it's impossible for me to be objective about Hale. Maybe Frank knows what he's doing and just scored the best trade of the year.

For the team, anyway. Not for me, personally.

I'm so confused.

"Here's a thought," Murph says, giving me a sideways glance. "Give Volkov the night off and put Hale in the net tomorrow night against St. Louis. Sink or swim. If he falls on his face, Frank will have to listen. Maybe we need a Plan C."

"Get out of my brain."

Murph snickers.

With only a few minutes left on the clock, I watch the scrimmage closely. Playing goalie isn't just about stopping goals. The goaltender has the best view of the game, so he drives the defensive strategy from the net. Being a goalie is really about communication and trust.

Unfortunately, Jethro seems to have left both communication and trust behind in Detroit. He's not getting through to his guys. And he's playing too far inside the net, a common sign of feeling vulnerable. He's not trusting the defense to stop breakaways or screen shots effectively, which makes him less effective at angle plays and more susceptible to long shots.

The scoreboard agrees. The scrimmage is 6-2 when the whistle blows. When Jethro removes his helmet, he's red-faced and panting.

I look away from that face I know so well. The one I still see in my dreams sometimes. How do I coach this guy? There's no rulebook for this.

"Hey, Coach?" Kapski skates up and steps off the ice. "Got a sec?"

"Of course." Our team captain is as solid as they come, and if he needs a word, I always have time.

He leads me over to the far wall where nobody can hear us. "I gotta ask," he says in a low voice. "Something wrong with the new guy?"

"Besides that disaster of a scrimmage?" My eyes flick involuntarily to the rink, where Jethro is pushing the net out of the way so the ice can be resurfaced. "Why are you asking?"

Kapski gives me a flat look. "You didn't introduce him to the room the night he arrived. And there's a rumor that you didn't want the trade. Is he staying?"

I pinch the skin between my eyes. "The trade caught me by surprise, because I thought we were going in another direction." I'm not a good enough actor to convince my perceptive captain otherwise. "And obviously, it caught Hale by surprise. I'll pull it together, and I'm sure he will, too."

He nods, like he's thinking it over. "Thing is, Coach, you like *everybody*. So I gotta wonder about this guy. I got curious and I googled him. You two were teammates once?"

"Uh-huh," I say quickly. "Long time ago."

His eyebrows quirk. "And you didn't get along?"

"Not always," I hedge, wondering how to end this conversation. "But that was kid stuff. He's, uh, a good guy. I'll get over my snit and figure out how he fits into our organization."

"Okay," Kapski says, still frowning. "Just let me know if I can help out? We don't have a lot of time to gel as a team. We got fourteen games in January."

"We do," I agree. "And we're going to be unstoppable."

He gives me a knowing grin. "All right. Later, Coach."

"Good work today," I tell him before he clomps off to the showers.

After he goes, I lean back against the concrete wall and stare up into the rafters. What the hell am I going to do about Jethro Hale?

NINE

Fifteen Years Ago

JANUARY

ON A SNOWY NIGHT right after the team wins a home game against Green Bay, Clay finally holds his damn party.

Jethro has pitched in as best he can. He helped clean up the apartment. He's gathered up all their valuables—except for the stereo speakers, at Clay's urging—and stashed them under his bed before wedging the bedroom door shut.

He doesn't trust people to respect his stuff, and he can't afford to be robbed. If it were up to him, he and Clay would be the only people who ever set foot in this apartment. He's half hoping that nobody will show up, although that would make Clay sad. His roommate still seems to think this party is the answer to all their problems.

So when their teammates start streaming through the door in their wet shoes, Jethro doesn't know whether to be relieved or annoyed. He opens a beer for himself and parks his ass against the wall of the kitchen, where he can see all the action at once. And, bonus, it puts him close to the drinks and snacks.

Clay has gone all out on the refreshments. There are two coolers full of spiked punch—a red version and a golden one. It's kept cold by giant ice balls with hockey pucks frozen into their centers. It's a detail that might seem like he's trying too hard. But coming from Clay, it just works.

Likewise, the food is a dazzling array of expensive-looking sausage meats and cheeses that Jethro can't pronounce. Platters cover the countertops. There are olives and pickles and some funny-looking candied nuts.

"Try this with a pita chip," Clay says, offering Jethro a bowl of dip. "It's made from roasted red peppers, white beans, and feta."

Jethro doesn't need the explanation. He'd eat anything Clay put in front of him. And the dip is exceptional, tasting of fresh garlic and lemons. The whole effort is classier than Busker, New York really deserves.

It doesn't take long before their apartment is heaving with people. Jethro recognizes about a third of them. Whoever they are, they seem pretty stoked to eat Clay's food and drink his liquor.

Jethro's vantage point allows him to watch Clay, whose smile shines on everyone tonight like he's a human lighthouse. He shakes hands and slaps backs as Jethro traces him through the crowd, growing more uncomfortable by the second. It's just plain weird to have all these people in their space, when he's used to having all Clay's attention to himself.

And it's dawning on him that Clay is *good* at this. He knows which joke will make you laugh. He knows what you want to drink before you even know yourself. Before he met Clay, Jethro didn't know that it was possible to be confident as well as anxious. Charming but also serious. Clay is the kind of guy you watch just to figure out what he'll do next.

Jethro opens a succession of beers and witnesses an entire flock of women surround Clay. With his easy smile and his rich-boy good looks, he's a magnet for female attention. Not that hockey players ever have trouble getting girls. Although Jethro is usually too busy or too broke to go out.

It's entertaining to watch a busty woman in a Brutes jersey practically climb Clay like a tree. He's perfectly nice to her in return, but he doesn't accept the crystal-clear invitation.

Poor girl. She doesn't know him as well as Jethro does, or she'd realize she's wasting her time. Clay isn't the kind of guy who'd drag her off to the bedroom in the middle of his own party. He's too busy recommending the cheeses and making sure his playlist is still cranking.

Eventually, she gives up and settles for a D-man named Rezinski. They sneak out a half hour later, his hands already up her sweater. Clay waves them off cheerfully.

"Jetty!" a teammate yells. "Beer pong!"

Jethro realizes he's been watching Clay for more than an hour, which is weird, even for him. So he turns to help some teammates count out beer cans on the wobbly dining table. He gets steadily drunker as the night wears on. Too bad they have practice at nine the next morning. Jethro knows he'll have regrets.

At three a.m. the apartment finally empties out, leaving Clay buzzing around, cleaning up bottles and cups.

"We can do that after practice tomorrow," Jethro says sleepily.

"Just checking for crumbs. And spilled beer. It stinks if you leave it."

Jethro is full of relief that the apartment is all theirs again, and he doesn't care about a few crumbs. He helps, though, before checking their darkened bedroom, which is happily unscathed. He brushes his teeth, then gets in bed, listening as Clay makes his final rounds, locking the door and shutting off the lights.

He's still feeling drunk when Clay comes in a few minutes later and promptly trips over Jethro's hockey bag which is still wedged awkwardly between the beds. He loses his balance and topples sideways toward Jethro.

Jethro, with a goalie's reflexes, catches him by the arm and eases him down on the mattress.

"Sorry," Clay says. "I'm kinda drunk."

"Same," Jethro says. "But that was totally the point, right?"

"Yeah, I guess." Clay stretches out beside him. "I talked to literally everyone, though, and never figured it out."

"Figured what out?" Jethro asks sleepily from a few inches away.

"What's wrong with the team vibe. Why the hell Laytner and Coach want to kill each other."

"Oh, now hang on," Jethro says, opening his eyes. "I heard some guys joking about this during beer pong."

Clay perks up. "Really? What did they say?"

Jethro props himself up on an elbow, and now they're so close that he lowers his voice. "They said Coach has a new girlfriend, and they hope shit won't go down the same way again. That maybe this time Laytner will keep his hands to himself."

Clay's eyes widen. "Meaning...?"

"Laytner slept with Coach's girlfriend."

"What?" Clay gasps, probably because their coach is sixty years old if he's a day.

"Apparently Coach likes 'em young. And after the team beat Muskegon, they were all at a bar, and she just couldn't resist."

Clay doesn't laugh. He covers his face with his hands. "This is terrible. That's the kind of grudge that lasts a *long* time."

Jethro doesn't have an opinion about this. He's watched plenty of people fuck up their own lives, and it doesn't even surprise him anymore. But Clay's shoulders are up around his ears again.

"How can you be drunk and stressed out at the same time?" Jethro asks. "It's a skill, dude."

"I'm special like that," Clay mutters.

Jethro clasps the muscle between Clay's shoulder and his neck. Rock hard, as usual. "You need to get called up to the big league, if only for the on-staff massage therapist."

"Seriously." Clay snorts, glancing over at him with a fond expression in his eyes. "I'd be all over that."

Jethro finds himself smiling back. Having survived Clay's party, he feels loose and happy again. Which is why he pulls off a tipsy maneuver, rising quickly to pounce on Clay, pushing his shoulders down onto the bed. "Relax, fucker. You got two goals tonight and then threw the best party to ever hit this shitty town."

Clay doesn't smile though. He sort of freezes.

Some people are too uptight for this world. So Jethro moves his hands to Clay's shoulders and squeezes. "Christ, ease up on the tension already." He looms over Clay and tries to work his fingertips into his shoulder muscles. But usually he does this from behind, so it's a little awkward.

Clay finally relaxes under his touch. He tilts his head to the side, giving Jethro better access to his left shoulder, which is always the tightest one.

Jethro uses both hands on that side—lifting his buddy's shoulder an inch off the bed with one hand and using the other to work into the muscle. Clay groans and closes his eyes.

It's late, and they should probably be sleeping. But Jethro gives it his best. He's led a frustrating life, where the hockey rink is the only place he ever feels useful. Growing up, he always felt crowded out at home by his mother's lovers and his sister's tantrums.

But it's different here with Clay. Their house is a sanctuary. And even if Clay is a rich kid, and the sort of golden boy that Jethro will never become, somehow, they're on an even footing. Clay has needs that only Jethro seems to notice. He has various hang-ups and tensions, and it's gratifying to sort them out with something as simple as listening to him vent.

Or with a slightly drunken massage.

"God, you are good at that," Clay mutters.

The praise lights Jethro up, even more than usual. He redoubles his efforts. But after another minute, Clay sort of twists to the side.

"I'm good now." Clay starts to sit up.

"What about the other side?" Jethro playfully pushes him back down again. "Dude." He pins one of Clay's thighs down with his own knee.

Clay goes very still, looking up at Jethro with heated eyes. He doesn't seem to be breathing.

For a second, Jethro doesn't get it. But then he looks down and sees why Clay is being weird all of a sudden. He's tenting his boxers, and when Jethro notices, Clay's body goes solid under his hands.

Their eyes lock, and Clay's are upset.

Seriously. Some people are too tense about *everything*. "Drunk, tense, *and* horny. You hit the trifecta."

Clay gives a strangled laugh.

"Relax. Jesus." Jethro lets go of him and flops onto his back beside Clay. Then he tugs down his own briefs. "Some problems are easy to fix, yeah?" He takes out his own cock, which is already thickening. Honestly, it's a surprise they haven't done this already. They share a tiny bedroom, after all. And a guy has basic needs.

At first, the silence from Clay's side of the bed is so deep that he wonders if he read the situation wrong. But Clay lets out a hot breath as Jethro drags a thumb over his own cockhead. That feels *nice*. So he starts stroking himself.

That's when Clay kicks off his boxers.

"There you go," Jethro narrates as Clay takes his own cock into his fist.

It's no surprise that Clay is beautiful down there, too. He's straight and long. And awfully engorged. Yeah, and Clay is already spanking it like there's a medal for the winner.

"Hey—bet I can outlast you," Jethro says, because hockey players can turn anything into a competition.

A horny grunt is Clay's only comment.

Jethro grins up at the ceiling. The beer is still fizzing through his bloodstream, and this contest is way more fun than beer pong. Seems like cheating would make it even more fun. So he reaches over and grabs Clay's stroking hand, causing him to gasp and lose his rhythm.

With a chuckle, Jethro raises Clay's hand to his own mouth, where he licks a generous stripe down Clay's palm. Then he replaces Clay's hand on his dick.

Clay says "nnngh," and the sound heats Jethro up a few degrees.

"Get it, man. You know you want to."

Clay wants to, all right. As he watches, Clay strokes faster, chest rising and falling on pace with a sprinter's. Jethro strokes himself slowly and rolls onto his side, enjoying the view.

"F-fuck." Clay locks his eyes with Jethro's for a split second before looking quickly away. Then he erupts like a fountain in his own hand and all over his T-shirt.

"Fuck," Jethro echoes just as his balls tighten. Because that was seriously hot. "Look what I made you do."

Clay just gapes at him for a second. It's a rare moment when he doesn't seem to know what to say. Then he grabs his messy T-shirt and pulls it over his head, wiping his hands on the balled-up fabric. He tosses it off the bed and sinks down onto his back with a satisfied sigh.

"Oh sure," Jethro grunts between strokes. "You're all chill for once. And I'm..." He bites his tongue and concentrates. It'll suck if he's gotten himself all boned up when he's too drunk to close the deal.

For a moment, Clay just stares at Jethro's fist, where his cockhead keeps appearing and disappearing. The scrutiny isn't helping all that much, suddenly.

But then Clay—the guy who somehow always knows what another guy needs—flicks Jethro's hand away. He leans over, and before Jethro can guess what's happening, Clay licks him from base to tip.

"Fuuuuuuck," Jethro rasps.

Now it's Clay's turn to snicker. And Jethro can't even take a breath before Clay is swallowing down his cock.

"Holy..."

Clay gives a good, hard suck, and Jethro's eyes practically roll back in his head. His body flashes with heat, and his balls tighten. "You're...*fuck.*"

Clay takes another drag, and Jethro practically levitates off the bed. He sucks in a breath and fights the orgasm that's building.

Because Clay's mouth is magic, and suddenly he doesn't ever want this to end.

But then Clay looks up at him from between his legs, eyes flashing with something like triumph. It's dark and weird and hot. Jethro's nipples ache, and his body's on fire. Then it's all over but the crying. "Look *out*," he manages before he comes.

Clay pops off him at the last second, managing to aim Jethro's cock at an angle so Jethro shoots jizz at his own chin. Then he pumps him two more perfect times, leaving Jethro wrung out like a dish towel and panting on the bed.

All he can do is suck in oxygen for a minute. He's also a little afraid to open his eyes. But when he does, Clay is looking down at him smugly. "Do you cheat at beer pong, too?"

Jethro's mind is too staticky to answer, and he doesn't even mind that much.

Clay, stark naked, leaves the room for a minute. Jethro hears the sounds of toothbrushing before his roommate reappears, still naked, this time remembering to step over the hockey bag on his way into his own bed.

Jethro lies there, stunned, even as his heart rate descends into a peaceful, sated rhythm. *Why was that so hot?* He wants to know if Clay thought so too, but he's never going to ask.

Five minutes later, Clay starts snoring. Jethro makes a half-hearted effort at wiping himself off. He lies there for a while, naked and startled and sexually satisfied for the first time in weeks. It takes him a while to slide into unconsciousness.

But then they both sleep like rocks until the alarm blares in the morning.

TEN

Jethro

THE COFFEE ON THE COUGARS' team jet is better than I'm used to, and the snacks they're serving are first rate. But the perks only make me grumpier.

What good are coffee and snacks if I'm not wanted?

Somehow, every interaction I've had with Clay is more awkward than the last. First the insults. And then yesterday's disastrous practice. Clay could hardly stand to look at me. Afterward, I didn't get a single note or word of encouragement. Even Murphy—his deputy—avoided me after practice. Like I might be contagious.

That was humiliating enough. But now there's an email in my inbox listing tonight's starting lineup, and my name is conspicuously missing.

I'm simmering mad.

It must be obvious, because David "Stoney" Stoneman, the team clown, turns to me in the seat next to mine. "You cool?" he asks. "You seem a little stressy."

"I don't get *stressy*."

"Sure, bud." He gives me a sidelong glance. "Must be my imagination. Wanna see my vacation pictures? The guys dared me to ride a horse. And I never back down from a dare. Check this out…"

47

I snort. "Do I have a choice?"

"Everything is a choice," he says in a chipper voice. "But you don't want to miss this." He opens up his tablet and shows me a photo of himself on a horse, somewhere on the beach.

And it is a funny photo. He's clutching the saddle horn for dear life. Even the horse looks a little nervous.

"I think of myself as a strong guy," he says. "But I could hardly walk for days after this."

"How come?" I hear myself asking.

"Riding a horse uses muscles you don't know you have." He shrugs. "Lots of clenching in the crotch area."

I laugh in spite of myself. "Where was this?"

He flips to the next picture and reveals a collection of hockey players wearing leis and holding coconut drinks. Stoney is kneeling in front of the group in... is that a grass skirt?

"Hawaii," he says. "After we got knocked out of the playoffs last year." He closes the tablet. "Bud, I'd give back my coconut bra if we could make it to the finals this time. You down for that?"

Am I? It shouldn't be a tricky question. I've spent my whole career in pursuit of the Cup, and I've had success beyond my wildest dreams. But the last forty-eight hours have aged me about a decade. My focus is shot, and my heart feels broken. It's not exactly the headspace of a champion.

"You know, I had a thought," says Stoney quietly. "Wouldn't it be sweet revenge if we made it further in the playoffs than your old team?"

"Yeah." I sigh. "Fuck those guys."

He grins.

I lean back in my plush seat and wonder if another championship is even possible for me at this juncture.

If it is, then I have work to do.

If it's not, then what am I even doing here?

"Hey—where're you going?" Stoney asks as I unbuckle my seatbelt and lift my coffee mug off the tray table. "I got vacation pictures from Mexico, too."

"Hold that thought." I get up and scan the rows of seats for Clay. No—for *Coach Powers*. I don't spot him anywhere, so I carry my mug toward the rear of the aircraft, peering into each row of seats.

"More coffee, sir?" asks a male flight attendant when I reach the galley. "I'm Harley, by the way. And you are?"

"Jethro. And yeah. I'd love some."

"Black, right?" He takes the cup.

"If you don't mind. And does Coach have an office back here?"

Harley gestures toward a door. "Right there." He returns my refilled coffee cup. "Ask Coach if he wants a cup? I haven't seen him yet today."

"Will do." I walk to the narrow door. I don't hear any voices on the other side, so I tap lightly with one finger. There's a muffled sound in response—maybe a "come in." I can't tell.

Regardless, I'm on a mission. I open the door and find Clay in a cramped space that's set up like an office. He's alone, and he's peeling his face from the surface of the table in front of him. When he gazes sleepily up at me, it's almost like stepping back in time. His eyes are soft and unfocused, the way he always looked first thing in the morning.

His eyes narrow when they focus on me in the doorway, and I pick up on a few interesting details. Like the imprint from the edge of his spiral notebook that's carved into his cheek.

Of course, I laugh, because that shit is funny.

Clay gives his head a shake, and scrubs at his face. "Something you need?" he growls, his voice thick with sleep.

I swallow my laughter as best I can. "Well, yeah, I wanted a word. But hold on." I lean out into the narrow hallway. "Harley, I think Coach could use some coffee."

The flight attendant hustles to press another mug into my hand, and I look down into the cup. The coffee has a heavy splash of cream in it—the way Clay always drank it. He was a bit of a hedonist. Cream in his coffee. Expensive cheese. Red wine, the glass propped onto his naked chest...

Okay, whoops. The fireproof vault creaked open for a second there.

Mentally shoving those memories back into the dark where they belong, I set the mug in front of Clay before easing the door shut. Then I slide onto the booth-like seat across the table from him.

And, whoa, it's a small room, so we're super close together now. I'm getting a first-row view of his cool blue eyes, the same ones that used to squeeze shut with pleasure whenever I put my tongue...

Shit.

Across the table from me, Clay's expression is stony as he takes a sip of coffee. "Well?" he says grumpily. "This is your meeting. What's the issue?"

"You should play me in St. Louis," I say, because there's no point in making small talk. After all these years, my skills haven't improved. "If you leave me on the bench, it looks like you're not sure about the trade."

Clay takes a slow sip and then grimaces. "Problem is, Hale, I don't give a fuck what other people think."

Maybe I should have stayed in my seat next to Stoney.

"And seriously," he continues, "is the starting lineup negotiable in Detroit? Because in Colorado it isn't. There's no suggestion box for how I start my players."

Hell. I catalog his features over the rim of my mug, and I see all the familiar signs of tension. The crease between his eyebrows. The tick in his movie-star jaw. The cool blue eyes. And an ache bleeds through my chest. How many times did we sit across a table from one another? Hundreds. And sometimes Clay was aggravated. But never at me. I was his port in the storm, and he was mine.

Those days are long gone. I can accept that, but the memories are *really* unhelpful.

And he's waiting for me to say something.

"Look," I say quietly. "I know you're in charge. I'm not here to ruin your day or question your authority. And I know you hate my guts for some reason."

His eyes widen in a flicker of surprise. But then he shuts it down and picks up his mug again. "Don't be ridiculous. I don't hate any player on the team."

"Please. Neither one of us wanted this trade. You made that clear already."

He scowls. "That was a mistake, and I apologized."

"But you're still punishing us both," I argue. "If you bench me, you'll look indecisive or out of step with your GM. I'll look like used goods. And we'll both look like losers."

He sets down the mug with a thump. "Make no mistake—the only way to look like a loser is to lose games," he says crisply. "Volkov is in the net tonight. You'll get your shot the minute it makes sense for the team."

"It was *one* bad practice," I point out. "And you avoided me like a bad disease."

"I'm not avoiding you! I'm showing you some grace, so you can take a minute to get your head around this trade, move your family to Colorado, and adjust to the goddamn altitude before you have to face another team."

"But I shut out St. Louis—"

"—last season," he grits out. "I can read a stat sheet, too. But I already said that this was not a negotiation. Because if I throw you in front of the net before you're ready, and it goes shitty, *then* how smart are we both gonna look?"

I blink back at him, and for a second, I only see the fire in his familiar blue eyes. But then his words sink all the way in.

He *expects* me to fail. He believes it.

I close my hand around my coffee mug and slide out of the booth. "Good talk."

"Jetty..."

I glance quickly at him, and his face tells me that he's just as surprised as I am that he used my old nickname.

"Sorry for the intrusion, *Coach*," I say heavily. "You can go back to your nap."

I spend the game on the bench, and it's a real gong show. St. Louis plays like a pack of stray dogs. Sharp elbows, sharp tongues, and very little discipline.

"Christ," the player beside me mutters. "They're like a classroom full of kids who can't hold it together the last hour before Christmas vacation."

"Keep your heads, boys," Coach says, pacing behind the bench. "We're not solving this problem with penalty points. Play a smart game, win shiny prizes."

From my seat on the end of the bench, I have to admit it's good advice. Also, I have to admit that watching Clay be *Coach Powers* is fascinating. He's a natural leader and always has been.

Except I wonder if he still lies awake at night, his neck muscles tight, wondering how to solve every little glitch in his team dynamics.

Yeah, I'd bet money on it.

Out on the ice, St. Louis is still up to their tricks. I watch their center take Stoney down in a blatantly illegal hit. The penalty is called, but only for two minutes, when it should have been a game disqualification.

The Colorado bench is *pissed*, especially a D-man named DiCosta. He's a big guy with Mediterranean features and a scowl. His hands are curled into fists.

Clay clamps a hand over DiCosta's shoulder pad. "Not your problem," he says calmly. "Let Dougherty take the fight."

I can tell that DiCosta wants to argue. And he wants to pound the offender into the ground.

"Not your problem," Coach repeats, his voice a warning.

And DiCosta actually listens. He meets Clay's eyes and gives him a quick nod. The players trust Clay, so he must be doing something right. More proof—Colorado pulls off a victory against St. Louis.

"Road points!" Clay shouts, slapping backs afterwards. "That's how we get 'er done!"

I almost catch myself smiling.

We all troop back to the dressing room, where I change back into my suit after playing zero minutes of hockey. On the bus to the airport, I take a seat alone. But then Tate, the team publicist, sits down beside me. He's a sleek guy with an impeccable suit and the slick manner of publicists everywhere.

My exact opposite, basically.

"Mr. Hale, I need to catch up with you for a minute. Welcome to the team." His smile is blinding.

"Thanks," I say with as much enthusiasm as I can muster. Which is not much.

"First of all, I need to give you the one-minute stump speech —if anything should happen in your life that a loudmouth on social media would make a fuss about, I need to be your first call."

"After I dial 911, right?"

He laughs. "I like a dry sense of humor. But you know what I mean."

"Yeah. I'm easy, though," I promise. "Been doing this job a while without the wrong kind of media attention."

"Then you're already my favorite," he says, opening up a leather folio containing a legal pad. He clicks a gold pen against his thumb. "Can I ask a few questions?"

"Sure."

"Do you have a partner? It helps me to know who's in your sphere."

Seriously? "Like you didn't google that shit already? No partner."

Tate laughs uncomfortably. "Well, I tried. But you keep a low profile. No social media at all?"

I shrug. "Doesn't suit my surly personality."

He laughs again, as if I were kidding.

"And thank God, right? The shit they must be saying about me right now." I shake my head. "I wouldn't want to know." Getting traded late in my career is deeply humiliating, and I sure don't want to read the comments.

He taps his pen against the pad. "It's not that bad," he says. "Just a few armchair morons who think they know hockey better than the pros."

"Uh-huh." I don't even have to look to know what they're saying. *Has-been. Should have retired already.* Ugh. I haven't even played a game for my new team yet.

"The thing is, you never show your side of things," he says. "You could have posted a triumphant pic in your new jersey. Or posted a sunset shot of the Rocky Mountains. The Motor City isn't the only place on Earth, you know? You could take charge of your own narrative."

My own narrative. "Yeah, because I'm so good at friendly chatter."

"What if I start the account for you?" Tate asks. "I'll put the posts in draft, and you can post the ones you like."

I probably won't like any of them, but I find myself nodding anyway. "Yeah, sure."

"Sweet!" he says with too much enthusiasm. "And I'll handle the comments section and shut down the trolls. Okay. Now back to my questions. No partner... so no family?"

"Oh, I've got one of those. My sister made herself unavailable to raise her kid, so my dad and I are doing that."

"Hell," he says, his smile fading. "I'm so sorry. And your family is moving out to Colorado with you?"

"Yeah, Liana found us a three-bedroom. My dad's name is Jeffrey Hale. And my kid is Toby Hale. Although it's best for everyone if those names never appear anywhere. They deserve their privacy."

"Understood." He scribbles them down anyway. Then he looks up at me. "There's one more thing we need to discuss. In a few days, we've got an upcoming announcement, and the team is sure to make some headlines."

"Oh yeah?" That doesn't sound good. "What kind of announcement?"

He drops his voice. "One of our players is sitting for an interview that goes live on Christmas Day. So what I'm about to tell you is strictly embargoed until then."

"Uh, okay?" Sounds like a lot of drama for a player interview.

"One of your new teammates came out as bisexual to the organization last year. Now he's engaged to a man, and they're going public with their relationship."

I give a slow blink. That isn't something you hear every day in hockey. "Which, uh, teammate?" I ask.

Tate frowns, as if I've disappointed him. "Hudson Newgate. The organization has known about this for months. Your teammates are all cool with it."

The subtext is very clear. I better be really damn cool with it, too.

"Sure. Of course." I give him a quick nod. *But big whoop, PR guy. Who on this bus isn't bisexual? Did you know I've seen your coach naked?*

It'd be almost worth it to see the look on Tate's face.

Almost.

ELEVEN

Clay

FOURTEEN HOURS after our victory against St. Louis, I'm standing in the grocery store, questioning all my life choices.

First, Christmas is two days away, so the store is packed. Second, I'm embarrassed to admit that three days off work feels like too many.

I suppose I could have flown home to Boston to eat Christmas dinner at my parents' table. But my sister Kaitlyn won't be there this year, because she wants to hang out with her boyfriend—a cardiologist at the hospital where she works in Seattle.

So here I am, wandering the aisles, trying to figure out what to cook to cheer myself up. The problem is that everything I put in my cart reminds me of cooking for Jethro. The yams remind me of the time I made him roasted sweet potato fries with paprika. And the broccoli reminds me that he used to like a version with garlic and butter and breadcrumbs.

In the condiment aisle, my eye is drawn to a jar of onion jam, which I haven't bought for years. But there's a flatbread I used to make with bacon, onion jam, and feta cheese.

And now I'm hungry for flatbread with bacon, onion jam, and feta cheese. So the jar finds its way into my cart, too.

It takes me half an hour to make it through the aisles, and then I make a tactical mistake by deciding to cook seared tuna for dinner. The seafood counter is crammed full of shoppers trying to purchase their seven fishes for Christmas Eve dinner.

I take a number and try to be patient. It's not like I have anywhere to be or anyone waiting at home for me. But it's crowded, and a little old lady bumps me with a surprisingly sharp elbow. When I take a step to get out of her strike zone, I accidentally bump another little old lady.

"Excuse me!" I say immediately. "So sorry."

She turns to me with an arch look. "Don't apologize for bumping into me, Coach. But I think you owe me an explanation for that midseason goalie trade. And make it a good one, because you haven't put Hale in front of the net yet. Makes me worry there's some issue with him. Is it his hip?"

Being grilled on my coaching decisions happens often enough when I'm recognized around Boulder and Denver, but I'm a little surprised by her vehemence. My fame isn't the same as the breathless hero worship the players get from fans. It's more akin to being a high school principal when he's out in the wild—everyone wants to lodge a complaint.

"Well?" she demands.

"Everything is fine, ma'am. We have to let Mr. Hale get his bearings here in Colorado so he can concentrate on his game." Luckily, my number gets called next, and I can excuse myself to ask the fishmonger for a nice tuna steak.

"That's an endangered species, you know," my critic sniffs.

"Yes, ma'am." I don't explain that a guy who always eats alone doesn't murder very many tuna. Or that I'd decided on fish for tonight, because it's one of the few things I never cooked for Jethro back in the day.

After wishing her a happy holiday, I take the tuna and finish shopping.

When I arrive back at my condo development, I find that

someone has helped himself to my private parking spot. The squatter drives an ancient minivan with Texas plates. I can see why it happened—the parking lot is jammed. Other people have families who visit over Christmas.

I spend a few seconds wondering if I'm a big enough jerk to call security and complain. But then I think of the potential gossip headline—*Coach Earning 2.5 Million a Year Tows Single Mom's Car Before Christmas.*

Yeah. No.

I park in the overflow lot, feeling grumpy. After unloading the car, I hoof it past the playground with my arms full of groceries. I notice a boy sitting listlessly on a swing, but I don't make eye contact. It's a little odd to see a kid alone out here in the snow. And he isn't wearing a coat. But he seems old enough to be on his own, and people get weird about strange men interacting with their kids, so I keep walking.

Suddenly, he calls out, "Hey mister!"

I stop as he jumps off the swing. "Yeah? Problem?"

"Can I use your phone? I need help."

"Uh, probably. What's the matter?"

He wanders closer, hands jammed in his pockets. "It's like this," he says, looking down at his Chuck Ts. "I snuck out of our new place, and now I don't remember which building it is. They all look *exactly* alike. And my phone is dead. See?"

He pulls an iPhone out of his pocket, the screen black.

Oh heck. I take in his broody face, green eyes... and a hockey sweatshirt from Detroit. My neck prickles. "By any chance are you Jethro Hale's kid?"

He gives me a startled glance. "Maybe. Who wants to know?"

I crack a smile because that's such a Hale-style answer. So suspicious. "Your dad and I are friends. I'm Coach Powers."

The kid's eyes widen like saucers. "*You?* You're the guy who's ruining my life? *You* got him traded?"

"No!" I argue. But then I stop myself, because a good management team doesn't ever admit to disagreements. I mean, this child probably won't phone ESPN and tip them off to internal strife in the front office. Although given his expression, I can't entirely rule it out. "It's complicated," I say lamely.

He glowers.

"But your dad and I have known each other a long time, and I'll help you find him. That's what friends do for each other." I set down my groceries and pull out my phone.

His eyes narrow. "You seem kind of shady to me," he says. "If you were such good friends, you'd probably know that Jethro's not my dad."

"Wait, what?" I look at him again and do a quick recalculation. So he's Hale's stepkid? But that's pretty wild, because he looks like Hale, prickly personality and all.

"He's my *uncle*," the kid says crisply. Like I should already know this.

"*Oh.* So you're Shelby's son. How is Shelby doing?" I never met her, but Hale was always worried about his sister.

The kid's face drops. "Well, she's in jail, which is why I'm having my life ruined by you and Colorado."

I gape at him. "God, I'm so sorry to hear that." My mind is full of questions, and I'm rapidly revising my understanding of Jethro's life. "Let's, uh, find your uncle. You know his number?"

He rattles off a number with a 313 area code, and I dial. Unfortunately, it doesn't connect. And my memory prickles with unease. "Does, uh, he use WhatsApp, by chance?"

"He didn't answer?" the kid yelps.

"Um..." I don't feel like explaining why the call won't go through. "Maybe he's showering or working out. I'll try WhatsApp."

"Maybe he doesn't want to take your call," the kid muses. "Can I have that?" He reaches for my phone, opens WhatsApp and taps out a quick text.

POWERS

I've kidnapped Toby. Send one million dollars and a family-sized package of Oreos.

"Um…"

"That will get his attention." Toby rubs his hands together and then shoves them in the pocket of his sweatshirt. "He's talking to the real estate lady with Grandpa. The place we're getting here is empty. So we have to spend Christmas at a *hotel*." He says the word like you'd say *maximum security prison*.

"I'm so sorry. Here, put these on." I pull a pair of gloves out of my pockets. "I've got another jacket in my car. Should we grab that?"

"I'm not wearing your coat," he sniffs. "Hey—do you know which building the indoor pool is in? I could maybe find my way back from there."

I pick up my grocery bags. "Sure. Toby, right? What grade are you in?"

"Fourth," he says, following me down the path.

"So you're…nine?"

"Ten. I got held back in kindergarten." He looks up and scowls, as if daring me to judge him for it.

"Cool. You like playing hockey?" I ask, straining for a safe topic of conversation.

"Not really."

Lord. I'm out of friendly chit chat already. Luckily, the app makes a ringing sound, and I grab for it like a lifeline. "This is Powers."

"Clay?" Jethro says in a strained voice. "Is Toby with you? What the hell?"

"Yeah. He's just having a little trouble remembering which unit you're in. They all look alike."

"He's outside? Christ. We're in 1202."

"All right. No big deal. We're on our way." I ring off and stick the phone in my pocket. "Come on, Toby. That way." I point towards building twelve, which is the one next to mine.

He sighs. "He's gonna be so pissed."

"Nah, he won't be," I say lightly. "Sometimes he just looks pissed when he can't figure out how else to feel."

Toby thinks this over. "Then he should stop doing that."

I can't really disagree.

As we approach building number twelve—a unit of six side-by-side townhomes identical to mine—one of the doors flies open. There's Jethro in the doorway, arms crossed, wearing a henley shirt that shows off his physique.

Predictably, he looks pissed. "Did you sneak out?" he asks Toby as soon as we're close enough to hear him.

"I was bored," Toby complains. "It's Christmas break."

As we get closer, Jethro steps back from the entrance, and I follow the kid into a completely empty condo. Jethro frowns at me, like he doesn't know what I'm doing here.

And, yeah, I'm not exactly sure myself.

"How'd you get past me?" Jethro asks Toby, who's slinking away.

"Climbed out the window," Toby mutters.

"Jesus." Jethro's shoulders drop. "Get your stuff. We can go back to the hotel."

"Whoopee," Toby says flatly. Then he disappears into a bedroom.

"Sorry about all this," Jethro mutters.

"Don't be sorry." I drop my voice. "He seems stressed. Told me I ruined his life."

Jethro looks even more exhausted than he did a moment before. "He's going through some stuff."

"I, uh, heard about some of it. Sorry about your sister. How long is she, um...?"

"It's hard to say. Parole is weird. She's in for a DUI with injury, plus drug possession. She got high with a friend and drove her car the wrong way in traffic," he says flatly. "Hit a barrier, flipped the car, and her drunk friend almost died."

"God. Poor Toby."

"It could have *been* Toby in that car." His face darkens. "We're obviously not over it. Sorry he mouthed off to you."

"Eh. Sounds like he needed to vent."

Toby reappears with his jacket and a comic book. "I'm hungry. Can we drive through McDonald's?"

"Nah, we'll get a real dinner with Grandpa after this."

Looking put out, Toby glances into my shopping bag. "Got any cookies?"

I stifle a laugh. "How about an apple?"

He brightens. "Sure. Thanks."

I lean over and root into my shopping bag. "Here we go."

Toby takes it, but now he's frowning at my groceries. "What the heck is *onion jam*?"

My neck heats for some stupid reason. And then I make it worse by looking up at Jethro.

For the first time since he arrived in Colorado, he looks back at me. Really *looks*. And for a couple glugs of my heart, we're right back in New York State. We're twenty-something idiots again, standing in our slummy apartment, getting to know each other one meal at a time.

I loved him. Right from the start, probably. The first time we sat down at our kitchen table together, I felt as if we belonged there together.

But he didn't feel the same way about me. And it will always hurt.

TWELVE

Fifteen Years Ago

FEBRUARY

AFTER THE GAME they just played against a Maine team, Clay knows he should be chilling out and feeling satisfied about the win. Instead, he's watching the door to their motel room with nerves fizzing in his belly.

As winter drags on, the Busker Brutes are finally clicking. Passes connect. More of Clay's shots find their way into the damn net. Their stat sheet has completely turned around, and a spot in the playoffs looks pretty likely.

Clay, as the high scorer, gets a lot of credit whenever a local journalist bothers to write up their team, which isn't that often. But he likes to think his impact on the team is bigger than some well-timed shots. He's been building morale for months, one back-slap at a time. The locker room isn't quite so tense and silent anymore.

Things are going well. So many things. And yet he's still eyeing the door at the motor lodge, wondering what's taking Jethro so long to come back with their pizza. Wondering if this is the night when Jethro will notice how needy Clay is for his company.

And worrying that he's about to throw a wrench into things, when maybe he should just fucking enjoy his life for a half second without sabotaging himself.

63

Finally, when he's almost convinced himself that Jethro fed the other half of the pizza to someone else, the key card lock buzzes and the door clicks open.

And there's Jethro, filling the door with his lanky body, a large pizza box, and an uncharacteristic smile. "Was that a great game or what?" he asks with no preamble.

"You know it."

Jethro had a clean sheet, and Clay had two goals. They're celebrating with a large pepperoni from the divey-looking place across the street from the roadside motel.

Clay gets up and grabs the pizza box while Jethro kicks off his shoes and sheds his coat. He tosses the box on his bed and opens the lid.

Jethro swoops in to grab a piece, sitting on the edge of the other bed. "The look on that winger's face when you stripped him in the third." He cackles before taking a big bite.

"I know, right? And the look on their coach's face when you shut him down for the millionth time." Clay smiles to himself as he tastes his first bite. "This sauce isn't as good as mine."

Jethro's agreement is instant. "How could it be?"

His heart swells, and he looks away so that Jethro can't see how happy this makes him. "Want to watch something?"

"Sure. Whatever."

This is part of their routine, of course. It doesn't matter whether they're at home or on the road. After a game, they eat a meal together, and they put on some TV to relax.

Clay chooses a red Netflix disc and slides it into his laptop, ignoring the TV on the hotel's credenza. The laptop screen is small, but that's totally the point. Jethro will have to sit right next to him on the bed after they eat the pizza.

That's how it always goes. They sit side by side—usually on the sofa at home but sometimes in a hotel room on the road. They watch a little TV. And after they're all good and relaxed, Jethro puts his hand down his sweats and takes out his cock. Or sometimes he casually slides a hand past Clay's hip and reaches right into his boxers without so much as a glance at him first.

Clay is always ready but never initiates. He waits for Jethro to make a move. Clay knows he's not fooling anyone—he always responds with the enthusiasm of a lotto jackpot winner, because that's how he feels every time they hook up.

Their repertoire is strictly hand jobs and blowjobs. But these days Jethro reciprocates both. The first time he went down on him, Clay almost fainted from joy. The sight of that sandy head bobbing up and down on his cock was more than he could stand. He had to close his eyes and recite hockey stats to avoid humiliating himself too quickly.

There are unspoken rules, though, and a long list of things they never do. Like kissing. That's off the table. And so is discussing *any* of this. The sex between them is strictly something that happens after dark.

Luckily, the winters are long in the Northeast, so it's dark a lot.

Only once did Clay manage to ask Jethro a question. It was last month, when they were lying panting on their backs, head-to-toe on Jethro's bed after a frantic sixty-nine.

"Did you ever do this before?" Clay had croaked. "Like, fool around with guys?"

"Well, yeah," his roommate had admitted quietly. "Couple times. You?"

"Yup. Once," Clay had said, feeling both relieved and jealous at the same time. Then he'd gotten up and moved to his own bed, like always.

After that single conversation, Clay has been careful not to push more boundaries. He craves more, though. He wants to kiss Jethro so badly that he dreams about it. Given the chance, he'd go in for long make-out sessions, until their skin is abraded, and their lips are bruised. And he wants to fall asleep pressed up against Jethro, kissing the back of his neck where his hair needs a trim.

His heart bleeds a little every time he climbs into his own bed alone.

Tonight, they eat their pizza and watch an episode of *Lost*. Clay can't concentrate. Especially when Jethro gets up and starts rooting around in his suitcase.

"Hey, have you seen my flask?" he asks.

Clay's heart dips. Because this is part of the routine, too—Jethro always does some drinking before the fun part starts. "I think you left it on the kitchen table. At home."

"What?" Jethro gives him an incredulous look. "And you didn't wanna mention that?"

Clay shrugs guiltily. "Why do you need it?"

Unfortunately, Jethro's reaction to this simple question is stronger than Clay anticipated. His face goes red, and his eyes narrow. "Are you trying to send me some kind of *message*?"

Clay feels all the joy leak out of him. He pauses the show on the laptop. "No. It was just a question."

Jethro is not going to let it go. He sits down on the other bed and glares at him. "Do you think I'm a drunk?"

"*No*," Clay insists. The truth is, he's rarely seen his roommate drunk. "Swear to God, I didn't plan some kind of TV-movie intervention. I just wondered..." He's afraid to finish the question.

"You wondered what?"

Good going, Powers. Way to ruin everything. "I just wondered why you always drink before we..." He clears his throat. "Because it doesn't, uh, feel great to be a thing you can only do after three beers or some Jack Daniel's."

Jethro's eyes widen and then immediately turn guilty. He doesn't say a word. He gets up quickly and ferries the empty pizza box into the hall. He makes a stop in the bathroom to brush his teeth.

Clay just sits there, panicking. He forced this conversation. Too bad he forgot to consider how awkward this might be, after he makes a mess of things. They're stuck in this hotel room together.

He's *such* an idiot. He could have just brought the flask along. He could be having a blowjob right now.

Jethro returns from the bathroom. He sits down on the edge of the bed again, facing Clay. "My father is a drunk," he says stiffly. "And my mother was, too, before she got wasted and drove her car into a telephone pole."

It takes Clay a moment to absorb this. And then horror blooms inside his heart. "*Christ*. I'm so sorry. I had no idea. That's... that's not how I think of you."

Jethro scrubs at his face. "But you're kinda right. The Jack is, like, part of a story I tell myself. Two lonely guys having some 'whisky and frisky.'"

Clay barks out a laugh. "That's an expression?"

Jethro shrugs. "I heard it once. Sounded familiar."

Clay's heart sinks a little more. "So, like, it's something you do when there aren't better options."

"Hell." Jethro's expression turns uncomfortable. "That's not what I meant, okay? But that's how it started."

Relief washes over Clay. It's not exactly a declaration of love, but he can work with this. "Fair enough," he says. Then he calmly takes off his shirt and tosses it onto his open suitcase. It's satisfying to watch Jethro's green eyes sweep over his body. "So I guess it's your call," Clay says. "If you can handle the *frisky* without the *whisky*. Just let me know."

Having said his piece, he gets up and heads for the bathroom to brush his teeth. He avoids looking in the mirror, so he won't have to lock eyes with his own desperation.

Pretty soon he runs out of things to do in the bathroom, so he turns off the light and emerges into darkness.

His heart leaps when he sees that Jethro is lying on *Clay's* bed. And he's buck naked, stroking his erection with lazy fingers.

God, the sight of him. All tight pecs and long legs. His shaggy hair on the pillow. It makes Clay bold. Instead of just sliding onto the bed beside him, he kicks off his clothes. All of them. Then he puts a knee on the mattress and swings his body onto Jethro's, straddling him.

Jethro goes perfectly still as Clay seats himself carefully, his cock already full mast and lining up with Jethro's. Clay can't help but admire their two lengths lined up together. What a sight.

Nobody says a word, and Clay is barely even breathing, until Jethro's hand closes around their cocks, making Clay hiss.

"Do you know," Clay asks in a husky voice, "that you're really fucking hot?"

Jethro's eyes widen. Because this is new, too. They *never* speak when they're together. But now he gazes up at Clay with heavy-lidded hunger, and slowly drags his palm over their cockheads.

Enchanted, Clay bends down and bites Jethro's nipple, causing him to gasp. He's already cottoned on to how sensitive Jethro is there. So he laves the puckered skin with his tongue, and Jethro groans.

Clay is on fire. His own nipples are tight, and his balls are already starting to ache as Jethro strokes them with his long fingers. Clay plants his fists on the bed, thrusting into Jethro's hand, and staring down at his pouty lips.

It's just too much. Too perfect. That must be why Clay throws caution to the wind, leans down, and kisses Jethro hotly on the mouth.

Jethro makes a shocked noise, and Clay would worry he'd fucked things up again, except Jethro gets over his surprise in the span of a heartbeat. He licks into Clay's mouth and pulls him down onto his chest.

Clay can't even believe his good fortune. Jethro's hands are everywhere, and Jethro's tongue is in his mouth. *God*, the taste of him. Clay is drowning in the glory of it all.

Until Jethro breaks their kiss, which makes Clay whine. But the goalie has a plan. He licks his palm and slides it back onto their cocks. Then he pushes his feet down on the bed and grinds his hips upward.

The next couple minutes are a little rough and a whole lot sexy. It's a hot, dirty grind that leaves Clay panting and nearing the limits of his patience. He gives Jethro the wettest, dirtiest kiss he can manage, because he's going to come. Right now, actually. He holds back a moan as he shoots into Jethro's hand and all over his cock.

"Fuck," Jethro groans into his mouth. Then he shudders, and Clay feels the heat of his seed as it joins the party. It's the dirtiest, best thing he's ever felt.

With a gasp, Clay shoves his face into Jethro's neck, enjoying the scrape of whiskers on his forehead. Jethro smells like shower soap and heated skin. Clay plants a single, sweet kiss on his neck while their hearts pound in perfect time with one another.

Not wanting to push his luck, he lies very still. And he wonders how long he can stay right here before Jethro comes to his senses and leaves him alone in his bed again.

THIRTEEN

Jethro

CHRISTMAS EVE ARRIVES at the Four Seasons in Denver. There's an impressive tree in the lobby, with soft white lights and shiny ornaments. There's also a special menu in the hotel restaurant, featuring a choice of Lobster Thermidor or filet mignon with a king crab crust and a roasted beef demi glaze.

"What the heck is *that*?" Toby demands.

"It's a steak," I say quickly. "You'll love it. It probably comes with mashed potatoes, right?" I prompt the server.

"It certainly can," the man says, because that's how it works at the Four Seasons. The customer is always right, even when the customer is a surly ten-year-old boy who's missing his mom on Christmas Eve.

My father, who's wearing saggy jeans and a *Mike's Repair Shop* sweatshirt while sitting in the center of a swanky restaurant, orders the Lobster Thermidor.

"Have you had that before?" Toby asks.

My father shakes his head. "No, but it has something to do with lobster *and* cheese. So what's not to love?"

I catch myself chuckling. But five years ago, if anyone had told me I'd be eating Christmas Eve dinner with my dad, I would have questioned their sanity. My father abandoned our family when I was six. Then he'd taken a multi-decade detour into alcoholism before getting sober about five years ago.

At first, I wanted nothing to do with our new-and-improved dad. I don't have a lot of time for people who never had time for me. But then he started showing up for my sister and Toby in a big way. So I grudgingly accepted him as a part of my life.

Then, last year, when my sister wreaked mayhem on the world and on my family, I no longer had the luxury of keeping my father at arm's length. He's five years into his sobriety and his redemption tour. And now that I'm legally somebody's parent, I couldn't get through the week without my dad's help.

So here we are on Christmas Eve, like a real family. This new version of my dad is a calm and quiet man—a little like me in that regard. Honestly, we have a lot in common, which is amusing and sometimes terrifying. I worry that I've inherited his bad heart and his penchant for abusing alcohol.

And I worry that Toby will, too.

Given the chance, my dad would still be back in Detroit, tinkering with engines at the garage where he worked, and planning his retirement. He's almost sixty-six years old. I pay him a salary as Toby's nanny, which means he hasn't had to start collecting social security yet. The unspoken plan is that I'll retire when my contract is up in eighteen months, and we'll revisit the plan for Toby's care.

But here we are instead, twelve hundred miles from home, linen napkins in our laps as we listen to a string quartet play "Silent Night" in the corner.

Toby and I both order the steak, and, damn it, when the food shows up, it's fantastic. The meat is tender as butter, and the green beans spike memories of the ones Clay used to make—with slivered almonds. He called them *haricot vert*, with a French accent, and

I teased him for days. "Just say *beans* like the rest of us, you preppy fucker."

Maybe it sounds like a harsh comment to give the guy who was feeding me. But that's how we were with each other. Clay had a slew of names for me, too. "Jethro the grouch" and "you broody fuck" both come to mind.

I take another bite, and the beans are perfect—buttery, with a nutty crunch. Clay is the only person I've ever known who cooked the same kind of food you might find at the Four Seasons. Young, stupid me thought maybe all rich kids could do that. One time I asked him where he learned to cook, and he'd winced. "Our, um, private chef taught me," he'd said. "I was ten or eleven when I started. Figured out that if I was helping in the kitchen, nobody would make me go do my homework."

That vault where I store my memories of Clay? It keeps drifting open, damn it. And the more I think about him, the more unsettled I feel. The man fed me every day with his own two hands. For an entire hockey season.

And then there's all the sex we had...

"Uncle Jethro?"

I look up and realize that I've been mowing down my food without speaking to anyone. Toby's steak is half gone, so I guess that's not so bad. "Yeah?"

"This is super good," he says quietly.

"Isn't it?" I agree. "What do you think we'd be eating right now if we'd stayed in Michigan?"

He flashes me a quick smile. "Little Caesars?"

"Possibly." I snort. "But it's the holidays, so maybe I would have gone all out. Extra garlic bread, maybe. Or a bag of Christmas Oreos for dessert."

Toby gives me an eyeroll. "You big spender."

"Amirite?" I wink at him and slide my fork through my mashed potatoes. I think they put a whole stick of butter in these, and I'm here for it.

"Mom and I used to make gingerbread on Christmas Eve." Toby looks suddenly crestfallen. "If we'd stayed in Michigan, maybe we could have gone to see her. I could have brought her some."

"We couldn't have," I remind him. And Toby should know this because we've discussed it already. "She's in a treatment facility."

"Even on Christmas?" He squints at me, as if maybe I'm pulling some kind of con on him. "That's mean."

"It's not mean," my father says, sipping his Coke. "It's what she needs to get her life back on track. She's lucky to get treatment at all."

The glance I send my father says *thank you*. I need his help driving this point home. Toby needs to understand that his mother suffers from a disease. But also that the treatment of it is dependent on her in addition to support and intervention.

There's no telling if my sister will ever get her life together. And neither Toby nor my father have any idea how many strings I pulled to get my sister into a pilot program for addiction treatment. I wrote a few checks to the right politicians and sent some hockey tickets to a state senator. That led to a phone call, where he asked me about my biggest concerns as a citizen in the great state of Michigan.

"Since you asked," I'd said, and then I'd told him how my drug-addicted sister had better access to drugs inside prison than outside it. I'd explained how I'd had to stop putting money in her commissary account once I figured out what she was trading it for.

Shelby is one hundred percent responsible for all four of the gray hairs I've counted on my head. But I still got her ungrateful ass into a medically assisted residential treatment program. The downside is that they don't allow visitors, which is hell on Toby. But if it gets her off the junk, it will be a small price to pay.

Toby stares down at the remnants of his dinner. "Maybe you can call the hospital tomorrow and see if they'll put her on Facetime."

I look at his sad face and silently curse my sister's name. I know she has a disorder and that I'm not supposed to blame her for it. But some days that's easier than others. "Bud, she's not allowed to accept incoming calls."

"What about making outgoing calls?"

"Um..." I don't even know what to say. I think I read that she was allowed to call us once she passed the sixty-day mark. And she passed it a week ago. "I'm not sure," I hedge.

He pushes his plate away. "Let's not even have Christmas. What's the point?"

Aw, hell. I search my heart for the right thing to say, and I don't find it. *Thanks, Shelby! Great work, here!*

"The point of Christmas is chocolate lava cake," my father says from the other side of the table. "That's what we need. I saw it on the menu."

Remarkably, Toby perks up. "Do we have to split one? Or can I get my own?"

"You can have one all to yourself," I say quickly. "It's Christmas."

No dessert could make a dent in the shitty week we're having. But for ten minutes maybe I can pretend.

On Christmas morning I wake up in my Four Seasons suite and check my phone. There's a text from Tate the PR guy.

TATE

Please check your email for an Instagram login.
Your password is COUGARS! and the "o" is a zero.
There are three posts in draft.

I guess that guy never takes a day off. I already regret saying yes to social media.

But I log in anyway and peek at the posts he's set up for me, preparing to hate them.

Except I don't. This Tate guy must be pretty good at his job, because he's chosen a few photos I don't hate. One of them is me in a Cougars practice jersey standing next to Stoney. I'm actually smiling, which is rare these days. There's also a photo of the Colorado mountains from the view of an airplane window, and a shot of my new Cougars jersey hanging in my stall on game day.

None of the captions offend me, so I post the one of the jersey, because why not make the publicist happy? At least someone on the team will like me.

Toby wakes up before long, and my father and I usher him toward the small pile of presents that we'd arranged on the coffee table in the living room of our suite. He's getting some clothes and comic books in addition to the gaming console, which suddenly seems like a really smart purchase.

"Omigod! Omigod! Where did you *get* this?" he gushes.

"Just got lucky," I say proudly. But the truth is that I paid triple for it on Ebay. And would have paid more if necessary. Anything to see this kid smile.

He takes it out of the package and holds the controller lovingly in two hands. Then his face crumples, and he shoves a hand in front of his eyes.

"What's the matter?" I ask, panic creeping into my voice.

"I just realized I can't show Trevor. Or play Ninjammers with him."

My dad meets my gaze across the room, mirroring my helpless expression back to me.

Shit. "Can I play Ninjammers with you?" I ask.

"I guess." Toby scrubs at his eyes. "You'll have to do."

***

Ninjammers, as it turns out, is nothing like the sporty games that Clay taught me to play back in the day. It's a juvenile fighting game with ostentatious weaponry and an incomprehensible plot line. After an hour, I've had almost all I can take.

"Kid, it's time for the Christmas brunch buffet," I insist.

"But we just started," he whines.

"I'm not sure you understand. There's strawberries and M&M pancakes, and you can go back as many times as you want."

He finally caves. "But bring your phone," he says. "What if Mom calls?"

So I bring my phone. I'm mowing down a plate of bacon and frittata when my father passes his phone to me across the table. "Hey, look."

"Is it Mom?" Toby asks quickly.

My dad shakes his head. "Just a news story about Jethro's new team."

"Hmm?" I ask, shoving cheesy eggs into my maw.

"You're gonna want to see this." He taps the screen.

When I glance down, I see a studio photograph of Hudson Newgate and the interview the publicist told me about. "Oh, yeah. I heard about this. Newgate used to play for Brooklyn, so they timed this story to come out right before the Brooklyn game."

"Did they?" My father's eyes narrow. "Kinda weird, right? Having this guy in your same locker room?"

My appetite takes a sudden dive. I put down my fork and try to figure out what to say. I can feel Toby listening, too. I guess this is what you'd call a teachable moment. "He's a great player, Dad. None of my business if he has a boyfriend."

"I suppose," my father says slowly. "Still weird, though."

I take a gulp of coffee instead of arguing with him, and it makes me feel cowardly. But I've never felt compelled to explain my complicated sexuality to my family or my teammates.

On the other hand, I've lived my life in a way that made sure I never had to. That makes me a chickenshit.

Toby looks up from his comic book. "Well, I think Newgate's cool," he says. "He's not just another hockey bro. Now he's a trailblazer. Because it's hard to be different."

For a second, I can only stare at Toby. It's pretty pathetic that a ten-year-old who's currently shoving half a pancake into his mouth did a better job explaining this than I did. "You know who else is pretty cool?" I ask. "You."

He looks startled. "Thanks? Will you play more Ninjammers with me after breakfast?"

I guess I earned that. "Sure I will."

FOURTEEN

Clay

CHRISTMAS DAY LASTS one hundred years.

The title of Newgate's article is: "On Winning Games and Coming Out." I read it approximately one million times, in between pacing around my apartment. The only useful thing I do all day is to order a nice bottle of champagne for Hudson and his partner to be delivered tomorrow on game day.

Tate, our head of publicity, sends a lovely email to the whole organization, where he reminds us that we don't have to read the comments. *Reading their shitposts is not your job. Letting them take up space in your head is not your job. It doesn't matter what they say about us. We're a strong organization, and we became an even stronger one today.*

It's great advice. So naturally I ignore it. I read all the damn comments and the ugly tweets, too. Some of them are gross. A few of them are violent. The more inflammatory the comment, the more likely they are to get a like or a share.

I know how algorithms work. The negativity shouldn't bother me, but it does anyway. I could not be more proud of being the coach of the first out player in the league.

But that doesn't mean I'm not worried for my players. I need them to feel safe and supported, so they can do their best work.

Pacing around my condo, I try to lay out the worst-case scenario for our upcoming games. A protest rally in front of the stadium. Or an empty arena, with all the fans staying home. Or fistfights in the cheap seats.

A text pings on my phone. It's from the publicist.

TATE

Stay cool, Coach! It's under control. There's a lot of action on StubHub, but seat prices are going up, not down.

Okay. Well. That's something, I guess. I do another lap between the kitchen, where my pizza dough is rising, and my home gym in the next room. I bang out some pushups. Afterwards, I catch myself looking in the mirror at my pecs, like a teenage dumbass.

On the one hand, it's important to stay in shape. I'd find it hard to ask my players to give me everything they've got while I'm sitting on the bench eating donuts.

On the other hand, I've caught myself dressing more carefully since Jethro turned up. And in the drugstore the other day, a box of teeth-whitening strips made it into my basket somehow.

God, it's loud inside my head. So I do the only thing I can—I hit the mat for another set of pushups.

The Brooklyn game is scheduled for the night after Christmas, and I can hardly sleep. It's almost a relief when seven o'clock finally rolls around, and I have an excuse to get up and go to the practice facility for morning skate.

Naturally, the first person I run into is Jethro. We manage to park our cars in the lot at the same time in adjacent spots.

Pull it together, Powers. I put on my Coach Face and climb out of the car. "Morning, Hale," I say as he joins me on the walk to the building. "How was your Christmas? Did Toby do okay?"

"We survived," he says. He's taller than I am, so I have to lift my chin to make eye contact. His green-eyed gaze socks me in the chest, the same way it always does. "He's taking the separation hard. But at least there's video games for that."

"Ouch. Does he get video chats with his mother?"

"No, and it's rough on him. He's giving me a lot of grief about going to a new school."

"I bet. If you need any help on the admin for that, Liana knows everything. She's handled new-school stuff before."

"We'll manage," is Jethro's response. It's so *him*, too. He'd rather chew off his own arm than ask for help or show an emotion.

Fifteen years ago, I didn't really understand that about him. I'd assumed there was something about me specifically that made him reticent. But it's a perk of adulthood in general—and my job specifically—that I have a deeper understanding about the myriad ways humans respond to pressure.

"Ready to skate?" I ask Jethro.

"So ready," he says. "Let's do this."

Inside, I watch some tape with Murph. "We can probably beat Brooklyn," he says after we review their recent game against Carolina. "It'll be a good matchup, though. You're not going to mess with the lines, right?"

"Nope. We're going to keep things steady. No experiments tonight."

"And in the net?" Murph asks, a teasing smile on his face.

Yeah, that's the big question. Do I play Jethro tonight? If I keep him on the bench for the third time, people are going to talk. On the other hand, tonight's game has its own stresses. It might make sense to keep to familiar patterns. "Let's go watch the scrimmage."

On the ice, Murph blows his whistle before skating lazily over to drop the puck for a face-off, while I watch from the sidelines. "Shake it off boys, and loosen up," he says before flicking the puck to the ice.

"Not gonna lie," he says a minute later as he glides up to the place where I'm standing in front of the bench. "Our guys all look kinda tense."

"Noticed that," I grumble. The scrimmage has a nervous energy that isn't typical before a home game the day after Christmas.

"Your guy Hale isn't helping."

I swing my gaze over to Jethro, who's playing too far into the net again. His forehead is creased in frustration, and his game-talk sounds irritated. "Noticed that, too."

"You putting him in tonight?"

"Still thinking about it," I say.

Murph shakes his head.

After they shower, the players wander up to the third-floor video room. I ask Murphy to take the meeting, and I flag down Jethro. "Could I see you for a sec?"

"Sure," he says gruffly. But his eyes are tense as he enters my office.

"Listen," I say the moment the door closes behind him. I sit at the side—in a visitor's chair. It's a move that says, *We're having a friendly chat, and you haven't been called into the principal's office.*

He remains standing, though.

"So," I say. "I'm putting you in for our Trenton game. We fly out tomorrow."

His shoulders slump. "In other words, I'm benched again tonight?"

"That's right. Tonight is a weird one. There will be a lot of unusual media attention, and I want everyone comfortable. So I'm not changing a single thing in our lineup."

He pinches the bridge of his nose. "Yes, Coach. Whatever you say, Coach."

I snort. "I don't even care if you're being sarcastic. I like the sound of it." I get up and slap him on the shoulder. "Now go watch tape and pretend to be interested."

Hale's eyes narrow. "I'm always interested, because I know I'll be playing that team again, whether it's tonight or not."

I hold back a sigh. "Then I apologize for my tasteless joke." I open the office door, refusing to be distracted by Jethro's disappointed face.

Before I can clear the doorway, I hear someone shout my name. "Clayzy!" I look up and see my sister running toward me.

"Hey! What the hell are you doing here?"

She skids to a stop in front of me, looking indignant. "Is that any way to say hello?" Then she throws herself into my arms.

"Well, hi," I say, my arms full of Kaitlyn. "It's so nice to see you. Although it's also nice when you call first. I'm having a busy day."

"I know, dummy," she says, wiggling out of my arms again. "I'm here *because* of your busy day. This is huge, and I wanted to witness it in person."

"That's cool, Kait. Ten bucks says your boyfriend is also working two hospital shifts in a row."

She actually smacks my arm. "I'd be here even if that wasn't true."

I laugh, but then somebody clears his throat. And I realize I'm blocking the door to my office, trapping Jethro inside. I move my ass out of the way, and as Jethro steps out, he comes face to face with my sister, who looks suddenly startled.

Then her eyes narrow. "So you're Jethro Hale. I'll be damned."

"And you're the sister," Jethro says. "Nice to finally meet you."

"Is it? I'll be keeping an eye on you."

"*Kait*," I warn, and my face is suddenly hot. She knows a lot about what went down between me and Jethro, but nobody else in this building does.

"I'm late for the video meeting," Jethro mutters, gaze darting down the hallway. "Excuse me." Then he sidesteps us both and hurries out of the C-suite.

I grab my sister by the elbow and tow her into my office. Before I close the door, I can see Liana watching us with open fascination. "Okay, what was *that*?" I demand.

"Hey, I didn't say *why* I'd be keeping an eye on him." Kait flounces over to my desk and sits on the edge of it. "I just worry about you and him in the same zip code."

"Well, don't, okay? Ignoring our..." It's still hard for me to figure out what to call it. "Our history is working for us so far. And while I'm happy to see you..." I sigh.

"Don't make snarky comments? Yeah." She pouts. "I know I shouldn't have. But there he was, you know? This guy who wrecked you. Fifteen years later, and you're not over him."

"That is not true."

She raises her eyebrows by a fractional degree but doesn't argue.

I shake my head. "Can we not talk about it? This day is complicated enough."

"True fact." She opens her shoulder bag and takes out a slender box. "I got you a present. For the big game tonight."

"Really? Is it a giant bottle of antacids?"

"No, Clazy. Just open it."

I take the box and lift the lid. The silk necktie inside is mostly blue, because Kaitlyn knows I'm too superstitious to wear a tie in any other color. But this tie has a rep-stripe pattern that alternates blue stripes with perfect rainbow stripes. It's the classiest Pride tie the world has ever seen.

For a long moment, I just stare at it.

"Come *on*," she says. "It's perfect. I squealed when I found it."

"Yeah," I say, my voice thick. "It's exactly the right tie. And I will wear it tonight."

"Then why are you making that pissy face? Wait—did you buy yourself the same one?"

"No." I lift the tie from its box, the expensive silk sliding against my fingers. "I'm pissed because I *didn't* buy myself this tie. I never bought it, and I don't know how long it might have taken me to buy it."

"Oh," she says quietly. "That's why you're so stressed out?"

"Well, yeah. This is a watershed moment for hockey. I'm the head coach—the guy who the players are trusting to carry the flag in this battle—but I've never been brave enough to let anyone know what this means to me personally."

"Okay." My sister's expression gentles. "And here comes Newgate, showing everybody how it's done."

"He's a goddamn inspiration." I dig my fingers into the muscle between my neck and shoulder, which is suddenly spasming.

My sister hops off my desk. "Sit," she says, pointing at a chair. "Let me work on that."

I do as she asks, because I'm not one to turn down a free neck massage. She circles the chair and digs her thumb right into the sorest spot on the first try.

"Look, I know you're going to be under a microscope," she says. "There will be trolls and haters…"

"Whatever. I can handle the haters. I can behave like a professional, even if I'm raging inside."

"Yeah, I know you can," she says soothingly. "Nobody is more professional than you. But please don't beat yourself up about the rest of it. You always put the team first. That's why you're still in the closet."

I look down at the rainbow tie in my hands, and I wonder if that's even true. "That's the story I tell myself, isn't it? When I got the assistant coach's job, I thought—I better zip my lip until I'm in charge. But after I got my promotion, I changed my tune again. I told myself that I couldn't be a distraction. I couldn't take the focus off the players."

"What did I just say about not beating yourself up? This is a big deal. Let yourself feel all the feelings."

There's a tap on the door, and then it opens and Tate, our publicity guy, slips in. "Hey Kaitlyn!" he greets my sister. "Happy holidays. It's good to see you again."

She finishes my massage with a pat on my shoulder. "You too, Tate. And does that mean I can ask you to scare up a ticket for me?"

He chuckles. "Sure thing. Hey, Coach?"

"Something wrong?" I ask. I'm so jumpy today.

"No—this is just a head's up. There's a news truck outside the facility."

"Fuck. *Here*?" I'd expected them at the arena tonight, but I don't want the journos harassing my players while they're trying to get into their gameday mindset.

He shrugs. "I'll give them a statement and explain that we don't do interviews until after the game. Just didn't want you blindsided."

"Thanks," I grumble.

"Hey—that's a great tie," he says. "Where'd you get it? I think I need one."

"Bloomingdale's," my sister says smoothly.

"Awesome." Tate jots that down on the notepad he's always carrying. "Listen, Coach, I just want you to know that it's an honor to be part of this organization. The way you've supported Newgate so bravely." He looks up from his notepad and gives me a blinding smile. "I couldn't be more impressed."

Both my shoulder muscles tense.

My sister clears her throat.

I let out a sigh. "Tate, that's a really nice thing to say, and you've been amazing to work with on this announcement. But maybe save that bravery trophy for Newgate. Because..." I swallow. "I'm also a queer man in professional sports. But I never did what Newgate is doing tonight."

Tate blinks. And then, to his credit, he recovers awfully fast. "Thank you, Coach, for sharing your truth with me. I understand how hard that can be."

"We're going to find out, aren't we?" I glance out the window, where a news truck is now visible in the parking lot. "Thanks for all your hard work. Safe to say that I appreciate it."

"Yessir," he says. "More updates later." Then he disappears, closing the door behind himself.

Kait gives me an amused glance and shakes her head. "Keep it together, Coach Powers. Tonight is going to be great whether you're ready or not."

I sure hope she's right.

Fifteen Years Ago

MARCH

SNOW IS THAWING into slush outside their hotel in Connecticut. The Brutes have just finished up a five-game road trip, where they picked up four points and secured their playoffs slot. And Jethro only let in one goal tonight, so he's in an uncommonly good mood.

He looks around the lobby, seeing a beer in every one of his teammates' hands. They're all in a partying mood, even if they'll be getting up at four a.m. for the bus ride home.

Clay, ever the social director, has brought his PlayStation to the hotel bar, and he's bribed a bartender to let him set it up with one of the bar's TVs. Jethro watches with amusement while Clay organizes a tournament—with brackets drawn on a napkin—for a driving game called *Track Wars*.

Jethro doesn't volunteer to play, but Clay puts him down as his partner anyway. Jethro isn't much of a gamer. He's never had the cash for a console and doesn't understand the controls super well.

Clay's competitive streak is clearly annoyed with him. "Fucks sake!" he crows after Jethro's car gets totaled yet again. "You have to downshift when the skid starts. See?" He reaches around Jethro's body and drags his thumb onto the right button. "Hit these both at the *same time*, or we're gonna lose in the first round."

Jethro, conditioned to listen to whatever Clay says, gives the move a try. "Cool. Thanks."

"Aww, look at you two!" crows Trey Duckson. He's a very stupid defenseman for whom there's no shortage of terrible nicknames. "You cuddle like that at home, too? So fucking gay."

There's instant laughter, and Jethro goes ice cold inside.

Clay releases him and straightens up, but Jethro tenses. This is the second time Duckson's made a comment like that, and Jethro wonders what Clay will say.

"Oh no!" his roommate bellows. "Is Fuckson *jealous*? Do you need a hug, too?" He throws his arms open and staggers, Frankenstein-style, toward the asshole.

"No! Shit." Duckson smacks Clay away with the hand that's not holding a cheap beer. "Just saying—all the love in the world can't make your boy a champion. Jetty is hopeless."

Your boy. Something uncomfortable slithers inside Jethro's chest. He can feel eyes on him, and it stings like a bad sunburn.

"Not as hopeless as that thing you call a beard." Clay lunges, trying to get a handful of the untrimmed nightmare on Duckson's chin. "Oh God, it *moved*. I think there's a family of possums in there."

Everybody laughs again. Everybody but Jethro. No matter how skillfully Clay skated around Duckson's comment, Jethro's still heavy with dread.

Not Clay, though. He claps his hands. "Okay, kids. Who wants to play next?"

Jethro forces himself to turn and pass the controller into someone else's waiting hands. Then he excuses himself to go up to use the bathroom in their room, and somehow never makes it back downstairs.

A few hours later, he hears Clay enter their hotel room. It's past midnight, and they're getting up at four. In spite of the late hour, Clay stops by his bed. "Jetty, you okay?"

No. He really isn't. And for the first time ever, he ignores Clay and pretends to be asleep.

Owing to a very long bus ride and the general air of exhaustion, Jethro is able to nurse his discomfort without Clay noticing.

Clay seems his usual self when they finally get home—moving around the kitchen, pulling things out of the fridge to see what's still edible. Sniffing the milk. Then he declares a state of emergency and drives off to the grocery store.

Jethro doesn't offer to help. He lays on the sofa, feeling hollow inside.

Somehow, these past few months, this apartment has become his favorite place on the planet. Good food and hot smiles from Clay. No judgment about anything. And, fine, all the sex he'd ever need. He's enjoyed it all without questioning it too much, like a hungry dog wolfing down a steak before someone snatches it out of his jaws.

But now reality presses in. This...thing between them. It isn't just a frantic scramble in the dark anymore. It got bigger without him really noticing. It can't last—he's always known *that*—but it's just now dawning on him that it could end really badly.

As soon as he hears the purr of Clay's German car, he gets up and hurries into the bathroom. He starts the shower and scrubs the bus ride off his skin. He unpacks his suitcase and puts his dirty laundry into the bag. When he emerges to head out for the laundromat, Clay is whistling to himself at the stove.

By the time Jethro returns with clean, folded clothes, the apartment smells like roasted garlic.

"Hey," Clay says from the sofa. "I already ate, but there's a plate for you in the oven."

Jethro feels an uncomfortable heat behind his breastbone.

"Thanks. Wow." *There's a plate for you* are words he rarely heard in his life. His mother seemed surprised each day when her kids got hungry for dinner. And annoyed when she had to do something about it.

He puts the plate on a tray that Clay bought for this very purpose and joins Clay on the couch. But he sits a healthy distance away. They watch an episode of something, and Jethro registers almost none of it. He's thinking too hard.

He steals glances at his roommate, watching the way the TV light plays across his attractive profile. What *is* it about that guy? Why does his husky laugh echo inside Jethro's chest? All the other people in Jethro's life seem dull by comparison.

Sitting here, in their shared space, Jethro always feels a contentment he can't quite name. A sense of belonging he's never experienced before. It scares him, how much he's come to rely on these quiet moments together. How much he craves Clay's company, his attention, his touch.

Like a plant turning toward the sun, he can't resist the guy. Fooling around has only made their friendship stronger. To Jethro, the weirdest thing about it is that it doesn't really seem weird.

The fact that he and Clay get off together would seem awfully fucking weird to other people, though. He knows this. Which is why Jethro keeps to his end of the sofa even after he's finished his chicken. His brain just won't shut off tonight.

Finally, Clay pauses the show. "Okay, what the hell? Are you just going to sit over there and worry?"

Shit. Jethro doesn't have anything smart to say. As usual. So he says nothing.

Clay doesn't let it go. He turns to Jethro with anger in his eyes. "Are you really going to let the dumbest man in hockey ruin your night?"

Oh boy. Clay is *pissed*. And Clay is never pissed at him.

"Come on," Jethro finally argues. "You can't tell me that you like people talking about us."

"But they're *not*. It was one stupid comment."

Jethro rubs his forehead. "I don't get it. You're the worrier. You're the one who thinks up ten new things that could go wrong every day before breakfast. Ten reasons we'll be stuck forever in the minors. Like that ref with the grudge? And Coach breaking up with another girlfriend? You're always ready to declare a disaster. And you seriously don't think the biggest risk is really..." He gestures helplessly. "*Us*?"

The blow lands. As Jethro watches, the fight drains right out of Clay.

Clay drops his head back onto the sofa and stares up at the ceiling. "Look," he says in a low voice. "You want me to move out? If you're so worried, I'll tell the guys that my trust fund payout went up, and I wanted my own space. Just say the word, and I'm gone."

This is not just a threat. He can tell Clay means it, and the idea is deeply unsettling. "I didn't say *that*, did I?"

"Either you're worried or you're not," Clay says tightly. "Which is it?"

A sick feeling rolls through Jethro. He's so confused right now. Clay is everything to him. But they're cohabitating in a fantasy world, where it doesn't matter who you fuck.

In the real world it does, though. Everyone knows that.

"Maybe we should live separately next season," he hears himself say.

Clay doesn't look at him. He just picks up the remote and restarts whatever it is they're supposedly watching.

Jethro puts the tray on the coffee table. He should get up and do the dishes.

But he doesn't. Instead, he does something really weird. He tips onto his side and rests his head in Clay's lap, uninvited.

For a moment, nothing happens except a few more lines of cheesy dialogue from "How I Met Your Mother." But then Clay's hand drops into his hair. Jethro closes his eyes when Clay begins to run his fingers through it.

Jethro shivers. It only takes another moment until he relaxes under the gentle touch of fingertips running along his scalp, and Clay's thumb stroking the sensitive skin at the back of his neck.

He knows this can't last forever. It really can't.

But maybe just a little while longer.

SIXTEEN

Jethro

THE UBER RIDE from my hotel to the arena shouldn't take more than a few minutes, but when the driver starts muttering to herself, I look up from my phone and realize it might take a while to approach the back entrance.

More than a dozen news trucks cluster in the drive circle, their satellite dishes reaching toward the sky like ugly metallic flowers. And there's a row of crowd-control barricades set up in front of the arena that aren't usually there.

When I see a group of people waving signs, my stomach drops. But then I read them and blink. *DROVE TEN HOURS, NEED TWO TICKETS!*

Those people aren't picketing, they're pre-gaming. It's like a strange little tailgate party, and the price of admission is at least one item of clothing in rainbow colors.

"Not sure I can get any closer than this," the driver grumbles, waving at a sawhorse guarded by a couple of cops. "You okay here?"

"Uh, sure." I could probably flash my team ID and get the car past the next pinch point, but there's no need. "Thanks."

"De nada," she says, and I feel a weird prickle at the base of my skull. I grab my gym bag and leave the car behind, threading past some bystanders and heading for the players' entrance.

"Excuse me," a policeman says. "You got ID?"

I pull it out of my pocket and hand it over.

He checks the ID and then looks me up and down in my game day suit. "Wait. You're the new goalie?"

"Yeah."

He hands back my ID. "You gonna play ever?"

"I've been wondering that myself."

He doesn't even smile. "Stay sharp. I'm counting on some play-offs action this year."

"I'll keep that in mind."

Inside, I make my way to my stall, noticing immediately that there's a skittish energy in the room. Tate is buzzing around like a nervous bee, his phone glued to his hand.

There's a special warmup jersey set out for me, and I hold it up for inspection. It's rainbow tie-dye in riotous colors.

Volkov, who will be in the net again tonight, weighs in from the bench next to mine. "Very bright," he says. "Like a unicorn vomit on jersey. But, hey, if Newgate have kink for this, I wear it."

Across the room, Newgate gives him the finger, and everyone snickers.

For the hundredth time in a week, I feel like I've stepped into someone else's reality. If you had told me at twenty-two that I'd be standing in an NHL dressing room listening to a Russian goaltender gently ribbing his queer teammate about a rainbow jersey, I would never have believed it.

I change into my workout gear as Tate makes another nervous lap of the room. "StubHub seats are up to fifteen hundred bucks," he says gleefully.

"You know what this means, right?" Clay's voice booms suddenly from the doorway. His hair is freshly cut, he's wearing a very sharp suit, and his tie is a tasteful blue with subtle rainbow stripes on it. "You boys have got to win this game. Can't make a big splash in the news cycle and then hand Brooklyn two points on the road." He rubs his hands together. And then his gaze sweeps the room, making eye contact with every player.

Every player except for me.

Yeah. Okay. I'm probably the last person he wants to think about today. Or ever.

I slide out of the room and head for the alcove where there are mats on the floor for stretching. My pregame routine used to take a half hour, but now I'm up to about forty-five minutes. It doesn't matter whether I expect to play or not. Staying this limber at thirty-seven requires a lot of effort.

On the mat, I start with big muscle groups. Quads and hamstrings. I'm stretching my hips when a face appears in the doorway. It's the man of the hour, Hudson Newgate.

"Hey," I say. "There's plenty of room. And only one of us made it onto the starting lineup."

"A little bitter, huh?"

"What? Aren't I hiding it well?"

He snorts and flops down on the mat beside me.

"You want the space?" I ask. "Maybe you need a break from people."

"Nah, distract me," he says. "Believe it or not, I don't really enjoy being the center of attention."

My heart rate bumps up a notch, because I can't even imagine what kind of a day he's having. "You okay? You feel solid? Do people keep asking you that?"

"Only all of them." He leans forward, stretching his hamstrings.

It costs me a lot, but I add, "For what it's worth—which is not much—I think you're really brave." *In a way that I could never be.*

"Thanks. But that's the funny thing; it's not about being brave. It's about getting to a place where my personal life is more important than what the hockey world thinks."

"Okay. I can understand that." Maybe? The truth is that I'm

incapable of looking at anything that way, because hockey *is* my life. There's no separation.

He shrugs. "Hockey can be so insular. And conservative, in the classic sense. We don't like change."

"Yeah. I'm just barely used to having quick-release blades."

"Exactly." Hudson leans into a stretch. "But where fans are concerned, somehow I ran out of fucks to give. Coach Powers made this possible, by the way. He's a great guy once you get to know him."

I crack a smile. "We played together fifteen years ago in the minors. Back when Earth was green."

He sits up and smiles. "No lie? You must have some good Coach Powers stories, then. What was he like as a teammate?"

"Uh…" I chuckle uncomfortably. When I think of twenty-four-year-old Clay, I don't picture him skating. I picture him stirring his homemade tomato sauce in our kitchen.

Shirtless.

But that's not the image I need right now. "He was flashy as a player. But always responsible, too. A natural leader. He had some of Kapski's dad energy even then."

"Yeah?" His smile widens. "Come on. Give me one good story."

"Well…he used to get the whole bus singing. One time he got the whole team to sing 'Bohemian Rhapsody.'"

Newgate laughs. "Please tell me there's video."

"Sad to say there's not. Another time the bus broke down before our dinner stop, and we were all starving. We ended up at this truck stop with a strip club but no restaurant. Coach wouldn't let us go into the club. So we're standing around helping the bus driver change a tire, and Clay sneaks into the strip club and asks for forty dollars change. 'Because strippers always have singles…'"

Newgate hoots.

"Yeah. He came out with the cash and bought out the vending machines for us."

The moment Newgate lifts his gaze toward the doorway, my neck heats.

"You telling tales?" Clay booms from behind me.

I turn around to find him leaning against the cinder-block wall, looking too classy for this world. "Just a couple," I say, suddenly embarrassed. It's a really inconvenient time to remember how attractive I used to find him. "In my defense, he asked me to distract him."

Clay suddenly looks worried. "You okay?" he asks Newgate.

"I'm *fine*." Newgate gets to his feet. "I promise. Just feeling really weird about being the diversity poster boy for an entire sport. No big deal."

Just the idea makes me want to climb out of my skin.

"Come and sign a few items for the auction," Clay says. "Then see the trainer."

"Yeah. Okay." Newgate strides out of the alcove. "Later, Hale."

"Later, kid."

I wait for Clay to leave, but he doesn't. "He's not a kid," he says.

"They're all kids," I grumble, tipping onto my back to pull my knees into my chest. "From one dinosaur to another. Am I right?"

Clay sighs. "Not gonna let that go, huh?"

"Nope."

He finally walks away.

SEVENTEEN

Clay

IT'S ALMOST GAME TIME. The arena is jam packed with fans. My players are about to make history. The number of news vans outside has swelled beyond my wildest imagination. We're the story of the hour.

And I'm a mess inside. A goddamned mess. I want to barf from nerves and then hide in a corner somewhere with a cool washcloth on my forehead.

Instead, I force my shoulders back and give my players a last-minute pep talk before warmups. "For some people, tonight is a big deal. We'll have new eyes on us." The room goes quiet, as it always does, because I run a tight ship, and this is a respectful team.

If only I felt truly deserving of that respect tonight.

"The thing is, though—we've already done the work that's led us here. We already know that being a team means more than passing the puck or covering each other on the ice. It means embracing every player's unique contribution. We understand that the strength of a team lies in its unity and the trust we place in one another.

"We support our teammate Hudson Newgate—and *all* our teammates—every night. So it doesn't matter who's out there watching or what they write about us in the news tomorrow. We already know who we are. We already know what to do when the puck drops. All we need to do is bear down and do it. It's time, guys. Let's show all our new fans how this is done. Cougars on three."

Murph counts to three, and then the room shakes with the force of thirty raised voices. Including mine. And Hale's, whose face I find unerringly in the crowd, even if I'm not supposed to seek it out.

In their bright rainbow jerseys, the players hustle out the door and into the tunnel. I stay to the back, clipboard in hand. The crowd gets louder as I draw nearer to the ice, which is wild, because the game doesn't start for another half hour. Warmups are usually for diehard fans only.

Not tonight. When the first players reach the bench, the crowd erupts with cheers. Bringing up the rear, I stop and stare at the spectacle of packed seats throbbing with fans in Pride gear. They're wearing rainbow hats and face paint. Many of them are waving signs, mostly on the theme of: *WE LOVE YOU NEWGATE.*

"Holy pepperoni," mutters Stoney. He hasn't taken off his skate guards. He's just standing there, gaping like I am.

I clap my hands together. "Let's go, boys. Clock's tickin'."

Newgate takes the ice, and the crowd screams. His face is bright red as they chant his name. "NEW-GATE! NEW-GATE!"

"Huh," Stoney says, stepping onto the ice with a couple other players. "If I kiss a dude, will they chant my name? Anybody wanna test that out with me?"

"You score a goal in the first five minutes, I'll kiss you myself," Kapski says. "Get a hat trick tonight, and I'll even give you tongue."

"NEW-GATE, NEW-GATE!" says the crowd.

Newgate skates toward center ice, where a couple of his ex-teammates from Brooklyn are waiting for him. We timed his announcement with this game for a reason.

The crowd erupts as he fist-bumps them one at a time.

My guys hit the ice for real, and I try to pay attention. This is my last chance to think about our plan of attack. Just because Brooklyn has some friendly faces doesn't mean they're going to hand us the win.

But it's no use. I keep staring down at my clipboard without really seeing it. In my head, I'm a scared teenager again, terrified to confront my sexuality. Keeping my eyes down in the locker room, wondering who'd kick my ass if they knew about me, hearing homophobic slurs casually tossed around and trying not to flinch.

Then I'm the loneliest guy on my college campus, working hard to charm everyone around me so they won't see what an anxious mess I am inside.

And then I'm in Busker, New York, slowly falling in love with Jethro Hale and feeling queasy every time I try to picture a future with him. For good reason.

Today the world has changed, at least for Hudson Newgate. Literally thousands of people showed up here tonight to tell him that he's enough just the way he is. That he can have a life without hiding.

It's awe inspiring. It's amazing. It's... stinging my eyes.

Damn it.

I force some cool air into my lungs, but it's not enough. I turn around and stride back into the tunnel. It's blissfully quiet, and I need a minute to myself. Or maybe several minutes. I take a slow, deep breath and exhale through my nose. But I'm actually shaking, and my hands are clenched into fists.

Let yourself feel all the feelings, my sister's voice repeats in my head.

Easy for her to say, when I'm the one shaking in the tunnel. I bend over and grab my knees, while each breath saws heavily out of my lungs.

After a minute or two, a shadow appears in my peripheral vision. And then a pair of goalie skates clomp into view.

I turn my head to confirm the inevitable. It's Hale, which just fucking figures. He's holding a cracked goalie stick.

"Kapski got me with a slap shot," he says.

I make no reply, because I don't trust the sound of my voice right now. Hale's the last person I want to talk to. So I don't. I stay where I am, my gaze on my shoes.

"C-Coach," he says, catching himself before using my actual name. "Uh, you okay? You don't look so good."

"I'm fine," I grunt. *Please go away.*

"But..." He hesitates. "Look, maybe I should go grab Coach Murph—"

"No!" I snarl, straightening up. "Jesus Christ! Just fuck off, already! Go get a stick, or go the fuck back to Detroit. Now is not the time. If I needed your help, I'd ask for it."

He throws his hands up as if in self-defense. "Christ almighty, I thought maybe you were having a heart attack. Just trying to be helpful, *Coach.*"

Then he stomps off, and I lean against the wall, my heart pounding. *Get a grip, Powers. Get a fucking grip.*

EIGHTEEN

Jethro

WITH NO HELP FROM ME, the Cougars beat Brooklyn in a close matchup.

Clay—who reappears behind the bench before anyone mentions his absence—coaches the game with great enthusiasm.

His eyes are suspiciously red. I keep sneaking looks at him, trying to understand what the hell is going on with him. As best I can tell, everything should be going great. He's coaching a winning team—one of the most-loved teams in hockey if the deafening crowd is anything to go by. And he just helped one of his players do what had once seemed impossible—to come out in a major-league sport in the classiest possible way.

The thing about Clay Powers, though, is that what you see is not always what you get. That lead vault where I keep my memories of him is seriously cracked by now, so it's not a stretch for me to picture him at twenty-four, building team morale one cheese plate at a time.

Even then, he was anxious. Those headaches. And the way he paced our small apartment trying to figure out what could be done to turn our donkey of a team into a stallion.

Coach Powers might have matured by fifteen years, but it's just dawning on me that the nervous kid I knew is still in there some-where. Still anxious about his choices. Still trying to get everything exactly right.

He's managed it tonight. That's for damn sure. As he coaches his team to a third-period victory, I watch and wonder why he was so upset before the game.

The fascination only goes in one direction. Somehow, Clay avoids looking at me for the entire game. Nobody else does, either. When the final buzzer sounds, the players' joy is palpable.

Clay is ebullient, patting backs and high-fiving players. His smile is wide, but his face is red with emotion, and his eyes are shiny. I have the strongest urge to push my way into the knot of people around him and grab him into a big, hockey hug.

But then I remember we don't do that anymore.

And I wonder if Clay still believes it's my fault.

NINETEEN

Fifteen Years Ago

APRIL

THE BRUTES ARE ON A TEAR. Game five of the first round of playoffs is a blowout, which means they'll advance to the next round. When the third period ends, the scoreboard says 4-0, and the skaters pile onto each other at center ice, like a pack of smelly puppies.

Clay scored *twice* tonight, and he's planning on scoring again when he gets home later. Because Jethro had a shutout and will totally want to celebrate.

He can't help it. His eyes lift to find Jethro at the other end of the scrum, laughing and spanking Laytner's ass with his goalie glove. His expression is more playful than Clay has ever seen it before.

Smiling to himself, Clay pats a few more backs as he heads for the bench to collect his stick. He's stopped by their coach. "Powers —my office after you shower? I need a word."

"Sure, Coach," he says automatically. But a familiar prickle of anxiety runs up his spine. They just *spanked* this team, and they're off to the second round of the playoffs. So why does Coach look grumpy?

He heads for the showers, trying and failing to figure out what might be wrong. Clay hasn't broken any rules. Well, not the written rules...

Hell. This can't have anything to do with Jethro, right? They've been careful. Haven't they? A locked door is a locked door. Although the cheap hotels where they stay on the road might have flimsy walls.

Shit. If there are rumors about the two of them? Jethro will lose his mind.

He cuts his shower short and hastily dries and dresses. He waves a comb in the direction of his overgrown hair and weaves through the celebrating bodies in the dressing room toward the coach's office.

Outside the door, he pauses for a moment. He drops his shoulders and lifts his chin before knocking. "Coach?"

"Come in." Coach is sitting behind his shitty little desk. The team's facilities are third rate, like everything in the bottom rung of professional hockey.

But Clay wouldn't trade it for anything, and now he has to wonder why Coach still looks pissed off. He takes the empty visitor's chair and waits.

Jethro is on a high after the win. Like everything is going well for a change. He follows his teammates to the Interstate, one of the few bars in Busker that stays open until midnight on weeknights.

"Yo—Jetty! Where's your better half?" asks Laytner.

He hears the little dig about the way he and Clay are always together but ignores it. Glancing around the bar, he says, "Dunno. Clay's gotta be here somewhere."

Except he isn't, which is super weird. He checks his phone, but there aren't any calls or texts. So he shoots him a message.

Hey! Dude. You okay? You got a flat somewhere?

No answer.

Yeah, that's strange. Clay would never bail on a celebration with the team. He's worked his ass off this season to shake up the dressing room and form a connection with every last guy. It's sort of obvious that Clay will be an assistant captain next season.

If he's not here, something must be very wrong.

"He must'a picked up a girl already," Duckson says with a snort.

"Right?" someone agrees. "Pretty-boy face. Nice car. Two goals tonight. I'm surprised we *ever* see him at the bar."

"Yeah," Jethro says with an awkward chuckle. But he feels sour at the thought. Which is weird, right? Clay can pick up some girl if he wants to. Just because the two of them are kind of...

He can't finish that thought without getting uncomfortable. There's no name for what they are to each other. Well, they're roommates. And teammates. But there's no *additional* word.

This is exactly the kind of thing he isn't supposed to be dwelling on, because nothing good can come from it.

Except now he's suddenly dwelling on it. He gets another beer and tries to make conversation. He watches Duckson challenge Boyer to a game of darts.

All the usual smack talk goes over his head tonight as he keeps glancing at his phone, wondering where Clay is. He still hasn't answered any texts. Which could mean one of two things.

Maybe Clay *did* take a girl home to their apartment. That's never happened before. It's awfully easy to picture, though. Clay has that kind of nice-guy charm that puts women at ease.

He shouldn't care. He really shouldn't. And, yeah, if Clay is going to ignore his team and ignore his texts, he must be with a girl.

Unless it's the second thing. Maybe he got into a car accident or some other awful bind.

Jethro puts down his beer and walks out of the bar. He gets into his junker and turns the key, listening to the rough engine warm up. Then he drives five miles back to the apartment building and parks beside Clay's BMW.

Okay. Well. Clay did make it home. That's good, right? So why does he suddenly feel ill?

With wary slowness, he gets out of the car, grabs his hockey bag out of the trunk, and walks up to the building. Lamp light filters from the blinds, which are always kept closed because... Because of what passersby might see if they glanced into the window on any given night.

So, yeah, there's no way for him to see inside, and that's why he's standing here, key in hand, feeling uncomfortable in a dozen different ways.

Finally, he opens the door and steps inside. Clay's hockey bag has been dropped unceremoniously by the front door, which is unusual. Jethro's discomfort redoubles.

Clay suddenly emerges from the dark little corridor to their bedroom, alone and fully clothed.

"Hey!" Jethro says brightly, mood immediately brightening. "You didn't come out to the bar. The guys were asking for you."

Clay folds his arms across his chest, his face doing something complicated. "Yeah. Uh..." He looks down at his feet. "I got some news."

"*Oh.*" Jethro mentally pivots, the way he's had to do his whole life.

News is like that. You come home from kindergarten one day, and your dad is gone—all his clothes missing from the bedroom closet. Or the phone rings, and your mom has been arrested again.

That kind of shit flies at you whether you're ready or not, but Jethro is still caught off guard, even when he should know better. "What news, man? Are you okay?"

Clay grabs some papers off the counter and thrusts them toward Jethro.

He takes them and reads the first couple of lines.

American Hockey League Standard Player's Contract
This Agreement, made and entered into this date, by and between the
Buffalo Blizzards LLC (hereinafter referred to as "Club"), and Clayton
Powers (hereinafter referred to as "Player")...

It takes a second to sink in. But then a current of joy sizzles through him, and he lets out an uncharacteristic whoop. "Holy *shit*, Clay!" He slaps the papers down on the counter and grabs his buddy by both shoulders. "You got called up?"

"Yeah," Clay whispers hoarsely. "I'm supposed to drive out tomorrow."

"Holy shit," he says again. "I gotta do round two without you?"

"Seems like it." Clay slowly lifts his eyes. They're surprisingly heavy, given this news. "The fucked-up thing is that I don't really want to leave."

"What? Sure you do," Jethro insists.

He's riding high on this sudden change of fortune. Because Clay isn't in a car wreck, and he's not fucking some woman in their bedroom. He's moving up in the world—exactly what Clay has been working towards.

And even if Jethro never expects it to happen for himself, he cares enough about Clay to be wildly happy.

Clay, though, is oddly silent and studying Jethro carefully at close range.

Jethro's hands are still parked on his roommate's shoulders. He gives them a squeeze, even though he suddenly has the sinking feeling that he's failing some sort of test.

It's not an unfamiliar feeling. He's failed plenty of tests in his life. And Clay is always a couple of steps ahead of him. Clay, who was always too bright and shiny for Busker, New York, or for the third-tier league.

Losing him will be a blow, for sure. In so many ways. But this is still a great moment. It's just proof that the universe understands that Clay is the best there is.

So then why does he look so apprehensive?

"You worried?" Jethro guesses, stepping back to give Clay some room.

Clay grabs the back of his neck. The gesture is so familiar now that Jethro feels a pang in his chest. "Not about the hockey. But..." Clay frowns, and his sentence dies.

"What's wrong?"

"We..." Clay clears his throat. "You and me. After the playoffs. I could come back."

"Come back? But they *signed* you." Did he read that wrong?

"For the summer," Clay clarifies. "I could be here. In Busker. Well, not for more than a few weeks. I'm invited to the rookie training camps in New York."

"Holy *shit*," Jethro whispers, because that's huge. A smile spreads across his face, picturing Clay doing drills with the greatest players in hockey.

"So...yeah. It's going to be a busy few months. But we could still be..." He clears his throat.

Jethro is silent, trying to take it all in. It doesn't help that Clay—who can always find the right words for everything—isn't explaining himself very well. "Be what?" He's going to need to have it spelled out.

"*Together*," Clay snaps.

"Oh," Jethro says with genuine surprise. "But..."

They won't be together, though. That's the whole point of this conversation. Clay is going to Buffalo and New York City, too. Jethro isn't.

Clay's face falls, like Jethro has failed yet another test. "God, never mind. Forget I said anything." He turns around and stalks into their bedroom.

"Hey," Jethro says, following him. "You know I'm kind of slow. What are you really asking of me?"

His roommate doesn't answer. He's cramming the last of his expensive clothes into a giant suitcase that's open on the bed.

"Clay—"

"Forget it," Clay says, sounding tired. "This solves all your problems, right? You were in it for the home-cooked meals and the blowjobs."

"Uh..." The truth is he loves the home cooked meals and also the blowjobs. But Clay is making it sound like some kind of exploitive situation. Which it wasn't at all. "Why are you being a dick right now?"

"Me? I am?" He zips the suitcase angrily. "Most days you don't even smile, yet just now you looked like you won the fucking lottery. Never seen you look so happy as when I told you I was leaving."

"Because you—you got *called up!*" he stammers. "How'm I supposed to look?"

Clay lifts one muscular arm and clamps a hand on the back of his neck again. He huffs out an angry breath, and Jethro can actually see his pulse beating beneath his Adam's apple. "Fine. You don't get it. You're allergic to feelings."

Jethro is, in fact, allergic to feelings. That doesn't actually matter in this situation, though, because neither of them is allowed to have any. Not *those* kind, anyway.

"Clay, if you think about this for a minute, you'd realize this is for the best. You and me are a no go. Hockey doesn't work that way."

Clay looks up only long enough to shoot a laser glare at him. "Yeah, I didn't say it was easy. But if you were the one driving away tonight, I'd be really fucking upset. Because...I *love* you, jackass."

"You're crazy," Jethro says before he can think better of it.

Clay's expression shutters immediately. "Message received."

"I didn't mean—"

"Yeah, you did." Clay manhandles the suitcase off the bed, looking everywhere except at Jethro. "I'm going," he says, arm muscles bulging as he grabs his bag and barrels toward the door.

The room is so damn small that Jethro practically has to leap out of the way to avoid getting clobbered by the big Samsonite bag.

Then he follows Clay into the living room. It's all happening way too fast. "Don't leave pissed," he says, trying to stop the tide that is Clay running away from him.

"Pretty sure I have to," he growls, opening the apartment door. He puts his suitcase outside and tosses his hockey bag out after it.

Jethro, wild-eyed, glances around their apartment. This can't be it. Clay can't leave like *this*.

"Wait, your gaming console," Jethro says.

Clay throws on his coat, and when he looks at Jethro his expression is more disdainful than Jethro would have ever thought possible. "Keep it. Maybe you'll actually remember me that way." He exits through the open door.

"Clay!" Jethro jams his feet into his shoes. "Hang on."

Clay doesn't hang on. He's got the BMW's trunk open. He jams the suitcase and the hockey bag inside and slams the trunk with a bang.

Jethro grabs his keys so he won't lock himself out, but Clay uses those two seconds to hop into the driver's seat. Jethro rushes towards the car as Clay closes the door and then cranks the engine. He's so eager to get away that all Jethro can do is stand in front of their shitty little porch and watch the headlights flare.

Jethro tries to meet Clay's gaze one last time, but the headlights blind him as the car careens out of its spot.

Clay's gone, and Jethro can barely process what's happened. He watches the red taillights until they've completely disappeared. Then he goes back inside and sits down on the sofa.

The furnished room looks the same as it did on the day he moved in.

The neighbor's TV rumbles through the thin wall, and it occurs to Jethro that it's the first time he's noticed it for weeks.

Clay is really gone. Of course he is. This was always going to happen.

We could still be together, Clay had said. But he was wrong. Obviously.

I love you, he'd also said. And that's just as ridiculous. Maybe even more so.

Jethro literally can't name another person who's ever told him *I love you*, including his own parents. If they ever did, it was too long ago for him to remember.

People don't say that to him, and Clay probably didn't mean it. Not really. He was just in shock or something. Clay gets anxious even when things are going well.

That had to be it. Because they both know that Clay can do so much better than Jethro. This thing between them was always going to be temporary. It's stupid of Clay to think otherwise.

And Clay isn't a stupid man. *In fact*, Jethro reminds himself, *he's probably over it already. He's probably accelerating onto 90 West, thinking happy thoughts. He must be.*

Jethro lies down on the couch and props his feet up on the opposite arm. He's still got his shoes on, which Clay would hate.

He closes his eyes. His brain unhelpfully sends him images of Clay in the kitchen, making jokes and stirring something on the stove. Clay in the shower, kissing the hell out of him, his golden fingers threaded through Jethro's hair.

The best moments of Jethro's life tend not to last. He already knows this.

And the sick feeling in the pit of his stomach? It won't last, either.

Probably.

TWENTY

Jethro

BY GAMETIME TWO NIGHTS LATER, I'm well-slept, well-stretched, and ready to play. Given my recent luck, though, I'm half expecting to see Volkov's name on the opening lineup. But true to his word, Clay puts me in the net.

It's about damn time.

The first period of the game isn't too interesting. Nobody scores, and I wish I could take credit, but Trenton looks a little shaky.

Unfortunately, so do the Cougars. The game gets chippy in the second. The Trenton players are acting like goons, and my teammates react by getting frustrated.

"Man on, Newgate!" I holler, just before he gets clobbered. And in the next play, Wheeler gets mowed down after I try to warn him.

Christ. Either they've all gone deaf, or they're deeply distracted. I end up playing tentatively, staying too deep in my crease instead of challenging the shooters.

Inevitably, a Trenton forward streaks down the left wing and fires a shot from the top of the circle. I'm slow to react, and the puck beats me high on the glove side. The red light flashes behind me, and now we're in the hole.

Fuck a duck. This is not how I wanted my first game to go.

I take a sip of water and push that thought out of my head. The puck drops again, and the Cougars try to rally. But our passes are just a bit off target. We get an ugly goal in front of the Trenton net. And then I manage to make a couple saves more by luck than skill. One shot deflects off my mask, and another puck catches my pad as I slide across the crease.

But I don't look sharp, and I know it. During a TV timeout, I skate over to the bench, spraying snow on the boards in frustration. Clay leans over, his face in a serious frown. "Hale, stop fighting the puck. Trust your instincts and trust your teammates. This team ain't that great."

"Like I didn't notice?" I say between clenched teeth. "If I needed your help, I'd ask for it. Sound familiar?"

There's shock on his face as I skate off after my temper tantrum.

I need to get my shit together, and I need to do it now.

After the next face-off, Stoney gets a breakaway, thank God, and we're up by one. But the third period seems to last all night, and we're scrambling in our own end. I'm deep in my net, leaving juicy rebounds that my teammates are struggling to clear.

I'm not the only one who's still playing sloppy, though. Trenton wants to win this thing with sharp elbows and illegal hits, and the Cougars respond with anger and careless passes.

"On your left, DiCosta!" I shout, and our D-man barely avoids getting flattened like a moth on a windshield.

It's like they don't even *want* to win this thing, and I'm so frustrated I could die.

Then the weirdest thing happens. A Trenton player named DiCosta challenges *our* DiCosta to a fight, and they almost go at it. But then *another* Trenton player fights his teammate instead. Strangest damn thing I've ever seen.

But the Cougars get some kind of lift out of watching Trenton implode. When play restarts, I can feel the tide turning. Passes start connecting. My own movements are more crisp, more confident. I challenge shooters, cutting down angles and smothering rebounds.

With a minute on the clock, we're still up by one goal. Trenton pulls their keeper and gangs up on our end, trying to push the game into overtime. It's a scrum in front of the net, and I'm forced to make an ugly, sprawling save that's definitely not highlight-reel material.

But it doesn't matter. I hear the sweet relief of the final buzzer, and my team pours off the bench to celebrate.

My first game for Colorado is a win. We've stolen two points on the road, even if the victory feels pretty hollow.

As we file off the ice, I catch Clay's eye, hoping for some sign of approval or encouragement. But his expression is unreadable, his gaze cool and distant. He turns away without a word, and I feel an unfamiliar pang of disappointment.

It's nothing a hot shower can't fix, and as I towel off and start to dress, my phone buzzes with a message. It's from my dad, a simple one-line text: *Proud of you.*

Hell. That's unexpected. I know my dad watches my games, but he's a lifelong Detroit fan. It isn't like him to use those words. *Proud of you.*

At least somebody is.

TWENTY-ONE

Clay

THE TEAM IS in high spirits after the Trenton game, and I get suckered into paying for drinks in the hotel bar. One of my players has braced his iPad on the bar, replaying the Trenton vs. Trenton fight on a continuous loop while the bartender scowls.

Across the room, Stoney and one of the rookies are doing shots of top-shelf tequila, while my credit card gently weeps from behind the bar.

The fact is we're the talk of the town, and we're on a winning streak. I should be elated right now. Instead, I just keep shooting glances toward the entrance to the bar, watching for Jethro.

I really fucked up with him. I gave him a tongue-lashing the other night, because I was mortified that he'd seen me in a vulnerable moment. But a coach can't do that.

If I wanted your help, I'd ask for it. He threw those words back at me tonight, and I totally deserved it.

Now he's avoiding the bar, which isn't a good move for a guy who still isn't gelling with his teammates. So that's probably my fault, too.

"Still not here," says Murph, who's suddenly at my elbow.

I turn to him so fast that pain stabs my neck. "Who are you looking for?"

"Hale." Murph shrugs. "Same as you, right?"

Fuck. Am I that transparent? "I just wondered if he was going to put in some face time with his team."

"Same," Murph grumbles, handing me a fresh drink. "Does he think he's too good for us? I already texted him my displeasure."

Hell. I really need to apologize to Hale. "Thanks for the scotch," I mutter, eager to get off the subject of Hale. Whenever his name comes up with the coaching staff, I can never figure out where to rest my gaze or my hands.

"You *bought* the scotch," he says cheerily. "Figured you might as well drink some."

I sigh. Then I take another sip.

"So what are we gonna do about Hale?" Murph asks. "He played like a rookie tonight."

My answer is cautious. "The trade is still raw. We have to appreciate that it's been disruptive to his life and obviously his game."

"He'd better figure it out fast," Murph says with a sigh. "This happens in hockey, right? And Liana is a miracle worker. I'm sure she's getting the family situated. Although the week between Christmas and New Year's is a weird time to move."

"That's right," I agree. "A weird time." I don't add that everything is more complicated when it's Hale. Everything.

"What's up, gentlemen?" Kapski asks, sidling over to us.

"Not Jethro Hale," Murphy snorts. "He should be here with the team. You seen him?"

Kapski frowns. "Nope. He didn't sign autographs with us after the Brooklyn game, either. Does he not get that he should show his face?" He pulls his phone out of his pocket and taps the screen a few times, then lifts it to his ear.

I take another gulp of scotch. Isn't there anything else we could be discussing? Another player? The shitty visitors' dressing room in Trenton? Our golf handicaps?

"No pickup," Kapski says. "The balls on that guy."

I'm familiar with his balls, offers up my stupid brain.

"Welp." I set my glass down. Somehow, it's already close to empty. "I think I'm done for the night." I tell Murph, "Cut the rest of the guys off in another half hour and make them go to bed. And be sure to get my credit card back."

"Will do," he says. "What's left of it anyway."

As I head for the elevator bank, I unpocket my phone and pull up the travel manifest. Hale is staying on the fourth floor, same as me.

On my way up in the elevator, I have a terrible thought. What if he picked up a woman? Maybe there's a reason he's too busy to come down to the bar.

My stomach bottoms out as I walk to room 407. Maybe this was a terrible idea.

When I pause at his door, I hear him talking on the other side. "I'm sorry this is so hard, Toby," he says, sounding exhausted. "It's not the scenario I would have chosen for us. But you can handle it. I know you can. It's going to be okay."

Oh hell. Talking his kid off a ledge isn't a scenario I'd anticipated.

"Good night, buddy," he says. "We'll talk again tomorrow." And then it's quiet again.

I count to three and then knock. He won't be happy to see me, but I need to do the right thing and apologize.

The door flies open. He must have been standing right on the other side. "Coach," he says.

I give him a quick scan, noting he's wearing nothing but low-slung sweatpants.

"Something you needed to discuss?" he asks. "Or did you come by to tell the dinosaur to take a Centrum Silver and go to sleep early."

I snort. Then I push past him into the room and close the door behind me.

"Look," I say. "This will only take a second. I need to apologize to you on a couple of points—the first one being that you are not a fucking dinosaur."

Goddamn stupid insult haunts me.

Goddamn his ripped abs, too, mocking me from a few feet away. And the happy trail running straight down from his navel.

And most of all—goddamn what my first coach called my *acute visual memory*. Seeing him in front of me every day? *Torture.*

He folds his arms, and I try not to watch the muscles bunch in his chest. "Well. Spit it out so I can get back to worrying about my kid and his freak-out over going to a new school. Then you can go back to ignoring me."

"I'm not *ignoring* you!" Then the three whiskies in my bloodstream make me add, "Like that's even an option. If it was, I'd take it. Every time I've spoken to you, I've fucked up. And I realize I'm making it impossible for you to have a functional relationship with the team. And to, like, socialize with us."

He blinks. "Nobody cares if I play darts with the rookies, Clay."

"Not true." I shake my head. "Kapski and Murph are hoping you start showing your face. Maybe some more interaction would..." I pause, because I don't trust the whisky to give decent coaching advice to a struggling player.

"Would what?" he demands. "Would make me suck less? Maybe it wasn't pretty, but we won the damn game. Why can't that be enough?"

"Is that enough for you, though?" I demand, taking a step forward. "Is this how you want the season to go?"

"*No.*" His expression darkens even further. "But I don't get a fucking vote. Nobody asked what I wanted, did they? Not your GM, not my old coach, not my wreck of a sister. Nobody in the *whole fucking world* gives a flying crap how I wanted this season to go. But I'm doing my goddamned best anyway."

He slams his jaw shut, and I note two things. One, that's the most I've heard him say in a long, long time. And two, we are standing very close. I can see the flecks of gray in his green eyes. His breath warms my face as his bare chest rises and falls with poorly contained emotion.

"Are you okay?" I whisper, taking a step back.

He takes a step back, too. Looks away. Collects himself. "Yeah, Clay. I'm just trying to play some hockey and get through the day. I don't know why you find it so hard to deal with me."

"You don't *know?*" I laugh awkwardly. "Maybe we should put you through the concussion protocol, because nobody's memory is that bad."

He waves his hands around. "It's been fifteen years since..." More hand waving. "Our whatever."

"*Our whatever*," I repeat slowly. "That's the sum total of your memory of me. Got it." I'm trying really hard not to get mad. But in order to actually get past our damn past, I need to acknowledge it. I need him to acknowledge it too, but I guess he's incapable of doing that.

"Come on, man," he says heavily. My frustration must be painted on my face. "I was a twenty-two-year-old bozo with the emotional range of a rubber band. You can't still be holding a grudge."

"A *grudge?*" My voice goes high. "You make it sound like I'm hung up because you ate the last cookie in the jar. Or you borrowed my favorite socks without asking."

"I didn't mean..."

"Didn't you? The problem is that I would have given you the cookie, the jar, and all the damn socks. I would have given you everything. Don't try to tell me I dodged a bullet. I always thought you were worth it. That's why I trusted you with my... with *every-thing*. But when it ended, you blocked my number."

His eyes widen. "Shit, I *did?*" He looks bewildered. As if he'd forgotten that detail. "God, I'm—"

"No, don't apologize," I say quickly, holding up my hands in surrender. "I recognize that we didn't have the same experience back then. I am not telling you how to feel. I'm just trying to explain

—but not excuse—my nasty reaction to your turning up. It took me a long time to bounce back from our breakup. Because that's what it *was* to me, okay? The end of something special."

He looks so flustered that I'm worried he'll bolt from the room. For both our sakes, I hurry to spit the rest of it out. "Again, it's not on you. And I won't bring it up again. But I'm sorry I was a dick the other night before the Brooklyn game. I've gone fifteen years without talking to anyone in hockey about...everything that happened. Because hockey doesn't work that way. Isn't that how you put it?"

"Shit," he whispers, his eyes wide. "That sounds like something I'd say."

"Yeah, and you weren't wrong." I take a gulp of air, fighting my way toward the finish line. "But after a decade and a half, one of my players finally gets his guy. So I'm having a really interesting week. If I took it out on you, I'm deeply sorry."

He swallows. "Apology accepted."

"Thank you," I say stiffly. "Good win tonight. We'll talk more about your game later. But I'm not sorry you're on my team. You're an extremely talented player. I've always admired you, and I still do. Thanks for letting me say all that."

His head jerks with a nod of agreement. So I give him what's intended to be a friendly wave, and I leave his room.

The sound of the door closing behind me is the sound of relief.

TWENTY-TWO

Jethro

AFTER CLAY LEAVES, I get into bed, his words echoing through my exhausted brain. *I would have given you everything. I always thought you were worth it.* When I was young and dumb, nobody ever said things like that to me.

Hell—nobody says them now. I don't even know what to do with words like that. So it takes me a long time to sleep. And when my alarm goes off the next morning, I wake up feeling groggy and unsettled.

The vault where I keep all my thoughts about Clay has been kicked wide open again. And now it seems like the contents of the vault aren't exactly what I remembered. Maybe it's not just a repository for good times and porn. There's some weightier stuff in there, too.

After dozing on the team bus, I follow my cheerful teammates to the airport lounge and listen to them chirp at Hudson Newgate as we wait to board the jet. Apparently, Newgate's picked up some new Instagram followers.

"Four hundred *thousand*?" Stoney says, scrolling through his phone. "That's, like, every gay dude in America. Some of these guys really work out, too. Huh. Nice deltoids on this guy."

"Don't forget the bi dudes," Wheeler says, elbowing him. "That's bi-erasure."

"I mean, who knew there were so many gay Canadians?" Stoney wonders aloud.

"Also, bi Canadians," Volkov chirps. "Do not erase them."

"Yo, it's not just dudes," Wheeler adds. "Plenty of women fans, too. Whoa, she's hot," he says, grabbing Stoney's phone. "Maybe you could introduce me to this one." He shows the screen to Newgate.

"Sure, I'll hop right on that," Newgate says. "Now get your asses on the damn jet, or we're never getting off the ground."

I follow them onboard, and take a seat near the front, alone. When Clay boards a moment later, I watch him greet Harley the flight attendant with a friendly smile. And I recognize the smile that Harley gives him back, like he's just won the lottery.

Clay has always had that effect on people. Even a scrap of his golden attention lifts your day to a higher plane. It's not just me who thinks so. He's magnetic. It's no accident that he's the youngest head coach in the league.

That's what makes our conversation last night so shocking, really. I always knew Clay was special. Everyone does. I just honestly never believed he could see me the same way. And I don't really know why he would. He was always out of my league, even when we played for the same league.

I would have given you everything. I always thought you were worth it.

If only it were true. And now I'm staring as he makes the turn into the aisle and files toward me. He glances down, giving me a friendly nod before heading toward the back of the aircraft.

So I guess that's where we are now—at the friendly nod stage. And I guess I can work with that.

He moves on, and I try to relax, even if our history has me churned up inside. I don't enjoy thinking about my twenty-two year old self. *Hockey doesn't work that way*, I'd said with the arrogance of a young punk speaking for an entire sport.

It makes me cringe.

The flight attendants make their announcements, and then the jet taxis down the runway and takes off. When my efforts to sleep fail, I scroll news coverage from our recent games.

It makes for some wild reading. There's some chatter about the Trenton on Trenton fight. But every news organization that covers sports, plus a few extras, declare the Brooklyn game a success. "A Bright New Era in Sports," shouts one headline. "Victory on Ice: Hudson Newgate Defies Odds and Critics in Emotional Game," shouts another.

"Queer Hockey Player Comes Out and Nobody Dies," declares a prominent blogger. Obviously, it's supposed to be tongue in cheek, but that joke would've hit too close to home when I was young. Slurs, threats, and fear were the norm when it came to queer men in sports.

Nobody wanted to have an honest conversation about it. Least of all me.

I tuck my phone away and close my eyes. Somewhere on this plane, Clay is probably reading the same news articles.

When I think of his red eyes at the stadium, something goes a little wrong in my gut. Fifteen years is a long-ass time to wait to start being yourself.

Beside me, Volkov is tucked against the window, snoring like a freight train. I sink a little more deeply into my seat and try to relax. I'm just dozing off when someone taps me on the shoulder.

I open my eyes to find Coach Murphy standing over me. "Sorry to interrupt you," he says, not looking all that sorry. "Can you come back to the office for a bit?"

"Uh, sure," I say.

Maybe they traded me again, says my subconscious. *Maybe Clay's apology was just for show.*

I follow Murphy toward the back of the jet. He pauses at the office's closed door and turns to me. "Listen, everyone who joins the team has a few onboarding conversations with the staff," he says. "You already met the trainers and the publicist."

"Right," I say slowly, not entirely following him.

"Doc Baker is the team psychologist," he says, shifting his weight. "He'd like to meet with you now."

"Oh. Sure." Every team has a sports psychologist, so I guess it's my turn.

"The usual rules apply," he says. "Anything you say is confidential, unless the doctor thinks you're a danger to yourself or others."

"Okay. Maybe he can make me suck less, yeah?"

Coach Murphy frowns at me and then walks away.

I tap twice on the door. "Come in," says a voice.

I open the door and find two people sitting at the table. One of them is Clay. "Take your time in here, guys," he says, rising to his feet and giving me another sturdy nod. "I'm going to go watch some tape." He slides past me and leaves the office.

I wonder what he *really* thinks about me spilling my guts to the team shrink. Because a few of the things churning around inside me have to do with a relationship Clay's worked hard to keep secret.

I sit down in front of Dr. Baker, who's a good-looking Black guy with glasses and a clean shave.

"Coffee?" he offers, pointing at a small pot. "It's fresh."

"I'd love some coffee."

He passes me the pot, and I pour myself a cup. "Look, I'll save us some time. I'm the new guy. It's not going great."

He laughs. "All right. You want to tell me why?"

"Because my life is a cesspool right now. Getting traded a year and a half before my contract ends was the most humiliating thing to ever happen to me. And my family issues keep me up at night." It's a lot of honesty, but it's also a smokescreen. If I talk about my game and my family, I won't stray into any of the confusing shit between me and Clay.

"Why do you think it's humiliating to be traded?"

Oh, please. "Why would you think it's *not?*"

"A trade takes two parties. Someone who wants you, and someone who doesn't."

"Detroit's opinion weighs pretty heavily on me. I won two cups with them, and they treated me like some garbage that had to be taken out. Then Coach Powers screamed his head off at the GM when he found out they took me without his approval. So, sure, tell me how I'm supposed to unclench."

He smiles. "I read your file."

Uh-huh. That's literally your job. "And?"

"And I noticed that you and Coach Powers used to be teammates."

That's not all we used to be, dude. "That's true. For a short while."

"Did you two get along?" he asks.

"Not always." *Not after I pushed him away.*

He rubs his chin. "Even so, it must have hurt to hear that your former teammate didn't really approve of this trade."

"It sucked," I say grumpily. "But Clay Powers isn't even in my top five problems. My family is taking the trade hard, which makes settling in pretty tough. Things will get better, though." *Especially if we can stop talking about Clay.*

"Your family didn't want to move? Tell me about them."

"Where to start?" Any shrink would have a field day with my family, so this is an easy little diversion. "I live with my father now, but he was purposely absent for most of my childhood. I became a parent to my nephew when my sister went to jail for a DUI and drug possession. Toby hates hockey, loves video games, and never misses an opportunity to tell me how I'm ruining his life."

"Shit." He sits back in his seat. "That's a lot to unpack."

"Isn't it just."

He sips his coffee, thinking. "Toby probably has abandonment issues."

"Well, sure."

"And now you have a matching set, thanks to Detroit."

I laugh because it's probably true. "At least I know mine are about business. Toby doesn't have that luxury."

"Hmm," he says, which is shrink talk for: *I'm humoring you right now*. "If you really believed it was only about business, you wouldn't be all up in your head about it now, would you?"

That's the thing about psychologists—they're too damned perceptive. "I can understand that it's just business to *them*, but I still feel peeved about it. They have a whole team to run, but it's my whole life they're fucking with."

"You understand it up here." He points at his head. "But it still hurts here." He points at his chest. "You're feeling the same kind of loss as if you got dumped, right? Suddenly the love of your life doesn't want you anymore. It shakes you."

I flash back to everything Clay told me last night and sort of sag into my seat. "Yeah, okay. Getting dumped sucks."

He grins. "So let's talk through it, and maybe we can unfuck your game. Hmm?"

If only.

Doc Baker tries, though. He takes me through some basic coping strategies. He talks a lot about setting aside my "inner narrative" and taking each moment as a new opportunity. I nod along in all the right places until our time is up.

I go back to my seat and unlock my phone again. Something else Clay said last night is niggling at me. It takes me ten minutes to find my phone's list of blocked numbers. Sure enough, Clay's 415 phone number is on the list. After a moment's hesitation, I unblock it and open up the text chain to read our final exchange.

And if I hadn't been cringing at my own behavior already, reading this would seal the deal.

I shove the phone into the seatback pocket and let out a quiet groan.

TWENTY-THREE

Fifteen Years Ago

APRIL

IT'S PAST MIDNIGHT, and Jethro is on his couch with a full flask of whisky.

That's right. His couch. Not *their* couch. He's painfully aware of how alone he is without Clay tonight.

After a truly hideous playoff game, he's bruised, both mentally and physically. He should be drinking a lot of water and going to bed. Except the bedroom isn't his favorite place in the apartment anymore. And forget the kitchen. There's nothing in the fridge except for stale pizza leftovers.

So here he is, marinating on the stupid sofa, emptying the contents of his flask way too fast and stretching out his legs because there's nobody around to take up the other half of the space. He might sleep right here. It would be easier than standing up and going to bed.

His ancient laptop is open on his gut. His sloppy fingers somehow find their way to the AHL stat sheets, where he looks to see how Clay's game went tonight.

The Blizzards won 4-1, advancing to the next round. He clicks on the score to get a breakdown, and a headline jumps out at him. *ROOKIE CLAYTON POWERS SCORES HIS FIRST AHL GOAL.*

Jethro isn't surprised. Not even a little. This is exactly what was meant to happen. Clay's the only one who couldn't see it.

He raises his flask to the empty living room. "Great job, you preppy fucker," he announces. "Told you, dumbass."

He closes the laptop and sets it on the wobbly coffee table. Then he opens his phone and squints at the text thread he had with Clay. There's almost nothing there. When you spend 24/7 with somebody, you don't need a lot of texts. Their last exchange was Clay asking Jethro to pick up some mesclun, and Jethro asking what the hell that is.

The last message says:

CLAY

NVM I will get it myself.

Jethro finds himself tapping out a delayed response.

JETHRO

U could have just said lettuce.

Saw you got a goal 2nite.

Told you! This is how hockey works.

Next year U will be in the big show. I will be here on the couch.

We lost 2nite. I got shelled.

He takes a gulp from his flask, and it burns going down. He's trying to get the cap screwed back on again—a guy has to be careful not to spill his last few swallows of whisky—when his phone beeps. It's shockingly loud in the stillness of the apartment.

He fumbles for the phone, which is trying to hide between his body and the couch cushions.

How many did you let in?

> We lost 4-0. We'll be out after the next one.

Way to fight for it.

> Fuck u! Really fuck u. I am fighting.

Got it. Not sure why you're texting me. I'm just your old roommate. You could be using this time to find a new one.

> Not getting a roommate.

No? Are you afraid he won't cook for you and suck you off? Or maybe you're afraid he will.

I think it's the second one.

You got used to having me around. You liked it. You liked me. But you wouldn't say so to my face.

That's fucking cowardly.

Now you're congratulating me from a safe distance. So gratifying.

Jethro reads each new text as it pops up. And each one fills him with growing irritation.

> Was just trying to say good game. UR the one who made it weird.

And that's your whole issue. You're afraid of things looking weird. You'll throw away something good just to make sure it doesn't look weird.

Jethro tries to think of a way to defend himself. He tries several times to type out something that makes sense. But it's no good. In the first place, he's drunk. And in the second place, part of him worries that Clay has a point. What they had together *was* really good.

But he's not like Clay. He doesn't have a guaranteed bright

future with a solid family who will support him if shit gets rough. Jethro only has hockey. He can't afford to fuck that up.

He backspaces over another rambling explanation, types *Fuck you,* and hits send.

It's callous, even for him. So he types: *I'm not getting another roommate because I can't have you.*

But it's the kind of text he'd regret in the morning, no matter how true it is. So he backspaces over that, too. He blocks Clay's number, so he won't be tempted to send it anyway. It's better to be callous than stupid.

And pining for Clay is stupid.

So he just won't.

He falls asleep clutching the flask in one hand and the phone in the other.

TWENTY-FOUR

Clay

FEBRUARY

ONCE WE GET through the holidays, our schedule is packed with important games. I'm living at the rink, but honestly, I love this time of year. The leader board is starting to firm up, but there's still plenty of opportunity for a team who wants it bad.

The Cougars do. We're riding in the number-two slot in our division, and my players are healthy. Both Kapski and Stoney are on pace to score more goals this season than they ever have before. Our penalty minutes are down, and our shooting stats are up. Ask anyone, and they'll tell you that we're on a roll.

Except, of course, for Jethro Hale, as every sportswriter likes to point out. His stats haven't improved, even though we've given him opportunities and he's working hard. He shows up to the rink early every day and is often the last to leave. He works out with the goalie coach and makes every video meeting.

He's even showing his face at the bar on the road, always nursing an NA beer and playing a little pool before heading upstairs. I can't fault him for not trying.

Still, his stats are crap. His save percentage hovers below ninety percent, and I'm running out of ideas, so I've called a Monday morning private meeting with goalie coach Bernie Demski and the GM.

On my way up the stairs to Demski's office, a voice stops me. "Coach!" It's Stoneman. "Got a minute?"

"Sure, Stoney." I pause, one hand on the banister. "What's on your mind?"

He waves a big manila envelope in the air. "I need you to make a contribution to the Cougars' vision board."

"Our...sorry?"

He squints at me like I might be a little slow. "Our team vision board. I'm putting together a huge collage of everything we want to achieve as a team—every image that uplifts us. Every goal. It's a way of opening your mind to all the best possibilities. Because if you can't picture what you want, then it can't come true."

"Okay..." This is the dumbest idea I've ever heard, and I'm trying to think of something positive to say. "Sounds a little simple. We've all got the same goal. Won't every player just give you the same photo of the Cup?"

Stoney gives me a look that suggests I've disappointed him. Then he shakes the envelope. "Nah, Coach. I'll bet I get a buncha shots of the Cup, sure. But first of all, when you walk past the board every day, that means something. It spins a little energy directly into your soul, or something. I saw a video on TikTok."

"Hmm," I offer warily. "Okay. What's the harm?"

He grins. "Knew you were cool, Coach. Get back to me by tomorrow, yeah?" He gives the envelope another shake and turns away.

I think about this project for another two seconds, and then call him back. "Hey, Stoney?"

He turns around. "You got something for me already?"

"Uh, no. But make sure you don't, um, decorate the dressing room with porn, okay? Just be mindful when you sort those photos." I point at the envelope.

His eyes narrow, and he gives the envelope a suspicious glance.

But then his smile brightens. "Don't worry. Imma edit that shit. It's going to be a masterpiece."

I head up the stairs, shaking my head. But I guess I shouldn't care if Stoney wants to focus on some woo woo. It's better than drugs, right?

Upstairs, I find Bernie Demski in his office, eating a post-practice granola bar and drinking a carton of chocolate milk. At seventy-two, Demski is the oldest member of our coaching staff, with a shock of white hair and bushy eyebrows that make him look perpetually surprised. He's been in hockey longer than I've been alive, and his expertise is unmatched.

Using two knuckles, I knock on the door frame. "Ready for us?"

"Course." He beckons toward the visitor's chair. "Want a chocolate milk? I got more." He gestures toward his mini fridge.

"No thanks." I'm a self-confessed food snob, and I couldn't choke that stuff down if I tried.

Frank Mullen steps through the door. "Hey all. Sorry I'm late. What's the update? How was practice today?"

"Close the door," Demski says, and I think *uh-oh*.

"That bad, huh?" Frank closes the door with a firm click.

"Well…" He sighs. "Hale is still up in his head. Feel like I've tried everything. The skill is there, and he's working hard. But the poor fucker can't get out of his own way. I thought we'd be doing better by now."

That's been my impression, too. Although I'm playing him every third game or so. Volkov needs the rest, and sitting on the bench isn't going to help Jethro get over himself.

Luckily it hasn't hurt us too badly. Yet.

"Goddamn it," Frank says, rubbing the center of his chest in a way that always makes me wonder if he should see a cardiologist. He glances at me, red-faced. "Gotta say, Powers, you kinda called this one."

Oof. "It's not like I'm happy about that," I say quietly. "Hale has still got what it takes. It's in there somewhere. All we can do is be patient."

"Is it?" Frank throws his hands in the air. "I'd feel better if he'd show us even a glimpse of his old magic. Maybe drastic action is called for."

My heart nearly stops. "What? Where would we scare up another goalie this late in the season?"

And Jethro would die if he could hear this conversation. I have to put the team first, sure, but we can't swing our players around like boomerangs. That's not how you build trust.

"You never know," Frank says. "I could make some calls. And, yeah, we'd look like idiots. But only until we won the championship."

I feel sick just talking about it.

"Kids, if I may?" Demski says drily. "You both need to slow your roll."

"Why?" Frank demands.

Demski tosses his empty milk carton into the trash bin. "I think Hale is going to pull through. I really do. And if you replaced him, the next guy might choke up worse. Let's not give every player in the conference the idea that there's a revolving door in front of our net."

"Good point," I say a little too loudly.

"Professional athletes are like thoroughbreds," the older man says. "Strong and fast, but occasionally skittish. Hale is a warrior. And, yeah, he's taking a little more time to settle in than we anticipated. But it's not a physical issue. His reflexes are still sharp, and his range of motion is top notch. Which, by the way, I can't say of Volkov this afternoon. I sent him to the trainers."

"Why?" Frank barks.

"His lower back feels tweaky. Talk to the trainer. I think they might want to rest him a couple games."

Hell. We all sit with this news a moment. Not that it's surprising. Goalies are prone to lower-back stress because they combine constant crouching with sudden, violent movement. Volkov had the same issue last season, too.

"I don't think Volkov's issues are any more serious than last year," Demski adds. "But talk to the medical staff. He might need a breather and some PT. And you'd rather heal him up now than during the playoffs."

"All right," Frank says, chastened. "Is Hale gonna hold it together for us? We'll need a third stringer, too."

"Where's Hale right now?" I ask Demski.

"Probably still on the ice." He shrugs. "I told the boys to call it quits, but he always stays behind to get a few more shots in."

"Great work ethic," Frank says, rising from his chair. "Too bad he can't convert that into performance."

"Maybe he can," I say lightly. "Bernie's right—this is no time to hit the panic button. Now if you'll excuse me. I need to see that trainer. And then talk to Hale."

I give them a salute and hurry out before Frank can make any more stupid suggestions.

TWENTY-FIVE

Jethro

EVEN WITHOUT A SHOOTING PARTNER, there's always something productive to do on the rink. Like working on rebounds. I'm tossing pucks at the boards, and then plucking them out of the air with my stick, when I hear the door to the rink bang open and someone stepping onto the rink.

"You need the ice?" I call out to whoever.

"Nope. Came looking for you."

Startled to hear Clay's voice, I miss the next fucking rebound. The universe doesn't want me to do anything right if he's watching.

I reach for another puck, but then hesitate. Why is Clay here? He never seeks me out when I'm alone. Since our wild talk in my hotel room, he's treated me exactly as he treats every other player—with a firm brand of civility they probably teach at coaching school. Never too warm or too chilly, and always infused with authority.

It's an improvement, I have to admit. Even better, he's played me in the net. And after every game—no matter how much I flail—he offers me a steady glance, a pat on the shoulder pad, and a positive word. *Good hustle.* Or, *You got the job done.* Even when I'm not, in fact, getting the job done.

He's been Mr. Supportive, while I'm stinking it up all over town.

"Afternoon," he says now, skating out to the bench to grab a stick. "Want me to shoot on you?"

"Sure. Is this a social call, or a business visit?" It comes out gruff, but if he has bad news for me, I want to hear it straight.

He picks up a bucket of pucks and skates to the top of the circle. "It's a business visit, Jethro. That's the only kind I make. No need to get stressy about it, as Stoney would say."

He drops a puck on the ice, and suddenly I don't have time to be a grumpy asshole. I refuse to let any of Clay's practice shots past me.

The first one is a wrister to the corner, and I snatch it out of the air. He follows it up with a five-hole shot that I deflect with my stick. My reaction is a little slower than it should be, and a bead of sweat rolls down my back.

"Not bad for a dinosaur," he says with a smirk, dropping another puck. "Let's see how you handle this one."

He winds up for a slap shot, and I brace myself, tracking the puck. It comes in low and fast, aiming for the bottom right corner. I drop into the butterfly position, my pads sealing the ice. The puck deflects off my right leg, skittering into the corner.

"Sweet," Clay says, already lining up the next shot. He flicks his wrist, sending the puck sailing high toward the left corner. I snap my glove up and catch it cleanly, holding it for a beat before tossing it back to him.

"Now let's speed things up." He drops several pucks on to the ice, setting up for a rapid drill. "How's Toby?" he asks.

I grip my stick. "I thought you said this was business."

"It is." The first puck fires high glove side again, and I snag it. "But how's Toby?"

"Hates the new school. Hates the teacher. Hates me." I get my stick on the next shot and send it sailing back to him.

He sidesteps it. "Is he just homesick? Or is it a bad classroom?" The next puck he sends me is a low blocker side.

I kick it out with my right pad. "Probably that first thing. But he's a ball of steaming hot anguish, and I spend an hour every night talking him down."

Clay gives me a thoughtful look, but he doesn't stop shooting. The next puck is a deceptive change-up, a soft shot aimed toward the five-hole, and I clamp my legs shut just in time to stop it from slipping through.

"Good one," he says, his voice professional but with a hint of something softer. He drops another puck and skates in closer, faking a shot before trying to deke around me. I push off with my left skate, sliding across the crease to meet him, my stick outstretched. He tries to flip the puck over my pad, but I manage to get my blocker in the way, sending the puck bouncing harmlessly into the corner.

By the time I look back at him, he's skated back to the top of the circle. He lines up again, this time taking a slap shot that rockets toward the top corner. Throwing my glove up, I feel the satisfying thud as the puck lands in it.

God I love this.

He drops another puck almost immediately. He skates in closer, snapping a shot at my blocker side. I deflect it with a quick flick of my wrist, sending the puck high into the netting behind me.

We continue this dance, him shooting and me blocking, each shot testing a different angle. This is what I live for, the rush of adrenaline with every save. High, low, glove side, blocker side, rapid-fire shots, and slow, deliberate ones. Sweat pours down my face and back, but I don't care.

I will not look like a chump in front of Clay. *Not today, Satan.*

Then, just when I'm so deep in the zone I could go on forever, he stops. He straightens up, cocks his handsome head to the side, and lasers me with a look that sees right through the tangled mess of a man behind these pads.

"When you got here," he says, "I thought you were playing too deep in the net—like you didn't trust your teammates."

"Accurate." I snort. "That's what happens when you've gotta learn a new team in a day."

He shakes his head. "Your on-ice perception is excellent. The best I've ever known."

Even at age thirty-seven, I'm not immune to a little praise. The compliment hits me right in the chest, and I swallow hard. "That's a nice thing to say, Coach. Too bad it ain't true lately."

"No, it is, Jetty. You don't trust the Cougars, and you don't trust me. But those are obstacles you could play through. What's blocking you is that you don't trust *yourself*."

"Bullshit," I mumble. As if there were anyone I trust other than myself.

"I understand why," he continues, ignoring my comment. "Detroit fucked you over. Toby is testing you to make sure you're not going to abandon him, too. Your sister, your dad, a new team, your legacy... there's a lot riding on you. It would screw with anyone's head."

"Look—isn't this kind of thing Doc Baker's job?" I lean over and brace my stick against my knee pads.

"Yeah, but..." He skates closer. "We don't have a lot of time to unfuck your game, per Baker's technical term. I'm pretty sure we're going to rest Volkov for three games. Starting tomorrow night."

Oh shit. "So you're good and fucked? Is that what you're trying to tell me?"

He leans over, too, matching my posture. We're closer than we've been in a very long time, and I see sudden humor dancing behind his eyes. "This is our workplace," he says primly. "We should avoid all discussion of getting *good and fucked*."

I laugh, startled, as a bolt of heat shoots through my veins. I know he's just being flip, but it's just too easy to recall the days when we stripped each other's clothes off and wrestled on the bed. The memory hits me like a heatwave, and the hot glance I give Clay is involuntary.

His eyes dart away, and I stand up straight and start gathering the pucks I've scattered with my stick. "Noted."

A smile twitches at the corners of his mouth as he rises to his full height. I can't help but notice a hundred small things about him. Like the way he's wearing a close-fitting, ribbed T-shirt, with its long sleeves pushed up on his strong forearms. And the light sheen of sweat on his forehead from the effort he expended shelling me with pucks.

All these years later, he's still blindingly handsome—maybe even more so than when we were young. And he's still so goddamn *good*. He's a good coach, and a good man, and patient with my miserable ass, even when I don't deserve it.

He's the whole package. And I'm the dumbass who blocked his number when I was young, just because he scared me so badly.

I was willing to give you everything.

Fuck. I've got to stop thinking about it. And I'd better start playing some great hockey this week, because I don't want to fail Clay Powers. It's bad enough that I did him wrong when we were young. I can't tank his championship chances, too. I won't be able to live with myself.

"Look, I can see you grinding your wheels already," he says. "But this is just another three hockey games in your life. If you can manage to be half as relaxed as you were a few minutes ago, it's going to be fine."

"Yeah, okay," I grunt. "Don't worry."

"I won't," he says with way too much confidence. "I just wanted you to hear it from me. And I wanted to ask if there's anything the organization can do to support you."

"No," I say quickly. "You've, uh, done plenty. I'm good. I got this. Thank you. I appreciate the chance." I glance up and our eyes meet. For a moment, the professional facade slips. There's something in his gaze, something that tells me he's working really hard to treat me like every other player.

But then he blinks and turns away, skating toward the bench. "Get some rest, yeah? See you tomorrow."

"Yeah," I mutter, watching him go. "Cheers."

By the time I gather up all the pucks and make it to the showers, the only guy left in the dressing room is Stoney. He's down on his hands and knees on the carpet. In front of him is a poster board and some rubber cement, the same materials Toby uses for school projects.

"Hey! Got a sec?" Stoney asks. "I need you to give me a photo for the vision board."

"The what?" I strip off my sweaty clothes.

"A picture of something you want most."

An image of Clay's smile floats through my mind.

"I know it's some woo-woo shit," Stoney says, "but this girl I'm dating swears by it. I'm gonna post it on the wall where we'll see it every day. Then the universe will, like, nudge things in our direction. It has something to do with magnets, I think."

"Magnets," I repeat as I head for the shower. If only the world worked that way.

"Think about it!" he calls to my naked backside. "It could change your life!"

If only.

TWENTY-SIX

Clay

THE DAY after my discussion with Frank and Demski, I'm giving a tour of the team's facilities to our new third-string goalie. Twenty-two-year-old Zack Walcott has been called up from the Cougars' AHL affiliate, the Rocky Mountain Raptors, in order to back up Hale.

I push open the door to the dressing room. It's set up for game day, with fresh jerseys hanging at every stall.

Walcott follows me inside. A guy's first time in a big-league dressing room is usually a moment for big smiles and a few sheepish selfies. Walcott only glances around with narrowed eyes, as if expecting something more. "Where are you putting me?"

He's cocky as hell for a kid from Saskatchewan who's never played a single NHL game. After introducing myself, he'd told me to call him "The Wall," explaining, "That's my nickname. I live it like a mantra."

Whatever.

"I think they have you over there." I point to a stall behind us, near the door. "And if you need anything, our equipment guy is Banks. You can usually find him in the sharpening room if he's not here."

"Thanks," he says coolly.

Kapski hustles into the room. "Hey! Just the guys I'm looking for," our team's captain says, thrusting a hand toward the newcomer. "You nervous?"

The kid smirks as he shakes Kapski's hand. "Nah, it's nothing I can't handle. Just looking forward to shooting my shot. Hale probably can't go three games straight without a fuckup, right?"

"Well..." Kapski laughs awkwardly. "We'll see how it goes, yeah? Glad you're fired up." When the kid turns away, Kapski meets my gaze. His expression says: *Can you believe this guy?*

Unfortunately, Hale has just stepped into the room. I scan his expression for a sign that he heard that exchange. I sure hope not, because Kapski didn't actually agree with the little asshole. He was just being polite. And if all goes according to plan, Walcott—no, *The Wall*—won't step onto the ice except for warmups and practices.

Hale is unreadable, though. He greets us with a quick nod and then crosses to his stall to remove his shoes as more players stream into the room.

Today, we're playing at home against Seattle. They're having a great season, and it won't be an easy game. I get busy working my usual routine, greeting players and checking in with the training staff. I'm wearing my sharpest suit and my luckiest tie, and I've watched every minute of tape we've got on Seattle.

But the truth is that I'm extra nervous about this game, and I don't like thinking about why. A month ago, I was pissed as hell to see Hale show up. Now I'm nervous he'll blow this shot, and Frank will find some way to make him disappear.

If that happens, Jethro's career is probably over. For reasons I'm unwilling to analyze, I'll be devastated.

Fuck me. It's going to be a long afternoon.

The game is hard fought from the first moment. By the end of the first period, we're tied at 1-1, although that score doesn't really reflect the way the game is going. Seattle is on fire, and they've had twice as much possession time as us. It's embarrassing.

Furthermore—as the entire state of Colorado feared—Hale looks a little shaky in goal. The puck he let in could have been avoided with sharper body positioning.

When it's time to address the team at intermission, I choose my approach carefully. A coach's anger can be motivating, but it isn't always the right strategy.

"All right, troops," I say, clapping my hands. "We step into the second period with a clean slate. Let's make good use of it. Seattle is on a winning streak, and they're feeling a little smug. Don't let them get away with that attitude. You're sharper than this. I need you to talk to each other. Newgate and DiCosta especially—pick a damn strategy for shutting down their winger. He keeps getting past you."

DiCosta nods, his face serious. "On it."

"Wheeler? Stoney? You look too tentative. Enough with the watching and waiting. Take back the puck and make some opportunities."

They nod at me, too, red-faced from exertion.

"And Hale?" I tread lightly here—not to save his feelings, but because I think he already knows what's missing from his game tonight. "I just want you to pretend it's *me* shooting at you. That'll get you angry for sure." The room erupts with surprised laughter. Even Jethro smirks.

Before long, we're back out there for the second period. Five minutes in, I'm sweating through my shirt. Kapski's line has found their mojo, but Jethro is still making everything look hard. His movement lacks fluidity, and his face is creased with discomfort.

When he skates over to the bench for a new bottle of water during the TV break, I can't help but ask, "You feel solid?"

"Yeah," he grunts.

"The Wall could go in," chirps the new kid from the other end of the bench. "I'm ready."

Hale's gaze moves at a leisurely pace toward the youngster and then back to mine. Behind his mask, he smirks at me. "Like I said, I feel good."

And whether or not it's true, Jethro makes several crucial saves during the latter period of the game, and we make it through regulation time with 2-2 on the scoreboard. He eats a Snickers bar during the intermission before the extra period, while I praise everyone's fortitude.

Then? We lose the game two minutes into sudden-death overtime, when Seattle scores with a flying saucer from the blue line. I curse as the lamp lights, and the fans moan their displeasure.

Hale, who missed the puck, sinks to his knees in front of the net, a sour look on his face.

"Fuck a duck," Kapski says. "We got a consolation point. But I wanted better before we head out on the road."

Didn't we all. I make a mental note to check that the Tums bottle is in my suitcase. I think I'm going to need them.

In the dressing room, I give out a lot of back pats before heading to my little arena office to make some notes about the game. I'm only in there for a minute before Frank knocks on the door and steps inside.

"Hey," the GM says gruffly. "Look, it's time. I'm gonna make a few calls, just in case there's another goalie on the block. Just to keep our options open." He winces. "But I swear I won't make any sudden moves without your buy-in."

Fuck. For a long moment, I study his lined face and search my feelings. Am I livid right now because that's a stupid idea? Or because I care too much about whether Jethro succeeds? "Frank, I don't see how another trade makes sense right now."

"It probably doesn't." He shrugs. "But I did this to us, so I owe it to the team to consider our options."

I scrub a hand over my face and briefly wonder if I remembered to charge my neck massager. "Do what you have to do. But, for the love of God, don't let *anyone* hear about it."

TWENTY-SEVEN

Jethro

DAYTIME GAMES ARE WEIRD. When I emerge from the arena, it's five p.m. and the sky is still bright orange. But my body is so tired it could be midnight, and I drive back to Boulder in a daze.

That game sucked.

I sucked.

I'm just lucky the score wasn't even more embarrassing.

You don't trust yourself, Clay told me yesterday, and it's hard to argue his point.

By the time I park at the condo complex, I'm fantasizing about a takeout dinner, a bad action movie, and an early bedtime. But as I unlock the front door, I hear the smoke alarm and Toby's high-pitched voice.

"Uncle Jethro!" he yelps when I walk in the door. "Help!"

Dropping my gym bag to the floor, I sprint through our newly furnished living room and skid into the kitchen, expecting the worst. There's no fire. Not that I can see, anyway. Toby and my dad stand at the kitchen island staring balefully down at a pan of burned cupcakes. There's a wisp of smoke rising off the cakes' blackened surfaces.

"Jesus Christ," I swear, my heart in my throat. "I thought somebody was dying."

"I am!" Toby wails. "I have to make three dozen cupcakes for the bake sale! Mom and I always made chocolate cupcakes, and I *promised!*" He looks up at me tearfully, and I feel my relaxing evening slipping away.

"The recipe just ain't workin' right," my father says. "When the tops are done, they're wet in the middle. This is our second batch."

"What if we bought some at the store?" I check my watch.

Toby looks scandalized. "But that's *cheating*. And I don't know why this won't just *work*."

"Did you follow the recipe?" I ask.

Toby narrows his eyes. "This isn't my first rodeo, Uncle Jethro. Mom and I made these all the time. I used the same recipe." He points to the back of the Hershey's Cocoa container, and something lurches inside my chest. I remember my mother making those cupcakes, too. She wasn't always a dysfunctional mess. Just most of the time.

Shit. "Any idea why it's not working?"

"Because Colorado *sucks*."

"Watch the language. And Colorado doesn't—" I stop short. "Hey, do you think it could be the altitude? I've heard that cooking in the mountains doesn't work quite the same way."

"So it is Colorado's fault!" my dad says with a chuckle. "The kid was right."

"Let's just fix it," I say heavily. "Let me change my clothes, okay? And then we'll...google it or something. Too bad none of us grownups knows how to cook." I loosen the knot on my tie.

"Wait," Toby says. "Your coach knows how to cook! The guy who ruined my life? I saw his groceries. Lotsa fancy stuff in there."

My hands freeze on my tie. Suddenly, I'm picturing Clay in the kitchen, a dish towel flung over his bare shoulder. He's tasting his spaghetti sauce with a wooden spoon, while talking hockey stats a mile a minute.

"You have him on WhatsApp," Toby presses. "Can I have your phone? I'll ask him to help me."

"We can't ask him," I say, shrugging off my overcoat. "He's probably not even home from the game yet."

"But this is an *emergency*," Toby says, lunging for the pocket of my suit jacket.

I groan as he taps my four-digit passcode into the phone. Clay probably won't see the message, so it won't matter. I go up to my room and change into some comfortable clothes.

When I return, I find Toby immersed in a WhatsApp conversation with Clay. "He says I need to adjust the liquids," he says looking up from the screen. "He wants to talk to you."

Sure he does. I'm the last person he wants to talk to after a losing game. "Give me the phone."

Toby hands it over. Hitting the little phone icon inside the app, I walk back upstairs to my bedroom and close the door.

"Hey," Clay says when he answers. It's a little jarring to hear his voice in my ear. "I understand you have a situation."

"Sorry," I say in a low voice. "I told him not to bother you. The world doesn't end if he can't make three dozen cupcakes by morning."

"He thinks it will," Clay says with a quiet chuckle. "I'll be over in five, okay? Unless you don't want me to come."

I sit down on the edge of my bed and flop back until I'm staring at the ceiling. "I guess... If we're not keeping you from something important, it would mean a lot to him if you can unfuck his cupcake game."

Clay laughs, and it's the same boyish sound I remember from the past. "Sit tight, then," he says. "This isn't rocket science."

"If you say so."

We end the call, and I lie there another minute on my new bed, staring up at the ceiling. *This isn't rocket science.* Weird how everything in my life kinda feels like that right now.

Ten minutes later I'm leaning against the counter listening in as Clay explains the situation to Toby.

"The problem is that water boils at a lower temperature in Colorado," he tells my mournful ten-year-old. "So recipes don't behave the same way in Boulder as they do in Detroit."

"What am I going to do?" Toby whines. "I said I'd bring three dozen chocolate cupcakes. And I..." He mumbles something.

"Sorry, you what?" Clay asks gently.

"I bragged about them," Toby says in a small voice. "I said they're so good they don't need frosting. Because frosting is gross. Mom used to dust them with powdered sugar instead." His face droops a little further.

I feel a pang in my chest at the mention of Shelby, but I stay quiet, letting Clay handle this.

"Okay," Clay says slowly. "Did you say what kind of chocolate cupcakes they were going to be? Because I have a chocolate and cream cheese cupcake recipe that works well even at altitude, and we could churn out three dozen pretty fast."

"Cream cheese?" Toby asks in a small voice. "That sounds a little freaky."

"No, it's amazing," Clay insists. "They're called black-bottom cupcakes, and my aunt Suzie has to bring them to every family picnic. Otherwise, we riot. Plus, they look cool without frosting. They're kind of swirly."

Toby chews his lip and then looks up into Clay's eyes. "Will you show me?"

"Yeah," Clay says, cuffing him on the shoulder. "I will. And I've got some cream cheese in my fridge. But I gotta ask—do you have a second muffin pan? Or this is going to take all night." He gestures at the small pan that only holds six cupcakes.

Toby shakes his head. "That's the one they had at the grocery store. We don't have a mixer either, so Grandpa and I took turns with the spoon."

Clay glances around our poorly furnished kitchen and seems to come to a quick decision. "Okay, here's what we're going to do. Get your ingredients and those baking cups and bring them to my place. We're going to do this right, and I don't feel like dragging my KitchenAid over here."

"Really?" Toby perks up immediately. "Okay!" He grabs the cocoa box off the counter, and then the bag of flour.

"Whoa, easy," I say as a puff of flour escapes into the air. "Go get one of our shopping bags out of the front hall closet."

Toby scampers off, and I turn to Clay. "You didn't have to do that," I whisper. "Learning to process failure is a life skill."

"So is learning to ask for help," Clay says, closing the carton of eggs and tucking it under his arm. "You should try it sometime."

My jaw drops, but before I can defend myself, Toby bounds back into the room with shopping bags and a big smile.

So I close my mouth and gather up the rest of the ingredients.

TWENTY-EIGHT

Clay

"REMEMBER—TURN THE MIXER ON *LOW*," I tell Toby. "Or the flour will fly around the kitchen."

"Got it," he says, reaching for the switch.

"Now add the liquid a little at a time." I hand him the Pyrex cup and stand back, hoping he's not about to spill chocolate and butter everywhere. It's getting late, and he's probably tired.

But he's careful. This is our third batch, and we've got our system down pat.

Meanwhile, Jethro is at the sink, giving me a heart attack every time I catch sight of him. He's wearing low slung sweatpants and a Detroit Lions T-shirt so threadbare that it should be illegal. He's washed every single mixing bowl we've sullied and hand-dried each measuring spoon between batches. That was always our routine—I cook, and he cleans up. So we're basically repeating history right now.

And fuck, now I have a visual for the future I always wanted with him. It's not very conducive to Operation Get Over Jethro.

That's on me, right? I could have given Toby a few pointers and left him alone. But baking is hard, and he needed my help. That's what I'm telling myself anyway. Because the alternative isn't very mature—that I wanted this exact moment in my kitchen.

And, well, I wanted Jethro to get another glimpse of what he's missing.

It's not very mature of me. I'm supposed to coach Jethro as best I can, and avoid drama. And maybe after tonight I'll remember how to do that.

At the moment, though, I'm kind of lost in the moment. There's jazz playing on my speakers, and the room smells like chocolate. I find it hard to stop sneaking looks at his strong body standing right there in front of my sink.

"Don't you think that's mixed enough?" Toby says, snapping me out of my reverie.

"Right." I shut off the mixer. "Easy does it. Last batch for the muffin tin."

"Maybe you should do this one," he says, handing the mixing bowl over to me. Then he folds his arms on the countertop and rests his head there, exhausted.

Jethro sets down his work and ruffles Toby's hair. "Listen, bud, it's past your bedtime. When you get the last batch in the oven, you're heading home to go to sleep. I'll take them out of the oven for you and finish cleaning up."

He picks up his weary face. "I'm okay. I got it."

Jethro shakes his head. "Nope. I'm calling it. Don't forget that it's me you'll be snarling at in the morning when you don't want to get out of bed."

Toby smirks. "Fine, but let me get 'em into the oven."

Luckily for all of us, that only takes a few more minutes and a dozen globs of cream cheese goo on my countertop. I slide the tray into the oven, and Toby sets the timer.

Then he allows Jethro to hustle him into his shoes and out the door. "I'll be right back, Clay," Jethro calls on his way out. "Let me clean that bowl."

"Take your time!"

The door closes behind them, and I take a deep breath. Maybe we needed this—a low-stakes lesson on how to be in the same room for a couple hours together without bickering over the past.

I put the last mixing bowl in the sink and spray hot water into it. I gather up the unused baking cups and tuck them back into the package and finish setting the kitchen back to rights.

Before long, Jethro is back, tapping on the door. After I let him in, he marches into my kitchen like he owns the place and commences washing up that last bowl. "You weren't supposed to clean up," he grumbles. "The kid really trashes a kitchen."

I take him in for a moment. The muscles in his forearms flex as he squirts dish soap onto the sponge.

"It wasn't so bad." Although now I have nothing to do while the muffins bake except breathe the same air with a man I used to love.

Maybe Jethro feels awkward, too, because once the bowl is clean and dry, he does a restless circuit of my living room, stopping to look at the family photos on the bookshelf and my lucky puck on its stand.

"What's this?" he asks, lifting the puck and flipping it.

"My first NHL goal."

"Against who?" He grins. "I need to know if it's a goalie I respect."

"Matti Korhonen."

"Nice," he says, setting it down again. He wanders onward, past the sofa. "Wait, what's this?" He plucks something off my coffee table. It's a curved thing, almost shaped like headphones, but not quite.

"That's..." *Shit.* "That's a neck massager. Kaitlyn gave it to me."

"Huh." He gives me a wry glance. "Do you look like a Star Trek character when you're wearing it?"

"Possibly. I'm not going to demonstrate." I cross the room and take it from him. The less said about neck massages, the better. It's

deeply embarrassing that I have an electric device to take the place
of his hands on my body.

I shove it in a drawer and slam it shut as if he'd found my dildo.

TWENTY-NINE

Jethro

WALKING around Clay's living room feels like walking around an alternative history of my life. His home is clean and bright. It's inviting and comfortable, which shouldn't surprise me. He always had great taste.

There's only one thing that puzzles me about this place. Why is he here alone?

"Hey, have you eaten?" he asks after we head back to the kitchen.

I shake my head. "Nah. I walked into the Great Cupcake Crisis and never got a chance."

He opens the refrigerator and takes out a container. "I've got some chili, and I'm starving. Want a bowl?"

I hesitate, but only for a second. "You know I do."

"Cool," he says briskly. "Grab some spoons, would you?" He takes two wide bowls from a cabinet, fills them with chili, and puts them in the microwave. "I'd offer you a beer, but you said you don't drink anymore?"

"Uh, no. No thank you."

"Okay." He gives me a sideways glance, and I can see him straining against the impulse to ask why not.

"It was a decision I made after my sister went to prison," I explain. "Too much substance abuse in my family. I live with my father, who's in recovery, and not drinking makes things easier on him. And also..." I swallow. "I always told myself I could give it up, and I wanted to be sure it was true."

He gives me a thoughtful nod. "That's a power move, Jetty."

"You can have a beer, though," I add quickly. "I won't even notice."

"I'm good," he says, removing the bowls from the microwave.

We set up our meal on the kitchen island, and I take a seat on a barstool.

"Hang on," he says, opening the fridge again. "We need sour cream."

I lean over the bowl and sniff. Then I let out a little groan. "Smells so good. How do you *do* that?"

"You're just hungry." He plops a blob of sour cream on my chili. "Here."

It's not just hunger. His cooking is so good that I regularly burned my mouth when I lived with him. I was that eager. I carefully test the temperature with a small taste, and then dig in. My first bite is sublime. It's meaty and rich, with just the right amount of spice and smoke. I let out a moan of happiness.

He gives me another sideways glance before picking up his own spoon.

As we eat, I can't help but flash back to our old life together, sitting at that shitty kitchen table. To distract myself, I glance around the room, taking in all the upgraded equipment. There's the mixer, a fancy espresso machine, and some kind of complicated-looking blender. Very civilized.

"Who are you cooking for these days?" I ask.

His spoon halts on the way to his mouth, and his blue eyes flash toward me.

I realize a beat too late how awkward I just made things. "Never mind," I say quickly. "Christ, I didn't think that through. I retract the question."

"Nah." He gives his head a shake. "It's just… I don't cook for anyone, except a couple weekends a year when I'm hanging out with my sister. So, yeah, it's kind of…" He sighs. "Humiliating? Depressing? Take your pick."

Whoa. "So you don't date?"

"No," he says quietly.

I'm full of follow-up questions, but I'm also aware that it's none of my business. So I take another bite.

He sighs. "I'm never dating women, Jethro. I'm not built like that. And I decided a long time ago that I can't date men, either. So it's just…hookups on summer vacation, always out of town."

I take that in, not trusting myself to comment. And unwittingly, I picture Clay in a Hawaiian shirt at a resort somewhere, flirting with the bartender. Slipping him his hotel key.

And then the bartender thinking to himself—*Fuck me, I just won the lottery.*

"Yeah, I realize it's weird," he says into my silence. "And I'll never know if it had to be this way, or if I complicated my life unnecessarily. I try not to think about it too hard."

I swallow a bite of chili and try to decide what I'm allowed to say about that.

"Whatever you're thinking, I'm sure my sister has already said it," he says. "It's lonely. It's stupid. It's unhealthy. I've heard it all before."

"That's not what I'm thinking."

He snorts. "Sure."

"No, really." Like I'm one to judge? "I mean… yeah, it sounds lonely. But you're not the only lonely man in hockey. What I *was* thinking, though, is that we're both kind of stuck in the same spots we were fifteen years ago. You're still the people-pleaser who puts everyone else's needs first. And I'm still the grumpy loner."

He gives me a startled look.

I say, "I was also thinking that me being perpetually single isn't very surprising. But I never expected that for you."

He blinks. "Why are *you* perpetually single?"

"I date women. In theory. But women seem to like the *idea* of me more than they actually like dating me." It's the sort of naked honesty that I can only provide after a very long day, while eating a bowl of the world's best chili. "After putting up with the long hours and the traveling, they expect their patience to be rewarded with a lot of fun times. They want a guy who's the life of the party. The kind who goes out of his way to impress their friends. But all I want is a hot meal and a movie on the sofa." And sex. But I keep that part to myself.

"Sounds like you haven't met the right one, then." He pauses between bites. "Charm is nice, but there are more important qualities." He studies me again with those familiar blue eyes, and I fight off a shiver. "You're kind of an acquired taste."

I bark out a laugh.

"No!" he holds up a hand for patience. "I mean that sincerely. A woman would have to really *know* you for a while to appreciate all that quiet strength and loyalty. That stuff is harder to see, but it matters more than a fun night in a bar. Whoever she was, she didn't stick around long enough to watch how hard you work. Or see you step up for your nephew and forgive your dad."

I'm still holding my spoon, but I forget to put it in my mouth.

"But maybe that's okay," he continues, "because you wouldn't have been happy with style over substance anyway."

Our gazes hold, and my heart does some kind of tumbling trick that I've never felt before.

Jesus. Even when I was a twenty-two year old fuckup, Clay saw me more clearly than anyone else in my life. That's a rare thing in this world. And I didn't even realize what I had.

The oven timer dings.

Clay reacts immediately, getting up to cross the kitchen. He takes our last dozen cupcakes out of the oven and sets them on the counter into the silence between us.

"Thank you for doing this tonight," I say quietly.

His cool eyes flip up to mine. "You're welcome. I'm sure you're exhausted, but these have to cool a few minutes before we can get them out of the pan."

I swallow the last bite of my chili. "Let's eat a cupcake. For quality control."

"*Quality control.*" He smirks. "But then there won't be three dozen. And I promised."

"Toby won't count them. And besides, we deserve this." I lean over the kitchen island toward the steaming pan. I grab one of the cupcakes by my fingertips, but it's hot. "Ouch. Dammit."

He snorts. "You could have taken one from an earlier batch."

"I don't like to follow rules. Now get over here, we're splitting this."

Clay takes a knife out of the drawer and circles to hand it to me. I make a clean cut across the cupcake's center, and steam rises from the molten chocolatey crumb, which is shot through with a swirl of cream cheese and chocolate chips. The scent of warm chocolate is intoxicating.

I set the knife down and reach for one of the halves. But Clay—fast as lightning—grabs my hand. "It's too hot. You're going to burn your mouth."

"So?" I say, even though all my attention is now focused on how he's holding my hand. I always liked his hands. And the way he used them to try to pin me down on the mattress...

"You were warned," he says, releasing me. "If you want a singed tongue, go right ahead."

My body temperature jumps as our gazes lock, which is probably why I say, "You seem pretty concerned about my tongue."

His blue eyes instantly heat, and I'm not the only one on the struggle bus, here.

He drops his gaze, breaks off a little piece of *my* half, and shoves it in his mouth.

"*Dude*." My voice is gravel. "Help yourself."

He gives me a hot smile. "Quality control is so important. You'd better taste it."

Then I do, only not the way he means. I grab the front of his shirt and brush his mouth with mine. Immediately, I'm swamped with memories. The scrape of his stubble against my lips and the scent of his woodsy shampoo.

He goes absolutely still, but it doesn't even slow me down. I tilt my head and kiss him softly. Somehow, it's a full-body experience. My skin prickles with awareness, and my pulse kicks in my throat.

Clay Powers is the only man I've ever kissed. Until this moment I never asked myself why, but I think I've always known the answer. I find plenty of men attractive, but none of them are *him*. What would even be the point?

Whatever my reasons, I still crave this. And now Clay craves it, too. His mouth softens against mine, and his lips part. He tastes like chocolate and my misspent youth.

Clay groans, snaking one hand around my waist. His other hand slides up my arm, clamping my biceps before skimming up into my hair.

I step in closer, still kissing him as my body flashes with heat. Our chests bump, and my heart beats a steady rhythm of *more, more, more.*

God. Our tongues tangle, and my body's a jet on the runway, engines humming and ready for takeoff. The only sounds are the glug of my heart and his fevered gasp as I inadvertently bump my thickening cock against his.

More, more, more. I let my hands wander down his back and onto his firm ass. The next kiss becomes a dirty grind. I run my hands under his shirt, in search of skin. I want to get him out of these clothes. We're going to end up on his couch, maybe.

Or not. Because suddenly it's over.

Clay wrenches himself away, and the warmth from his body is replaced with cool air. My eyes flip open to see him step back. He puts both hands on the stone countertop and drops his head.

"Fuck," he says, between rapid breaths. "No. I can't, Jethro. *We* can't. Hell. It's just...a terrible idea."

My body feels otherwise.

"Sorry," I mumble, not knowing what else to say. And, yeah, I didn't mean to go there, but for a minute he liked the idea. A lot.

I pick up my half of the cupcake and shove it into my mouth. The taste of warm chocolate explodes against my tongue.

I have no idea what just happened here, or what to do about it. But right now, I'd trade the best cupcake in America for another taste of Clay.

THIRTY

Clay

I SPEND the next day in shock, trying not to lose the thread of every conversation I have at the office. Luckily, it's a day off for the players, so I don't have to face Jethro. I don't have to look him in the eye and remember the way I plunged into his mouth with the enthusiasm of a championship diver off the high platform.

Ugh. I'm such an idiot. I took a difficult situation and made it impossible. Right before a road trip.

Then, forty-four hours after the world's most explosive kiss, we head to Toronto, where I can't hide in my office.

Instead, I'm being tracked through the hallways under the arena, greeting players, answering questions, and trying to stay out of Jethro's way. I can't look him in the eye yet. I'm embarrassed, I guess, even though he'd been the one to make a move.

And, fine, I'm a little miffed. He should understand by now that I've always had more feelings for him than he could reciprocate. Kissing me on a whim isn't cool.

Every time I think about the gross impropriety of a coach fooling around with a player, I die a little inside. Luckily, he seems to be avoiding me, too.

I can't say the same for his agent, Bess Beringer, who's been stalking me through the arena. She's chosen tonight to show up and support her player. I'm pretty sure that involves yelling at me, because I keep spotting her hovering in the near distance, waiting for her chance.

So I handle it like a grownup, ducking into the men's room when I suspect she's about to pounce.

I'm standing at the sink, washing my hands in peace when Bess pops the door open like a red-headed poltergeist and fixes me with a stare. "When you're done hiding, I'd like a word."

Busted. "I'm not hiding. I'm a busy man. And I get that you're here to support your players, but I don't know what we can solve during the last hour before gametime."

"Plenty," she says, holding the door open. "Give me five minutes of your time."

Having no choice, I step into the corridor and stand patiently against the wall.

Bess gets right to the point. "This is a pivotal moment in Hale's life, and also in your season. It's been more than a month, and he still seems spooked. So I'd like to know what you're doing about it."

The image of running my fingers through his hair springs to mind. *Fuck!*

"The whole organization is supporting him the best way we know how..." *By letting him kiss me and then freaking out over it.* "...by giving him our full attention."

"Besides bestowing him with the sunshine of your winning personality," she snips, "what exactly does that mean? I'd like to hear some concrete steps you're taking. Has he gotten extra time with the sports psychologist?"

"He can have all the time he wants with Doc Baker, Bess. We ensured he had the obligatory talk with the doc, but I'm not aware Hale's booked any follow-up appointments."

"Make him!" she thunders. "He happens to be terrible at taking what he needs."

He took it in my kitchen. "Fine. I'll be sure they speak tomorrow.

What else?" I'm not enjoying this conversation, but I'm glad Jethro has an agent like Bess in his corner. She's a bulldog.

"Let's talk about this kid you called up to be Hale's backup this week. What's his deal? He seems to spend a lot of time explaining to Twitter that he's a heartbeat away from his NHL debut. Look." She whips out her phone to show me a post by Walcott.

I see a bunch of emojis I don't understand, and, *Probably getting my big chance tonight, I heard!*

"What I want to know is—heard from *who?*" she demands.

Hell. "From nobody. I'm starting Hale in the net tonight, as you well know. The kid is just..." I sigh, and think of Stoney's poster board, the one where he's pasting everyone's dreams. "What do they call it? Manifesting."

Bess promptly rolls her eyes. "It's *manifesting* to get a tattoo of the Stanley Cup on your groin. Telling social media that you're a better goalie than a hockey legend is just obnoxious."

"Agreed. I'll have somebody talk to him before the night is out."

"How about immediately?" She flings her arms wide. "I overheard him asking Hale if he wanted a coffee to help him stay up late enough for an eight p.m. game, Toronto time."

For fuck's sake. "I'm on it. Not every good hockey player arrives with passable manners."

"Find him some manners in your equipment room, before I cover his mouth with hockey tape."

"Noted," I say with a sigh.

She drops her gaze. "Look, both Hale and I realize he's underperforming expectations, and that it's a problem. But you can't solve it by hanging him out to dry. Nobody works harder than Hale."

"Yes, ma'am. Agreed."

By the time the puck drops and the game starts, I have a tension headache. A doozy. The pain climbs up my shoulders and into the base of my skull as I watch Toronto win the face-off and skate away with the puck.

Every game is hard, and some are harder than most. But this one starts out badly and quickly gets worse. Toronto scores on us about eight minutes into the game. The goal is a perfect storm—my D-men miscommunicate and lose the puck to a winger who moves it into our zone with speed, luck, and possibly even a little voodoo.

Three minutes later, the same player tries a wrist shot that Jethro can't see because Wheeler dives into his line of sight to try to save the play.

It goes in. We're down two in the first period.

Sometimes I can just feel a team's momentum dropping off a cliff. And that's what happens to my Cougars tonight. It doesn't help that the Toronto crowd is deafening, their energy roaring through the barn every time their team touches the puck. It's like a physical force, pushing us off the puck, throwing us off our game.

As our defense falls apart, Jethro takes a beating, both physically and mentally. His reactions are slightly mistimed, and I can see the frustration building in the set of his shoulders, the tightness in his jaw. He's still fighting, but the puck seems to have a mind of its own tonight.

We manage to beat them back for another ten minutes, but it's like trying to hold back the tide with a broom. Toronto's next goal is a blistering slap shot, leaving Jethro too little time to react before it's sailing past his glove and into the back of the net.

The arena explodes. I grip the edge of the boards, my knuckles white. We're down by three, but it feels like thirty. My guys are skating like they're in quicksand, their reactions always a step behind.

Jethro makes a few good saves as the period winds down, and I let myself hope that maybe we've weathered the worst of it. Maybe we can regroup during intermission, come out strong in the second. That's the speech I give the boys, at least.

But hockey, like life, rarely goes according to plan.

As the second period starts, it's like watching a car crash in slow motion. Toronto comes out flying, their sticks a blur, their passes tape to tape. They're playing like they can read each other's minds, while we're fumbling around like strangers on the ice.

Five minutes in, they score again. It's a deflection off one of our own players, a cruel twist of fate that leaves Jethro sprawling uselessly as the puck trickles over the line. The goal horn blares, salt in the wound.

"This is a fucking travesty," barks the rookie goalie from the far end of the bench. "The Wall could have stopped that."

"For the love of all that's holy, shut your damn mouth," pants Kapski, who's red-faced and dripping with sweat. "You're not helping."

I couldn't have said it better myself. But as the game grinds on, I find myself watching Jethro more than any other player. He's over-committing on shots, leaving himself vulnerable to rebounds. His body language screams desperation.

And then Toronto scores again in a beautiful tic-tac-toe play that leaves Jethro completely wrong-footed. Before I've even caught my breath, they score again on a soft goal that squeaks through Jethro's pads, the kind of shot he usually stops in his sleep.

I feel physically ill as I catch Murph's eye and give a slight nod. He knows what it means. We've been here before, just not with Jethro. Not yet.

As Jethro skates to the bench for a TV timeout, his eyes are distant, unfocused.

"Hale," I say, keeping my voice low and steady. "You're done for the night. Walcott is going in."

For a moment, I think he might actually argue. His eyes flash with pain. But then it's gone, replaced by a dull acceptance that's almost worse.

He nods once, sharply, and pushes past me to the bench.

Walcott heads out to the crease, looking radiant. It's never easy coming in cold, especially not when you're already down 6-0. I'd bet a hefty sum of money that every player on my team would rather slap that smile off his face than work with him.

But here's the thing—the scoreboard doesn't care. And with a wild-card goalie in the net, my boys have to shift their focus. They'll have to protect him because he's a young, untested punk with more gab than sense.

They're professionals, so they do what must be done. The third period is much more stable. The D-men pull it together just enough to turn the gushing wound of our defensive strategy into a trickle. Then Stoney gets a goal off a breakaway, which lifts morale a little further.

Walcott makes several decent saves in a row before finally letting one in. But the pendulum has swung, so the setback doesn't ruin us. Kapski gets us another goal two minutes before the merciful blare of the horn ends the game.

I've never been so grateful to hear a sound in my entire life.

The team is deathly quiet as they leave the ice and trudge back toward the visitors' dressing room. Bess shoots me an evil glance in the corridor as I pass by, but she's too smart to try to argue the substitution.

I did what I had to do, by pulling the only lever I had to pull.

In the dressing room, the silence is deafening. Jethro sits in his stall, still fully dressed except for his skates and helmet. He's staring at the floor, and I know he's replaying every goal, every mistake, in his mind.

I want to say something, anything. But I don't. I can't. Not here, not now. Not with the eyes of the team, the media, and what feels like the whole damn hockey world on us.

"God, that was sick!" Walcott says brightly into the silence. "Talk to The Wall, Toronto!"

Abruptly, Jethro stands, sending his helmet to the floor with an angry bang. There's murder in his eyes.

Every head turns, and my head gives a brand-new throb as I brace myself for whatever is coming.

But he merely stomps out of the room toward the coat lockers. I hear a loud crash—the sound of a fist connecting with a locker door.

The whole room winces, except for Stoney, who explodes. "For fuck's sake!" he yells at Walcott. "Your saves were solid, but you weren't alone out there, dumbass. Get that into your head. And I *know* it was you who tried to manifest your dick pic onto my mood board."

The rookie closes his mouth, thank God, but the damage is already done. Morale is in the basement. My headache pulses, a steady drumbeat of pain that matches the ache in my chest. I hope to God that Hale didn't injure himself trying to take out his frustrations on a locker.

I'm failing him, I realize. If I were a better coach, maybe I would have known what to say. Maybe I could have avoided this debacle.

And forty-eight hours from now, in Montreal, if we play out this drama again? I might not survive it.

"Here you go, Coach." Gabby from the travel team hands me a key folio. "Room 1810, a junior suite. Gold level! Looks like the Fairmont upgraded you."

"Thanks," I say, taking the key.

The Fairmont is a grand old place. One of the benefits of growing old in hockey is cashing in on travel perks; I've stayed in this hotel at least once a year for my entire career. They know me by now. In addition to the beautiful room on a high floor, I'll probably find some gourmet snacks waiting for me.

As I take the elevator up to the suite, I'm thinking I'd trade away all the perks for a different outcome from tonight's game.

I exit onto my floor with my carryon bag, sleepily studying the placards to determine how far I am from my room. I pass the Gold Lounge, which I'm way too tired to enjoy tonight and roll to a stop in front of 1810. There's a chime for the elevator alcove, and I glance over my shoulder to see Hale stepping from a car.

His tired eyes narrow as he trudges to a stop in front of the door to 1808. "Are you lurking here in the hallway to give me pointers? I already know how badly I played tonight."

"Just trying to get into my room." I swipe the card in front of the key reader.

His frown lines deepen as the door unlatches. He pulls out an identical card and swipes into 1808. "Good night," he says grumpily. He follows this with a mumbled, "If only."

My room is as big and beautiful as I expected. There's a fireplace on one wall and thick carpets underfoot. There's a silver plate with three French macarons waiting beside a bottle of sparkling water.

There's only one thing wrong—the adjoining door to Jethro's room. It's already hard to get any emotional distance from him, but now he's on the other side of the damn wall.

Yay. What a shitty coincidence.

But it makes sense, when you think about it. We've been in pro hockey for the same number of years, and his loyalty program balances must look just like mine. We're both Gold Level dinosaurs with our 1000 thread count sheets and our macarons.

I don't even like macarons.

I'm so tired.

Ten minutes later I'm ready for bed and lifting the covers when I hear a knock on the adjoining door. My hand freezes on the quilt.

The knock comes again. "Clay," says a muffled voice. "You up?"

Fuck. I cross the room, unbolt the door, and yank it open. "It's late, Jethro. Can it wait until tomorrow?"

He stares back at me in flannel shorts and another threadbare T-shirt that shows off his muscular chest. "Do you want me to quit?"

"*What?* I want you to go to sleep."

He shakes his head, as if I haven't heard him. "Gun to your head —do you wish I'd just retire? It's bad enough being the guy that

Detroit threw away. I don't want to be the guy who fucked up Colorado's shot at the Cup."

I blink. "Are you for real? You can't just *quit*. This isn't Starbucks."

"I could," he says gruffly. "You know it's true."

I stare. "You'd walk away from...what, fifteen million dollars? Because you had *a bad game?*"

"It's not just a bad game! *Christ*. It's six weeks of shitty playing. I'm sure your GM is already calling around just in case he can find another trade. Don't pretend like I'm the only one who ever had a crazy idea."

I turn around and march over to the bed I was so close to getting into. I perch on the edge and put my head in my hands. "Jetty, listen. I don't think I'm the right person to help you right now." I'm too twisted up about him to give good advice.

"Nah, Clay. You don't understand. You're the *only* person who can give me advice. Nobody else ever believed in me. I'm not talking as a goalie, but as a person."

My head swings up to take him in. These are not the kind of words that ever come out of his mouth. "That cannot be true."

"No, it is," he says, crossing the room to sit beside me. "I'm trying to look at this rationally. I don't want to be that guy who holds onto his career with his fingernails while everyone wishes he'd just get a clue and go. You're the only one I trust to tell me the truth."

I take a breath. "Jetty, no. This isn't how it ends for you. This is just the panic talking."

"Is it, though?" he asks. "My stats have *never* looked this bad."

"Yeah, that's called a slump. Or a bad case of the yips. It happens to everyone, but you get over it, right?"

"If I thought that was true," he says in a voice more broken than I ever thought possible, "we'd both be asleep already."

This is new territory. Even when we lived together, we never would have had this conversation. Jethro hadn't doubted himself like this. Or if he had, he never spoke about it.

The irony. Back then, I would have done anything to hear his most vulnerable thoughts. All I'd wanted was for him to crack open a little bit and share more of himself.

Now I'm out of my element. "Look, when you're seventy years old, you'll still be a better goalie than half the league. I know this, but somehow, you've forgotten. And no amount of yapping on my part is going to convince you. The only way out of this hole is to try to believe it yourself."

"Fuck," he says, clearly miserable. "I've never not known what to do."

I rub the achy spot on my shoulder and try to think. "When's the last time you remember feeling confident? When you played the game without getting up inside your head."

He looks up, his dark-eyed gaze steadier. "That's easy. It was three or four days ago, when I was practicing with you."

I swallow. "All right. And the time before that?"

He shrugs. "Detroit, I guess. Right before my life blew up. The stakes didn't feel so high."

I think that over. "If you walked into this room ready to quit, then the stakes just got a whole lot lower. If you've accepted the idea that you'll be leaving the game when it's time, then what's one more try? Got nothing to lose."

He stares up at the ceiling a moment. "Yeah, I guess," he whispers. "That's not a bad way to look at it. I'm sorry to dump out my bag of crazy at your door. But you did trade for me."

I snort. "And I've got the king-size bottle of Advil to prove it."

He smiles, and then we sit quietly together for a thoughtful moment. Eventually, he turns to look at me again, and we're so close together—and on a *bed*, for crying out loud—that my pulse kicks up. I'm not proud of it. But it's late, and he's all rugged muscle and stormy eyes.

I sense the exact moment when he feels it, too. Although it's subtle. A widening of his eyes. His pulse visible at his throat.

And I need to shut it down. "Jetty…"

"What?" He sounds defiant. "I can practically hear your gears grinding over there. And then there's this." He sits up and squeezes the muscle between my shoulder and my neck. "I'm over here beating myself up over my failure to evolve. Meanwhile, you still have the same neck ache you've had since George W. was president."

I close my eyes, because he's right, and also it feels good. I'm so tense my shoulders are like bricks.

"Look," he whispers. "Getting shipped to Colorado is the most humbling thing that's ever happened to me."

"You said," I murmur as his fingers get a better grasp and squeeze.

"It's not just the hockey," he says. "You're the best person who ever walked into my life, and I can't believe it ever made sense to let you walk out of it. I just wanted you to know that I finally realize that. And I'm sorry."

It's the apology I never thought I'd hear. For a long beat, I forget to breathe. Meanwhile, Jethro kneels behind me on the bed. Now *both* his hands find their way onto my aching shoulders.

I take a gulp of air and roll my neck to release the tension. I don't speak, because I'm afraid what will come out of my mouth. But I can't hold back my groan.

"There you go," he whispers, his strong hands starting a slow massage. "I was always happy to do this. Made me feel useful, but never used. I liked how competent you were. Always knew what to do—except for this one thing. You *needed* me."

I close my eyes, because it's true. I needed him. But then he decided he didn't need me.

"And then later on," he says, his voice barely above a whisper as he works me over with a firm grip. "…I was just looking for a good reason to touch you. I'd rub your neck. Get you nice and loose. Your shoulders would drop. And when you were ready, you'd tilt your head to the side. You'd make room for me. And that's where I'd put my mouth."

He's right. It went exactly like that. He'd lower his head and suck...

Just thinking about it makes my nipples tighten.

His hands continue to work their magic, and I'm trapped in a time warp. I'm twenty-four and desperately in love with the grumpy goalie from Detroit. And, fuck me, but the thirty-nine-year-old me can't seem to move on.

I tilt my head to the left and hold my breath.

He doesn't make me wait. Jethro leans down and slowly traces the sensitive skin of my neck with soft lips. His tongue finds a sweet spot at the back of my jaw, and the gentle scrape of his stubble lights me up like a flare.

He seizes the moment, his tongue in my ear. His hand sliding around to my chest. He's several kisses in before I can gulp in a breath. "Jethro, wait."

He stops. Immediately.

As soon my brain absorbs a little more oxygen, I feel a flare of irritation. "Why did you really come in here tonight? Was it for this?"

"No," he says immediately. "But I wanted to see your face. I wanted you to tell me it would be all right."

My heart gives a squeeze that's half love, half anger. "God, we're complicated. This is already a terrible idea, and you're kind of a mess tonight."

"True. But you really think I'll be more of a mess if you let me suck you off?"

The question goes straight to my groin.

Sometimes I hate Jethro Hale. I really do.

THIRTY-ONE

Jethro

MY HEART IS POUNDING. If he rejects me, it will kill me. Now that I finally understand that there is more to life than hockey. And that I probably already ruined any chance I ever had at a future with Clay.

He lets out a hot breath, and I wish I could see his face. Then again, my bravado might not hold up if I had to look him in the eye. He'd be able to read my desperation as easily as he reads an opposing team's weaknesses.

"We can't," he finally says.

"Why?" asks the blood pounding in my veins. And other places.

"A player and a coach?" He puts his head in his hands. "Do you even have to ask that question?"

"You really think the rules are the same for us?" I snort. "There's no coercion here. And you sure weren't my coach the first hundred times we got tangled up together."

He groans, and I like it. It's the sound of a man who never forgot how hot we are together.

"Besides," I press. "Who's going to know?"

"Me," he says grumpily.

I put my hands back on his shoulders and squeeze gently, and he seems to melt under my touch. "You want me to go? I'll go now. But I still haven't heard a real objection."

"You want to know the real problem? Fine." Suddenly he stands, whirling to face me. His color is high, and his eyes are flashing the most beautiful shade of blue. "It will *mess with my head.* I can't just blow off steam with you and shake it off in the morning. I never could. Happy now?"

Oh shit.

"Oh shit," I whisper. "*Clay.*"

He looks away, his expression pained. I stand up and cup his face with one hand, gently turning it to me. "I'm sorry. I'm an ass." I stroke his cheek with my thumb. "I never meant to mess with your head. And this is *not* just blowing off steam for me. It really never was."

His face reddens, and he moves from my grasp. "Damn you, Jethro—seriously—for saying every damn thing I wanted to hear, but fifteen years too late." His eyes flash with anger. "You have the worst timing in the whole damn world."

Like that's even a surprise? "No wonder I got shelled tonight, then," I say.

He gives me a look of profound exasperation, and I brace myself to be evicted from the room.

"What the hell am I going to do with you?" he asks.

It's a fair question.

But then Clay answers it, and not the way I'm expecting. Suddenly, his hands land on my chest and he gives me a shove, forcing me roughly backwards. My knees hit the bed, and I topple onto the mattress.

"You are a giant pain in the ass," he says in a graveled voice.

"I'm sorry to hear that. I really like your ass."

The growl he makes is full of violence, and his mouth has curled into a snarl. He leans over me, bracing both hands on the bed. Then he drops down to give me the angriest kiss in the history of kisses.

For a split second my reflexes fail me. Clay's kiss is all pressure and heat, and all I can do is lie there and take it. But I'm a greedy man, so I catch on soon enough. I pull him into my arms and then down onto my chest, the way I've been aching to do since I walked into this room.

He growls again, forcing his tongue into my mouth, as if to teach me a lesson.

I don't need schooling on this, though. I'm riled up and ready as I slide my tongue against his and moan.

"I hate you," he says fervently, in between deep pulls of my mouth.

"Okay," I slur.

"You're a force of chaos in my life," he says before nipping my bottom lip.

"I know."

"Stop it," he demands. "Stop being nice."

There's a problem with angry kissing—you both have to be angry. And I'm not. As Clay deepens the kiss, I'm so filled with relief that I could cry.

I thought this was gone forever. I thought I'd driven away the only person who ever loved me. But here he is, trying to fuse his body onto mine. So I stroke his back with reverent hands, and I soften my mouth under his, taking everything he's giving me.

Our kisses roll on. Time stops, and nothing matters. Not my save percentage. Not my reputation. Not all my scary responsibilities. Just this. Just him, and the burning need to get closer.

Clay moans, making a sound like he's in pain. And maybe he is, because there's a very hard cock lined up against mine, asking for relief. Good thing I know what to do with that. I press an elbow into the mattress and roll us both so I'm on top.

He gazes up at me in surprise. Like he can't figure out how we arrived at this moment where I'm snaking a hand down his body and yanking down the waistband of his boxers. I slip a hand inside and wrap my palm around his hot length.

"Fuck." His blue eyes look dazed.

I'm still half afraid he's going to tell me to stop. But fortune favors the bold. "Take off your shirt," I demand.

By some miracle, he does, shucking it off to reveal toned abs that make my mouth water. I don't resist. I kiss my way down his stomach, making his skin tremble.

"Christ," he pants.

Kneeling, I nose across his V-cut. My movements are slow, lazy, but inside I'm chaos—heart pounding, limbs shaky, mind staticky with desire as I finally reach my prize and kiss the tip of his erection.

He shivers, then sinks his fingers into my hair.

"Mmm." I take him into my mouth, breathing in the warm scent of his skin as a drop of saltiness hits my tongue.

He curses, and his hips twitch.

Triumph flares inside my chest. His desperation does things to me that I haven't felt in years. I take him deep and give a hard suck.

More cursing, which makes me grin. And then a pair of hands scrambles for my shirt. "Take this off," he says. "Take it all off. I want to see you."

I sit up tall and tug off my T-shirt, flexing all the muscles in my chest.

"What, is this the Chippendales?"

"You asked for it," I point out.

He sighs. "I did. Go on, then. If I'm going to break all the rules, I might as well get the full experience."

I'm not a fan of his rules, but I'm too smart to argue. I stand up and drop my shorts, kicking it away with the enthusiasm of someone who's getting exactly what he wants. And then I wrap a hand around my aching cock and give it a few slow pumps.

Clay makes a pained gasp. "Bring that over here."

"In a minute," I tease. But the truth is I'm desperate to be touched, and I only hold out another few seconds before I climb onto the bed and sink onto his body, skin to skin, the way I crave.

And as I lower myself down for another kiss, I take in his flushed face, and heated eyes that only mirror my own expression. He groans when I kiss him, and I moan as he slots his tongue into my mouth again.

Then the kiss catches fire, my nerves snapping and popping like live wires in a thunderstorm. Our hips churn, and our hands are everywhere at once.

"Slow down," he pants into my mouth.

But I can't take it slow. I don't even remember the meaning of the word.

"Baby, *slow*," he says.

Baby. Nobody calls me that. I think I like it.

He rolls to his side, taking me with him. He runs a hand down my flank, and his lips find my neck. His stubble has me breaking out in goosebumps as his questing hand finds my sac and strokes.

"Don't want it to end yet," he whispers hotly in my ear.

I take a gasping breath. "I like your hands on me."

"Yeah? How about my mouth?"

I moan.

He snickers. "Hold on a sec."

I breathe deeply while he rolls away, grabbing something off the floor. I hear the snick of a bottle opening and a moment later he returns to kneel on the bed. When he touches me again, slicked-up fingers find my sac.

"Jesus," I gulp as my arousal climbs. The wet heat of his mouth suddenly envelops my cock, and I make an unintelligible noise. "Clay," I gasp as soon as I remember to breathe. "*Yes*."

His response is smug silence and brain-melting suction.

I thread my fingers through his hair and wonder what I did to deserve this. And maybe he's *still* trying to teach me a lesson, because his pace is relentless. Like he's trying to make sure I remember everything I once gave up.

"Cl-clay," I try again as my spine starts to tingle. "I'm close."

He backs off a little. But then his slick fingers wander past my taint and into my crease. When he breaches me, I take a shaky breath. We never did this. I'd thought about it, though.

The sensation is...odd. I haven't decided if it's pleasurable, but I part my legs anyway. Whatever Clay wants, I want, too.

With a groan of approval, he leans in to distract me with his wicked tongue.

And wow. I'll never get sick of that. After a couple of minutes, I'm gripping the sheets with both hands. Then his finger makes a beckoning motion inside me, and I almost levitate off the bed. *Holy...*

He hums around my cock, and the vibration makes my limbs tingle. "Clay, I..." That's as far as I get.

Suddenly everything is white noise and splendor. I'm coming and cursing and seeing stars. I let out a shout and bear down on his wicked finger, and the sensation drenches me in pleasure until I'm panting. Until I can barely remember my own name.

After, I have to work to catch my breath. I open my eyes and find Clay staring down at me with heavy-lidded eyes, jacking himself.

"Let me."

He shakes his head. Then his jaw softens, and his eyes close, and he makes a low, soft sound as he comes. It's the most moving sight I've ever seen in my life.

I only hope he won't hate me for this later.

THIRTY-TWO

Clay

WITH MY HEART STILL THUMPING, I stare down at the mess I made of Jethro. The bed is wrecked, too. There's probably a metaphor here, but I'm too spent to find it.

He's watching me with calm green eyes and sex hair. "We need a shower," he rasps. "Come on."

"I should…" I almost say *go back to my room*. But I'm already there.

"Hey," he chides. "You can give it an hour at least until you start regretting me."

I suppose he has a point.

Dumbly, I follow him into the bathroom, where he calmly walks over to the shower and cranks the faucet. As he tests the water temperature with one hand, I doubt the reality of this moment. Did I really just push a hot, naked goalie down on the bed and then suck him off while teasing his prostate?

On a team road trip? After a disaster of a game?

Did that really just happen?

"Clay," he says, grabbing a bottle of body wash. "Get your ass in here."

I do it because I'm weak. There's water sluicing down his hard body, and it's easier to step into the shower than to argue. Also, I'm kind of fascinated by the sight of his hand washing his abs clean.

"Huh. You told me I'm a mess tonight," he says. "But maybe I'm not the only one."

Another good point. "We shouldn't have done this. And we can't do it again."

"Why?" He adds more body wash to his palm and runs a firm, soapy hand all over my chest.

It feels so good that it takes me a moment to respond. "Because it's inappropriate! A coach and a player?"

"We've been over this," he says. "Morally, there are no gray areas here. This isn't the same as if you hit on Walcott—*call me The Wall* —or something."

"Gross." I give him a murderous glance. "Thanks for that image in my head."

He chuckles. Then he spins me around until I'm facing the tiles and grabs the meat of my shoulders. "I never finished my massage."

I drop my head and notice that my shoulder stiffness is largely gone now. "I think I'm cured."

He kisses the center of my neck. "I care about you, Clay. I hate to see you tied in knots."

I lean my forehead against the tile and sigh. "Your timing is terrible. I'm not kidding that we can't be a couple. It's not a moral issue—but my career would not survive the gossip, Hale. If I'm fucking around with a player, the owner will fire me. He's about a hundred years old, for starters. But honestly—he'd have no choice. Everything the team has achieved would be swallowed up in a big, salacious story. The PR guy would probably burst a vessel just thinking about the headlines."

"Hell." He leans his cheek against my shoulder and wraps his arms around me. "I'm not here to ruin your career."

"I know," I mutter, my throat closing up.

"And it's only fair."

"How do you figure?"

He kisses my neck. "Back in New York, it was *me* who said we couldn't be a thing. I chose hockey. So why shouldn't you?"

"*Jethro*," I gasp. "I'm not trying to get even with you."

"Yeah, I know," he says gruffly. "So how about we don't waste time talking anymore. Not tonight, okay? If this is all I get, then I need to make the most of it."

My heart clenches. "Okay," I whisper. "It's a deal."

He turns me around again and presses my back against the tiles. His expression is as vulnerable as I've ever seen it. Fifteen years ago, I would have shaved a whole year off my life to get him to look at me the way he is right now.

His green eyes close as he kisses me slowly.

I meld my body to his. The warm water rains down on us. And for one night at least, I have everything I ever wanted.

THIRTY-THREE

Jethro

I WAKE UP SLOWLY, because I don't want to wake up at all. I'm sleeping on my side, naked on soft linens, my hand curled around Clay's hip.

It's perfect. Except that his phone alarm is playing a tune that's slowly becoming louder and more insistent.

Beside me, he groans and rolls over. Blue eyes flip open and regard me through a sleepy haze. It's like looking straight into my past. All those dreamy mornings waking up in Busker, eating breakfast in our kitchen before morning skate.

But only a moment passes before his gaze slides away from mine. He sits up, grabs his phone, and silences it. "I need another shower," he announces.

"I'm sure you do," I say with no small amount of smugness. We went three rounds last night. I wasn't sure my thirty-seven-year-old body could manage a feat like that anymore. But it turns out that with Clay, anything is possible.

He doesn't smile. The walls are already going up as he slides out of bed and pads naked into the bathroom, his hair wild, his phone in hand.

Reluctant to head over to my own room, I stare at the ornate plasterwork on the ceiling. A morning sports podcast comes on, echoing off the shower tiles. The chatter feels like a shield.

We can't do this again, he'd said. I can't argue with him about it. I can't be the reason he loses his job. And while it's tempting to lie here and force him to deal with me again, I'm not going to beg for his attention. I still have my pride. So I slide out of bed and go back into my own room without a word.

My body feels pleasantly used as I walk into the shower for a quick rinse. A little sexual exhaustion is both unfamiliar and nice. It feels like my soul was cleansed all the way down.

Still, I wonder whether Clay will avoid me like a disease for the rest of the season.

That wouldn't be worth it.

Although it sure was fun.

When I show up to our team breakfast forty minutes later, several players look up from their cups of coffee to give me troubled looks. One of the rookies actually crosses himself.

For a second, Clay's paranoia catches up with me. Why are they staring? Where is Clay?

I spot him at a table in the corner, ensconced between the GM and Coach Murphy. He doesn't look up from the conversation.

The ugly truth hits me—my hideous performance last night has everyone spooked. Like I might be contagious. Or, more practically, that I might do the same in Montreal tomorrow night.

I fill a plate and find a seat at the table with Kapski, who's too good a captain to scowl at me, and Stoney, who rarely scowls at anyone.

"Hale," Stoney says. "I need something from you."

"Is it a scoreless game?" I salt my eggs. "Take a number."

"You never gave me anything for the vision board," he complains. "I need a picture from *everyone*."

I snort. "Just grab that shot of twenty-seven-year-old me eating Fruit Loops out of the Cup and call it good."

"Buddy, we can't live in the past," he says loftily. "We need to be forward-thinking."

"Stoney," argues Kapski, putting down his toast. "Every photo on your board was taken in the past. That's how time works."

He frowns. "Maybe draw me something. That would be special."

"I don't draw," I grunt, trying to drown myself in my coffee mug.

When I feel eyes on me, I glance up and spot Clay watching me from across the room. Our gazes lock for a split second, and I wish I could rewind the morning to the moment I woke up at peace in his bed.

He quickly looks away, and I go back to my eggs.

———

The bus leaves an hour later for a practice rink outside Toronto. After that, we review tape for tomorrow's game, and I have a Zoom meeting with the goalie coach. Together, we painstakingly review every single error I made during last night's horror show.

Fun times.

At four, we board the jet to Montreal. After we reach cruising altitude, I lean back in my chair and close my eyes to catch up on some extra sleep. A guy my age can't stay up all night having sex without repercussions.

"Hale?"

My eyes fly open to find Dr. Baker standing over me. "Uh-oh," I say. "Are you looking for me?"

He beckons. "Let's have a chat."

"Hell," I say, unbuckling my seatbelt. "I was going to nap."

"Then you should have pretended to be asleep," the psychologist says as I follow him down the aisle toward the office. "I mighta fallen for it."

"Next time."

He gives me a friendly grin and holds open the door. We settle on opposite sides of the little table, and I speak first. "I suppose you're wondering why I played so badly last night. Why I keep getting worse, instead of better. You and everyone else."

"It hadn't crossed my mind," he says. "I really just hauled you back here to ask what picture you're putting on Stoney's vision board."

"Dude."

He snickers. "Yeah, I noticed you're still struggling, and I wondered if you had any thoughts about it and how you're feeling today."

"Um..." *Sexually satisfied, but otherwise hollow?* "It's been a rough patch. And everybody else's anxiety about it isn't helping."

"I'll bet." He drums his fingers on the table between us. "So what did you put on Stoney's board? Serious question."

"Nothing," I admit. "I don't believe in that stuff."

He shrugs. "Fair. But let's pretend for a second that the exercise has value. You cut out some pictures of how you want your life to look, paste them on the board, and suddenly your life will head in that direction—like a freight train on a greased track. So what would be on Jethro Hale's personal vision board?"

"Why?"

"Because I'm asking," he replies with frustrating calmness.

"Um..." I'm almost too tired to play these games. "A glove save? A clean sheet? Another championship ring."

"Really? That's all?" The words drip with skepticism. "This isn't the team board; this is just yours to fill up. So what else is on there?"

"Um..." *Just Clay's face.* And some of the meals he used to cook for me. "Black-and-white cupcakes and chili."

He laughs. "Okay, now you're on the right track. But a guy needs more than hockey and food. You're thirty-seven and your current contract—which is probably your last—will end in eighteen months. What then?"

"Christ," I curse under my breath. "Like a lot of guys, I have no idea. And are you *sure* this is what we should be talking about? You think staring into the void is going to unfuck my game for tomorrow night?"

He leans back and crosses his arms. "I think there's no harm in it. And I think your personal vision board needs some work and probably always has. Maybe your core belief is that hockey is all you've got in your life…"

"Hockey and cupcakes," I remind him.

He ignores the interruption. "And suddenly hockey and you aren't working so well. Maybe hockey is fixing to dump you out on your ass. That would fuck with anyone's concentration."

My jaw ticks. "It's not all I have," I argue. "I have a nephew who needs me. His smile would be in the center of this hypothetical board."

"Admirable," he says. "But give me something for *you*."

"Why? And how does that help me midseason?"

"The thing about the tough questions is that it's never the right time. But they're out there waiting for you anyway. There's never a convenient day for unfucking your life. That's why we have to do it a little bit at a time. So what's the *first* thing you'll do when you retire from hockey, whenever that might be. Take me through it."

"Um…" I sigh, and I'm suddenly so tired my eyelids feel heavy. "Maybe I'll think about going back to school."

He perks up a little. "Really? What were you studying in Wisconsin?"

"I left to go to the minors before I had to decide," I admit.

"Were you sick of school?" he asks.

"Nah." I shake my head. "But I found it hard to balance academics with hockey, and my grades were always rocky. I needed to keep a certain GPA to keep my scholarship. And then my sister…" I stop short when I realize this conversation won't do a thing to cheer me up.

"Your sister?"

"She got into some trouble during the spring term of my junior year. I left school for two weeks to move her out of a bad situation. I missed some midterms."

"That sounds like a tough spot," he says. "You've been bailing her out your whole life, huh?"

I rub my forehead. "Some people just aren't built to survive this world. She's one of them. It doesn't matter. I dug myself a hole, and when my drafting organization offered me a contract in Busker, I felt like I had to take it. If I waited, they'd find some other goaltender. And I might have lost my scholarship anyway."

Doc Baker nods thoughtfully. "So you took the contract and made the most of it. Barely a full year later, you made it to the big leagues."

"Yeah, I did okay. Especially since I was just a kid who didn't know his ass from his elbow."

"With a great survival instinct," he says. "Nobody survives like you, right? Three championships is almost unheard of. Still healthy at thirty-seven. Would you say it's still fun?"

"Of course."

"Okay, but what else is there for you?" he asks. "If you went back to school next week, what would you study?"

"Sports management," I say immediately. I've always been interested in the way teams function.

"Cool," he says. "And hobbies? What else—or *who* else—in your life deserves more attention?"

"Um..." I immediately picture Clay in his kitchen, making cupcakes with Toby. And then I picture him underneath me on the bed...

Doc Baker watches me, waiting.

"Um," I repeat. "I don't know. I've been kind of busy."

"I know," he says quietly. "But that may be why it's so hard for you to unfuck your game—because it matters too much. It's all you've got."

Clay told me largely the same thing last night. But this conversation is exhausting. "I don't see how this is going to help me shut out Montreal tomorrow."

He nods. "It might not. And what happens if you get benched tomorrow in Montreal?"

My gut shifts uncomfortably. "Then I get benched. It happens. I'll just have to sit there and watch that smug rookie start his first big-league game."

"That will suck," he says bluntly. "And you'll move past it. But that's easier to do when you have more going on in your life than trying to prove to the Detroit organization that they're a bunch of idiots."

I hate it when he can see inside my brain. I hate it so much.

"So," he continues, "I want you to try to really dig in and think about what else is on the Jethro Hale vision board. A degree in sports management, maybe. A new hobby. A new relationship."

"Now *that's* unlikely," I grumble, picturing Clay's hustle into the shower this morning. He made it very clear that we weren't going to be a thing.

"You say that," he says in a chipper voice. "But I want you to visualize it anyway. I don't care about photos and glue, unless you're into that. Imagine yourself outside the stress of hockey. Outside your current obligations. Can you do that for me?"

"Sure," I agree, because it might get me out of this room faster.

"Great. I'll ask you to report back next week."

I get up in a hurry. "See you then." *Unless the GM trades my ass before then*, I mentally add.

THIRTY-FOUR

Clay

"I VOTE to start Walcott in the net tonight," Demski says through my laptop's speaker. "That's our best shot."

I've braced myself for hearing this, but my stomach riots. "Take me through your thinking."

"Hale is obviously cracking under the pressure." He takes a swig of chocolate milk. "Putting the cocky kid in the net tonight is not ideal. But I think it's the best call. Nothing against Hale, but he needs a mental break."

It's a damn good thing I packed my antacids. "So the idea is to rest him, not punish him," I say slowly, trying out the idea.

"Exactly," Demski agrees. "He's got the yips, and that partly stems from trying to avoid this exact scenario. But the truth is you get benched, and nobody dies. If you play the rookie tonight, he won't have to dread it anymore. We'll be helping him hit the reset button."

"We all need that sometimes," says Murph. "I get it. But can the Walcott kid handle this? I don't know what he's capable of because he never shuts his mouth."

"You'll find out soon enough," Demski says. "This is important. You gotta change the conversation, guys. The definition of stupidity is doing the same thing over and over and expecting a different result."

It's not, unfortunately, the only definition of stupidity. Another definition involves getting naked with your troubled goalie and making game night even more stressful for both of you.

I've spent part of the last twenty-four hours beating myself up over it. Hale was in a rough place. He needed to talk. He needed a coach, a friend.

He didn't need a blowjob. And neither did I. No matter how spectacular.

Murph asks another question, but it's hard to concentrate on tonight's decisions when I'm consumed by what happened *last* night. God, I'm such an idiot.

The call with Demski ends eventually, and Murph closes my laptop. Neither of us gets up right away, even though we're crammed into yet another tiny stadium office that was probably meant to be a closet.

"I'll tell Hale that we're starting Walcott in the net," Murph says slowly. "He deserves to hear it from us instead of reading it on the starter sheet."

"Agreed. But you find the kid," I say quickly. "Tell him his parents need to watch the game. *I'll* go find Hale."

I'm not looking forward to this conversation, but I won't shrink from it.

"All right," Murph says. "Whatever you say."

After he leaves, I drop my head and take a series of slow breaths. I couldn't keep my dick in my pants, so my discussion with Hale will be personal—something it should not be.

Like a prisoner heading for the gallows, I get up and head for the dressing room. I don't spot Jethro. Instead, I see Stoney sticking his vision board to a wall with poster putty.

"Check it out, Coach! Almost everyone has chipped in. Except for you, I might add."

Ignoring the dig, I scan the collage. It's very elaborate. There must be over a hundred pictures, artistically pasted in overlapping patterns. The Cup features prominently, as does Cougar Blue. I take a minute to scan for inappropriate imagery. We'll let reporters in here later, and I don't need the bad press.

I'm not paranoid, either—someone's vision for the team is apparently a view of Margot Robbie in her Barbie-pink bikini. But Stoney has handled this with discretion, by giving Ms. Robbie a large sign to hold that covers her breasts and torso. The sign has Sharpie text that argues for tape-to-tape passes and clean hits.

"Good work, Stoney. I hope this brings us some magic."

"You betcha, Coach. Feel free to pitch in. I saved you a corner." He points at the upper left side. "Everybody's getting in on it. Even Jethro Hale gave me something today."

"He did?"

"Right here." He taps the board.

I squint at the images. "Is that a...?"

"Cupcake," Stoney says. "He called it a black-bottom cupcake. He says cupcakes are very motivating. And he said this—" He taps another image. "—is a lucky symbol. And we need all the luck, so..."

I blink as I realize what the lucky symbol is. Two oak leaves. "Double Oaks," I say slowly.

"Yeah, he told me I had to put them like that—sorta crossed in the middle." He shrugs. "Don't know what it means. But I'm here for it."

I slap Stoney on the back, make an excuse, and walk away quietly.

But it's loud inside my head. Before Jethro came back into my life, I assumed he'd forgotten all about me. I would have bet he'd never remember the name of our old apartment complex, which was not the most memorable spot on Earth.

He remembers plenty, though. And he wants me to know it.

And, damn. It was easier to stay professional when I thought he didn't care.

After ten minutes of searching for him, it seems like he's nowhere in the arena. My last stop is the sharpening room, and there he is, standing at the sharpener, testing the edge of a blade with his thumb.

I stop short in the doorway. "What are you doing?"

He looks up calmly. "Sharpening my skates. You've heard of it?"

"You still do it yourself?"

"If you want something done right..." He tests the blade again and turns off the machine. "You looking for me?"

I glance at Banks, our young equipment guy. "Give us a minute?"

Wide-eyed, Banks slides out the door and closes it with a solid click.

"It's about the game tonight," I say, bracing myself.

Jethro looks calmer and more rested than I feel. He obviously got some sleep last night. Our Montreal rooms weren't adjoining, thank God, but I'd spent the night tossing and turning, alternating between stress dreams about the game and sex dreams involving Jethro. Takes a rare man to mix those up on a single night, so I guess I'm special.

"Just tell me," he says quietly.

I swallow. "We're starting Walcott."

"All right." He tests the blade again.

"It's not personal," I blurt.

He glances up, and his expression hints at amusement. "Jesus, Clay. I know that. Not born yesterday."

"Okay. Thank you." I stand there awkwardly for another beat before I realize that's all we need to discuss. "Um, see you later."

He smiles and shakes his head, as if I've done something amusing. "Later."

THIRTY-FIVE

Jethro

I'VE SAT out lots of games in my career. A season has eighty-two games, and starting goalies usually play fifty or sixty of them. They spend plenty of time on the bench.

But this game feels different. Like a harbinger for the rest of my life.

It's kind of a dark thought, but luckily, I've got a hockey game to distract me and a damn good seat for it.

Montreal is a good team this year, and I've always liked playing here. The fans' passionate shouting sounds better in French, especially since I can't understand the shitty things they're probably saying about us.

Our guys are playing well tonight, but so is Montreal. Kapski puts in some serious effort moving the puck down the ice, setting up scoring chances, but nothing quite lands like we need it to.

From my spot on the bench, I study Walcott's every move. The kid's posture is textbook perfect—shoulders square, glove held high, stick blade flat on the ice.

Between plays, there's an unmistakable cockiness in the way he taps his posts, in the exaggerated way he stretches after each whistle. It's the kind of swagger you'd expect from a rookie getting his first big start.

He makes his first save less than three minutes in. Good start for the kid. But Montreal keeps pressing, and our defense is scrambling.

After another few minutes, we finally get a decent offensive push. Stoney threads a beautiful pass to Newgate, who fires a rocket at Montreal's net. Their goalie snags it out of the air, making it look easy. Like I once did.

"Nice try, boys!" I chrip. But I feel antsy, like I should be out there, too.

The game stays scoreless, but it's not for lack of trying on Montreal's part. They're outshooting us two to one, and Walcott is starting to lose his swagger. He's making the saves, but his rebound control is shaky. Our D-men are struggling to clear the puck.

"Tighten it up out there!" Clay barks from behind me. I glance back and catch his eye. He looks as tense as I feel.

Just past the eight-minute mark, we get our first power play. This is our chance to swing the momentum. Kapski wins the face-off cleanly, and we set up in Montreal's zone. For a minute, it looks promising. We're moving the puck well, creating chances.

Then disaster strikes. Newgate's pass gets intercepted, and suddenly Montreal's on a shorthanded breakaway. The whole bench leans forward as we watch their forward bear down on Walcott.

The kid comes out to challenge, but he's a split second late. The forward dekes, Walcott bites, and...

Red light. The first blood of the night is spilled, and unfortunately, it's ours.

I check Walcott's face. He looks white.

"Shake it off, Walcott!" I call from the bench.

He mutters to himself. Resets his stance.

Our guys push back, but Montreal smells blood in the water. They're all over us, peppering shots at our net. Walcott makes a glove save, and then deflects one with his stick. But he's started to move jerkily, second-guessing himself.

Clay makes a noise of distress as Montreal's winger fires a routine shot from the point, the kind Walcott could stop nine times out of ten.

But he hesitates, caught between blocking and catching, and the puck sails right past his glove. The lamp lights again, barely three minutes from the last goal.

The arena erupts. Walcott looks like he wants to melt into the ice.

I glance over at Clay, who's conferring intensely with Murph. Two goals inside of ten minutes. On instinct, I start stretching. Neck rolls. Ankle movement. Calf stretches. I barely even realize I'm doing it.

The atmosphere in the arena shifts up another gear, the Montreal fans high on their early success and hungry for more.

Meanwhile, Walcott's body language has completely changed. Gone is the cocky rookie from the start of the game. Now he's hunched slightly, his movements jerky and uncertain. I can practically taste his anxiety from here.

Don't give up like that, I mentally coach him. *You're so fucking young.*

Clay makes a line change, hoping to slow things down and give Walcott a chance to regroup. For a few minutes, it seems to work. We manage to keep the puck in the neutral zone, trading harmless dumps back and forth.

But then Montreal's star center intercepts a sloppy pass at their blue line. He streaks down the ice, our defensemen scrambling to catch up. Walcott comes out to challenge, but he's too aggressive, too desperate to make up for the earlier goals.

When the center fakes a shot, Walcott drops into the butterfly, and I'm watching a horror movie, the kind where you want to shout at the screen—*don't open that dooooooor!*

With a flick of his wrists, the Montreal center strikes, lifting the puck over Walcott's shoulder. The goal horn blares for the third time in less than fifteen minutes.

The kid stays down on his knees, staring at the ice like he can't believe that happened.

Clay strides down the bench. "Hale, you're in," he barks.

I'm already reaching for my mask and a water bottle. As I stand, I catch Walcott's eye as he skates towards the bench. His face is pure devastation.

"Hey," I say as he reaches the gate. "It happens. You'll bounce back."

He doesn't reply, just gives a jerky nod.

Taking a deep breath, I glide onto the ice. The familiar chill hits me.

As I skate to the crease, I hear Clay's voice behind me. "Lock it down, Hale."

I tap the posts, settling into my stance. The ref is taking his time, so I look up into the nosebleed seats. They're full. Montreal has one of the largest arenas in hockey, with over twenty thousand seats. I've stood here many times, often playing well, sometimes playing poorly.

What's one more night, right? No reason to get too tangled up over it.

The puck drops, and I settle in. The scoreboard has my guys a little spooked. "Watch the corner, Newgate!" I call. "Move back, DiCosta!"

Montreal looks smug, and maybe a little too relaxed. We can work with that. I come out of the net a little bit, opening up my angles. Watching for Montreal's first big challenge. They'll test me to see if I'm as shaky as Walcott.

It doesn't take long. Their winger fires a quick snapshot from the slot, but I'm ready. I track it all the way, snagging it cleanly with my glove. The familiar smack of rubber hitting leather hits me like a drug.

"Gorgeous!" Kapski shouts as he skates by.

I clear the puck to the corner and play resumes. Our guys seem to find their rhythm again. We manage to keep Montreal to the outside for a few shifts, but they're persistent.

With about two minutes left in the period, they catch us on a bad line change. Suddenly it's a two-on-one rush, gunning for me. Their center carries the puck, eyes darting between his winger and my net.

There might be twenty thousand pairs of eyes on me, but that's not what I'm thinking about as time slows. This is really just a math problem. Angles and timing. The center's decision versus my reaction.

I've been here so many times before. I'm ready when the center makes a perfect pass across to the winger. As the winger winds up for the one-timer, I push hard to my right, extending every inch of my body.

The puck leaves his stick like a rocket. For a heart-stopping moment, I think I've overcommitted. But then I feel it—the satisfying thud of the puck hitting my pad. I kick it out to the neutral zone, and our defenseman clears it down the ice.

The Montreal crowd groans in disappointment, but I hear our bench erupt behind me. As I get back to my feet, I catch Clay's eye. He gives me a quick nod that's all relief.

"Keep pushing, kids!" I shout, tapping my stick on the ice. "It ain't over."

For the game. Or for me.

Two hours later, we lose the game. But we lose in overtime. That's right—my boys battled the score to 3-3 by the end of regulation time. I made at least thirty saves, and I didn't let a single goal in until the game-winner, when Montreal got an ugly goal off a messy rebound situation.

After the buzzer, I'm drenched with sweat and almost too tired to skate off the ice. But I'm also…

What *is* this mysterious emotion I'm feeling?

It might actually be joy. Huh.

Before I reach the tunnel, Kapski hug-tackles me. "Some losses feel like wins," he says, thumping me on the back. "You left it all on the ice tonight."

He's right, and I'm already feeling the effects. But it's the good kind of exhaustion—the kind that means I've earned it.

I make a beeline for the dressing room and take off my skates. I want a shower, but I'm waylaid by Tate as he leads two journalists toward my stall. "Mr. Hale, do you have a moment?" Tate asks.

There's only one acceptable answer. "Of course." I rise to my tired feet and wax on a smile.

"That was an impressive performance tonight," says the guy from ESPN. "What would you say turned your game around?"

I'm too tired to laugh, but it's tempting. It's such a backhanded compliment. *Why didn't you stink it up out there again tonight, Mr. Hale?* And because I still have a teenage sense of humor, my gaze jumps right to Clay, who's standing a few paces away.

Athletes are superstitious people, and it's tempting to credit this win to the nonverbal pep talk Clay gave me after my last disaster of a game.

"Well." I chuckle, sounding exhausted. "Every slump has to end sometime, doesn't it?"

Unfortunately, he isn't completely satisfied with that answer. "What have you and the coaching staff been working on since you arrived in Colorado?" He shoves the mic into my face again.

I glance at Clay again, and inwardly snicker. "Just the basics," I say with a straight face. "Drills in the net and physical conditioning. They've been very patient with me. But I've been playing in this barn for years, and all that experience has to kick in sometime, right?"

Behind me, somewhere in my gear, my phone starts ringing. My family wouldn't call me at this hour if it weren't important. I reach back and paw around until I find it. I check the screen, and it reads *MAPLEWAY REHAB CENTER.*

"What is your goal for the rest of the season?" another journalist asks.

"Um…" I hit Accept with my thumb. "I'm really sorry. I have to take this."

Over the journalist's shoulder, Tate frowns at me. Then he makes a slashing motion with his hand.

"I *really* have to take this," I insist, and he scowls. "Sorry." I slide around the reporters and edge toward the corridor leading to the showers. "Hello? Shelby?"

"Hi," she says, and I can barely hear her. "It's me. I watched your game."

I blink. "Shelby, you haven't spoken to us in months. Your kid asks me every night when you're finally going to call. And you called to talk about hockey?"

There's a silence on the line, and I mentally curse myself for taking a swing at her two seconds into our first call in months. I meant to do better. But she's so damn frustrating.

"Shelby—"

"Jethro—" We both try to speak at the same time.

"I'm sorry," I break through. "Talk about whatever, Shelby. It's good to hear from you."

She sighs. "I didn't call to talk about hockey. Not really. But it's hard to know where to start. I realize how hard I've made everything, and I'm sorry."

I close my eyes and lean back against the wall. It's loud around me in the locker room, and it's loud inside my head. "I can take it. Whatever," I say in a fit of eloquence. "But would you please call Toby? He's just barely holding it together."

"In…Colorado?" she asks. "He's with you? I asked the director to let me watch one of your games as a reward. She told me you play for Colorado now." Shelby sobs. "I didn't even know. I was picturing you and Dad and Toby in Detroit together."

My heart breaks a little. "We're still together. But, yeah, Toby had to start a new school. He'll tell you he hates it, but it's not going all that bad. He has a couple friends. He joined the robotics club."

"What's...what's that mean?" she asks tearfully.

"Swear to God I don't even know. He tried to explain it to me. Something to do with LEGO and computer programming?"

We both laugh uncomfortably.

"Thank you for watching over him," my sister says, her voice thick. "I know you think I dumped him on you."

You did. "I'll always look out for Toby," I say because it's true.

"Do you know why?" she asks.

"Um..." Is there an answer to that question that won't get me in trouble?

"Because I'm an addict, Jethro." She sobs again.

"I know, babe." My eyes prickle.

"I know you know!" she wails. "But I never said it out loud until this month. I didn't even want to come to this place. I only did it because it sounded better than jail. And Jethro—I relapsed here."

"In *rehab*?" I can't even disguise my dismay.

"Somebody's mom brought her a fix," she says, sniffling. "I took it from her. Even after all that work getting detoxed, I stole a needle and shot up. Then I got so sick I thought I'd die."

God, Shelby. You idiot. I take a deep breath instead of saying it aloud.

"Jethro, I thought I deserved it. That's the thing you never got about me. I do all my stupid shit because I didn't think I was..." She sobs.

I bite down on my lip.

Her voice is thick with tears as she continues. "There was a nurse who sat with me for twelve hours while I detoxed again. I said, 'It's late, just go home to your family.' And she said, 'I stayed because you need someone. And you're worth it, Shelby. Even when you're a mess, you're still worth saving. We're all worth saving.' But I realized…I *never* believed that before."

"Shel, Jesus." My eyes burn and fill, and it startles me. I haven't cried since the nineties. "Of course, you're worth it."

"You say that…but…" She hiccups. "Not everyone is you. Not everyone knows where they belong."

I gulp in air. Someone moves into my peripheral vision, and I turn away instinctively.

"Jetty." Clay's voice is quiet. Worried.

I give him a quick head shake. *Everything is fine. Nothing to see here.* He backs away.

"Will Toby be okay?" she manages.

"Yeah," I grunt. "He's…yeah. If you call him, he'll even be great."

"I'll do it. Tomorrow. At 3:30."

"We're an hour behind," I grit out. "He needs to hear your voice."

"Okay," she squeaks. "I don't know how to look him in the eye. I can't tell him the truth—that I always thought he'd be better off without me."

"That is *not* true."

"Careful, Jethro. You must have thought it sometimes."

"Well…" This conversation is killing me. "It's been hard watching you self-destruct for twenty years. I never know what to think."

"I know," she says quickly. "We've, um, talked about that a lot here. I'm working on it."

All the fight drains out of me, and I sag against the wall. "Okay. I'm sure you're trying."

"You don't have to be sure," she says. "But I'm still doing it anyway. Now I got to go. Good comeback tonight. Sorry you didn't get the win."

"I'll live."

"Jethro, I love you. Just wanted you to know that."

My throat closes up. "Love you, too, Shel." *Even when it's hard.*

We fly home late. Sagging in my seat on the jet, I get messages from three people.

First there's Toby. He congratulates me on the game. *Too bad you didn't get the win*, he says, echoing his mama exactly.

I tell him thanks. And I tell him he's up too late.

I *don't* tell him that I talked to his mom. Shelby has spent the last couple of decades failing to keep her promises. It's better not to get his hopes up.

This time, though, it feels different. I want it to be different. For both of them.

The second text is from Doc Baker.

> God that was fun to watch. But this doesn't mean we're done. Gonna be asking you about that vision board.

> I'll get right on it.

The third one is from Clay, who is texting me from somewhere on this same jet.

> Are you all right?

> I'm fine. Dealing with some sister drama.

> Is Shelby okay?

I close my eyes and wonder what to say. I'm trying to be as honest with him as I can, so he'll know that I'm trying with him. But some shit is so ugly that I've always hidden it from him.

> When we lived together, I used to listen to you talk to your sister on the phone. And I was so jealous of how easy it sounded. Mine was always in trouble. I've bailed her out my whole life, but she and I could never just talk.

I'm lucky. Kait and I are close. But don't forget I have two brothers I barely know.

Yeah, okay. But there was a lot of pain I might have avoided if I were better at dealing with her feelings.

And also my own.

I get that.

She tried to harm herself. She told me that the reason she's been such a wreck for so long is that she didn't believe she was worth saving.

Oh fuck. That's got to be hard to hear.

Yeah, like I could have told her I loved her, you know? Maybe it would have made a difference.

You were in over your head with her. If it's any consolation, I knew you loved her. Even if you didn't talk about her much. I knew you worried.

Well, thanks. She and I are gonna have to take things one day at a time I guess.

Hang in there.

I'm fine. If you're that worried you can invite me over later.

You know I can't.

Yeah, I do. If things were different though...

Maybe I've overstepped, because he doesn't respond. I put my phone away and fall into the easy sleep of a guy who didn't let anybody down tonight.

"PITTSBURGH HAS a formidable first line and a strong PK team," Murphy says from the front of the video room. "But when a team can rattle them, the defense usually falls apart. Watch this clip."

The video begins to play again, and I have a pen poised over my notepad. But I haven't actually written anything in a half hour except for *Buy coffee pods* and *Drop off dry cleaning*.

So far, March has been a blur of arena lights and coffee cups. Outside, the Colorado winter still has its icy grip on us. But inside the rink, things are heating up. We're in the thick of it now—that late-season push where my guys are tired and sore but hungry. I see it in their eyes during these video meetings, but it's most apparent on the rink when they dig deep for that extra burst of speed even when their muscles are screaming.

Glancing around the room, I take an inventory of our many blessings. Newgate's on fire, racking up points like he's got something to prove. Wheeler—taking notes with a gold pen—recently rehabbed a bout of bursitis faster than expected. And Volkov's back isn't giving him too much trouble lately.

In the corner, DiCosta still has a black eye. He's taken more than his share of bruises, blocking shots with a reckless abandon that makes me wince and applaud at the same time.

Stoney looks a little sleepy, but only because he probably got up early to work out before practice. He's dragged that vision board of his to every game we've played, in every city. It's starting to look a little ragged in the corners, which feels like a metaphor for all of us.

And Hale... well, Hale's been Hale. Solid most nights, brilliant on others, with only the occasional hiccup.

He turns his rugged chin in my direction, catching me staring at him. And I look away quickly, which is just as damning as if I'd kept staring.

Oops. I wish I could say this never happens. But it totally does.

A moment later, I get a message notification on my watch.

> Something you need, Coach?

My face burns, and I don't respond, because I won't be the guy who's texting during Murph's video review.

A moment later, I get a new text. It's a picture of a little kid suited up for hockey—skates and all—fast asleep on the bench.

> This is me if Coach Murph doesn't wrap it up soon.

I smirk before moving my eyes back to the video screen like a good boy.

After saying all those soul-bending things to me last month, Jethro has pretty much done everything I've asked of him. He hasn't knocked again on my door at a hotel, and he keeps all our public interactions strictly professional.

But we message each other daily. It's mostly simple things, like funny hockey videos and jokes. Sometimes I ask how Toby's doing, and the news there is good. Shelby calls him weekly, and it's made everything better for the kid.

Also, our old team—the Busker Brutes—is having a fantastic

season this year, so we exchange stats and yack about their odds of winning the championship.

The problem is that it's all killing me one text at a time. He's always right across the room, where I can see him but never touch him. I miss the hell out of him, just like I did after our split.

This time it hurts worse, if I'm honest. Last time I was angry at Jethro, because I thought everything was his fault. Now our distance is my choice.

Jethro said it bluntly enough—I'm choosing hockey over him. It's a little more complicated than that, but my heart doesn't know the difference. Especially on the nights I dream about him. In my guilty dreams, we have a lot of sex. I wake up hard and ashamed with no outlet for my frustrations.

It's not like I have any other entertainments in my life. At this point in the season, I'm living on coffee and game tape, strategizing for our playoffs bid. It's grueling work as I search for any edge I can find to put us ahead of the pack.

This is a huge moment for me. Other years, I've been pushing just to make it into the playoffs. This time I want to finish the regular season in the top two.

It's not just about bragging rights; it's about setting ourselves up for even more success. The higher we finish, the more home-ice advantage we'll get later—like facing a lower-seeded team in the first round, sleeping in our own beds, and having our fans behind us.

Every point matters. So every practice matters. Every game matters. I'm running myself ragged because I think we could go the distance, and not at all because I need a distraction from thinking about Jethro.

Nope. That's not why.

No way.

My wrist vibrates again, and I look at the screen like a trained dog who's heard the dinner bell. It's Jethro again.

I have something for you. I'll come by your office later.

The first response I think of isn't exactly platonic.

Sometimes I hate my brain.

"And we'll leave it there for now," Murph says at the front of the room.

I pop up out of my chair and head for my office. I need to shake off these feelings, stat. So I get down onto the rug, where I hold the plank position for sixty seconds before starting a set of pushups. This will get my blood flowing in a productive way.

"Um, Coach?"

I sit up so fast that I bonk my head on the padded armrest of my office chair. "Shit."

"Careful," Liana says from the doorway as I extricate myself from the floor. "You all right?"

"Of course. What's up?"

She frowns at me. "There's a risk assessment meeting starting now?"

"Oh. Hell." I grab my legal pad off the desk and head back out again.

"Should I bring you a cappuccino?" she asks, giving me a skeptical look. "You look a little ragged."

"That's my default setting in March," I argue. "But, yeah, I'd love one. Thanks."

When I reach the small conference room, I apologize on my way through the door. "Sorry I'm late. Who wants to start?" I sit down at the head of the table. Murphy is there already, along with Tate from PR, Kevin Tang the head trainer, and both our team doctors—Doc Whitesmith who's our medical doctor, and Doc Baker.

"I'll go," the trainer says. He pushes a sheet of paper in my direction. "There aren't any surprises on here. Volkov is holding up, but we're sending him to the massage therapist every forty-eight hours.

Wheeler's bursitis is cooperating. There's a few more knees and ankles on here, but nothing you don't already know."

"That's great, Kevin. Thanks."

Usually, he gets up and leaves at this point, but I see him hesitate. "There's one more thing I'd like to mention, but I didn't put it down on the sheet."

"Go ahead," I say quietly. If he didn't write it down, then it's sensitive, and everyone in this room knows to treat it that way.

"Pierre is making me nervous," the trainer says, playing with his watch band. "He's jittery. Red eyes and the sniffles. I just...got a bad feeling."

Which means coke, probably.

I glance around the table at the other uneasy faces. Sadly, illegal drugs are all too common in pro hockey, and Pierre is a twenty-three-year-old hothead who likes his substances.

"Any proof?" Murph asks.

The trainer shakes his head.

"We could do a random drug test," the doctor says. "Force the conversation."

"Oof," Murphy mutters. "Maybe *after* we clinch our playoffs spot?"

I kick Murphy's foot under the table. "That kind of thinking won't solve any problems. How about asking Kapski to casually check in with him? If it comes across as friendly concern and not judgment, there's a chance he'd open up to his captain."

"Yeah, okay," Kevin says. "That could work. I'll talk to Kapski."

"I'll ask Pierre for a chat," Doc Baker says. "See how he's feeling."

"Good. We'll all keep an eye on him," I add.

The trainer leaves, and Tate and Doc Whitesmith give their updates. Nothing too serious there, so I start to relax.

The meeting is just breaking up when Liana swans in with a tray of espresso drinks. After we dive for them, Murph and Doc

Whitesmith depart, leaving Tate, who's eyeing me nervously. And Doc Baker, who is communing with his cappuccino.

"Hey, Coach?" Tate clears his throat. "There's something I wanted to show you. It's nothing to worry about," he says, even if his expression says otherwise. "I just wanted to keep you in the loop."

"All right. Let's have it."

He opens his laptop.

"You need privacy?" the team psychologist asks.

"Doubt it," I grunt.

Tate makes a strangely uneasy face. Then he turns his laptop so the screen faces me. It's on Pickr, a popular photo-sharing site.

It's a picture of twenty-something me asleep on a team bus. I'm seated next to Jethro, who's also asleep. We're leaning toward each other, my head on his shoulder, his head against mine.

The sight of our boyish faces, blissed out and at rest, makes me take a sharp breath. But then there's the caption: *Look! It's Jetty and Powers back in the olden days, acting like a couple faggots.*

Blood drains from my face.

"It's really nothing," Tate says. "Just another dumbass on the internet. The pic isn't new, although the caption is."

A long beat goes by before I find my voice. "How did you find this?"

He chews his lip in a rare display of discomfort. "Since Newgate came out, I've been expanding my Google alerts for the team to include, um, some unsavory keywords."

"Like faggot," Doc Baker suggests. I'd almost forgotten he was here.

"Yeah, and a bunch more." He shrugs. "Honestly, it's barely worthy of our notice. I just thought you'd want to see it, since..." He hesitates.

"Since I disclosed my sexual orientation to you," I say quietly.

He gives a single nod.

Doc Baker, unflappable as always, asks a question. "Are there more photos of Hale or Coach? And was the photographer an old teammate of theirs?"

"Probably," Tate says. "This is the poster's profile." He changes the tab, and we see the photographer's home page. It's titled *BladzeOfGlory*. "It's all hockey stuff. He stopped posting ten years ago. You recognize him, Coach?"

I glance at the more recent thumbnails, and one of them is a selfie. I do, in fact, recognize the guy. *Duckson*. I haven't thought of him for years. He was always throwing around the f-word.

"He's an old teammate," I say numbly. Then I get up and open the conference room door. "Liana!" I yodel. "Find Hale for me."

I flip back to the old picture and stare at the screen. For the second time, the image hits me right in the gut. We look so fucking *young*, our faces untroubled in sleep.

"Let's not panic," Tate says, watching me. "It just took me by surprise."

The door opens a few moments later, and Jethro walks in. When he sees the odd collection of people in the room he frowns. "Something wrong? I was just coming up here to give you this." He sets a small paper bag on the table.

"What is it?" I ask, trying to keep up with the conversation. I'm still reeling inside.

"Chocolate-covered pretzels. We made them for another bake sale. I found something Toby could make without a rescue operation. See?" He pulls a tin out of the bag and pops the top off it. It's full of pretzels coated in dark chocolate with tiny blue sprinkles. "He did Cougar blue, for luck."

Doc Baker reaches into the tin, takes a pretzel, and pops it into his mouth. "Oh, hell yes. These are great."

"Thanks." Jethro looks pleased with himself. "Now what did you need me for?"

Without a word, I turn Tate's laptop to face him.

Jethro squints at the screen. And then he *laughs*. Not just an awkward chuckle, either. "Wow," he says, grinning. "I bet Fuckson took this, right? That asshole. So predictable."

The look I give him does a poor job of hiding my reaction. *You think this is funny?*

"What?" he demands. "This photo has been here...how long? Nobody cares. And didn't you tell me once not to let the dumbest man in hockey ruin my day? Could swear that was you."

"Yeah, but..."

Doc Baker's and Tate's heads swivel back and forth like spectators at a tennis match. They're both clearly fascinated by this exchange.

"But *nothing*," Jethro says. "Since when do we care about randos posting shit on the internet? There's a guy on Reddit who swears I had a nose job last season." He touches his nose, which—like so many other players'—has a bump from being broken by a puck at some point in his career. "Relax, Clayzy."

"Clayzy?" Doc Baker chuckles. "That's a good one."

"Old nickname," I mumble. Then I reach for the laptop and scroll slowly through the other fifteen-year-old shots.

On some level I know Jethro's right—this old picture doesn't matter. But my heart is thumping anyway. I feel naked right now. Like anyone who looks at that photo will read my old heartbreak like a book.

Many of the other photos are poorly focused and poorly composed. Digital cameras just weren't great back then, especially with a dingus like Duckson behind the lens.

But still, it's like peering into the past. There's our coach's scowl. And our captain—Laytner—with his too-long hair and square jaw.

"Kinda curious..." Tate says slowly. "If you two were pals back in the day, then why does the whole team think you hate each other?"

The question sort of echoes against the walls of the conference room.

And I gulp.

THIRTY-SEVEN

Jethro

CLAY GOES STILL. But I know him well and sense the panic flaring behind his facade. His vibe reads trapped animal.

"We were teammates," I offer. "And roommates for a short time. But not every friendship survives a season with the Busker Brutes and a cramped apartment."

"*Huh*," says the psychologist.

Clay clenches his jaw. He's still scrolling through the photos which are, thankfully, mostly of Fuckson's stupid friends.

At the end of the gallery, another shot of us rolls into view. I don't remember this moment, either. We're at the rink, wearing practice gear and standing in the dressing room. I'm smirking, like maybe I just chirped another player and made the other guys laugh.

As incriminating evidence, the photo wouldn't turn heads except for one thing. Clay's expression in the pic stops my heart. He's watching me with naked adoration. Like he's never met anyone as perfect as me.

I can't look away. I've never seen any photos of us together. Honestly, the look on his face is hard for me to process. Although

Clay has been very clear with me, until this very second, I don't think I believed him. Not all the way down to my gut.

Now I'm staring at the evidence. If love had a face, it's the one he's wearing. It shouldn't shock me, but it does. At twenty-two, I clearly wasn't ready. Nobody had ever loved me before—not self-lessly—and I hadn't loved anyone, either.

I didn't know what it felt like to fall for someone. I didn't understand what was happening to me. And Clay's love scared the hell out of me.

It's all so obvious now. I let myself believe that I couldn't date a guy, because that was easier than facing a scary new thing.

I look up at Clay at the same time he looks up at me. Our gazes clash for one potent second, before he looks away. He bends down and kills the tab, then snaps the laptop shut. He hands it to Tate. "Thanks for showing me this."

"Sure thing," the publicist says, snagging a pretzel. "It's nothing to worry about."

"Right," Clay says quietly.

Doc Baker looks between us, a question in his eyes. But he follows Tate out of the room, leaving me alone with Clay.

As soon as the door closes, Clay drops into a chair, a dazed look on his face.

I sit down opposite him and wait for him to speak. But he doesn't. "Clay, are you seriously freaking out?"

He sighs. "No."

I'm not convinced. I push the pretzels toward him. "Here, taste these. Toby insisted I bring them to you. He's proud of them."

Clay looks at the tin like he's never seen it before. He takes a pretzel and bites it. "All right. Good work, team. Although it's not really baking."

"Oh, *please*," I complain. "Even this was a challenge for me. It took me a minute to figure out that we needed to chill them on wax paper. The first batch is permanently glued to one of our plates.

And it was super messy. There was chocolate, like, all over my body."

Clay's eyes heat. "Jethro."

"It's a literal fact. You're the one who made it weird."

He rubs his forehead. "Tell Toby the pretzels are great. But you could have called me. I promised him I'd help out with the next bake sale."

"Seriously?" I flop back in the chair and look at the ceiling. "I *couldn't* call you. I wasn't going to put us in that position. You'd feed me dinner again, and then I'd hump your leg like a horny animal."

"*Jetty*." He takes another bite and shakes his head. "Yeah. Fine. I get it."

"Do you?" I press. "Did you know I also called the travel department and told them I prefer hotel rooms on lower floors?"

He squints at me. "Why?"

"So we don't end up in bed together!" *Jesus*. "Don't be dense. You told me you needed distance, so I'm giving you distance. *All* the distance, Clay. There ought to be a championship I could win. Because you're not the only guy who has a lot of distractions. I fucking dream about you."

He stops chewing. "You do?"

"Of fucking course!" It comes out shouty. "I know I'm some kind of late bloomer, and I already fucked up my chance with you. But I'm coping, okay? I want to win you a damn Cup, too, so you can have what you really want in life. I don't get why you're freaking out about an old photograph. There's no scandal. There's no *us* to terrify anyone. So calm your tits already."

He stares at me.

"What?" I ask.

"You seriously told travel you like the second floor, so we never end up in adjoining rooms?"

"Well, yeah." I shrug. "Because if we did, I'd be knocking on your door again, looking for a loophole. I'd be dragging you over to the bed and tying you to the headboard."

He swallows roughly, and his Adam's apple bobs.

"Yeah, I know," I say. "That would be a terrible idea, because you'd just run from me in the morning, and we'd start this whole pain loop over again, am I right?"

Those clear eyes edge away from me. "Probably."

"Yeah, I thought so. But that brings me around to a very important point. For the love of God, don't give Duckson any power over your headspace. He doesn't deserve it. He's just a smack talker. He doesn't actually know we were once a thing. And now we're *not* a thing, no matter how many dirty dreams I have about you, or how often I wonder what it would be like to be your dishwasher in chief again. So. Why. Are. You. Worrying?"

He props his head in one hand. "You make a few good points. It's just..." He trails off. "I don't spend a lot of time second-guessing my job or the decisions I make in this building. But lately I spend a lot of time second-guessing my personal life."

I study his frown, wishing I could kiss it away. I know my strengths, and I'm better in bed than I am at discussing the heavy shit. "Are you second-guessing your whole life because I showed up in it? Or is it because Newgate came out? Or is it because you're almost forty, and you're having a midlife crisis?"

"All of the above?" He eats another pretzel.

"So you're having a difficult year. Aren't we all." I kick him under the table. "But screw Fuckson and all his stupid pictures. He played, what, three NHL games before he got bounced back to the minors?"

"Did he?" Clay asks distractedly.

"Yeah. But that's my point—every guy in those photos left hockey a decade ago. They're still dining out on their old war stories, because that's all they've got. You have a big career and a team that could win you a championship ring. You can't get all up in your head over Duckson, because, as I reminded you earlier, you gave me the *worst* hard time about reacting the same way to him fifteen years ago."

The corner of Clay's mouth tips up for the first time. "Fuck me, I did, didn't I?"

"Yeah. And secondly, if you don't do the crime, you shouldn't do the time. If you let him get to you, then my sacrifices here count for nothing." I spread my arms apart and flex. Ridiculously. "This is what you're missing. So there better be a good fucking reason."

"God, will you stop?" He gives me an exasperated glance and swats across the table at me. "I get it. Point made."

I do another ridiculous flex because the room's sole window looks out on the running loop, where exactly nobody is standing. "You gonna calm down now?"

"Yes," he says grudgingly.

I push back my chair and get up. "Good. I gotta go do some squats, so I can out-lift the youngsters who want me to retire. And also, so I can look good naked."

Okay, maybe that last comment was a little over the top. But on my way out the door, Clay gives me a hungry look that makes it all worth it.

If I have to suffer, so does he.

THIRTY-EIGHT

Clay

WE PLAY Minnesota on March thirteenth, with Hale in the net. He gets his first shutout for Colorado, and the scoreboard reads 4-0 after the third period. The whole bench erupts with joy, because this win clinches our playoffs spot.

March *thirteenth*. It's the earliest clinch date of my coaching career. That has to mean something.

Right?

Immediately after the game, the crotchety old team owner calls me to congratulate me, and I try to sound humble. "It was a group effort. We're working hard, here."

He clears his throat in my ear. "Great to see that our backup goaltender isn't stinking it up anymore. At least against a crap team like Minnesota."

"He's doing well, Mr. Silbert," I say mildly. "At this point I'm more worried about Volkov's back and Wheeler's knee." *And Pierre's potential drug problem.* "We'll try to stay on top of it all."

"See that you do," he says.

We all celebrate in our own ways, I guess. Jethro shows up to drink NA beers at the hotel bar. Kapski passes out woven bracelets to the whole organization that say, *THIS IS A COUGARS YEAR.*

At the bar, Stoney makes a big show of ordering a frame for his vision board, which is looking more tattered every game. "Double-thick Plexiglass," he says. "We can take it everywhere we go."

Jethro nudges him. "But won't that mess with the magnetism?"

"It doesn't work that way!" Stoney says. "Nice try, though. Just for that, you owe me another photo."

After dropping about a thousand dollars on drinks for the team, I retreat to my hotel room at one in the morning. I'm still buzzing inside, my head full of strategies and petty anxieties.

We could win the Cup. But in order to do that, everything has to go *exactly* right.

Even though it's late, my phone lights up with an incoming call. Naturally my brain leaps to Jethro. I can't think of anyone else who'd call me at this hour.

Oops. Or maybe I can. It's Kaitlyn's face who appears on the screen. And it's her voice yelling in my ear after I answer the phone. "OMIGOD CLAZY! THIS IS AMAZING! WHEE!"

"Kaitlyn, ouch. I wouldn't think a doctor would be so callous with my hearing."

"Where is the love?" she demands. "I stayed up late to congratulate you."

There's a two-hour time difference in her favor, but I don't point that out. "Thank you. Now I just need another dozen miracles before I can wrap my entire body around the Cup."

"We're going to have the *best* party when you guys win. Even Dad will have to say proud things about you because some of his doctor friends are hockey fans."

I snort. "I don't want to win this thing for Dad, Kaity. I want it for me." It's been years since I worried about what he thinks.

"I know," she agrees. "But I'll enjoy it anyway. I'm petty like that. What else is going on with you? I haven't heard from you in ages."

"That's because nothing else is going on with me. Hockey is all I think about."

Well, hockey and Jethro. But it's almost the same thing.

"How are things with Jethro Hale?" she asks, exhibiting the same freaky intuition she's had her entire life.

"Pretty good. We've reached an understanding."

"Whoa. What *kind* of understanding?"

"The kind where we're friendly with each other and things aren't as tense anymore."

"Wow," she muses. "And how did that come to pass? Was there yelling involved?"

"There was some yelling," I say carefully. "But then I explained to him that our breakup had affected me more than it ever did him, and I apologized for acting badly when he turned up in Colorado."

She whistles. "That's...wow. Very mature of you."

"I'm actually good at this coach thing, Kait. Give me a little credit."

"What did he *say*, though? What does he think happened all those years ago?"

I laugh. "You're just loving this, aren't you? My drama is so entertaining. Better than TV."

"Don't judge. And don't cliffhanger me. What did Jethro say when you admitted your feelings for him?"

I sigh. "At first, not a lot. But later he was really nice about it. He said he regrets the way it ended. And that if he'd been older and wiser, we might still be together."

There's a silence at the end of the phone.

"Kait? Did I lose you?"

"I'm here," she says. "Just trying to process this. He...he told you he might be in love with you, too?"

"Not like that," I say quickly. "Can't imagine those words ever coming out of his mouth."

"But *still*," she gasps. "He's all, like, 'Hey we were amazing together. I get that now. Okay, bye'?"

"Well..." I screw my eyes shut. "He was open to more, but it's a nonstarter. I had to shut that down."

Another gasp.

"Kait, seriously. A player can't date a coach."

"I know that," she insists. "But what I don't get is how you're so calm about it. The love of your life said he wants you back. And you're, like, 'No can do! See you at practice.'"

"Kait! I'm not dead inside. But there are literally no other options here, unless I *quit my job*. Which, as you pointed out five minutes ago, is going better than ever before."

"But that's just so depressing!"

"I KNOW!" I shout. "It sucks! I spend half my time trying not to think about it! And in case you wondered, this conversation isn't helping!"

She sighs. Tragically. "I think I hate him even more now, and I didn't think that was possible."

"Don't hate him. Jeez." I sigh, too. "He's a good guy."

"He stomped on your heart," she grumbles.

"The thing is...he wasn't wrong fifteen years ago. I wish he'd been able to talk to me like a grownup and tell me I wasn't the only one who cared. But there was almost no practical way we could have stayed together and still had our careers."

"You thought there was," she points out. "And he didn't try."

"He didn't," I agree. "But what if it's nobody's fault? Maybe it was just easier to blame him. Easier, but wrong."

"Maybe," she mumbles, because Kait is as fair as she is loyal. "But what about the future? How many years does he have left in hockey?"

"Another season probably."

"That's not so long," she says.

I laugh. "Feels long, though."

"There's a dirty joke in there somewhere."

"*Kait.*"

She snickers. "Okay, hear me out. The Cougars win the Cup three months from today. And then Hale retires in a blaze of glory. You two could be a couple then, couldn't you?"

"I guess. Maybe." It's not like I haven't had this thought before. "It's not like I can ask him to do that."

"Can't you?" she presses. "Both your lives have been built around hockey—with no compromises. Maybe he's a little sick of it, just like you are."

"I didn't say I was sick of it."

She sniffs. "You didn't say it out loud. But I know you. You'll win the Cup. And then go home to your empty apartment and wonder what you're supposed to do now."

That sounds depressingly plausible. "I thought you called to congratulate me, not psychoanalyze me."

"Can't help it. Occupational hazard. Oh—one more thing. I'm pregnant. With twins."

I sit up fast. "Wait, what?"

"Two babies, due in September. A boy and a girl."

"Wow, Kait! Congratulations." My throat tries to close up around my words. This is big. Kait is in her late thirties, and it wasn't all that long ago when she was convinced she'd never have a family.

"Isn't it amazing? You're the first in the family to know. You want to know why?"

"Why?" I ask, still trying to imagine my baby sister pregnant with twins. My mind is blown.

"Because I knew you'd get it. And I knew you wouldn't ask me when Raul and I are getting married. Which I appreciate."

"Are you? Not that I care." My sister's boyfriend is a sharply dressed Puerto Rican doctor a few years older than her. I've always thought he was great.

"We'll probably get married eventually. But it's not top of mind. We're both excited about the pregnancy."

"Of course you are," I say sleepily. "Twins. I'll teach them to skate."

"I love you, Clazy," she says, her tone a little weepy.

"Back at you, too, Kaity. Thank you for telling me."

We ring off, and I turn off the lights and make myself comfortable on the bed. The Twin Cities' lights twinkle in the river outside my window.

Rolling onto my side on the king-sized bed, I think of my sister and her boyfriend, happy at home in Seattle, starting their family together.

I've always known that my life wouldn't look like that. It's a choice I made. But I'm old enough to wonder how things might have been different if I'd chosen another path. If I'd prioritized a relationship and a family over the glory of professional sports.

Somewhere in this same building—probably on a lower floor in another king-sized bed—Jethro is sleeping alone, too. We have our reasons.

It's just that sometimes—like right this second—it feels like a waste.

THIRTY-NINE

Jethro

APRIL

THE REGULAR SEASON slowly grinds toward the finish line. Day in and day out, I play hockey. I go to practice. I go to the gym. Then I do it all again.

My stats are showing a lot of improvement, but one thing never changes—I watch Clay a little too hungrily each time we're in the same room.

We still text, but lately I've forced myself not to reach out much. He asked for space, and I'm trying to give him that, for both our sakes.

On the home front, things are a little more upbeat. My father's health is stable. Toby seems more settled in school, where he's made two friends, Kavi and Dave. "They'll never be Trevor, but they'll do," he'd told me.

Our condo is nicely furnished now, and I lead a surprisingly domestic life for someone who's always been single and never intended to have a kid. I've been stocking the place with groceries, because I know the playoffs are going to hit me like a freight train. With the help of Clay's assistant, I've found a pediatrician for Toby who's accepting new patients. I even made it to parent-teacher conferences.

The brightest spot of all our lives is that my sister has made good on her word; every Monday night she calls Toby, and they talk. It's made a huge difference for him. He's more relaxed now that he can tell she's doing okay, and he knows she still cares.

I still feel like I'm bailing water out of the ship rather than sailing it, but it is what it is.

On a quiet Friday night, on a tiny break between the end of the regular season and the start of the playoffs, I find myself staring into the refrigerator, contemplating what to have for dinner. There's been no significant improvement to the Hale family kitchen skills, so we eat a lot of frozen food, and I'm a little sick of takeout.

Toby has Robotics Club, and I'll be picking him up from school around six o'clock. So I get a wild hair. "Hey, Dad, what do you think about going out? I'm in the mood for Japanese."

"Yeah, maybe," he says. "If they have other stuff besides sushi."

I've been working on expanding Toby's palate, but Mr. Old School doesn't share my passion for trying new things. "This place I found has ramen dishes and chicken skewers. I know you'd like it."

"All right," he says grudgingly.

At six, we swing by the school. Toby bounces toward the car looking happy to see us. "Are we going out?" Toby guesses as he slams the car door. "Pizza, maybe?"

"Sushi," I say quickly before my dad can jump on the pizza train.

"Cool. Is it close? I'm starved."

"Buckle up, kid, I'll have you there inside of ten minutes."

"Okay. I guess I can make it. Hey—did you hear when the last day of school is? Grandpa said *May twenty-third*! That's, like, a whole month earlier than in Detroit!"

It's actually three weeks earlier. I'd already checked. And I'd already been just as surprised as Toby. "Weird, right? I bet you like Colorado a little better now. They go back earlier in the fall, though. There's no such thing as a free lunch."

"Free lunch is totally a thing," he says. "There were kids at my old school who have free lunch tickets. And I won't care if they go back earlier if I'm in Detroit, right?"

I hesitate. "Why would you be in Detroit, pal? There's another year on my contract. You'll have to pull that scam the following fall."

The backseat is very quiet, and now my father is looking studiously out the passenger window. I wonder what these two have been discussing.

"But..." Toby finally says. "If you win the Cup, then you might retire, right? Going out on a big note?"

"A high note?" I ask. "Who said that?"

More silence.

I glance toward my father. "Dad, were you speculating about me retiring?"

"Not speculating," he says. "Just thinking aloud. If your team goes all the way, I thought you might call it quits."

It's not a ridiculous idea. But it's also not a great topic of conversation. "I can't even think like that right now. Anything could happen."

"Yeah, I know," he says. "But I was trying to explain to Toby that just because school gets out in May, we might not go right back to Michigan. Your playoffs season could go deep into June."

"God willing," I say, stopping at a light.

"I can't wait to go home," Toby says. "It's going to be awesome."

"Yeah, buddy," I say with a sigh. "Just don't plan next year without me, okay?"

"Okay," he says sullenly.

It's only a few more minutes until we reach an upscale commercial street in central Boulder, and I even get lucky with a parking spot. The restaurant is a bright and popular little eatery that gets good reviews online. Through big front windows, I see an attractive mountain mural and maybe twenty busy tables.

"Looks full. I hope there's no wait," my father says, because optimism isn't a Hale family trait.

"Let's ask before we worry." I pull open the door. I'm hit by the fresh scent of soy sauce and sesame, and my stomach grumbles.

A slender man with a riot of earrings greets us. "Konnichiwa. Table for three tonight?"

"That's our hope."

He looks over his shoulder. "Give me five minutes," he says, "I'll get a table ready."

"Thanks, man. Appreciate it." I grab a menu off the host's stand and hand it to my father so he can find something besides raw fish to order.

"Mmm, dumplings," he says appreciatively.

I scan the tables to check out people's entrees. And my gaze snags on two men in a booth together. They're both laughing about something, leaning in the way you would on a date. And I'm a little shocked to realize that one of them is my teammate, DiCosta. And his date? The excellent interior designer he recommended to us back in December.

Casually, I pull my phone out of my pocket and fire off a text to Clay.

> Does DiCosta have a boyfriend?

He must be glued to his phone because he answers immediately.

> Yeah, why are you asking? He's pretty private about it.

> No reason. Just spotted them at Little Zen Garden.

> Ooh. Get the spicy salmon roll. It's my favorite.

> Good tip.

I stash the phone in my pocket and glance toward DiCosta

again. It's amazing to me that Clay heads up the most queer-friendly team in the league, but he's still not out himself.

It makes me wonder—what if I hadn't run from him all those years ago? Would that be us sitting there?

My attention to that table must tip off Toby, because he suddenly says, "Hey, there's Carter!" And before I can stop him, he zips over to stand at the end of their booth. Uninvited, he starts chatting up Carter. If I had to guess, he's telling him how he reprogrammed the LED lights in his room to pulse to the music he plays on his Bluetooth speaker.

DiCosta glances up and catches me watching them. I lift a hand in greeting, and he gives me a nod before picking up his chopsticks.

"Gentlemen?" The host approaches. "Your table is ready." He gestures toward a spot on the opposite side of the room.

I cup my hands by my mouth. "Toby," I say just once.

His head swings in my direction, and I beckon to him.

A minute later, we're all seated at a table by the window, and my father is still studying the menu.

"I was just telling Carter about the lights," Toby says. "I wasn't bothering him."

"I'm sure you weren't," I agree, trying to keep the peace. "But they're having a nice conversation, and I wouldn't want us to interrupt."

"Might be a date," Toby says.

"A date?" my father scoffs. "There's no way DiCosta has a boyfriend."

"You never know," I say mildly.

He closes his menu and laughs. "Oh, please. Your whole team can't be fags."

My heart lurches. "Dad, don't ever use that word."

"Why?" He shrugs. "Nobody can hear me."

"I can." I look directly into his florid face. "It's offensive."

His eyes bulge. "To you? Come on."

My heart pounds against my ribcage because I know what I

have to do. "Dad, it's not okay to make assumptions about anyone's sexuality. For the record, I'm bisexual. I'm attracted to men as well as women," I add, in case Toby doesn't know that word.

Saying it aloud is awfully weird. I'm not sure I ever have. And now my father is staring at me with wide eyes.

Suddenly, he bursts out laughing, dropping the menu on the table and tipping his head back in glee. "Nice one, Jethro. Very funny."

"Uh, I don't think he's kidding," Toby says, studying my face, which is probably as red as a tomato.

My father's laughter dies. "No, he is. Tell Toby you're joking."

I hadn't planned to discuss this tonight, but I slowly shake my head.

He gapes at me. "You can't be serious. I'd know. And you never had a..." He grimaces. "Boyfriend. *Jesus*."

"I did," I say quietly. "Once. A long time ago."

His eyes bulge, and his face reddens. The man has a heart condition, and I wonder if I'm going to be dialing 911 in a second. But then he takes a deep, gulping breath and looks down at the table. "Jesus Christ, why are we discussing this in a public place?"

"But you said nobody can hear us," Toby chirps.

I can't hold back a snort. "Right. And this conversation is probably overdue. I'm not ashamed of it, by the way. Not anymore."

My father looks up sharply. "Did something happen?"

Yeah, I lost Clay. "No. There's no story. I was just young and dumb back then. I thought I cared what other people think." The implication is clear. *People like you.*

"Goddamn it, Jethro." My father gives his head a shake of disgust. "You're always pushing my buttons. Always trying to put me in my place."

"It's not like that at all," I insist. "I'm not looking to have a long conversation about it. But it's not okay to use slurs. Even if they didn't apply to me, it's still not cool."

My father looks like he wants to snarl at me, but the waiter picks this moment to approach the table. "Have we decided what we want?"

"I have," Toby says brightly. "Can we please have the gyoza to start? The large size. Fried. And can I have the shrimp tempura and an avocado roll?"

"Yessir. And you, sir?" He turns to me.

"A dragon roll, four pieces of tuna nigiri, and the spicy salmon roll. That's my ex-boyfriend's favorite."

The waiter writes that down without even blinking, while my father looks mildly nauseated.

Toby, though. He watches me with bright eyes and a proud smile.

So I know I did good.

FORTY

Clay

"TRAVEL IS LOCKED DOWN FOR SEATTLE," Liana says via the smart speaker on my kitchen counter. "I have you in a suite. We're removing the bed from the second bedroom and installing a conference table and video equipment."

"Cool," I say, tossing zucchini slices with minced garlic. I'm meal-prepping ahead of the playoffs.

"Tomorrow you've got morning skate, followed by a risk-assessment meeting, followed by video review and strategy."

"Yup. Hold on. I need to drain my noodles."

"Coach? What are you making?"

"Lasagna. It freezes well in individual portions."

She huffs. "I know a private chef who could feed you during the playoffs. You have more important things to do with your time."

The problem is that I don't, in fact, have better things to do, or anyone to do them with. "Cooking calms me down. We've been over this."

I'm not exactly calm, though. Not by a big stretch. Exercise and cooking are my only healthy outlets, and neither one of them is quite cutting it tonight. So after we hang up, I go to the pantry, pull out a bottle of single malt that I'd been saving, and pour myself a dram.

With military precision, I make eight individual lasagnas in Pyrex containers, with various fillings and toppings, and I place seven of them in the freezer. The last one goes into the oven as I pour myself another whisky.

And then I feel guilty for the whisky, so I put on my sweats and do a few sets on the weight bench in my home gym.

There's nothing on TV that can hold my attention, and I don't have anything new to read. So while I'm eating my lasagna, I text my sister. She responds a few times. But then:

> Sorry Clazy, GTG! It's date night. Time for dinner and mocktails!

She sends me a photo of her and Raul all dressed up to go out to dinner. They're glowing. Both of them.

My heart lurches, and I smile at the screen like a fool.

> Have a great night. Eat an extra dessert for me.

> The twins will fight you for it.

I set the phone down and top off my whisky. It's going to be another long, lonely night.

It's hard to do pullups when you're drunk.

These are my thoughts from the damp wood chips beneath the pullup bar on the playground. I'd been trying to metabolize the liquor through exercise, but the damn bar was slippery.

At least there's nobody around to witness my hijinks. It's dark and cold, and nobody is interested in the playground. Including me.

I lie back on the wood chips, my breath making visible puffs in the chilly air. There's almost a full moon tonight, which is probably why I can't see any stars.

Or maybe my eyes are just unfocused. It could really go either way.

"Clay?"

Someone is calling my name. I'm not in the mood to be interrupted, so I close my eyes.

"*Jesus.*"

A body lands beside me with a thud, and two warm hands touch my cold face. "Clay, baby. Open your eyes."

I do, and the only thing I see is Jethro's worried face. "Hi. Is something the matter? Did I forget a meeting?"

He makes a noise of disbelief. "Are you...*drunk*?"

"Maybe," I hedge. "If I was, it wouldn't be a big deal."

"It would if you froze to death," he snarls, and it's way hotter than anyone has a right to make a snarl sound.

"You're very hot," my mouth says. "In a rough way. I always went for prettier guys until I met you."

He blinks. "Um..."

"Thinking about your scruff on my sac makes me hard."

He closes his eyes. Then he opens them again. "Okay, here's what's going to happen. You're going to get up and walk back to your condo with me."

"I like this idea," I say, picturing him naked. But then I sit up too fast, and the motion makes me nauseous. "Uh-oh."

"What? Are you hurt?"

I hold up a hand for patience, then I take a cautious breath of cold air. After a moment, the squidgy feeling passes. "Okay, I'm ready."

He braces a hand under my elbow and carefully helps me to my feet, like you would with somebody's granny. "There we go. Good work."

"Well, duh. I still squat over three hundred. And you should see my bench. Keeps the pecs looking fiiiiiine, you know?"

"Like I hadn't noticed," he mutters. "One foot in front of the other, hot stuff. Let's move."

"You're very bossy tonight," I say with a yawn. "Kinda dig it."

He sighs. Then he tucks me against his side and wraps an arm around my waist.

It's nice. *Really* nice. "Why are you out here, anyway?" I ask.

"I did a big grocery shop. But somebody took my parking place, so I dropped the food off at home and parked in the back lot. How did *you* end up out here?"

"Hmm." I think it over. "Well, my sister is having twins."

He stops walking abruptly, which means I do as well. "*Tonight?*"

"No," I say quickly. Or at least I say it as quickly as my mouth will move, which is not that fast. My lips feel weirdly heavy. "In Sheptember."

"Ah," he says "Sheptember. Makes perfect sense why you'd be on your back on the cold, hard ground. It's going to be, like, thirty tonight." He nudges me forward, like an equestrian encouraging a horse.

"I had some whisky," I explain as we walk. "And I wanted to do some pullups. I really just needed to get out of my house."

"Right. But why?"

"It's really quiet there. All the time. I don't have friends. And now my sister is having twins and probably marrying Raul and I'll never see her again."

He's quiet for a second. "You have lots of friends."

"No. No. Nope. Coaches don't have friends. People hate them or fear them or kiss their asses. But they doesn't have friends." I burp. "They usually have a family, but I skipped that part."

"You're just stressed out because the playoffs are coming," he says.

"Maybe," I admit. "I used to yell at you for drinking to calm yourself down. You drank to have sex with me."

He groans. "We aren't talking about that."

"Yeah, I know. It's against the rules. I wouldn't need whisky to have sex with you, though. Just saying. Stone sober works great. Or drunk, honestly. I could still suck you off like a champion."

"Maybe think about keeping your voice down."

"Sure. Whatever. I can't remember why that matters."

"You'll remember in the morning, trust me." He wraps his arm a little more tightly around me. "Okay, time to do a few stairs. Ready?"

"Yeah."

He half drags, half carries me up the steps to my building. Then he frisks me for my keys.

"I like you handsy. Do that again."

Sighing, he opens the door and ushers me inside. "Dude, your kitchen is a mess."

"Lasagna."

"Ah. Did you put the pesto and zucchini in it?"

"Yes!" I exclaim. "Great memory."

"It's not hard remembering all the things you did for me. I'll never forget that shit. Now let's get you to bed. Is that upstairs? You're going to need some water and Advil."

"It's too early to go to bed," I argue.

"Clay, you can hardly stand up," he says, tightening his grip around my shoulders.

I lean into his sturdy frame and bury my nose in his flannel shirt-jacket. He looks so buff in it, but also cuddly. "Why would I want to? You feel so good."

Another grunt of irritation. Then strong arms maneuver me up the stairs. "Come on. Into bed you go."

That *sounds* promising, but the look on his face is all business. "You don't text me anymore," I blurt out. "Not like you used to."

He deposits me on the bed, then pulls my socks and shoes off one at a time. "You wanted space, and a good professional relationship. So I'm giving you space. The professional part is a work in progress, seeing as I enjoy watching you lift weights in the gym. But I guess nobody's perfect."

"Oh." I make a mental note to use the gym at work more often.

He pulls off my sweatpants. "Where do you keep your medicine?"

"Kitchen drawer," I mumble, pulling the comforter up. I'm cold from lying around on the playground like a dummy.

"Stay put," he says.

I don't, though. I stagger to the bathroom and pee, then brush my teeth. When I return to the bed, he's fetched me a glass of water and two pills, which I swallow carefully. My stomach still hates me a little.

Jethro leaves the room again without saying goodbye. I hear him bumping around downstairs, probably checking the lock on my back door and turning out the lights.

Come back, my heart whines.

Surprisingly, he does. Five minutes later he kicks off his shoes and sits down on the bed beside me. He leans back against my upholstered headboard and catches his knees in his hands. "How worried should I be about you right now?"

"I'm not going to barf."

"That's not what I mean," he says quietly. Then he reaches down and runs his fingers through my hair. "Not like I'm one to talk, but you're kind of a mess, Clayzy. You seem really down at a moment when another guy would be on top of the world."

His hand in my hair feels so good that I almost forget to answer. "I'll be okay. I always am."

He peers down at me before flattening himself on his belly, still watching me like I'm a puzzle he can't quite solve. Then—and maybe I've actually begun to hallucinate—he kisses me. It's a real kiss, too. Slow. With soft lips that make me shiver.

I arch up off the bed and let him know how much I need more of that.

Miraculously, he tilts his head and kisses me again. And again. But each one is a little softer and a little briefer than the one before.

Then he stops, leaving me panting and hungry for his mouth.

"Are we going to fool around now?" I ask as my body yells *more more more.*

He shakes his head.

"Then what was that for?" I demand. "Just...torture?"

He runs his fingers through my hair again and cups my face. "We can't fool around."

"Sure we can. You're not taking advantage of me."

"No kidding. Even drunk you're better at making decisions than most people. And I'm not trying to be patronizing. But you told me we weren't doing this, and I'm following instructions. I don't want to be another regret of yours, okay? That's not fair to me."

Shame burns my neck. "You're right. I'm sorry. But you started it."

"I wasn't trying to start anything." He gives me a soft kiss on the chin. "But you're in kind of a dark place. I need you to know that I care about you. Don't forget that."

"Yeah, I won't. And neither will my dick."

He smirks. "I'm counting on it. And if we ever go to bed again, it will be when both of us are all in."

"Parts of me are all in right now. I must not be very drunk."

"Sure you're not," he says with another smirk. Then he flops onto his back beside me. "Now go to sleep, Clay."

"Are you staying?" I ask greedily.

"For a minute," he says. "Close your eyes."

I do it. But I also roll toward him and park my head on his strong chest the way I've always wanted to.

He lets me. He wraps an arm around me and rubs the achiest part of my shoulder.

"Sorry I'm such a wreck tonight."

He sweeps the hair off my forehead. "Honestly, it makes me feel better to know that you can be a fuckup. I didn't know you had it in you."

I try to think up something witty to say in reply. But I just fall asleep instead.

Sunlight blazes in my face. I wake up with a start, and then groan as my head gives an unhappy throb. I have no idea what time it is, but I can hear my phone alarm going off somewhere in the house.

I'm alone in bed, like always. But an image of Jethro leaning over me in the dark swims into my mind.

That really happened, right? I rub my temples. It seems improbable that Jethro came over last night and put me to bed with kisses. But the glass of water he brought me has been refilled. And the bedroom door is closed. I never do that.

I gulp down the water. Then I stagger downstairs, wondering how big a wreck my kitchen will be. I'm pretty sure I trashed the place last night making lasagna.

I stop dead at the bottom of the stairs. The kitchen is sparkling clean. Every dish has been washed, and the counter gleams. My phone is on the charger.

Oh Jethro.

There's a note, too, on a Post-it.

You don't owe me anything, but I wouldn't say no to one of those lasagnas in your freezer.

I start the coffee and sit down on a barstool, listening to the silence of my apartment

FORTY-ONE

Jethro

WE WIN the first two games against Seattle at home with Volkov in the net.

I celebrate by baking up the lasagnas that Clay left on our doorstep after that weird night when he got drunk. There was a sealed envelope inside the bag, with a note addressed to me:

> J—
>
> Yikes, right? When I make a mess, I make it big.
>
> Thank you for sorting me out. That was totally above and beyond.
>
> I appreciate you more than you can know.
>
> C

I guess we're even now, because I seem to remember showing up at his door feeling particularly messy a couple months ago.

Although Clay has begun avoiding me at the rink again. Maybe he's embarrassed.

Or maybe he's just very busy trying to win a championship, and I'm a whiny little bitch.

But at least I have lasagna for dinner.

"Where did this food come from?" my father asks as I'm serving it onto plates.

"It's from my secret gay lover." I hand him a plate.

"Hey." He gives me a sour look. "You're the one making it weird now. I haven't made a single comment. Why do you have to keep bringing it up?"

Because it amuses me and irritates you. "The lasagna is from Coach Powers. I did him a favor the other night, and this is like a thank-you note."

My father gives the plate another look. "Huh. Wow. He cooks?"

"Yeah. It's his hobby."

"Damn useful hobby." He opens the silverware drawer and takes out three forks. "Let's eat."

"*Toby!*" I call upstairs. "Dinner!"

"Coming." Footsteps thump on the stairs. It's kind of shocking how loud a boy who weighs seventy pounds can be.

We all sit down, and I lean over the plate and sniff. I get a whiff of garlic and homemade tomato sauce.

"What's the green stuff?" Toby asks suspiciously.

"There's basil and a layer of zucchini. It's so good you won't even notice you're eating a vegetable."

He looks unconvinced.

I dig in. The sauce is bright and zesty, the pasta is tender, and the cheese is crisp on top and gooey inside. It's heaven.

The only thing that could make it better is if Clay were sitting across the table, too.

My family agrees that the lasagna is fantastic. I can tell, because nobody speaks for a while. We're too busy eating.

"Mom called today," Toby says eventually.

"But it's not Monday," I point out.

"I know!" He beams. "She's back at the regular jail now."

"*Oh*." I swallow. "Already?"

"Yup," he says. "She can call me any day she wants."

"That's great," I say hollowly. Although it isn't. There are drugs in jail, which boggles my mind. And while I know my sister wasn't lying when she told me she wants to stay clean, I wonder how she's going to do that when temptation strikes.

"She said you wouldn't be happy," Toby says, licking his fork. "She said you'd worry."

"Well, it is *jail*," I say lightly. "Who'd be excited about that?"

"I am." He shrugs. "When we go home for the summer, you can bring me to see her every week."

"We'll see," I say automatically, like every parent everywhere.

"Why do we have to *see*?" Toby demands. "When we're home again, it'll be easy to go there."

Sure, kid. Easy to watch your mom relapse. "Look, we'll see her, okay? I just don't know when. Let me get through some more games and we'll see what happens."

He tosses his fork onto the plate with a clatter. "You're not even *playing*," he says. "How hard could it be?"

I take a slow breath, so I won't start yelling.

"Toby..." my father says wearily.

"I *hate* Colorado," he says. Then he shoves his chair back and runs upstairs.

My father takes another bite of lasagna, holding his comment until after he hears the door slam upstairs. "He just misses Shelby."

"I know."

"It's not gonna stop, though. He needs to move home. *I* need to move home. I don't have anyone here."

Except for me. I don't say it, though, because I don't need verbal confirmation that I don't really count. I've known it all my life. "You shouldn't have put that idea in his head about me retiring," I say. "That's not your call."

He lifts his eyes heavenward. "Really? You win the Cup, and you're going back to training camp in August? How many championships does one man need?"

I eat my last bite of lasagna. Then I set down my fork. "What do you think I'm going to do with myself in Detroit, anyway? I can't even think about working for my old team, not after the way they treated me."

He shrugs. "You'll take a little time and figure it out, either this year or next. Either way, your boy needs his mama, and our life is there."

On that depressing thought, I swap my plate with Toby's and finish the scraps he left behind.

Nobody can dent my appreciation for Clay's lasagna.

Not even my father.

FORTY-TWO

Clay

GAMES three and four are in Seattle. We load up the jet with our best players, equipment, all our hopes and dreams, and fly off to do battle against a young team that I *know* we can beat. Even so, I spend the entire flight holed up in the office, worrying over my starting lineup.

There's plenty to think about, but I spend most of my time mulling over my choice of goalies.

On the one hand, I don't want to mess up our momentum. The "if it ain't broke, don't fix it" school of thought would have me playing Volkov again. On the other hand, we're still wary of his lower-back issues and trying not to tire him out. I'll need him in the next round, too.

Everyone has an opinion. Murph wants to put in Hale. The GM thinks I should play Volkov again, but my gut says he's wrong. And I can't decide if my gut is telling me the truth, or if I'm every bit as tangled up over this question as Jethro and I used to be, well, tangled up together, naked and sweaty.

Needing more input, I text Coach Demski, who's traveling with us to Seattle.

You awake? I need a consult.

Gimme five, I'm in a hot hand of poker.

Sometimes I forget that other people think about things besides work.

Demski rolls in a few minutes later. "Thanks for your patience. I won fifty bucks off your D-men."

"No problem. Let's talk about game three."

"Play Hale," he says easily. "He's looking strong. We need to keep Volkov rested."

"Yeah, I was thinking that. But I'm also worried about breaking momentum."

He taps the table thoughtfully. "Game three after a two-game streak is always a tough win. Seattle will come out strong. They're fighting for their lives. Nothing about this game is going to feel like the last one. So no matter who you play, they're going to get a workout."

"True." I lean back in my chair. "I just needed to talk it out."

"You seem tense," the older man says. "Don't forget this is supposed to be fun."

"*Fun?*" I snort. "I don't think the owner cares how much *fun* I'm having. We need to win."

"Of course we do," he says easily. "And winning is totally fun. But you have to try to enjoy the journey. Otherwise, your players are going to pick up on your anxiety. They're going to think you don't believe in them, and that will affect their play."

I give him a skeptical look. "Is this some kind of goalie superstition?"

"Nah, just good advice from an old man. Athletes are like dogs —they can smell your fear. So you gotta find a way to embrace the moment." He gets up. "Excuse me, I gotta embrace the moment, too. If I win a few more hands before we land, I can buy the wife a nice gift to apologize for missing our anniversary again."

After the door closes, I lean back and shake my head. *Enjoy the journey.*

Thanks, pal. Now when I feel anxious before the game, I'll be worrying that it's contagious.

Demski wasn't wrong about game three. Seattle comes out of the chute with their fangs out and ten thousand hometown fans on their feet before the puck even drops. Their energy is electric, bordering on desperate.

I watch Jethro settle into his crease, tapping the posts. We're up two games, but playoff hockey is a different beast entirely. One bad bounce, one moment of lost focus, and the tide can turn in an instant.

Hale knows that, I remind myself. *He's been here before.*

As the first period gets underway, Seattle comes out flying. Their forwards are everywhere, swarming our zone like angry hornets. Jethro makes his first save less than thirty seconds in, kicking out his right pad to deflect a low shot from Seattle's top scorer.

"Nice one, Hale!" I hear Kapski shout as he clears the rebound.

But Seattle won't be discouraged. Five minutes in, Jethro's up to six saves. Our guys are on their heels, struggling to match Seattle's intensity.

Then it happens. Seattle's star center threads a perfect pass through traffic. Their winger one-times it, the puck a blur as it rockets towards the top corner. Jethro pushes off hard, stretching every inch of his frame.

For a split second, I think he has it. Then I see the red light flash behind him.

The arena explodes, and so does my brain. Jethro slams his stick against the post in frustration. It's only one goal, but it feels like more. Seattle's played us even through the first two games. Now they have the crowd behind them and first blood.

"Shake it off, boys!" I hear Kapski yell, trying to rally the team. "Plenty of hockey left!"

But Seattle is alive with hope. They keep coming in waves, and it's all my D-men can do to keep us in the game. And Jethro makes save after save, some more desperate than pretty. By the end of the first period, the shots are 18-4 in Seattle's favor, but somehow, we're only down 1-0.

As Jethro skates off the ice, our eyes meet. His jaw is set, his expression grim. He knows this is no way to win.

I give an impassioned speech during the intermission that I probably won't remember later. Lots of hand waving and *you can do this.*

But the second period starts much the same way. Seattle is relentless, and we can barely get the puck out of our zone. Ten minutes in, Jethro's made another dozen saves when disaster strikes —their defenseman winds up for a slap shot from the point. DiCosta skids over to block it, and the puck deflects off his shin pad, changing direction completely. And before Jethro can adjust, it's in the back of the net.

2-0 Seattle. And an own-goal.

DiCosta gives a shout of frustration. And Jethro's face is bright red when he lifts his mask for a drink. It's not anyone's fault, really, just a bad bounce. But I can see the anguish radiating off both of them.

Finally, our guys seem to wake up. We start to push back, generating some offensive pressure of our own. With two minutes left in the period, Newgate threads a beautiful pass to Pierre, who buries it top shelf.

2-1. About fucking time.

I give another sermon in the dressing room on the theme of *we're still in this thing.*

But Seattle is still in this thing, too. They fight us for every inch of ice, every loose puck. Jethro makes a couple of big saves to keep us within one. Then, with ten minutes left, the refs miss a blatant high stick on Wheeler. No call.

I'm livid, shouting at the officials. It should have been a power play for us.

Instead, Seattle is back in our faces. Their forward drives hard to the net, and in the ensuing scramble, the puck somehow squeezes through Jethro's pads and over the line.

3-1 Seattle.

Jethro's furious. At the non-call, at himself for not squeezing the pads tighter, at this whole damn game. He whacks his stick against the crossbar, earning himself a warning from the ref.

We pull him with two minutes left, desperate for a miracle. Hale glowers from the bench while Seattle's goalie stands tall, buffeting our shots.

When the final horn sounds, the scoreboard reads 3-1. As the team files off the ice, I can see the disappointment etched on every face. We let an opportunity slip away. We could have put a stranglehold on the series. Instead, we've given Seattle life.

In the locker room, I keep my post-game speech short and to the point. "We got outworked tonight, plain and simple. But it's one game. We'll get our revenge in forty-eight hours."

The post-game rituals seem to last forever. But when the room clears out, I catch Jethro's eye. He's sitting in his stall, putting on his shoes, his expression still pissed as hell.

"Hey," I say, sitting down beside him. "Forty-two of forty-five shots, man. That's hardcore. Better than ninety-three percent."

He gives me an incredulous glance. "That game sucked."

"Not your save percentage, though."

He gives his gym bag a kick of frustration. "Are you this patronizing to every player who has a bad night?"

"Jesus Christ. Are you this rude to all your coaches?"

We're standing now, facing off against each other, both of us angry.

"Let me ask you this," he says quietly. "Did you sweat a lot over the goalie decision for tonight?"

I hesitate.

"You did, right? You got a cramp in your neck wondering if you could be objective about putting me in the net. And now you're going to go stare at the ceiling in your room and brood about it some more."

Get out of my brain. "Hale, it's not like that."

He gives me a look of fury.

"Last bus to the hotel leaves in five!" the GM's assistant calls.

Jethro grabs his bag off the floor. He gives me a macho goalie look, all bushy eyebrows and cynicism. "Don't stew over it, Clay. We can both take this loss like men."

"Whatever that means," I grumble, because I've always hated that expression.

He strides away from me without another comment, leaving me perfectly positioned to admire his ass.

Like a man.

———

Two hours later I'm spread out on the silken king-sized bed in my expensive hotel suite. And staring at the ceiling. It's a nice ceiling, but it's not helping.

Tomorrow is going to be a busy day of setting up for game four. I'm supposed to be sleeping, but I'm brooding about the second line's positioning. And also about that bad call from the refs tonight. And about that last, punishing goal from Seattle.

Most importantly, I wonder if there's anything I could have done tonight to coach the game to victory. I'll never know the answer.

But there's one thing I *know* I could have done better.

I grab my phone off the nightstand, open our messaging app, and bang out a text.

> I'm sorry I was patronizing. I didn't mean to be.

A reply pops up a minute later, and it's the eye-rolling emoji. And then:

> Don't stew over it.

> Oh you should talk, at 1:30 in the morning.

> I'm not stewing over the game.

> Then why are you up???

> Family crap. But I know you're lying there doing a play by play with your neck in that electric massage thing.

With an angry groan, I yank the stupid massager out from under my neck and fling it onto the carpeting. The thing doesn't work anyway.

> I was just trying to be nice.

> Yeah, don't do that. You can't be all up in your head about me and win the Cup.

Frustrated, I stab the call icon and wait to see if he'll pick up.

"Yes, Coach?" Jethro's voice says a moment later.

"What is your point?" I demand. "What do you want from me?"

"A lot of things," he says silkily. "But I can't exactly reach through the phone and grab your dick. And you took that off the table, anyway. Or you tried to, but as far as I can see, it's not working."

"Of course it's working! What are you talking about?" I'm so frustrated right now I want to throw the phone across the room.

And the stupid truth is that if he were here right now, I'd do whatever he wanted. Plus some more. Maybe then I could fall asleep.

He sighs. "Look. I can't play hockey if I'm worrying about disappointing you on a personal level. And you can't make good tactical decisions when you're carrying the weight of my teetering career on your conscience."

"I'm not," I insist. "That wasn't our problem tonight."

"My mistake, then."

I sigh.

"Look," he says. "You *chose* this. Your whole life is set up to win this championship. So go do that, no matter what it costs. Tonight was a shitty game, but I'm not going to crumble. I'll work my ass off any time you put me in the net. But it's your job to use me like any other weapon in your arsenal. Deploy me or don't. But don't second guess us both, because it's not helping."

There's a tight band of discomfort around my chest, because the truth hurts. "You've been heard."

"Clay, I need the Cougars to keep winning. The minute we lose, I'm on a plane to Michigan, dealing with family stuff. So try not to let that happen right away, yeah? Be brutal. Play me or don't. My time with this team is short either way, so make it count."

I wince at every blow he delivers, because every one of them is a direct hit. This is exactly why we keep experienced athletes on the roster. They can see the bigger picture.

But something else he just said is bothering me. "Is everything okay with the family?"

He's silent for a second. "Clay."

"Hey—I ask about everybody's family. Pierre's girlfriend is pregnant, so Liana is sending a fruit basket. And Dougherty's kid just got braces and a teddy bear from the team."

Jethro snorts. "All right. Here's the Hale family update—my felon of a sister finished rehab and got transferred back to genpop. My kid wants to spend time with her this summer so we can all watch her relapse."

Oh shit. "Well, Mr. Hale, the team usually sends roses for this kind of family milestone. But Liana can probably recommend a thornless arrangement if we're worried about shivs."

He barks out a laugh. "That's nice, Coach. But a team who really wanted to show their love would send a carton of cigarettes. I've heard they're like gold inside."

"You're right. Nothing says *we care* quite like contraband tobacco. I'll ask my assistant to update our gift policy."

"See that you do."

I smile up at the ceiling. Talking to Jethro makes me feel less lonely. But he needs me to coach the team as if he's just another player.

If only I could figure out how to do that.

FORTY-THREE

Jethro

AFTER I HANG up with Clay, I put the phone down and turn off the light. I close my eyes, imagining him somewhere in this same building, doing exactly the same thing. I can picture him lying in bed so clearly, one arm curved around his head on the pillow. It's hard to believe that was once my nightly view.

Near the end of our doomed relationship in Busker, we finally started sharing a bed. I think it happened by accident the first time —like he was too sexually satisfied to get up and cross the room to his own bed.

Or maybe it was me. I can't even remember anymore. All I know is that I liked it, but I tried not to think too much about it. I didn't want it to mean anything.

Still, I'd wake up in the night and listen to him breathing slowly beside me. I didn't realize it at the time, but it was the sound of peace and acceptance. It's taken me all this time to understand that I loved him. I loved him as much as I was capable of loving anyone.

He loved, me, too. And his brand of love was a purer sort than I'd ever experienced before. His love didn't come with a price tag.

My family has always been more complicated. And it never lets up.

Earlier tonight, when my father had called me after the game, I'd assumed it was to say something consoling. Or at a minimum, to bitch about the ref's bad call.

But nope. He hadn't mentioned the game at all. "Guess what? Your sister is up for parole," he'd said with obvious excitement. "I need you to write a letter in support of her progress. We're all writing letters."

"Wait," I'd said, panicking. "Not Toby. You can't tell him about the parole hearing. She's not getting out, Dad."

"She might. I have a good feeling."

"Dad," I'd groaned. "Don't tell him."

But I knew my request had come too late. Now my anger is keeping me awake. Shelby's lawyer had warned us that parole is a very erratic process. It's not fair for Toby to dream about his mom getting out when the odds are so low.

My father blew it, and I'm not even around to handle the damage. And now I'm supposed to write a letter? *Dear parole board. I love my sister, but literally anything can happen if she gets out. Please let her out anyway because there are drugs inside your prison. And even your rehab facility. What the hell are you even doing?*

Okay, not that version. I'll have to workshop it.

I roll over and push my face into the pillow. If Clay were here, I wouldn't be thinking about hockey or prisons. I'd be face down on him. I wouldn't squander his attention, either, like I did when I was young.

It's been hard dredging up the past, and realizing all the ways my younger self was stupid.

It's been hard realizing that I still love him but can't have him.

Meanwhile, it's been hard in my boxer shorts. I slip a hand beneath my body and past the waistband of my underwear. I close my hand around my hardening cock and sigh into the sheets.

Clay. I just told him to stop thinking about me. But the only way I'm going to be able to fall asleep is if I get off to the image of his hands on my dick.

I stroke myself in earnest. I bring myself right to the edge.
But what brings me over in the end is the memory of his smile.

FORTY-FOUR

Clay

MAY

IT TURNS out that Seattle gave us all they had in game three. They fall apart during game four, and we seal the deal on the series in game five.

I celebrate by drinking a single beer.

Then it's on to round two in Dallas. We lose the first game. Badly. I don't sleep a wink afterwards. An angry call from the owner doesn't help.

And I keep thinking about what Jethro said. *Your whole life is set up to win the Cup. So go do that.*

I switch things up for the next game, changing my defense pairings and putting Hale in the net. We win the second game. And the third one, too.

Most days start early and end late. My life is happening at warp speed. There's always a decision to be made. Always an issue to solve. Another meeting with the coaching staff. Another risk assessment with the trainers. We're monitoring Pierre's disposition and Wheeler's knee and a hundred other factors that could all make a difference.

I barely sit down, and when night falls, I either fall into a dead sleep, or I stare at the ceiling, thinking through our plays.

Hale told me to stop thinking about him. And somehow, I do it. It helps that he barely makes eye contact lately and I'm too exhausted to think of anything other than hockey.

But whatever we're doing, it works. When I put Hale in front of the net against Dallas again, he lets in a single goal all night long, and we end up taking the series in six games.

Suddenly, we're headed for the conference championship against Edmonton. We've leveled up. This is the furthest I've gotten in my coaching career.

This is it. My big moment.

And I celebrate by having a giant migraine on the first night.

"You okay?" Liana asks me before we head out to the ice.

"You okay?" Murph asks me behind the bench.

"You okay?" the trainer asks me, probably because I'm squinting.

"I'M FINE," I snarl at all of them. Because I have to be fine. I have my clipboard clutched under one arm with the starting lineup clamped to it.

Edmonton is an older team than Dallas, and Hale has played with a few of their starters before. So I put him in the net to kick off the series. He starts off strong, stopping everything during the first period.

But familiarity works both ways, and Edmonton is determined to pick apart our game. When they find the right keys to unlock our defense, Hale starts getting shelled. I end up putting Volkov in for the third period, because we need a change of dynamics.

From the other end of the bench, Jethro's jaw looks as tight as mine as we manage to push the game into overtime.

My headache tightens its grip, and I throw up during the break.

If this is the kind of fun Demski wants me to have, I might need to look up the definition of the word.

FORTY-FIVE

Jethro

WE MANAGE to win the first Edmonton game during overtime, but we don't make it look easy. Hessler—a solid defenseman—tweaks his ACL. Newgate struggles.

And Clay? He looks like death, his face pale and clammy. It's a migraine for sure.

I want to text him and check in, but I'm not a hypocrite. I can't tell him to treat me like any other player and then coddle him.

On our day off, I do a lengthy practice with Demski and a heavy workout, but when Clay announces the starting lineup for game two, I'm not on it.

It's a blow, but if I were him, I'd probably play Volkov again, too. It sends the right message to Edmonton. *We figured out how to beat you and we're going to do it again.*

Unfortunately, we drop game two, and so I'm on for games three and four, where we split the results.

I'm on the bench for game five, and we win, but not decisively. Volkov struggles, missing a second-period shot that my dad could have stopped.

At least that's what my dad says when he bitches about it afterward.

We fly back to Canada for game six, and when the starting lineup comes out, Volkov's name is on that one, too. My first reaction is wanting to punch something. Since I'm a professional, I don't.

The bench it is. At least I have a good seat for the game. And it's hairy from the first drop. Edmonton comes out swinging, desperate to stay alive in the series. They score within the first two minutes, catching Volkov off guard with a quick wrist shot from the slot.

The hometown crowd roars, and the tension on our bench ratchets up several notches. That goal wasn't supposed to happen.

After the face-off, our guys fight back. We answer the goal at the ten-minute mark. But on the other end of the ice, it's clear to me that something's off with Volkov. His body language is stiff. He makes a few good saves, but he's fighting the puck on every shot. I watch him grimace as he gets up after a particularly awkward stretch to make a glove save.

"You seeing this?" Stoney mutters from beside me on the bench.

I nod, my eyes never leaving the ice. "Yeah. He doesn't look right."

Edmonton scores again late in the first period. This time it's a soft goal, one Volkov should stop easily but doesn't. He fishes the puck out of the net, frustration etching his face.

During the intermission, the locker room is tense. Clay gives a pep talk, but he glances over at Volkov with concern. Our starting goalie is sitting quietly in his stall, rolling his shoulders.

The second period gets off to a great start when Newgate puts up a goal. But things go sideways when Edmonton scores twice more in quick succession. Volkov is clearly struggling, his movements more labored with each passing play. After the fourth goal, Clay catches my eye and gives me a slight nod.

"Hale," he calls out. "Start stretching. You're going in at the next break in play."

Every head on the bench turns in my direction. And it's almost like the loud soundtrack of the arena dims for me. I'm going in, and I'm going to stop the bleeding on this shit show.

The TV timeout arrives, and as I strap on my mask and grab my stick, Clay gives me a pat on the shoulder. "Lock it down," he says, his voice low and intense.

But I don't need any encouragement. After fifteen years of professional hockey, I know just what to do.

I skate out onto the ice, tapping the posts as I settle into the crease. The opposing team is all smiles.

Yeah, yeah. Doubters.

The puck drops, and it's on. Edmonton steals the puck on the first face-off and proceeds to test me early, peppering me with shots. But I'm ready. I make a flashy glove save on a breakaway attempt, and I can feel the game's energy shift.

"You want more of this?" I taunt Edmonton's captain as he skates by. I remember when he was a rookie during my fifth season.

Midway through the third period, we're still down 4-2, but my defensemen seem to feed off my attitude. Their play becomes sharper, more focused. Edmonton's captain trips Stoney and gets called for it, so we get a power play.

And *boom*. Kapski scores. The Edmonton fans groan. It's 4-3, and every player hunkers down for a battle. No one is going to back down. The players get chippy and the elbows fly.

With two minutes left in the game, the speed of play accelerates to a screaming blur. Edmonton is on their heels, desperately trying to get the puck back. They ice it on a poke check, giving us an offensive zone face-off. Clay calls a timeout, gathering the team around him.

"Alright, boys," he says, his eyes blazing with intensity. "This is our moment. We won back our chance. Let's not waste it."

As the puck drops, time seems to slow down. Kapski wins the draw cleanly, getting the puck back to DiCosta at the point. He fires a rocket through traffic. I hold my breath as I watch it sail towards the net, deflecting off Stoney's stick and past Edmonton's goalie.

Our bench explodes. We've tied it up with less than a minute to go.

Sweat's dripping into my eyes, but I'm jazzed for the overtime period. After the break, both teams stay scrappy, but neither can find the back of the net. Then, five minutes in, Newgate intercepts a pass at our blue line and takes off. He's got a step on the defenseman. I lean forward, my heart in my throat.

Newgate dekes, the Edmonton goalie bites, and suddenly the puck is sliding into an open net. My team goes absolutely berserk.

We've done it. We're moving on to the final.

There you go, Clay. I look for his cleanly shaven face among the playoff beards, as my teammates pour onto the ice in celebration. As I join the pile at center ice, I catch Clay's eye.

He's grinning from ear to ear.

FORTY-SIX

Clay

"THE *FINALS*," my sister gasps into my ear. "Are you freaking out?"

"I don't freak out," I tell her as the elevator climbs to the ninth floor of my hotel. It's one thirty in the morning.

"Pfft. Nobody is too macho to freak out," she insists. "I bet you screamed like a first-timer at a Taylor Swift concert."

I laugh. "If we actually win the whole damn thing, I might just do that."

"The *finals*," she repeats. "Maybe even Dad will notice."

We both laugh. *As if.*

"Clay, I'm taking off from work and flying to Colorado. Can you get me a ticket for game one?"

"Yeah. You and the boyfriend."

She squeals.

"Hey, you feeling okay?" I ask her.

"I feel *great!* My brother is going to the finals! Whee!"

Laughing, I get off the elevator and start looking for room 912. "Goodnight, Kait."

"Night, Clayzy! Congratulations!"

Tucking the phone into my pocket, I turn down the corridor.

And stop dead when I see Jethro leaning against the wall, watching me.

And, fuck, he looks good in his game-day suit, a lazy smile on his face. My stomach does a swoopy thing that it's not supposed to do when I look at him. "Hey," I say, swallowing. "You looking for me?"

He shakes his head. "I wasn't. But I was about to open my door when I heard your voice."

"You're on this floor?" I ask stupidly. Since he'd confessed that he'd requested rooms on low floors, I wasn't expecting to see him.

"I guess the Fairmont just really loves to upgrade me." He pulls a key out of his pocket and swipes into... I peek at the room number. 910. It's the one adjacent to mine. "Congratulations, Clay. I know this means a lot to you." His door opens, and he steps through, dropping his gym bag on the other side.

The door is about to swallow him up, and I'm not ready. "That was a hell of a game, Jethro. We're going to the finals because of the way you played tonight."

He glances over his shoulder at me. "Thanks, Coach" he says slowly and deliberately. "You take care now."

Then the door closes behind him with a sturdy click. I remain there in the hallway, forgetting to move. Tonight, I was given a passport to everything I ever wanted.

So why do I feel like the thing I *really* want just disappeared behind that door?

Eventually, I remember to unlock room 912. Walking in, I pass a door which clearly adjoins Jethro's room. He's right there.

Fuck. This is some kind of karmic test, isn't it?

I go through the motions of getting ready for bed. I fire up the shower and wash all the gametime sweat off my body, and I hang up my suit. I brush my teeth. I find a complimentary bottle of imported water and a fruit bowl on the table. There's a fancy chocolate on my pillow. The spoils of the rich and successful.

But I just feel hollow inside. Tonight, I reached the greatest achievement of my career, and I don't have anyone to celebrate with besides my sister.

I sit on the edge of the bed and drop my head into my hands. If we've won the Cup ten days from now, I will be a very, *very* successful hockey coach. But I will still be lonely as fuck.

Without really thinking about it, I slip off the bed and walk to the set of doors separating our rooms. I unlock and open my side, then knock on his.

For a moment, I don't think he's going to answer. I can't blame him. I made the rules, and now I'm the ass who's thinking about breaking them.

Then I hear a single word on the other side of the door. "Clay?"

"Yeah."

"Did you just knock on my door?"

"Yeah."

I hear the bolt slide, and he opens the door partway. He's bare-chested, and my eyes dip down to take in my favorite abs, an athlete's eight-pack, and a sandy brown happy trail running down the center of his stomach.

When I remember to raise my eyes to his, they're squinting at me. "Did you want something?"

Yes. I swallow. "Great game tonight. You...you amaze me."

His jaw hardens. "Really, Clay? That's what you knocked on my door to say?"

"Um..." I'm so busted.

He rolls his eyes. "Just don't take a step closer."

My heart drops. "Why?"

"A guy only has so much willpower."

Oh. We stare at each other for another long beat. Then he licks his lips, and I feel it in my sac. "And if I did take a step... Then what?"

He glares at me. "Take it and find out."

On tonight of all nights, after an exciting conference win, it seems I've got the self-control of a squirrel in a nut shop. So of course, I step closer.

Jethro's eyes darken. Then his hands land on my chest, and he pushes me bodily back into my own room. "Just remember. *You* knocked on my fucking door."

"I...I did," I stammer as my knees hit the bed.

"This was *your* idea. You confusing son of a..."

I never find out how that sentence ends because he pounces, basically tossing me down on the bed. I'm on my back, and he's covering my body with his heated one. His kiss is almost brutal in its vigor—all firm lips and scruff.

At first, I match his angry energy. Mouth locked onto his, I arch my back, pressing up against his chest. Jutting a knee between his muscular legs, I'm like a wrestler who won't be pinned.

Then his tongue slides into my mouth, and I hear myself moan. He tastes like heat, and he tastes like *him*. I stop fighting, my body going willingly slack under his.

Our kiss goes straight to nuclear. His kiss is deep and my body is on fire. If I could form a thought right now, I'd wonder if the hotel's sprinkler system were up to code.

But thinking is overrated, while Jethro's angry kisses are not. I take everything he's giving me, and my body begs him for more.

He groans, rocking his hips against mine before coming up for air. "Christ," he pants, pushing off my chest and glaring down at me. "You confusing fucker. Am I never getting over you?"

I run a hand up his strong chest, the way I've wanted to since he opened the door. "Been wondering how that works for years. Haven't figured it out yet."

All the fight drains from his expression. He lowers his body back onto mine, green eyes inches from my face. "Are we doing this?"

"Yes," I say quickly. But I don't wrap myself around him the way I want to. Not yet. I'm the one who keeps changing the rules, because my resolve crumbles every time I look at him.

Jethro watches me, like he can see the confusion inside my soul. He leans down and gives me another kiss. It's quick. Too quick.

"Look," he whispers. "This is a bad idea. But I want you anyway."

"Yeah," I manage. And then I give into the temptation to grasp his shoulders and pull him onto my chest. "So finish what you started."

Confusion flickers through his eyes.

"Our first time," I say. "I was twenty-four, kinda drunk, and half in love with you. And you said, 'Hey buddy let's get off together! What could go wrong?'" I lift my hips off the bed and grind my cock against his. "You feel that? Fifteen years later and still going strong."

He lets out a breath before kissing my neck. "You gave me a whole fricking PowerPoint about why you can't fool around with a player. So how do you think this ends?"

I screw my eyes shut and say, "I don't know, Jetty. I just wish I could be twenty-four again for one night. I want to love you and not think about the consequences."

FORTY-SEVEN

Jethro

MY HEART IS POUNDING SO HARD I'm sure Clay can feel it. I'm still lying on top of him, almost nose to nose.

He wants sex, and I'm the dumbass who's arguing with him. Why am I like this?

I guess because I've been trying to do things right for once in my damn life. I'm trying to be honest with myself. "You make it so damn hard," I mutter under my breath.

"Likewise," he says, grinding up against me. "But what if we were just...the *old* us? One more time. Nobody would ever know."

He's right. Canada's best luxury hotel chain has provided us with complete privacy.

"I used to wait for you to come home. Knew I'd get to touch you," Clay says, running a hand down my back and onto my ass, making me shiver.

"Yeah?" Pushing against my wiser instincts, I kiss him slowly.

"Yeah," he murmurs against my lips. "Every night. Couldn't wait until you walked through the door."

"Y-yeah," I admit shakily. "Me too." Talking about this is a brand-new experience, though. For all the sex we used to have, we never discussed it.

He runs his thumb across my upper lip. "You never let on that you cared. You were so fucking casual about it. Just leaning over in the middle of a TV show and putting your hand down my pants."

"Thought I had to be that way. Talking about it would have been too..." I blow out a breath. "Too real."

"Yeah," he says quietly. Because he gets me. He always has.

"I didn't ask questions because I was worried about the answers. I was worried one or both of us would find reasons to stop."

He bites his lip, and it makes me want to bite it, too. "Mostly I didn't mind. I liked the suspense of wondering what you were going to do with me. And when you'd decide it was time."

I sink my hips a little lower onto his. "After dinner, we'd sit on that ratty old couch..."

He grins. "That piece of shit."

"Sometimes I'd rub your shoulders." I move my hands to his shoulders now and squeeze the muscles there. "If you got too tight, you'd get one of those headaches."

"Mmm," he says, closing his eyes as I begin to knead. "More."

I slide off his body. "Sit."

Blinking at me, he sits up. I maneuver behind him, opening my legs to straddle his hips before grabbing his shoulders again. "This was one of my approaches," I whisper into his ear. "After I worked the kinks out, I might suck on your neck." Demonstrating, I lower my mouth to his shoulder and drop a kiss. Then another one.

Clay goes very still. Then he tips his head to give me better access to the soft skin of his neck.

"Yeah, you loved it. Got super horny whenever I used my tongue."

"Who wouldn't, though?" he mumbles.

"This was only one of my tricks. Sometimes I'd reach over and start playing with you." I slip a hand around him and then dip into his underwear to palm his hard cock.

He lets fly a string of curses. "Goddamn holy fuck."

"Back then, you'd bite your lip," I remind him. "You weren't as vocal. Like you didn't want to make a big deal out of it."

He leans his head back onto my shoulder. "I didn't want you to stop."

"Don't worry. I won't." I stick my tongue into his ear.

He groans. Loudly.

Getting Clay riled up had been my favorite hobby. "I used to think up ways to make you crazy."

He lets out a gasping chuckle. "It worked."

"Yeah." Although now I understand that daydreaming about sex was just one of the ways I avoided thinking deeper thoughts about the two of us. "I was a tease sometimes." I lighten my touch just to prove the point.

He growls.

"Before I met you," I say while slowly stroking him, "I'd fooled around with guys before. A little slap and tickle. Jerking a buddy off."

He makes a horny gasp and thrusts his cock into my hand.

"Always knew that I found guys attractive. Never wanted to put a label on it. But then came you." I withdraw my hand suddenly, and Clay makes a noise of protest. But then I raise my palm to his mouth. "Lick it."

He does.

I slip my hand back to its favorite place. "You changed me," I say, as I start to jack him again. "You..." I use my free hand to tilt his jaw towards my mouth. "You did this."

I take his mouth in a badly angled kiss that's more tongue and ambition than skill, but it only takes a moment before we're both panting.

"I remember," he says shakily. "One night I just went for it. We were in a hotel. Like this." He twists away from me, sliding out of my grip. Then he yanks off his underwear and removes his T-shirt.

He kneels on the bed, naked. The perennial golden boy. Tanned skin, toned body. Camera-ready face. Way out of my league. Or so I'd always thought.

But now he's crawling toward me, pushing me down into the pillows before kissing me senseless.

I'm so turned on. And I feel so lucky. Then and now. Same as always.

The kissing continues as he rides my hips, pausing only to yank my boxers down. Then we're skin on skin, raring to go. I'm twenty-two and desperate. And I'm thirty-seven and in love. I'm a total mess inside.

But Clay is here and nothing else matters.

"Jetty," he whispers, bracing a hand on the mattress and looking down at me.

"W-what?"

"I'm really the first guy you kissed?"

I am almost too turned on to answer questions. "I said so, didn't I?"

"Am I the *only* one?"

"Yeah. 'Course."

Clay likes this answer. A lot. The kiss I get next is blistering hot. Then he kisses his way onto my neck and down my throat. Onto my chest. "Am I the first guy who blew you?"

"Yeah," I answer heavily. "And you're sure as hell the only guy I ever blew, then or since."

He looks up, blue eyes flaring. Then he continues on his path, kissing and tonguing his way down my body until he's reached the promised land. He licks me from base to tip. And when he takes me into his mouth, I have to throw back my head with pleasure. My skin prickles, and my nipples tighten, and I can't believe my good luck.

Except I don't want to just lie here and be serviced. My inner twenty-two-year-old is in the mood to get messy. "Flip around," I urge Clay. "I need to suck you."

With his mouth around my cock, he groans. I feel it in my balls.

But then he does what I ask, and we scramble to rearrange ourselves diagonally on the giant bed.

"Hi," I say to his erection, which is dark red and straining. "Remember me?"

Clay doesn't have any time for my jokes. He grabs my hair and shoves my head toward his cock.

I take the hint, nuzzling him and skimming a loving hand over his sac, making him groan. "The first time, I tried to fake this," I say, brushing his tip with my lips. "I wanted you to think I knew what I was doing."

"Didn't care about your technique," he mumbles. "Wanted you so bad."

Hearing this lights me up, and I sink into the heady work of pleasuring him. He tastes clean and salty, and it's the best kind of sensory overload. Every place I touch him makes him shiver.

He's torturing me at the same time, with kisses and tongue. It's hot and dirty and a revelation. But it's also deeply familiar. For years, I'd forgotten how this felt—the unique cocktail of lust and equilibrium that I've only experienced with Clay. I think I needed to forget it in order to survive.

I'd never been "the one" for anybody, certainly not a catch like Clay. I hadn't understood that what we had together was rare.

Clay groans, then pulls out of my mouth. He flips his body with the grace of an Olympic swimmer and kisses me deeply. My hand fumbles between our bodies, taking both of us in hand.

He nips my lower lip, and I stroke us toward the finish line.

"Baby," I gasp, because his blue eyes are closed, and I need to see them.

His bright gaze flips onto mine.

"I love you," I say to him for the first time in my life.

"Fuck," he says artfully.

Then we smash our mouths together and come all over the expensive hotel bedding.

Clay

I WAKE up pancaked against Jethro's back.

Unlike last time, I don't panic. I kiss him between the shoulder blades.

"Sleeping," he mumbles, and I grin.

Adjusting my neck on the pillow, I tangle our feet together. Then I watch his back rise and fall as he snoozes on.

I love you, he'd said last night. I hadn't had the spare brain cells to say it back, but we both know I feel the same way.

For a few moments I revisit my favorite daydream where we win the Cup, Jethro retires, and I get to have everything I ever wanted—an epic career victory and the love of my life.

But of course, the reality is that we could lose. And win or lose, Jethro might want to finish his contract. Another season would be worth millions to his bank account.

My happy ending would require sacrifice on his part, and that sucks. But I can't help dreaming about it.

In my defense, it's early and I'm in bed with a man I've loved for over fifteen years. Also, he's naked.

Jethro rolls onto his back suddenly. "It got loud in here."

"What?"

He glances over at me with sleepy eyes. "I can hear how loud you're thinking."

"Only about ordering coffee. How about an omelet? Should I get room service?"

He thinks about it. "Pancakes," he says. "Two eggs, two pancakes, and bacon. With maple syrup."

I rub my bare belly. "I like this idea. Coffee?"

"Am I breathing?"

I start to slide out of the bed, but he catches my hand in his.

"I'm taking it as a good sign that you want to have breakfast," he says. "Last time you lit out of the bed like your ass was on fire."

With my thumb, I rub the backs of his fingers. "Nothing got easier since then."

"I know," he agrees.

"But I'm doing a shitty job pretending that you don't matter to me. That *we* don't matter."

"Agreed," he says a little smugly. "Order the food in room 910. That way I don't have to move yet."

"Good idea." If the room service delivery person is a hockey fan, they won't wonder about the goalie in the coach's bed.

"Plus, I'm always happy to buy you breakfast after you put out for me."

With a snort, I walk naked into his room to order our meal.

We're full of pancakes and drinking coffee in bed when Jethro picks up his phone and taps a contact. And when the call connects, I hear it answered with, "Cougars Clubhouse, this is Avery speaking."

"Hello, Avery. Is this the travel desk?" he asks.

"Yes, Mr. Hale. Is there something we can help you with?"

"Yeah, I hope so. A while back I gave you a preference for lower floors when we travel. But last night they put me on the Gold Level, and I had a *really* lucky night." He looks me dead in the eye and winks.

"It was a fantastic game," our employee gushes.

"Thank you. I'm a superstitious guy, so I'd like to keep the good times rolling. If you could put me on the club level when we travel next week, I'd appreciate it."

"Anything for our players," she says. "Can't wait to see where I'll be sending you—Detroit or Carolina."

"Me too. Thanks." He clicks off and takes a sip of his coffee without comment.

"Superstitious, huh?" I ask.

"Yup. I have the uncanny suspicion that the location of my hotel room affects my odds for blowing you on the road next week."

"Risky, though," I point out, even as my cock gets a little heavy.

He watches me over the rim of his cup. "If you say we can't, I'll understand. But Clay, this doesn't get easier after the finals."

"I know," I say automatically. "As long as you're a Cougar, we can't ever be a real couple."

But what if he retires? my heart asks.

He tilts his head at me, almost as if he can hear my thoughts. "And if I should happen to retire in a blaze of glory, it still doesn't help. I can't keep my father in Colorado if I'm not under contract. He wants to go back. Toby wants to go back. I dragged them here out of obligation. But if that obligation ends..."

The coffee turns to battery acid in my stomach. "You'll have to leave if you're not playing for Colorado? But if you're playing for Colorado, then..."

He nods when he sees that I understand. There's no magic solution here. Just bad choices everywhere I look. And to think that I woke up this morning wondering if we had a chance.

I love you, he'd said. But sometimes that's not enough.

I'm still processing this when someone knocks on the door. "Coach?"

Jethro's gaze locks on mine. We're naked in this bed, two sets of breakfast dishes piled messily onto a rolling cart, clothing strewn around the floor. But nobody panics. We're in too deep for that.

"Two minutes," I call. "Gotta get dressed."

We both slip out of bed. Jethro sets his cup down on the room service cart and rolls it quietly through the door and into his own room, like a naked service worker. Then he returns to grab his underwear off my floor.

He stops on the threshold, though, as if waiting for me.

I go to him, and he takes my chin in his hand and kisses me softly on the jaw. "To be continued," he whispers in the barest voice.

Pulling him close, I put my lips beside his ear. "I love you, Jetty. Only you."

He steps back, gives me a sad smile, and shuts my half of the double door with a very quiet click.

I use the next ninety seconds to pull on my pants and a T-shirt. "Sorry," I say, opening the door. "I was having a lazy morning."

"Can't say I blame you," says Doc Whitesmith, the team physician. He's followed into my room by Kevin Tang, our head trainer.

"Uh-oh," I grumble. "Don't take this the wrong way, boys, but seeing the two of you in my hotel room first thing in the morning can't be good news."

Whitesmith slowly shakes his head. "It's Volkov's back. He's in a lot more pain than he let on. The pain has sharpened, and now it's radiating down his legs."

"Aw, hell." I feel sick. "So it's a disc?"

"Probably a herniated disc," the doctor hedges. "We'll send him for an MRI tomorrow, first thing. I didn't bring him up here because that fool is insisting he's good to play. He gave the usual speech— *Russian machine never breaks!*"

Oh, Volkov. "If he has a serious disc injury, I'm not playing him no matter how hard he whines. He could have permanent nerve damage if we don't intervene, right?"

The trainer nods. "We'll have to see the scans, but the course of treatment would be rest, cortisone shots, the works."

"Yeah. Sorry, Coach," the doctor says. "I got a bad feeling."

"Okay. Keep me posted. And I'll make sure the other goal-tenders are aware."

They depart a minute later, and I stand in my quiet hotel room, trying to steer my brain back onto the finals. I take out my phone and message Jethro.

> Were you eavesdropping?

> You call it eavesdropping. I call it being well-informed.

> Your well-informed ass is going to be playing a lot of hockey next week.

> That's what I'm here for, Coach. Not just another pretty face.

> Make sure your pretty face is on the jet in two hours. We've got work to do.

He sends me a saluting emoji.

FORTY-NINE

Jethro

"YOU'RE COMING OVER to watch the game, right?" Newgate says to me in the airport parking lot. "I'll text you my address."

Detroit is playing Carolina tonight, and the outcome of their series will determine our opponent for the next round.

God, let it be Detroit. I want to face down those fuckers and win.

"I'll try to get there," I explain. "Depends on what the kid is up to." I feel guilty that I've barely seen Toby these last few weeks. He's already out of school for summer break, which leaves him and my father basically waiting around for the playoffs to finish.

"Hey—what if you brought Toby with you?" Newgate says. "There'll be a lot of food, and also cookies. Jordyn would be pumped to see another kid in the house. Day camp hasn't started yet, and Gavin tells me she's already bored."

"Okay, yeah. Maybe he'll come with me," I say, hedging because Toby isn't always in the mood for new people. "I'll ask his lordship if he's free tonight."

Newgate gives me a quick grin. "All right. Later."

I get into my car and head home. "Hey Siri."

"Yes, champion?"

I almost deserve that description this week. "Call Toby."

"Calling Toby."

But the phone rings out. No pickup. And his voicemail is full. "Call Dad, Siri."

"Calling Dad, champion."

But he doesn't pick up either, which is odd. Unless they're grocery shopping or something.

I drive home feeling a little worried. And then I let myself into a silent house. "Hello?"

My own voice echoes back to me. They're not home, which isn't that strange. I guess. So I take my suitcase upstairs to unpack.

That's when I find the note on my bed.

Jethro—

Great game last night. We know you're tied up for another ten days now, but we couldn't wait. I scored a couple last minute tickets to Michigan and we went home to visit Shelby, and to show up for her parole hearing.

—Dad

With an angry shout, I ball up the note and throw it against the wall. Then I pull out my phone and text him.

> You can't just take the kid to another state without my knowledge or consent. That isn't how custody works.

No response.

I've been banging around my condo for a good fifteen minutes by the time he replies, and the breezy tone makes me feel ragey.

> Just landed! Sorry. It was a quick decision. Toby is so pumped to be home. And it's important to show up for your sister.

He follows it up with a photo of Toby smiling in an airplane seat like he just won the lottery.

Fuck. I'm so torn. I want Toby to have his mom, but this wasn't the way to do it.

> Ask yourself why you felt the need to sneak out of town without telling me. Does that sit right with you?

> Didn't think you'd want to interrupt your pregame routine to discuss the idea. You've barely been home in the last four weeks. Don't lose your shit over this. We're doing great.

I lie down on my bed and sulk. I'm exhausted. I'm angry. My personal life is running off the rails, and I'm under a lot of stress at the office.

But then I think about Clay, and I feel a little calmer. What would Clay do in this situation?

He'd go watch the game at Newgate's.

So that's what I do.

Newgate and his fiancé live barely a mile away in a townhouse complex that's a bit grander than mine. The front door opens even before I can knock. "Hey!" Newgate says, grinning at me in the doorway. "Wasn't sure I'd see you. No kid?"

"No kid. That's a long story. But I'm happy to be here. Brought some sodas." I hand him a case of Spindrift.

"Come on in," he says. "Game is at the four-minute mark. No score yet. Who are you rooting for, anyway?"

"Tough question," I admit, following him into a generous living room with a fireplace. My teammates are scattered around on the furniture and spilling onto the floor in front of the TV. "I guess I need Detroit to win so I can finish them off myself, *mano a mano.*"

He grins. "Fair. That's how I felt about Brooklyn right after they traded me. But it gets better."

"I'm not sure I believe you, but that's okay. My anger keeps me warm at night."

He laughs. "You've met Gavin?"

His fiancé waves from a dining table that's spread with food. "Come make yourself a plate, Jethro."

"I made the cornbread," a little girl says. She's about Toby's age, I guess, although I'm not great with kids' ages. "Nice finish last night. Especially that last save."

"Thanks, kid. I'm feeling pretty good about it myself."

She gives me a big smile.

I make myself a bowl of chili with chips on the side, and chat with Gavin while keeping an eye on the game.

"Who were you close to in Detroit?" he asks me, nodding toward the screen. "I know how rough it is getting traded."

I glance toward the screen as if I need a reminder of who's actually on that team. "You know...toward the end I had a lot going on at home. It kind of took me out of the mix with those guys."

My team captain wasn't all that understanding about it. I remember having to blow off an early season practice to fill out some paperwork for Shelby, so she could get into that treatment program.

"I need to know you're serious about hockey," the twenty-five-year-old captain had said to me. Like I hadn't been serious about hockey since he was learning his times tables.

The truth is that most of my friends had already retired, and I didn't feel as much respect for the new crew as I used to. Maybe that was their fault.

Or maybe it was mine. *Hell.*

"Fuck 'em, then," Gavin says cheerily. "Whether they go down tonight, or go down next week, they're going down."

"Works for me," I agree, because I want to see the head coach weep on TV.

The first period ends at a 1-1 tie, though, and I go into the kitchen to put my plate in the dishwasher and get another soda.

When I return, the room is filling up with even more hockey players, including "The Wall" Walcott, who's standing awkwardly against the stairway banister, holding a beer and looking sheepish.

"Look who it is," I say, slapping him on the shoulder. "You must have gotten a phone call this morning." I'd imagined they'd call him up again. During the playoffs, a team can carry a bigger roster, so they probably put a couple of goalies on high alert.

"Yeah," he says slowly. "I was kinda surprised after how the last game went for me. Thought they'd leave me in the minors forever after that." His face reddens. "I came here tonight looking for you, though."

"How come?" I ask, my eyes flicking toward the TV screen to check that the second period hasn't started yet.

"Wanna apologize," he says. "I was such a dick before. You're, like, a legend, and I thought I had to be..." He swallows hard. "... overconfident just to make it through the day. Then I bombed anyway. And now it's permanent. My first start in the NHL will always be a blooper reel."

Somehow, I manage not to laugh. "Buddy, listen up. We've all got that blooper reel. And if you plan on making a career in hockey, you're going to do a whole lot more stupid shit. I made a lot of dumb mistakes, some of them in front of twenty thousand people. That's part of the job. Why should you be any different?"

He reddens further. "Thanks. I appreciate that. I want to earn it, you know?"

"Then maybe try a little less bluster and a little more humility. It won't make the hockey any easier, but when stupid shit happens, it's easier to recover from it."

He nods. "Yeah, I'm getting that."

The front door flies open and Carter steps inside, holding a platter. "Greetings! I come bearing cookies!"

A cheer goes up from the crowd in front of the TV, and Jordyn lets out a happy shriek. "Ooh, what kind?"

"They're M&M cookies, but I only used blue M&Ms because go Cougars."

Behind him DiCosta appears, chuckling and shaking his head. He nudges Carter into the room and closes the door behind them. "I don't know who's going to eat the rest of those M&Ms."

"We can eat them during the off season," his boyfriend says. "Here, kids." He passes the platter into the scrum of hockey players.

I could be watching the game in the comfort of my quiet condo with my pick of the furniture. But it feels important to be here in the mix, so I step through the crowd, looking for a place to sit.

"Here, man," Newgate says, moving his ass over a couple feet. "You can share this thing with me." He indicates a beanbag chair that he's leaning on. "It won't turn you bi, I promise."

A few people chuckle.

"Thanks." I drop down next to him. "But whatever chair you have to sit in to turn bi, I already sat in it back when I was a youngster."

Newgate is silent for a second. Then, when he realizes I'm not kidding, he laughs. And several curious heads turn in my direction.

A moment later, the second period starts, and all those heads turn back to the game.

I don't know why it took so long in hockey for a player's sexuality to stop mattering. But somehow it has. Because in this room, at this moment, the outcome of the Eastern Conference final is more interesting than whether or not I'm attracted to dudes.

When the cookie platter comes my way, I take one. And I make a silent toast to progress.

And then I watch Detroit lose 3-1 to Carolina.

FIFTY

Clay

___

JUNE

THE PRACTICE RINK outside Raleigh is already loud, but when Murph blows an ear-splitting whistle, I actually wince.

"Let's go!" he cries, skating over to the face-off circle to start the scrimmage. "We've only got a half hour!"

"Coach," Liana says from my right side. "You have a call with the venue in twenty minutes."

"Thank you."

"Coach?" the head trainer says from my left side. "I need fifteen minutes after practice."

"All right, Kevin. Schedule it with Liana."

And so on. My life is happening in a higher gear than I even thought possible.

Last night we lost game one at one a.m. during the third over-time. My guys fought like warriors. Hale only gave up three goals in a five-hour game, and the last one was only the result of a really unlucky bounce.

We're already exhausted. I let everybody sleep in until noon, and then we all bussed out to a practice rink for a strategy session and a practice.

Murph drops the puck again, and I focus on the scrimmage. Per my instructions, we're running a few new defensive plays. But the point of this practice is to shake out our nerves.

I could feel it in the video room earlier—a thrum of staticky energy. Players hunching forward in their chairs to get closer to the screen. Sharp eyes. Tapping feet. They're all a little spooked by leveling up to the finals. And so am I, if I'm honest.

There's exactly one man in the organization who isn't jittery, though. And that man is Jethro Hale. He's like a rock in the middle of a roaring river, calmly making notes on his pad during meetings and fending off attacks during practice.

Even now, as his teammates skitter around him in hyperdrive, he's hunkered down in the net and stopping everything that flies his way.

"Hale looks really solid," Demski says from the bench.

"Agreed," I say tightly.

"Gotta say he's been great with Walcott, too."

"Really?" I can't imagine that Jethro has much patience for the twenty-something blowhard.

"Totally. Hale is like the alpha dog who sets the mood for the pack. He isn't panicking, so nobody around him feels the need to panic, either."

"I wish that would rub off on me," I mutter. But then I want to kick myself, because *rubbing off* is something Jethro and I do with some frequency.

Like last night. We're both on the club floor of the Raleigh hotel. Our rooms don't adjoin, but they're across the hall from each other. And it's pretty easy to walk three paces into one room instead of another.

So Jethro walked into mine, and we spent fifteen minutes making each other come before we fell into a dead sleep for nine hours. Then we ate room service naked and started our prep for game two.

It's stupid. It's risky. But I don't want to stop seeing him.

"Walcott is a changed man," Demski says. "He put away his ego.

Now he's trying to make his contribution on the ice and not Snapchat."

"That's good to hear. Even if we don't need to lean on him."

Demski's eyes are trained on Jethro, who's casually manning his station, calling out defensive moves and keeping a lock on his end of the ice. "God willing we're going to make magic, Coach. I got a good feeling."

The next twenty-four hours roll over me like a Zamboni, and suddenly it's time for game two. At ninety minutes before game-time, I've already answered four dozen questions, eaten six Tums, and sweated through two shirts.

We need this win so bad. We can't give up two games' worth of momentum.

The tension in the room is electric. Stoney's vision board has been dragged to North Carolina, where it's covering the opposing team's logo in the middle of the rug. Nobody is laughing at that thing anymore. They're too busy taping their sticks and stretching their hamstrings and saying their prayers.

Suddenly, Stoney bursts into the room in a panic. "Where's the doc! Need him in the bathroom. Something's wrong with Pierre!"

My heart takes an express elevator down to my guts.

The next ten minutes are the lowest point of my coaching career. We find Pierre huddled on the floor in front of a toilet, sweating and ranting in French. His pupils are blown, and his face is the color of a tomato.

I call 911, while Doc Whitesmith checks his vital signs. "What did you take?" he asks repeatedly.

"*Qu'est-ce que t'as pris?*" demands Boudreau, our other French-Canadian player.

But Pierre is not making sense.

Minutes later, the paramedics arrive, start an IV, and check his heart. Murph and I have a hurried argument about who's going to the hospital with him.

"It can't be you," Murph growls. "I'll go."

Helplessly, I watch them leave. Then I walk directly into the equipment room and put my face against the cool tiles of the wall.

This is my fault. When the trainer tipped us off, I should have acted more forcefully.

"Coach?" Jethro sticks his head into the little room. "It's chaos out here. You okay?"

"*No*," I shout.

Jethro's eyes widen. He steps into the room and closes the door. "Take a breath."

I pick up a skate and hurl it at the metal storage shelves. The sound blasts through the confined space loud as a freight-train crash.

"Clay." He backs me up against a rack of hockey sticks and puts his hands on my shoulders. "*Settle.*"

But my breaths are coming in gasps. "He told Kapski he'd stopped."

"Yeah, he lied. Addicts do that."

"*Fuck!*" The urge to smash something overtakes me again. But Jethro's a step ahead of me and he grabs my hands.

"Get a grip," he whispers. "And do it now. That guy is going to be okay."

"You don't know that."

"He got immediate care. And the body can take a lot of punishment. Ask my sister."

I suck in air. He's got a point. And I don't have time to throw a tantrum. "Okay, okay. Fuck."

"Stay here another minute," he says soothingly. Then he actually kisses my forehead, like I'm a kindergartener who's upset over the last cookie. "Breathe."

"Okay, okay," I pant.

He steps back from me at the exact second the doorknob turns.

Loud voices filter through the gap as Kapski sticks his head inside. "Uh, Coach?"

"He needs a minute," Jethro says firmly, ushering Kapski out and then following him. "But I got something to say." Jethro gives a piercing whistle. "Hey, hey. Can I have a minute of your time?"

The room quiets down immediately.

"I don't speak up much around here," Jethro says. "Because you kids seem to know what you're doing, and also my record kinda sucked when I got here."

I move to the doorway to check my players' faces. I see a mix of confusion and worry.

"Today, though, I've got the kind of experience that matters. My sister is an addict. She overdosed on my bathroom floor once. But she's still around, putting gray hairs on my head."

There's a stunned silence. Then Stoney says, "We shoulda seen it, though. Before he ended up shaking on the floor by the toilets."

"Maybe," Jethro says. "But I've been down that road, too. I'm a champion at blame as well as hockey. I've seen guys more fucked up than Pierre go to rehab and win a ring the next season. When he wakes up tomorrow morning in a hospital bed, with his family looking terrified, what do you think he wants to hear? That we blew the game worrying about him?"

Nobody says anything. But they're listening.

"Panicking won't help," Jethro continues. "We've got an hour to remember how to be great. It's the finals, guys. Our teammate messed up bad. He's going to have a lot of regrets about tonight. You're probably angry at him. Maybe you're mad at yourself for not paying enough attention. But if you blow up your focus, it's not helping him at all. Don't make it worse for him tonight, okay? Let's just get this done."

From the doorway, someone starts clapping. It's Doc Baker, the team psychologist. Then Coach Demski joins in. And Kapski.

Then the whole room.

Okay. Well. Jethro is better at this coaching thing than I am tonight. He just did my fucking job for me.

I look at my watch and step into the center of the room. "Warmups in nine minutes."

"Suit up!" Kapski shouts.

Slowly, my guys pick up their rattled selves and go back to game prep.

FIFTY-ONE

Jethro

THREE HOURS after my big speech, we're up 3-1 with two minutes left on the clock.

We're playing so well I could cry. Passes are sharp. The defense is on point. We hit that moment when the speed of play accelerates to blistering. Carolina is skating for their lives, and taking chances.

I see a play developing at the blue line, with a well-guarded pass to Carolina's sniper. My mind is essentially a supercomputer at this point—weighing angles and measuring outcomes at the speed of light.

There's no time, and I have to commit to a strategy before I can see the release. I dive to the right just as he fires at the same exact corner I'm covering.

Smack. Right into the glove.

Our bench erupts. As the ref takes the puck from me, I get a look at Clay. He's waving his hands over his head, smile bright.

I turn my head, panning the crowd. Time slows down. The fans are a smear of Carolina red, with dots of Cougar blue. Their screams of frustration are an aural blur.

"Great save!" my captain says as he drives toward the face-off circle.

It was, in fact, a great save. My life's work is so well captured in this one moment. The sweat and the muscle burn and the shriek of the crowd. The glory on my teammates' faces.

I'm thirty-seven years old. I've seen everything that hockey can do.

I've seen guys cry on the bench. I've watched a fight between two coaches that ended up on HockeyBrawls.

I've seen a puck get lodged in a player's playoff beard before the dude accidentally shook it loose and scored on himself. And a guy get a compound fracture so bad that his bone stuck several inches out of his leg.

This is all I know. It's a big life. And I don't know how I'm going to let it go when the time comes.

———

After our win, there's the usual blur of media outlets waiting to pounce. But Tate chases everyone out of the dressing room except for team members and staff.

Clay walks in, holding his phone. "Guys, I have some fresh news about Pierre."

The room falls quiet.

"First of all, he's stable, a bit more responsive, and has not required resuscitation."

Faces all around me start to relax.

"But they're monitoring him for heart, kidney, or neurological issues caused by an overdose of cocaine."

Everyone flinches.

"This is a serious health risk for him, and a sad day for the team. We'll be monitoring his care. And we'll be doing a lot of work around the organization—and I'll personally take the lead on this —to find out how we could have done a better job of supporting him before things got this bad. My only hope is that we can all learn something from this. And I commend you all for the work you did here tonight. I know he'll be proud of you, too."

The applause is brief but loud. In a mood that's pretty somber for a team that just won game two of the finals, we peel off our sweaty gear and head for the showers.

In my hotel room, I realize how sore my bad ankle is as I change gingerly into my pajama pants. My phone rings, and Toby's face appears on the screen.

"Hey, kid. It's *late*."

"I knew you'd say that," he chirps. "But I stayed up to tell you congratulations."

"You watched the game?" Toby is not exactly a hockey fan.

"We totally watched. Grandpop says we have to watch 'em all because you probably don't have so many left."

I snort. "Does he know something I don't?"

"He said if you guys win it all, you'll probably retire."

My ankles might like that idea, but it's not my father's call.

"Guess what?" Toby asks brightly. "I saw Mom today."

"You did?" I sit heavily on the end of the bed.

"She's doing *so great*. Grandpop said we can go back in three days. Also? Mom needs more money in her account to make phone calls. She wants to call you."

"Mm-hmm," I say, promising nothing. I've kept her commissary account low on purpose, so she can't trade for drugs. "I'm pretty hard to reach these days."

"She knows. She said to tell you she's proud of you."

"Well, shit," I whisper, the sentiment hitting me unexpectedly hard. I can't think of another time when Shelby's said something like that.

"She said it's hard starting over, and she bets your ankle is killing you. But you're doing really well. She also said she watched the last Detroit game on TV the other night and the commentator mentioned you. They said it's a damn shame they got rid of you."

I laugh. "Did they? I missed that." There was so much chatter at Newgate's house that I didn't hear a word of the commentary.

"Grandpop signed me up for day camp at the Y, because Trevor is doing it. I get to see him every day for two *weeks*."

I flop back onto the bed, phone pressed to my ear. "That makes me happy, bud. I wish I could have done that for you."

"Are you mad at us?" he asks in a squeaky voice. "You haven't called Grandpop at all. I know it's weird we didn't tell you before we left Colorado."

I hold back a sigh. "Buddy, I'm not mad at you. I'm a little irritated at your grandpop. But it's not the kind of thing I can't get over." *For you*, is the unspoken end of that sentence. Toby deserves a family who isn't constantly at war, like mine had been. He deserves a happy childhood, with day camp and friends and regular visits with his mom.

"Okay, because I think he's really proud of you, too. You should have seen him yelling at the TV screen." Toby laughs.

I pinch the bridge of my nose. The thing that Toby doesn't understand is that it's easy to be proud of someone when they're winning. It's how you treat them when they're losing that matters. "Let's hope game three is just as successful."

"You got this!" he says.

"And tell your mom I said hi, and that I will put three hours' worth of calls in her account."

"Cool!"

I sign off with Toby. And now I'm lying on the bed, too tired to finish getting ready for bed. Until there's a knock on my door.

That's motivating, so I pick up my weary body and open the door for Clay.

He slips inside, still wearing his suit and rumpled shirt, a troubled look on his face. "Hey."

"Hey yourself."

He crosses his arms and leans back against my door, looking uncomfortable. He's not even staring at my mostly naked body, which isn't like him.

"Do I have to do everything around here?" I gripe. Then I cross to where he's still hovering, and I kiss him.

His hands fly to my shoulders, and he kisses me back. Thoroughly. But he still looks troubled when I release him.

"Clay," I say with a sigh. "Come on." I loosen his necktie. "Take off this getup. Check out my shower. Relax. You earned it."

"Did I?"

"Yes, fool." I thread the tie out of his collar and aim it at a chair. Then I slip his jacket off his shoulders. "At ease, captain. You're off the clock."

He sighs and starts in on his shirt buttons. "We've got one guy out with the kind of back injury that can fuck you up forever. And one guy who thought it was worth risking his *heart function* to take some uppers."

"Yeah, that sucks. But they'll both be okay eventually. You gettin' all bent over it won't actually help. You do know that, right?"

He leans his forehead against my shoulder with a thunk. "I guess."

"Aw, baby. No." I run my hands through his hair. "You're just tired."

"Am I? What are we doing, Jetty?"

"We're doing our best."

"Hockey's all I have, and I'm fucking it up."

I laugh. "Says the winning coach who just beat Carolina in their own barn."

"How come you're so wise tonight? In the dressing room, you knew just what to say."

"Eh. Because I've had to develop endless patience with people who make bad decisions."

"I love you," he says quietly.

My heart swells. "I know. Now take a shower because it always calms you down."

He walks wordlessly into my bathroom, and I'm calling it a win.

FIFTY-TWO

Clay

WHEN I RETURN to the bedroom, naked and clean, I do feel calmer. Jethro was right. He can't brag about it, though, because he's stretched out in bed, asleep.

I take a trip around the room to turn off various lights and bolt the door. Then I lift the covers and slide into bed.

This is a new experience for me. Jethro and I have shared a bed before, but only after sex. We never did sleepovers just for the sake of it, but I'm just assuming he's cool with it.

I'm thirty-nine, and I've never had this with anyone. I crave it. I want someone to come home to at the end of a long day.

And I want that someone to be Jethro.

Pressing my luck, I roll towards him to wrap an arm around him.

It doesn't go that well, because he wakes up with a jerk. "*Shit.*"

"Sorry. Should I go?"

"No fucking way," he says, reaching for me. "You just bumped my bad knee is all."

"Your *knee?* What's wrong with your knee?"

He nudges me the other direction—onto my hip—and curves

his body alongside mine as the big spoon. "Clay, I'm thirty-seven. Everything hurts after a game. That's just Wednesday in my body."

"Oh." I relax onto the pillow. His arm feels good around my waist. I close my eyes.

"Clay?" he whispers after a minute. "Can I ask you something?"

"Yeah?"

"How did you handle retirement as a player. Like...the first week?"

My heart kicks into a higher gear, because Jethro said the word *retirement*. I can't let on how much that excites me. "The first week sucks," I tell him honestly. "That's the 'what the fuck have I done' moment."

"You had a bad injury, so it must have been terrible," he hedges.

"Awww." I reach back and pat his hip. "Somebody followed my career but never said so."

"Shut up. It was on ESPN."

I smile in the dark. "So, yeah. I didn't have a lot of choice about retiring. I was twenty-nine at the end of that season, with a bad fracture from a playoff game. I had surgery. Turned thirty in a cast."

"Ouch."

"Yeah, nobody wants a thirty-year-old with months of rehab. Skaters aren't valuable at that age. So I had to grit my teeth and announce my retirement. But then job offers started trickling in. Some TV stuff. Scout work. And then a coaching job. Assistant coach at a Big 10 school. It would probably be the same for you."

He's quiet for a second. "I don't know. You've got a college degree and charm for days. I'm not as employable as you."

"You're right. Who'd want a multi-championship winner with a fifteen-year pro career in a niche position when they could have a dozen retired forwards who never saw any playing time?"

He just grunts.

"You don't need to solve this ahead of time," I say quietly. "But Jetty—there's so much out there, and you have so much to give. This only seems scary because it's a big unknown."

No comment again, but he puts his palm in the center of my chest and rubs slowly.

I like it. I like everything about this. So I tuck my body a little more tightly against his. "Hmm. I wonder if I can fall asleep like this? Or if it's too distracting to have your dick so close to my ass."

His hand freezes on my chest. "Clay."

"Yeah?"

"Would you ever let me fuck you?"

"Sure."

"Really? Have you done that before?"

"Yes and no." I choose my words carefully. "I've topped guys, but I never let anyone top me. But you have to remember that the only sex I have is on vacation, with strangers, and it just never seemed like a good idea." Too much trust involved.

His hand slides off my chest and ends up on my ass. "But you'd let me?"

"Oh yeah."

He groans. "Like soon?"

"Not tonight. Your knee is bothering you, for starters."

His head thunks into the spot between my shoulder blades. "Okay. Well. Something to look forward to."

"How about this? Show me a clean sheet for any game in this series, and I'll leave the stadium immediately to buy some lube."

He laughs against my back. "I've *got* lube. And now I've got a woody, too."

"Better stop some pucks, then."

"Clay."

"Hmm?"

"Roll over."

I do, but I watch out for his knee. Now we're nose to nose, and I'm staring into his serious green eyes.

"Gonna hold you to that promise. Now kiss me goodnight."

I lean in, and the kiss is a hundred percent Jethro—it doesn't fuck around. It's bossy and fast.

In other words, it's the best thing that ever happened to me.

"Now go to sleep," he says, rolling onto his back again. "I gotta rest up so I can get a clean sheet in game three."

I snort. Then I fall asleep about ninety seconds later.

FIFTY-THREE

Jethro

ALAS, I do not get a clean sheet in game three. We're still playing great. Before the final buzzer, we've got five goals.

Unfortunately, Carolina has four. Two of them were lucky, one of them was a complete miscalculation on my part, and the final one was offsides and should have been disallowed. But the ref Clay screamed at didn't see it our way.

Still, a win is a win, and I'm in the mood to celebrate. I text Clay after the post-game madness.

> Come over. I'll be home alone. Unless you think it's too risky.

> I'm in. I'll wear a hoodie. Maybe that sounds kind of James Bond, but it pays to be careful.

> James Bond didn't wear hoodies. But if you're really worried, I'll leave a door open for you. Come in the back.

> Oh baby.

> !!!

:)

I'm drowsing when Clay arrives in my bedroom. "Is that you? Or am I being robbed."

"Gonna rob you of those boxers."

Apparently, we're still capable of joking around like rookies, because he does, in fact, steal my boxers a moment later.

And then we stay up way past our bedtime.

* * *

Game four goes a little better for me. Carolina plays like they're out of gas. By the middle of the third period, it's 3-0 in our favor. Their coach calls a time out, and I skate over to the bench.

"Don't let your guard down," Clay is saying to the team. "Don't underestimate them. Defense will be everything as they get desperate. Help Jethro keep a clean sheet, okay? I want it *bad*."

I don't even dare to make eye contact with Clay after that comment.

"If we can shut out Carolina tonight," he adds, "forget the bar tab. I'll buy everyone a pony."

There's a rumble of laughter, the loudest of it from me.

Maybe there are some sexual favors at stake for the other team, too, because Carolina makes a big push and slides a goal between my skates in the last two minutes of the game.

I'm only partly mollified by DiCosta's goal right before the final buzzer, and we go home with a 4-1 win. The series is three games to one, which means we could end this thing in Raleigh.

The next day I get a text from my dad. *Call me* is all it says.

That sounds grim, so I return it in a hurry. "You rang?"

"Yeah, kid. Nice streak you got goin'."

I relax a little. "Thanks. How's Shelby?"

"She's great, Jethro. So great. Can't wait for you to see for yourself. Meantime, I could fly Toby out to Raleigh to watch the game. You got two tickets?"

"Sure." I rarely use my comp seats. "You want to come to a game? They're yours."

"Of course we want to come," he says, as if this were a regular occurrence.

I buy them airplane tickets and find them a hotel room. On game day, I wait for them in the hotel lobby, stealing a few minutes from my busy schedule for a quick hello.

I'm checking my watch for the fifth time when the revolving doors push open and Toby strides in. He's wearing shorts, a Cougars tee, and a big smile. "Uncle Jethro!"

"Hey!" Something catches inside my chest as he runs toward me. "Dude! I haven't seen you in ages! Nice shirt."

He laughs and throws his arms around my hips. "I got a foam finger, too! I'm gonna cheer really loud."

"I could use it. How you been?"

We sit down on a sofa, and he starts blabbing at me about day camp. "The free swim is better than the lessons. They make everybody take lessons. Volleyball is cool, but we're riding horses next week!"

"Wow. I've never ridden a horse."

"Never?"

I shake my head.

"Mom told me not to do it unless they have helmets. So I asked, but they totally have helmets."

"Well, that's good to hear," I say uselessly. That would have never occurred to me. Worst guardian ever.

"Grandpop went on a date," he says next.

My eyes lift to my father, who's standing awkwardly to the side.

"What?" he demands, his face reddening. "It's just a date. Everybody dates."

I shrug. "That's cool. You're the one making it weird, not me."

He rolls his eyes.

"Where'd you meet her?"

"She bought the house next door!" Toby says. "Her name is Greta. She makes really good cookies. She calls them Snickerdoodles, but they aren't like a Snickers at all."

"Bummer. Still nice of her, though."

"Yeah," Toby says. "She comes over after dinner a *lot*."

"Twice," my father corrects. "To play cards."

"Cool." I bury my smile.

Several of my teammates breeze into the lobby through the revolving door. "Lunch in ten," Kapski says with a wave. "Third floor."

"Aye aye, Kap."

"Wait!" Toby says, springing up. "Can you sign this, Mr. Kapski?" He pulls a Sharpie and a pack of hockey cards out of his pocket and thrusts them at Kapski.

"Sure, buddy."

Toby collects a few signatures, something I've never seen him do before.

"This is new," I say to my father. "He's never been a hockey fan."

"His Michigan friends are," my father says with a chuckle. "They told him that if Colorado wins, those cards would be valuable."

"So he's a little opportunist?"

My dad just shrugs.

Then Clay appears, and Toby swoops in on him, too. "Hi, Coach!"

"Hey, Toby. Mr. Hale." He stops abruptly, smiling at my kid and then my dad. He puts his hands in his pockets. Then he pulls them out again, like he forgot how to stand still. "Are you ready for the game?"

"Yeah, but are you?" Toby demands. "I got a lot riding on this."

Clay cracks a smile. "I'll do my best, okay?"

"If you win, I'll make you cupcakes," Toby says.

"Hmm." Clay crosses his arms across his chest and seems to

think about it. "You know, it's been a while since we made those, and I could use another one. All right. It's a deal. Now I'd better get upstairs. Later, guys." He trots off.

"Don't forget the cream cheese," I tell Toby. "And now I think I have to go with them for lunch."

"Is the food good?" he wants to know.

"Yeah, bud. But while we eat it, they play video of the other team and talk strategy. It's not really about the food."

"We're getting hot chicken," my father says, a hand on Toby's head. "Buddy, wait for me by that plant?" He points at a potted tree by the check-in desk. "I just gotta talk to your uncle a minute."

"Sure. Bye, Jethro." He bops over to hug me again. "I'll scream loud."

"You do that."

"Look," my dad says after Toby scoots away. "I'm sorry I didn't ask your permission about the trip to Michigan. I know that custody document has your name on it—but you weren't *home*."

"Yeah," I say gruffly. "I know I haven't been around."

"I'm not judging," my father adds. "You got a busy life. But so do we, and it's not in Colorado. The boy needs Shelby."

Does he, though? And does Shelby deserve him? "We'll talk more when the series is over," I say. "Promise."

"Fine. We'll be rooting for you." He gives me a quick smile.

"Thanks, Dad. It means a lot." I hold out my hand for a shake, but he grabs me into a quick, hard hug instead.

I'm so startled, I forget to say goodbye.

Upstairs, during Murph's video review, I surreptitiously pull out my phone and message Clay.

> Sorry my kid mugged you in the lobby.

> Sorry I was so awkward.

> You know, I noticed that.

I've literally never done a meet-the-family thing. I mean I still haven't. But it made me think about it.

Toby's already a fan. I'll make sure he keeps his word about those cupcakes.

See that you do.

FIFTY-FOUR

Clay

WE LOSE game five in front of Jethro's family, my sister and her boyfriend, and a packed Carolina crowd. Simply put, my guys succumb to the pressure of the moment. They went into the first face-off looking rattled. Carolina scored first, and our guys never recovered.

Jethro, to his credit, didn't get rattled until the third period. He held the score to a 2-2 tie until the last ten minutes of the game when he let in two flying saucers.

The series is 3-2 now. We're still up. We can still close the deal with a single win. But we're no longer on a roll.

Over the next seventy-two hours, I give more renditions of my "Shake it Off" speech than you'd hear at a Taylor Swift concert. "Let's do this at home, boys! Let's close the deal in our own barn, in front of our own fans. It'll only be harder if we take this thing to game seven."

And so on.

My sister and Raul fly to Colorado and set up camp in my guest room, which means I don't see Jethro privately at all for a couple nights. I'm probably too busy, anyway. The only time I take a break from hockey is to visit Pierre at his new Denver rehab facility and assure him that the team doesn't hate him.

"We're going to win this thing. You watch," I tell him.

It's all bluster. Suddenly it's game night again, and I don't feel ready. Surely I could have worked a little harder. Run through a few more plays. Analyzed a little more tape.

There's no way to stop time. Stacks of news trucks park outside the arena again, I'm down to my last clean dress shirt, and there's a stain on my lucky tie.

Is this what greatness looks like? I ask myself in the mirror in the arena's restroom.

It will have to do.

I make another nervous lap past the stretching mats, and then through the trainers' room, where Jethro is having his ankle taped. "Something wrong with your ankle?" I bark.

Both the trainer and Jethro look up at me with pitying glances. "Nothing new, Coach," Kevin Tang says. "Just his usual soreness, magnified somewhat by all the action he's seeing."

"But I like action," Jethro says with a teasing lilt. "Planning on a clean sheet tonight, boss."

I give him a glare that implies I'm too strung out to be thinking about anything but hockey.

"Coach? A word?"

I whirl to find Tate standing there, a frown on his face. My chest goes tight because the PR guy wouldn't interrupt me before a game if it weren't important. "Sure," I say a beat too late. "In my office."

The fifty-pace walk into my little office seems to take all year. What could the issue be? A breaking story about...?

I start to sweat as I close the door. "What's the issue?"

"A journalist is asking for quotes on an obnoxious little piece he's running."

Suddenly I'm lightheaded.

FIFTY-FIVE

Jethro

FROM MY SEAT on the trainer's table, I see Tate approach Clay. I can't hear exactly what's said, but Clay goes white. And then they both disappear.

My stomach dives. There's no reason to believe that someone is running a story about me and Clay. But that's where my mind goes anyway. And if it happens to be true, then everything Clay worried about will come to pass. The narrative will make a sudden shift from success to scandal.

I spend a long couple of minutes in the dressing room before Clay reappears, his mouth tight. "Hey Coach?" I call, flagging him down. "You got a second?"

His gaze finds me, and he gives a quick jerk of his chin. I set down the stick I'm taping and hurry after him into the equipment room. "What's the matter?" I blurt out the second I step over the threshold.

He leans against the sharpening table, a thoughtful expression on his face. "Just a nasty story brewing about Pierre's overdose. Tate had to warn me in case I'm asked about him tonight."

My jaw unclenches. "*Oh.*"

"I had that same reaction," Clay says quietly. "For a second, I worried about…"

"Yeah," I agree quickly. "Same."

He gives his head a shake. "Go win this game, Jetty. That's all that matters tonight." He gives my shoulder a squeeze on his way out the door.

But I don't move for a moment. I take a deep breath. And then another one. It's hard to admit when you've been selfish. But it's true. We can't go on like this, waiting for disaster to strike.

Clay was right. Something has to give.

But the clock doesn't give a damn about my little midlife crisis. It's time to put my skates on. Then come the pre-game rituals. On-ice warmups. The national anthem. The whole nine yards. This is the soundtrack of my life.

The arena is so packed it's shaking. And when the announcer does the starting lineup, player by player, the crowd swells with a cheer after every name.

Usually, I tune this part out. When we're moments away from the start of the game, I like to use this time to think about the challenge to come.

But not tonight. I feel a prickle of awareness as the echoing voice cries, "Number 31, Jethro Hale!"

I lift an arm and wave to the crowd. It's an uncommonly enthusiastic gesture for me. Toby's out there somewhere watching with my dad. And maybe my sister is watching from the prison TV room.

But they aren't the reason I'm feeling so much right now. It's because I know this could be the last time I hear my name announced in the arena.

Do I really have the guts to pull the retirement trigger? I guess we'll find out.

But now it's showtime. And we're as ready as we can be.

When the puck drops, the first period kicks off like a tidal wave. It's a blur of shouted defensive advice, quick saves, and near-misses. We're playing our hearts out.

Heading into the second period, we're up 1-0 on a wrister from Stoney, but it's far from a comfortable lead. Carolina is skating like a pack of overcaffeinated greyhounds. Their captain dekes our winger and shoots the puck. I scramble for it. My ankle twinges as I make a particularly athletic save, but the adrenaline keeps me going.

In the second period, Kapski scores to extend our lead to 2-0. The crowd is electric, sensing how close we are. Time seems to slow down for me. I hear every satisfying smack of the puck against the boards, the shouts of my teammates, the taunts from the opposing players.

"You slow fucker," their center sneers into my face as we fight over a rebound. I flick the puck away from him and grin.

I'm having fun right now. Who'd want to put an end to this kind of fun?

Clay's voice is already hoarse as he makes a speech during the break, while the trainer retapes my ankle. "We're twenty minutes away from history. Twenty minutes from etching our names on the Cup forever."

Twenty minutes. His words send a shiver down my spine. It would be wild to see our names together after all this time. *Fifteen years and twenty minutes.*

"But it's not over yet," Clay continues. "They're going to come at us with everything they've got. This is when champions are made. This is when legends are born."

I watch as he locks eyes with each player, his intensity infectious.

When he turns to me, he says, "Hale, you've helped carry us this far. One more period. Twenty more minutes of the brilliance you've shown your entire career. I know you've got it in you."

His faith hits me with physical force. It's easy to forget that I stood in his hotel room a few months ago and offered to quit.

What a wild year it's been.

As Clay wraps up his speech, the energy in the room rises. We're ready. We're hungry.

"Cougars on three!" Murph shouts.

He counts down and then the room erupts in cheers and stick taps. As I file out with the others, I catch Clay's eye one more time.

Twenty more minutes. *We've got this.*

Time to bring it home.

The crowd is loud as the ref sets up for the face-off. I stretch. I breathe. I wait.

He tosses it down, and the other team comes out swinging. Lots of quick passes and chaos. One deke and a blind transfer later, they get off a shot into my corner, and I can't get there in time. The lamp lights, cutting our lead to one.

Fuck a duck.

I lift my mask, take a drink. I try to shake it off. Suddenly nostalgia over last games seems stupid. Maybe we're taking this to game seven. Maybe we're doing this again in forty-eight hours.

But then Stoney gets a breakaway. I stop breathing as he weaves toward the goal and sets up against their goalie. The lamp lights, and the arena explodes!

3-1 with ten minutes left. We can taste it now.

They're the longest minutes of my life. Every play feels crucial. Every clearance is our season's make or break. My heart is pounding so hard I can barely hear the crowd's roar.

But the clock keeps ticking down, and that's all the Cougars need. The horn finally sounds, and I straighten up in disbelief.

We've done it. We've won the Cup. My teammates pour onto the ice, sticks and gloves flying. I glide forward and the joyous pile consumes me, laughter and tears raining down around me.

We fucking did it.

The arena's lights glint off the Cup as it's passed around. When it reaches me, I clutch it with both hands. It's heavier than I remember. And it hits me that this moment—this perfect, glorious moment—might be my last act as a professional hockey player.

A few years back, one of my teammates goaded me into bungee jumping with him in British Columbia. I teetered there on the platform, unsure if I was going to do it until the moment I actually jumped.

That's me right now. Half of me wants to stay here on the platform. The other half feels the ache in my ankle and the weariness in my bones and the rightness of going out on top.

I take one last look around the arena, trying to commit every detail to memory. Then I lift the Cup high above my head and let the roar of the crowd wash over me one last time.

FIFTY-SIX

Clay

I'VE NEVER HAD SO many hours of joy in one night. Every smile lifts me higher. Every back pat. Every shout of victory.

Even the champagne shower I'm treated to in the dressing room is a blessing.

The place is packed with players, families, and media. Every ten seconds I'm hit with another cry of "Hey, Coach!" and then I'm shaking someone else's hand, and trying to give intelligible sound-bites to people who'll be covering our victory.

"Clayzy!" my sister manages to shout at one point. "Over here!"

I swim through another clot of people to find my sister, her baby bump, and Raul. They're beaming at me. Then I happen to glance at the couple beside them. My parents.

I blink. "You came?"

My mother laughs. "Congratulations, Clay. This is really something. Your sister said we shouldn't miss it."

I'm startled again as my father pulls me into a hug. "The youngest coach in the league gets it done in game six!" he says proudly. "I guess we won't be needing that hotel room in Raleigh tomorrow night."

"No you won't," I say, recovering. "Didn't know you'd become a hockey fan, though."

He shrugs. "I'm not. But I'm a fan of yours, Clay. I'm sorry if I wasn't always so understanding of your career. Middle age has a way of showing you all the things you've missed, though."

"Thanks?" I try to wrap my head around this development. "Sorry I'm tied up here for a while. It would be great to visit with you guys."

"Tomorrow," my mother says, reaching out to pat my arm. "We know it's a big night. How about brunch?"

"Brunch sounds great," I say. "I'll be there."

My mother kisses my cheek. As I wander back into the chaos, I'm still a little dazed.

Two hours later, I reek of champagne and cigar smoke. Players' families and the press have cleared out. The players are finishing up long-delayed showers and taking selfies with the Cup, before they head off to party at a nearby club.

I've never stayed so late at the arena or gotten tipsy in the locker room. I find myself wondering how much an eventual Uber to Boulder is going to set me back, before remembering that money doesn't matter. Not tonight anyway.

The only thing that matters is this team. This moment. This victory. I put my fingers in my mouth and whistle. "Guys? Can I have your attention?"

Wet heads turn in my direction. Everyone looks jubilant. "I've given you a lot of speeches this year. But you're going to have to forgive me one more. Because I can't leave here tonight without telling you how proud I am. How humbled I am by your effort and your sacrifice. The only way we arrived here tonight was by all of you giving a hundred percent, and then some."

I glance at each man in turn, and they're all smiling. Naturally, my gaze rests for an extra beat on Jethro. He's got his feet kicked up onto an exercise ball, like a guy in a lounge chair. His arms are crossed as he gives me a lazy grin.

God, I love that man, and I don't have the first idea what to do about it.

"I know you didn't do it for me," I say. "But thank you for making me the proudest man in hockey. My gratitude for you runs deep, and I can't believe I have the best job in the world. Can't wait until our championship rings show up. I've been saving space right here." I lift my hand in the air, and everyone laughs. "So thank you and good night."

There's loud applause. Kapski jumps up and waves his hands. "I just want to echo everything that Coach said. I have so much faith in all of you, and it's an honor to be your captain. Does anyone else have anything they need to say before we head out to party until dawn?"

More applause, and then a hand goes up. Jethro's.

My heart stumbles a little as he kicks his feet off their perch and stands up. "Team, look, I appreciate your patience with me this season. Took me a while to become the goalie you needed."

"But you got there!" Stoney calls. "Timing is everything! Timing and vision boards!"

"Yeah, about that," he says, shoving his hands in his trouser pockets. "I never really *envisioned* that this day would come for me, but I'm making a new vision board, kids. Tonight was it for me. I'm out."

My heart stops.

"Your man over here..." He points at Volkov, who had to watch tonight's victory from the box. "He's doing his rehab so he can lead you to another victory next year. I need to do the smart thing and make my exit with grace."

I'm hearing all these words, but my heart can hardly believe them. And somehow my eyes are hot, and my throat is closing up.

"Besides," he adds. "There's another consideration..." He gazes directly across the circle, right at me. As if asking permission for... something?

I nod. Whatever it is, I'm ready.

"...Your coach is the most amazing guy I ever met. But he said he won't date me until I leave the team." Jethro shrugs. "So there you go. I'm pretty much in love with him, so it makes quitting easier."

"*Jetty*," I gasp.

Newgate laughs.

The GM blanches.

DiCosta snorts.

Everyone else stares.

"So, yeah, that's a wrap for me. It's been an honor to play with you guys. Thanks for listening."

Everyone starts talking at once. I stand where I am, rooted to the floor, completely floored that Jethro would go there tonight.

But mostly I'm overwhelmed by the idea that he'd do that for me. That he'd do the brave thing and step away from the only life he's known for fifteen years, and tell the whole world that I matter to him.

"Hey," he says a moment later, arriving at my elbow. "I know that was...yeah. I should have cleared that with you ahead of time. But I'm ready to give you everything I have, and I just couldn't wait."

"Well it's..." I clear my throat. "It's a big deal to hear you say it," I say, finding the courage to look straight into his deep green eyes. "I'm not really used to everyone seeing me as an actual human with his own life. But you're worth a little awkwardness, Jetty. You've always been worth it to me."

He grins, and it makes him look ten years younger. "Can we get out of here?" he asks. "Are you going to the club with the guys?"

"Not anymore." I grab my suit jacket off a hook and turn toward the door.

Someone hoots at us. I think it's Stoney, but I don't turn around to see. I let Jethro walk me out into the corridor, and then out into the parking structure. "I was going to Uber home after all that champagne."

"I don't drink, so it's your lucky day," he says, putting a hand on my back. "I'm over here."

He guides me to his SUV and opens the passenger door for me, handing me into it like a gentleman.

I'm not that drunk, but it doesn't matter. As soon as the door closes, I sink my head into my hands and relax for the first time in... Well, a long time. It's been months since I felt like I wasn't holding up the whole world.

A warm hand lands on my knee, and I realize Jethro is seated beside me, but he hasn't started the car. "I'm okay," I mutter.

"I know," he says quietly. "But maybe we just need a minute after that."

"God. That's the truth." I pick my head up and sink back into the seat. "I've never been so happy. But I also feel about a hundred years old."

He laughs. "Good thing I'm attracted to older guys."

I manage a snort.

He turns to me in his seat, and moves his hand to my shoulder. "Where are we headed? Toby and my dad are at my place."

"Kaitlyn's at mine." I shake off my daze and look at him. He's watching me with patient eyes. "There's always some obstacle with us."

"You say that." He runs a hand through my hair. "But I'm knockin' them down as fast as I can. You're not my boss anymore. I don't have to call you Coach anymore, unless that's a kink you have. Then we'll talk."

I let out an exhausted chuckle. "No issues there. Jetty—I want this. I really do. But I'm not letting myself get too excited about it yet. Because you just made a huge decision. You don't have your future planned. And I know you need to get on a plane to Michigan."

"Yeah, that's all true," he says quietly, stroking my cheekbone with his thumb. "But I want this too. For me."

My heart does a flip flop.

"And there's a couple of details you don't know," he continues. "My sister's parole hearing was this morning, and they approved it."

"Whoa." I throw my head back against the headrest. "Holy shit. She's out?"

He shakes his head. "No, but she will be within the month. I don't know exactly how that's going to go. But she wants to move back into my father's house and parent her child. She wants to petition for an end to my custody of Toby."

"Oh wow."

"I'll spend the summer in Michigan with all of them. If she does well, she'll regain custody. Then I won't have to stay there, Clay. After a few months, I could be anywhere."

"*Oh.*" Hope bubbles up inside me faster than the champagne I was showered with earlier. "You mean, like...Colorado?"

"Now he gets it."

"Jethro." I lean over the gearbox and put a hand on his chest. "Listen, I'm trying so hard not to leap to conclusions here. I never thought it was possible to get everything I ever wanted inside of three hours."

He smiles at me. "I don't know when you became the cynic and I became the optimist, but I'm kind of digging it."

"How long," I demand suddenly. "How long until you go back to Michigan for the summer?"

"Couple days, probably."

I make a frustrated sound. "Can I visit? I don't want to go a whole summer without you."

He blinks. "Hell yes. I can get away for a weekend, too. We could have a getaway on Lake Michigan somewhere. Just don't make vacation plans without me. I don't want to hear that you took your annual sex trip to Italy or wherever without me."

I laugh, because I can't even imagine wanting that. Everything I want is in this car. "Drive me home. Sneak into my place. Kaitlyn and her guy are probably asleep."

He hits the ignition button. "You don't have to ask twice. I'm there."

FIFTY-SEVEN

Jethro

I WAKE up in Clay's bed at nine a.m.

By nine fifteen, we're kissing like porn stars.

Last night we fell asleep about four minutes after arriving in his bedroom, and now we're making up for it. I've got him pinned to the mattress. The sheets have been cast to the floor, along with the thin collection of clothing we were wearing.

Somewhere in the back of my mind, I'm aware I want to fuck him, but owning his mouth is too much fun. So is rutting against him and listening to him moan as I hold his hands down against the pillow.

He shifts a knee between my legs to give himself better leverage and thrusts his hips up against mine.

I roll us both onto our sides and skim a hand down his ass. "This is mine now," I pant into his mouth.

"Is it though?" he asks between kisses. "Don't remember seeing a clean sheet in your last game."

I groan. "Seriously? Do I have to come out of retirement for a few games just to fuck you? Is the new schedule out?" I try to think of a guaranteed shutout. "When do we play Buffalo?"

He laughs against my swollen lips. "There's lube in the bedside table."

I dive for the drawer with the same enthusiasm that saved several shots from Carolina last night. I grab the bottle. And when I turn back to Clay, he's lifting his knees, catching them in his hands. Offering himself to me.

The blatant invitation makes me groan. "Man, and they said the first day of retirement would be sad. Respectfully disagree."

He drops his head and laughs. "Glad to hear it."

I position myself between his legs and open the bottle, slicking up my fingers and then rubbing them into his crease.

"Aw, fuck," he gasps. "Yeah. You need pointers?"

I shake my head. "Women have asses, too."

"Ah."

"Breathe." I penetrate him with my finger, and he lets out a slow breath, taking it.

"I could be jealous right now," he says, bearing down, his abs rippling. "But it's handy that you know what you're doing."

"Good answer." I stroke inside him and his breath stutters. "You play with yourself like this sometimes?"

"Yeah," he says, his chest flushing with desire.

"You ever think about me when you do it?"

He winks at me. "Once or twice."

"You get off on the fact that I didn't fool around with any guy since you. Well, I get off on the fact that you haven't let another man inside you. It's only gonna be me for you."

His arm muscles flex as he holds his knees. "So you say."

Laughing, I grab the lube again. I work him up to two fingers, and then I tap his spot.

He hisses. And suddenly nobody is laughing. I make a beckoning motion with my fingers, and Clay practically levitates off the bed. "Oh yeah. Fuck."

"We're getting there." I lube up again and try three fingers. It takes him a minute to relax and let me in.

But I'm a patient man. Besides—it took me fifteen years to really let Clay inside my heart. And I'm still learning.

"Now, do it," he urges, arching his back. "Fuck me," he adds, just in case I've forgotten the agenda.

"Condom?"

"Do we need one?"

I shake my head. I've been tested. "You're it for me, Clay. There's nobody else."

"Then what are you waiting for?"

As usual, Clay asks all the right questions.

FIFTY-EIGHT

Clay

I WATCH Jethro's face as he lubes himself up. There's nothing more beautiful to me than his thoughtful frown. I thought so back then, and I still think so now.

With the same careful deliberation he uses for everything, he lines himself up. Then he locks his green gaze to mine. That penetrating stare that I love so much. When he enters me, it's the single sexiest moment of my life. And the sensation of going from too empty to impossibly full.

Above me, he blows out a breath, like he needs a moment to calibrate to our new reality.

This is real. Finally.

"You feel incredible," he whispers. Then he leans down to kiss me.

"So do you."

"Gonna move now," he says after another kiss.

"Kind of hoped you would."

He braces his hands on the bed and experiments with a slow thrust. "You good?"

"So good," I whisper.

He shivers. Then he fills me again.

Bit by bit, kiss by kiss, we pick up the pace, until he's nailing my spot on every stroke, and I'm clutching his shoulders, hoping he never stops.

"Holy... I... stroke yourself," he says through gritted teeth.

I grab my dick and give it a tug. I sink into the bed and look up into his straining face. It's perfect.

"*Clay*," he warns.

"Go. Take it."

With a groan, he thrusts, and his whole body shakes. I feel the heat of his seed inside me, and that's what finally takes me there—that and the expression on his face. Like he's too overcome to breathe.

"Holy..." he says again. Then he pulls out and collapses on my chest.

"That was..."

"Wow." He yawns, and I run my fingers through his hair.

"Shower?"

"Sure," he slurs. "In a minute. Don't want to go anywhere. Ever."

I hold him so closely I can feel his heartbeat against mine.

Thirty minutes later I exit the bathroom, leaving Jethro in there toweling off his hair. In the bedroom I pick up my phone and find a text from my sister.

KAITLYN

I'm afraid to come upstairs.

Yeah I brought someone home.

You think? The room was shaking.

"Oh shit."

"Problem?" Jethro pads into the bedroom.

"Uh, no. My sister is texting me."

> Mom and Dad are on their way over. We're
> supposed to have brunch?

"Oh shit."

"You keep saying that."

I wince. "Yup. So my parents are on their way here, and we're all going out to brunch."

Silence. I look up to see horror on his face. "Brunch?"

"You're probably starving," I point out.

"Not hungry enough to think a sit-down with your extended family a half hour after fucking you through the mattress is a fun idea."

I bark out a laugh. "My parents won't know."

He sighs. "You sure this is a good idea?"

"No," I admit. "But I care more about you than them. And I'm not ready for you to leave."

"Okay," he says, wiping the last drops of water from his shoulders, while I admire his naked body. "It's your funeral."

I open the drawers of my bureau and locate a polo shirt that's a little long on me. It should fit him fine. "Wear this. Let me find you some khaki shorts."

"Or I could just make a break for it out the back door."

"Not another back door joke," I say, pulling out a shirt for myself.

He sighs again. "I must really love you."

"You must. Now hurry up. It'll be less awkward if we get downstairs before my parents arrive."

Except when I walk downstairs, Kaitlyn is standing in the kitchen with a glass of water, pointedly looking up at the ceiling.

"What are you doing?"

"Checking for damage," she says.

Jethro makes a groan of dismay as he follows behind me.

When my sister catches sight of him, she almost drops her water glass. "Omigod. *Him?* Clay!"

"What?" I grumble.

Her eyes are wide. "This man broke your heart! And he's a huge risk to your career. *God*. If this gets out…"

"Baby," Raul says from the sofa where he's paging through one of my magazines. "I'm sure Clay knows what he's doing."

"Raul, I appreciate you," I tell her boyfriend.

My sister growls, and Jethro just looks freaked-out.

The doorbell rings at this awkward juncture, and it's the first time I've been glad to have my parents interrupt a conversation with my sister. I leap toward the door and answer it.

"Morning!" my mother says. "We've been up for hours, but I'm sure you needed to sleep in."

"Or something," mutters my sister.

"Morning, Mom." I give her a quick hug and shake my dad's hand. "Let me get my keys, and we'll head out to a place I like…"

Jethro is already shaking his head. "We drove my car."

"Oh. Right." I clear my throat. "Anyway, I would like to introduce you both to Jethro Hale. He's my…"

"Goalie," my father finishes, holding out his hand. "Great work last night."

"Thank you, sir," Jethro says, adding a firm handshake. "I'm glad it all came together."

"We're so happy for all of you," my mother says primly. "What an accomplishment. Will you be joining us for brunch?"

Bracing myself, I take a deep breath and prepare to explain.

But Jethro beats me to it. "I would love to crash your brunch. Your son has great taste in food, and this is the first day I'm allowed to be his date in public."

The look of deep confusion on my parents' faces would be funny if it weren't so uncomfortable.

My sister winces.

Raul turns a page in his magazine.

"His…what?" my father manages.

"Mom, Dad, Jethro is my boyfriend," I say as levelly as I can.

"Your...what?" my father repeats.

Jethro frowns at me. "Hang on. You're not out to your *parents?*"

My mother gasps.

My father's mouth flops open like a grouper's.

"Oh shit," Jethro whispers.

"*Clay,*" my mother squeaks. "Really? All those times I asked you when you were going to meet a nice girl? Why didn't you just *say* something?"

"Why didn't you stop asking?" my sister counters.

"You can't date your *goalie,*" my father says, horror in his voice. "Jesus Christ, the scandal!"

The scandal! Of course he'd latch onto that.

Then again, I guess it's better than unfiltered disgust. I sigh.

"So, yeah, about that," Jethro says, scratching his beard. "I retired after last night's game. I don't want to cost Clay his job. But you should know that we met in our twenties. This isn't some wild hair. Give him a little credit."

"Oh," my father says slowly, his gaze jumping between us. "And now you're retiring, for...?" His synapses seem to suddenly fire. "For *Clay?*"

"Oh, Dad." My sister puts a hand in front of her eyes. "This is why people need therapists."

"Yes, for Clay," Jethro says firmly, and suddenly my eyes are stinging. "And for my ankles. And because I've been doing the same thing for so long, I forgot what else is out there."

"Well said," my sister crows. "Maybe you're not as bad as I thought."

My father rubs his forehead. "Well. Congratulations to you both, I guess."

"Thank you." And honestly, that could have gone worse.

"Can we eat brunch now?" Kaitlyn asks, hand on her belly. "Kind of desperate, here."

Jethro pulls his key fob out of his pocket. "Let's go. My treat."

My sister gives him a sideways glance. "You think you can butter me up so easily?"

"Pretty sure I can," he says. "I've had a pregnant sister, too, and I know how this works. What would you do for a pancake right now?"

"Almost anything," she says, following him toward the front door.

"See? Easy peasy," he says.

My parents and I follow them out, with Raul bringing up the rear.

"Clay," my mother says, pausing before we reach the cars. "I apologize. All these years, it just never occurred to me that you..."

"Are gay," I say. "I guess I knew you guys wouldn't be assholes about that. But I spent my whole childhood being the Powers child who never quite fit in. Wasn't that eager to add another thing to the pile."

She shakes her head as we arrive at Jethro's car, where he and Raul are sorting the six of us into two groups. "I'm still sorry."

"Don't worry about it, Mom," I say. "I have no regrets."

For the first time in years, it's really true.

FIFTY-NINE

Jethro

SINCE IT'S A WEEKDAY, the restaurant isn't too slammed. We get a table right away. I make sure to seat myself beside Clay. And as soon as the food is served, his hand lands on my knee under the table.

To a casual observer, our party of six wouldn't look that interesting. But to me, this moment is a goddamn miracle. I can hardly believe I'm really here, dressed in Clay's clothing, sipping coffee with his parents. Like a real couple would.

Part of me might always secretly believe that I don't deserve him —that I've pulled off some kind of elaborate scam to call him mine. The miracle is that Clay feels the same way about me. His thumb strokes over my kneecap, and I know he's happy I came along, even if it's a little awkward.

I steal a glance at his handsome face, lit with enthusiasm as he and his sister bicker lightly over the definition of Eggs Benedict and whether bacon belongs in a Bloody Mary.

Clay's mother turns to me. "And where are you from, Jethro? Where is your family?"

I chuckle. I mean, you'd just have to. "Grew up in Detroit, but my father and my nephew have been here in Colorado with me this season. I have temporary custody of my sister's kid while she's incarcerated."

The poor woman's face contorts into surprise and horror before she can stop herself. "That sounds traumatic. I'm sorry for your troubles."

"It's been a tough couple of years," I agree. "But my sister seems to be pulling herself together."

"And your nephew knows you're there for him," Clay says with a proud smile. "Great kid. Sharp, and with a willful personality like his uncle's."

I snort. "That's very diplomatic. Thank you."

"No, it's important," he says. "Grit makes the man. Ask any coach or employer."

"It's true," his father says mildly, and I catch a flicker of disbelief on Clay's face, like he's not used to his father agreeing with him.

"Do you boys have plans for the summer?" his mother asks.

Boys. Like we're a couple of college kids. I grin.

"We're working on it," Clay says. "Jethro has to go back to Michigan for a couple of months. But we'll find some weekends to spend together. And I'm told he could be back in Colorado this fall." He gives me a glance that's full of hope.

"I have a lot to figure out," I admit. "Thinking about going back to school. I didn't get to finish my degree like Clay did."

His father's face lights up. "Where were you in college?"

"Madison."

He gives an approving nod. "Go Badgers."

"That was a lifetime ago," I say wearily. "I wouldn't go back there. I'm thinking of looking at Boulder."

"Really?" Clay says with unguarded interest.

"They have a sports management program," I mutter, because it's hard for me to talk about this. It's hard to share my big ideas when I don't know yet what's possible. "I'm just looking into it. Not sure what they're looking for on an application."

"*Please*," Kaitlyn says, forking up pancakes. "They'd be lucky to have you."

"Did you know we work with that program?" Clay asks.

"What? No." I shake my head. "All I've done so far is read their website."

"Yeah, we take five students a season. As interns." He winks.

"Dude." I snort. "I'm not going to be your *intern*."

"Why not? You already know how I take my coffee."

"But think of the scandal," my sister says. "We can't have a scandal."

There's laughter all around, but Clay's is the loudest.

After brunch, we say goodbye to the rest of the Powers family. Clay gets a back-slapping hug from his dad that leaves him red-faced, and a lingering hug from his mom. "Don't be a stranger," she says to both of us.

So, yeah, that could have gone worse.

"Well," Clay says, as we watch them drive out of the complex's parking lot, "it feels like I had to win a championship to get my father's respect. But I suppose he's just mellowing."

"I'm mellowing," I point out. "It happens."

He shakes his head. "It's stupid that I care."

"It isn't." I know this for a fact because I also spent years wondering why my family couldn't just be normal.

"Thank you for coming out with us," he says, turning to me. "That couldn't have been easy."

"I don't do easy," I remind him.

"Look, I'm going to Uber it into Denver to get my car," he says.

"I could drive you."

He shakes his head and lifts his chin toward the door of my building, where Toby is emerging. "I think you're needed elsewhere."

"Uncle Jethro! Where've you been? I gotta show you my new game." He comes running towards us.

"Hey! I'm sorry. I had some things to do after the game." I give Clay a sideways glance, and his blue eyes gleam with amusement.

Toby stops at my side. "Hiya, Coach. Thanks for making my hockey cards more valuable."

"You're very welcome. I can probably get you a signed jersey for your memorabilia collection. You could put it up on your wall or sell it on Ebay. Your call."

"Hey, thanks!" he says brightly. Then he turns to me. "Come on! This game is the coolest."

I reach out and ruffle his hair, and he doesn't even squirm. "All right, I want to see this thing. And then we're going to plan the rest of our summer together."

"Cool." He reaches out and grabs my hand.

Clay shoves his hands in his pockets and takes a step back. "All right. You two have a nice day. I'll see you around."

"Wait," I say. "Not so fast."

Clay pauses, his eyes darting from me to Toby as I free myself of Toby's grip and take a step forward.

Then I just hug him in the June sunshine. Like other people do.

And he hugs me back, just like that.

"Call me later," I say. "We'll make some plans."

"You can bet on it."

I give him a quick kiss on the temple and step back. Toby is wide-eyed with curiosity as I give Clay a wave. "Later."

"Later." He gives me one more smile before he turns to go.

SIXTY

Jethro

AUGUST

MY SUITCASE IS SO STUFFED that I have trouble zipping it up.

"You should have let me ship another box," my sister says. "That's going to weigh a ton."

"Not a weakling," I grumble, even though she's right.

Last night we all went shopping for school supplies at Target. Toby and Shelby loaded me down with notebooks and highlighters. A dictionary and a thesaurus. I also own a new calculator and mechanical pencils.

I put my foot down, though, when Toby wanted me to buy a 3-ring binder with superheroes on it.

"They have a Detroit hockey one," he'd said.

As if. "I don't need a binder, kid. But you pick one out for yourself."

My first college class in over fifteen years starts tomorrow. I'm taking just one course while I officially apply to the program. Getting my feet wet, basically.

I'll also be taking some scouting trips for the Cougars, looking at young goalies in the junior leagues. Trying to spot the next legend in front of the net.

I can't wait.

The suitcase finally zips shut, and I ease it onto its wheels. "All right, Shelby. The room is yours. You can break out the ruffles or whatever."

"Ruffles?" She puts a hand on one of her bony hips and gives me a stare. "Bitch, please."

I laugh, and her eyes sparkle.

Four weeks ago, we stood outside the women's prison for forty minutes until the gate opened at last, and Shelby ran out. She's painfully thin and looks older than thirty-five. But she is off drugs, going to daily NA meetings, and doing great.

Since then, she's been sleeping on one of the bunkbeds in Toby's room. I'd offered to bunk with my nephew and give her my bedroom, but Toby insisted he wanted her close. He's over the moon to have her home.

"You take care of yourself," I tell her now, and it comes out sounding stern.

"I will," she says, her smile fading. "I promise, Jethro. And I'm going to test every week, so you won't have to worry."

The testing is probably humiliating, but it's part of the program that Shelby's lawyer has laid out so that she can legally regain custody of Toby. As of this week, my father is Toby's emergency legal guardian. But Shelby has a plan and a new job at a coffee shop.

"Bartending pays better, but coffee-shop hours work better with Toby's schedule," she'd told me.

I roll my suitcase out of the room as she says, "You take care of yourself, too, doofus."

"That's easy," I insist. "I'll get plenty of sleep and eat a lot of Clay's cooking."

My dad is waiting at the bottom of the stairs, car keys in hand. "Ready?"

"Absolutely," I say, trying not to look like I'm straining to carry this monster of a bag down the stairs. "Toby!"

"Yeah?" he calls from his spot in front of the TV, where he's wringing the last few days out of summer vacation by watching a superhero movie in his PJs.

"Come say goodbye."

The sound of the movie pauses, and he joins us in front of the door.

But my sister hugs me first. "Have a safe flight. Text us when you get home."

"I will," I promise. "Walk me out, Toby."

He does, barefoot. I roll my suitcase down the walkway and then heft it into the trunk of the car where my father waits behind the wheel. As Dad starts up the car, I turn to Toby. "Look, I got something to say to you."

"What?" He gazes at me, suddenly serious.

"You know how I call you 'my kid,' and not 'my nephew,' and sometimes people get confused?"

His forehead wrinkles. "Yeah, it's weird."

"Not to me," I say with a shake of my head. "I know you got your mother back, but you'll always be my kid. It's going to be weird not seeing you all the time. I'm really going to miss you."

"Oh." His eyes get soft, and then his gaze darts away.

"Maybe we don't say it enough, but I love you," I tell him. "And you can call me at any time, for any reason."

He sniffs. "Thanks."

"I mean it. I'm keeping your room the way it is, because I know you're going to want to visit. You and your mom."

"Yeah," he says. And then surreptitiously wipes his eyes on his sleeve.

"Come here." I hold out my arms, and he steps into the hug. "I know you like it here better, but there will always be a place for you in my home. That never changes."

He takes a sniffly breath. "Bye, Jethro."

"Bye, kid." I give him one more squeeze, and then let go. My eyes are burning, like they used to when Clay chopped onions in our tiny apartment.

My dad beeps the horn, but I take another minute to wave to Toby one more time before he walks back into the house.

It's a quiet drive to the airport, and my dad has a Tigers game on the radio. After he pulls up at the Delta departures area, I open my door.

"Wait," he says, grabbing my wrist.

I pause and turn to him.

"Just want to say thanks," he says. "It's been a tricky couple'a years around here. But you stepped up for Toby and your sister. And you put up with me to do it." He clears his throat. "I hope you and your guy are happy together. You deserve that."

For a long beat I'm literally speechless. "Thanks, Dad," I choke out eventually. "I appreciate that."

I'm so surprised that I almost walk off without my suitcase, and my dad has to honk the horn before I remember to turn back and fetch it out of the trunk.

Five hours later, I'm watching for the damn thing to show up on the baggage carousel in the Denver airport when someone lets out a whoop.

I turn around and spot Clay jogging toward me. I only get a moment to brace myself when he leaps into my arms. "You made it!"

"Right on time," I say, my smile slightly crooked. "You didn't have to pick me up." It's a forty-minute drive.

He hip checks me. "I wanted to, Jetty. It's still the preseason, and my schedule isn't off the rails yet." He steps back and scans me from head to toe with bright eyes. "You're looking tan."

"That's from standing around at Little League." One of Toby's friends is baseball crazy, so Toby reluctantly joined his team.

"Well, it isn't from our beach trip." Clay snickers.

"Clearly." We'd rented an Airbnb in Traverse City, where it proceeded to rain all four days. We'd spent all our time in bed.

"I have dinner already prepped," Clay says just as my bag appears on the carousel.

"Hold that thought." I lunge for the thing and drag it off the belt. "Actually, whatever your dinner plan is, I'm in. I don't even need to hear it."

Clay chuckles. "All right. Come on."

He leads me to the parking structure and heaves my bag into the back of his SUV. "Christ."

"I know. Toby made me buy school supplies."

He bleeps the locks, and we get into the car. I wait for him to start the engine, but he doesn't. He turns to me and pulls me into a kiss.

Aw, yeah. I kiss him back. "See? This is what I came for. Not your cooking."

"Mm-hmm," he says, kissing me again. "Even if it's sous vide steaks in garlic butter with French beans and scalloped potatoes?"

My stomach rumbles as he releases me. "Okay, the cooking is a close second."

He laughs as he starts the car. "Glad to hear I'm still first," he says. "Did I mention the chocolate mousse?"

I groan as he reverses out of the parking spot. "Drive fast."

SIXTY-ONE

SportsNight Weekend Profile

"Denver's Power Play Couple"

By Ivy Dean

Clay Powers made more headlines in hockey last season than most coaches ever dream of. Midseason, one of his star players, Hudson Newgate, became the first pro hockey player to come out as bisexual, and then went on to marry his partner. Newgate, the Cougars organization, and Coach Powers were lauded for their inclusiveness.

Not six months later, Coach Powers became the second youngest head coach in the history of the sport to win a championship and then Coach of the Year.

Powers also oversaw the season-changing addition of veteran goalie Jethro Hale to the Cougar squad last year. "It's a great honor to play for my old

friend and former teammate Clay Powers," Hale
said on the night of their triumph.

Every sports news outlet was in Denver that night to
cover the Cougars winning the Cup. But few
people know what happened after the champagne stopped flowing.

"Coach closed the doors to the dressing room and
said a few words to the team," said David Stoneman, Alternate Captain and jersey number 66.
"He thanked us. Told us how proud he was. Then
the captain spoke, and when he was done, he
asked if anyone else wanted to say something."

Stoneman laughs at the memory. "So Hale raises his
hand and he tells us he's retiring. He didn't even
tear up or anything. It was totally unemotional—
the way you'd rattle off your coffee order. And
then he said, 'Besides, your coach said he can't
date me until I leave the team.'"

When asked what happened next, Stoneman shrugs.
"For a second, nobody knew whether to believe
him. But Coach turned red, and I realized it was
true. Those two always had sort of a weird energy
between them. And now I guess we all know why.
I'm happy for 'em."

That was six months ago. The romantic partnership
between Powers and Hale flew under the radar as
the new hockey season got underway. The
Cougars got off to a fine start in the preseason
with Andrey Volkov back in the net after a
successful back surgery this summer. Upstart
Zack Walcott is his occasional relief.

Jethro Hale is employed as a part-time scout for the
Cougars and is still a familiar face at the Boulder
practice facility and the Denver arena. The press

only picked up on the deeper relationship between Powers and Hale this month, when the two started house hunting in the tonier sections of Boulder.

They ultimately chose a grand four-bedroom with a fantastic kitchen and mountain views.

"We're gonna have some sick parties on that patio," Stoneman said about the purchase. "The team is pumped up."

Let's hope they're also pumped up to win another title this year. Central Colorado will be watching.

The End